DO NOT REMOVE
CARDS FROM POCKET

Adam Homo

ADAM HOMO

FREDERIK

PALUDAN-MÜLLER

TRANSLATED BY

STEPHEN I. KLASS

INTRODUCTION BY

ELIAS BREDSDORFF

1 9  8 1

The Twickenham Press

NEW YORK

Copyright © 1980 by Stephen I. Klass
All rights reserved
Printed in the United States of America
Library of Congress Cataloging in Publication Data
Paludan-Müller, Frederik, 1809-1876. / Adam Homo.
Includes bibliographical references.
I. Title.
PT8162.A713   839.8'116   81-58568
AACR2
ISBN 0-936726-01-6
ISBN 0-936726-02-4 (pbk.)

This translation

is dedicated to the memory of

my brave and much loved parents

David and Ruth Klass

CONTENTS

PART TWO

PART THREE

INTRODUCTION

BY ELIAS BREDSDORFF

Frederik Paludan-Müller was born in 1809 in a small town on the Danish island of Funen, where his father was then a parson —eventually he became Bishop of Aarhus. His mother was highly gifted, a poetic and sensitive woman, who died insane in 1820.

After matriculation in 1828, Paludan-Müller studied law but did not take his degree until 1835, by which time he had established himself as a highly popular poet. Young Paludan-Müller was good-looking, something of a dandy and a lady-killer, and his literary idols were first Heine and then Byron, whose influence in Denmark—as in many other parts of Europe—was very important in the 1830's, indeed so strong that it often surpassed that of Sir Walter Scott, who wrote: "Nature has mixed in Lord Byron's system those passions which agitate the human heart with most violence."

The peak of Byronic influence on young Paludan-Müller is to be found in his verse novella entitled *The Dancer* (1833), a poem clearly inspired by Byron's *Don Juan* and written in the *ottava rima* which Byron had revived. When many years later Georg Brandes, the Danish critic, spoke of Byron's influence, Paludan-Müller made what was intended as a disclaimer: "When I wrote *The Dancer* I had only read a couple of cantos of Byron's *Don Juan* and very few of his other works." But he added the revealing admission: "All the same, I was then, like so many others, passionately fond of the English poet."

Paludan-Müller had borrowed the main motif in *The Dancer*

from the love story of Juan and Haidee in Canto Two of *Don Juan*. Dione, a young and beautiful dancer, loves and is loved by Count Charles, whose crafty mother, however, persuades him not to marry below his own station. But when evil rumors are circulated about Dione, Count Charles challenges the person who questioned her honorable reputation and is killed in the duel. His death makes her lose her sanity, and she drowns herself.

What fascinated contemporary readers were both the Byronic spleen and the poetic realism of this verse novella, set in Copenhagen, with vivid pictures of the Royal Theatre and the young dancer, Miss Dione, a typical Bournonville ballerina. The story of the two lovers is tragic, not because they are separated but because it is implied that happiness is something denied the human race.

The Dancer made Paludan-Müller the darling of the Danish reading public, which had grown tired of the early type of Danish Romanticism with its naive simplicity and its devotion to ancient Nordic motifs. Elegance, piquancy and "modernism" were what they found in this poem.

In 1834 a mythological drama entitled *Amor and Psyche* was published, and also a narrative poem entitled *The Fall of Lucifer*. From then on Greek mythology and Old Testament stories remained important sources of inspiration for Paludan-Müller.

Intoxicated with his early success, he was disappointed and bitter when a volume of poems which he published in 1836 was torn to pieces in a leading Danish literary journal, especially because of the implication there that he had been highly overrated as a poet. While working on a polemic reply, published as a booklet entitled *Trochees and Iambi* in 1837, he was taken seriously ill with typhoid fever, and the illness came to change his life in more than one way. As a young student he had been attracted by motherly women, much older than himself, especially by his mother's cousins; the oldest one for a time became a sort of mother confessor to him, and for a time he was in love with the middle sister, who was unhappily married. Now that he was very ill, Charite Borch, the youngest of the three sisters, but still seven years older than himself, devoted herself entirely to looking after the patient, who was removed to her mother's house. Charite was a deeply religious woman, who, unlike her two elder sisters, was not very attractive in outward appearance.

x/

The illness also resulted in a spiritual crisis, mirrored in the description of Adam Homo's nervous disease:

He seemed to feel his reason overthrown,
In which wild ferment, just as if they hated,
Soul and body burst and separated.

Here the poet has described his own experience. At times Adam's soul withdraws, scared and silent; at other times it throws itself violently into the fight, without recognizing friend or foe, but insanely getting them mixed up. When Adam wakes up, he sees his mother sitting at his bedside. When Paludan-Müller woke up, Charite was at his bedside. The description of Adam's convalescence makes it clear that his crisis, like Paludan-Müller's, had been one of life and death.

It was not long before Paludan-Müller and Charite Borch were engaged, and in 1838 they were married. Shortly after their marriage they went to Paris, where they stayed for nine months, and then to Italy. They were away from Denmark for two years, and it was during this time that Part One of *Adam Homo* was written. It was published in 1842 and had a somewhat mixed reception, for both critics and readers were uncertain about the interpretation of this torso. It was only after Parts Two and Three had been published in December, 1848 that the poem was fully understood and appreciated, and it has remained an important classic in Scandinavian literature ever since.

Paludan-Müller continued to write verse dramas and narrative poems based on Greek mythology; there followed *Venus* (1841), *Tithon* (1844) and *Adonis*, his last poem (1874). His main biblical poems are *The Death of Abel* (1844), *Cain* (1861) and *Paradise* (1862). Other poems with ancient motifs are *Kalanus* (1854), *Ahasuerus* (1854) and *Benedict of Nursia* (1861).

Though mainly a poet, he also wrote some prose works, notably the story entitled *The Fountain of Youth* (1865; translated into English by H. W. Freeland, 1867), and a novel cycle in three volumes, *Ivar Lykke's Story* (1866–73).

After their marriage Paludan-Müller and his wife lived a sheltered and isolated life, in their Copenhagen flat in the winter and in quiet Fredensborg in the summer. Charite became not only his muse but also acted as a keen watchdog, doing her best to prevent others from breaking his isolation from the world. In his book *Two Visits to Denmark* Edmund

Gosse describes his own successful attempt in 1872 to gain entry as a young Danophile to the elderly poet whose work he had come to admire. "In those days," Gosse writes, "to a Danish pilgrim, the vision of Frederik Paludan-Müller at Fredensborg was like that of Victor Hugo in Guernsey or that of Tennyson at Farringford to a French or an English worshipper." And it was only due to the cunning of Dean Fog, Gosse's fatherly friend and protector, that Gosse managed to penetrate into the home of the Danish poet, whom he calls "an incorrigible hermit."

His mature works are all inspired by Christian faith and by a philosophy of renunciation. A constantly recurring theme in his poetry is death, for death in blind obedience to God meant for him the liberation of the soul from the vanity and sin of the world.

He died in December, 1876 at the age of 65.

Adam Homo, Paludan-Müller's main contribution to literature, is at one and the same time a realistic novel set in Denmark in the 1830's, the story of a man's life from the cradle to the grave (and after), and a theological didactic poem. Its hero, whose Christian name and surname both mean Man (in Hebrew and Latin), is an anti-hero, a man "Attempting all, not once for all his labor/Choosing right." We see him reaching the highest social level while at the same time throwing away all his intellectual honesty and all his idealism, and discarding every fundamental value. By contrast, Alma, the woman he loved but rejected in favor of a wealthy baroness, develops spiritually while sinking socially. The apocalyptic ending tells the story of what happened after Adam's death, when two advocates plead their opposite cases for the salvation or damnation of his soul in the heavenly Court of Justice. When ultimately the soul is weighed and the scales go down towards Hell, Alma saves him from damnation by putting the weight of her love on the scales, and she accompanies him to Purgatory in order to save his soul. Paludan-Müller, the devout Lutheran Christian, here accepted a Roman Catholic idea of the possibility of intercession by one person for another, and also of an intermediary stage between death and final judgment (Purgatory) and the eventual salvation of purified souls (Apocatastasis).

In his preface to *Trochees and Iambi* Paludan-Müller wrote: "As far as I am concerned, Dante has confirmed my conviction that no one will become a truly great writer until he has obtained a basic view of life and of the meaning of life, so that it penetrates all his writings as a fundamental harmony, or shines through all the light and shadow of his pictures as a primary color." The quotation is important, for Dante's *Divina Commedia* is undoubtedly one of the important inspirations behind Paludan-Müller's Danish human comedy. Behind Alma, who leads Adam through Purgatory to Paradise, Dante's Beatrice is clearly distinguishable. And so is Gretchen in Goethe's *Faust*, for through *Adam Homo* resounds a clear echo of Goethe's worship of "das Ewig-Weibliche." It has been said (by F. J. Billeskov Jansen) that the *Divina Commedia* is a poem about the salvation of a man, *Faust* an explanation of human nature, and *Adam Homo* an accusation against man. Whereas the *Divina Commedia* is about a human being who is saved, *Adam Homo* is primarily about a human being who fails and falls.

In 1840, the year before Part One of *Adam Homo* appeared, Johan Ludvig Heiberg, another prominent Danish poet, published an apocalyptic comedy entitled *A Soul after Death*, a witty verse drama, the anti-hero of which was intended to represent the average Dane, or at least the average Copenhagener of the period. In Heiberg's comedy we meet the hero only after his death, when his soul wanders full of self-confidence towards the gates of Heaven, where he expects to be well received, having been an ordinary, decent, law-abiding citizen. But at the heavenly gate he is interrogated by Saint Peter and finally rejected after his abysmal ignorance about the essence of Christianity has been revealed. He then attempts to gain entry into Elysium, the pagan paradise, where he reveals to Aristophanes an equally shocking ignorance of the spirit and ideas of ancient Greece and of the classics. Finally, he is admitted to Hell by that hospitable and gentlemanly door-keeper Mephistopheles, and the subtle irony of the play is that here the soul of the Danish "Mr. Everybody" feels himself to be at home and perfectly happy, for Hell is nothing but a replica of the soulless and superficial life that he had led when he was alive.

I am not suggesting that Heiberg's play influenced Paludan-Müller in any way, but the ideas behind the two poems are similar, though Adam Homo cannot possibly be described as an average Dane. His background, his education and his final elevated social status certainly prevent him from being regarded as a nineteenth-century Danish Everyman. When asked by Georg Brandes which part of the poem he wrote first,

Paludan-Müller without hesitation replied that the two lines he wrote down on paper first of all were the following (from the end of Canto Ten):

HERE LIES ADAM HOMO PEACEFUL 'NEATH THIS LAND,
BARON, GEHEIMERAAD, AND KNIGHT OF THE WHITE BAND.

And that is not how the average Dane died.

Another contemporary countryman of Paludan-Müller, only four years younger, whose name springs to mind when discussing *Adam Homo* was Søren Kierkegaard, whose mature work may also be seen as a condemnation of the way in which eternal values were rejected by the times in which he lived. In *Either/Or* he complained about the times, not because they were evil but because they were despicable (*ussel*), totally lacking in passion and greatness. The first part of this work describes and ridicules the aesthete, the Byronic spleen-man, and is among the finest satires in European literature. Like Paludan-Müller, Kierkegaard had also been an elegant and witty dandy; he also revolted against his own former existence and became obsessed with the problem of what the essence of Christianity was. For him Christianity was a paradox which must be personally experienced by the individual, in isolation. Using his own metaphor, to be a Christian was to be "alone in a small boat in 70,000 fathoms of water."

There is in *Adam Homo* a distinction between a *true* existence and a *bogus* existence, and it has rightly been pointed out that this distinction makes Paludan-Müller, no less than Kierkegaard, a forerunner of modern Existentialism.

In many ways Kierkegaard and Paludan-Müller are parallel figures, living at the same time but not necessarily influencing one another.

It might be added in this context that in 1840 a young Russian author, M. Lermontov, wrote his important novel entitled *A Hero of Our Times*, a book which—against a different philosophical background—also condemns and rejects the times in which its author—and its anti-hero—lived. But, of course, no one in Denmark knew about this work till decades later.

Adam Homo has left its mark on later literary works. Most prominent among these is Henrik Ibsen's verse drama *Peer Gynt*, the manuscript of which was completed on the island of Ischia off southern Italy in 1867. It was Ibsen's negative counterpart to his earlier verse drama *Brand*, about the uncompromising Christian who forgot that God is also *deus caritatis*. *Peer Gynt* is a biting satire against many of the qualities, as well as the lack of qualities, which Ibsen considered typical of contemporary Norway. As a young man Peer Gynt is full of potential and promise, but he invariably takes the easy way out, and it is part of his nature always to go "round about" instead of tackling problems and facing issues. Ibsen's play, too, is related to Goethe's *Faust* but much more directly to *Adam Homo*. "Frailty, thy name is man" could have been the motto of both works. Solveig, the girl whose trust Peer betrayed, is Beatrice, Gretchen and Alma at one and the same time. When as an old man Peer Gynt has reached rock bottom, he again meets Solveig, whom he let down, and she tells him that the only place where he has been his true self is "in my faith, in my hope, and in my love." So it is Solveig who saves Peer from being totally discarded as a human being, just as Alma's love rescued Adam from damnation. Both Adam and Peer are weak and pitiable characters, covering their inner emptiness behind elegant phrases and a homemade philosophy adapted to each new situation.

The echo of the philosophy of *Adam Homo* resounds in many works, right up to Isak Dinesen's stories in which each human being must be obedient towards God's intention for him.

Two women stand out in *Adam Homo* as saintly, almost Madonna-like characters, Adam's mother and Alma Star. The former teaches her little boy the meaning of the verb *to be*, perhaps the most frequently quoted stanzas (at the beginning of Canto Two), by bringing in the analogy of animals who live instinctively according to the plan of the Creator, while human beings have the freedom to choose:

> "Look, see the little bird!" his mother said,
> As Adam stared at it while it progressed
> Along the sky. "It's dipping to its nest
> Over in the meadow just ahead.
> Just hear it sing while it prepares a bed
> For all its young, so tiny and so blest.
> To sing, to fly, to feed their family,
> That, Adam, is what birds would call to be."

(The image of the black snail in the following stanza is less successful, for black snails prefer rain to sunshine.)

We get to know Alma in two different ways in *Adam Homo*, partly in the description of her first meeting with Adam at the dance, their engagement, her father's birthday party, etc., partly by means of the many sonnets in which she reveals her inner self and her conviction that all life is will. Alma's sonnets break the metrical form of the *ottava rima* used in the narrative part; they form part of Canto Six and of Canto Eleven (the lyrical poems in Alma's Remains, in which other metrical forms are used).

Among the other female characters two of the most important, both treated by the author with scorn and irony, are Countess Clara, who plays with Adam as a cat with a mouse, and Baroness Mille, the target of Paludan-Müller's rage against female emancipation. When Adam first meets Mille at her father's manor house he sees two copper etchings:

One was a full-length portrait of George Sand,
Of modern novelists by all odds queen,
In male dress, with a horsewhip in her hand,
Smoking a cigar with earnest mien.
The other showed the Germans' own Bettine
Before her mirror, at her writing stand,
Looking at herself as her hand spurred
A nimble pen whose squirts were all but heard.

George Sand, whose real name was Aurore Dupin (1804–76), was the famous spokeswoman of female emancipation and of the right of women to be guided by their hearts; she used a male pen name and dressed like a man. Bettine was Bettina von Arnim, née Brentano (1785–1859), a German feminist author who belonged to the circle of Goethe's friends and later married Ludwig von Arnim.

Here as elsewhere in *Adam Homo* Paludan-Müller reveals his profoundly conservative views, according to which women should be content to be good wives and good mothers and should not trespass on the long-established prerogatives of men.

Almost all the male characters in *Adam Homo* are treated with scorn and derision. This is true also of Adam's father, the Reverend Peter Homo, a scheming rationalist who encourages his son to break his engagement to Alma so that he can marry the wealthy young baroness instead. By the time Paludan-Müller wrote *Adam Homo*, his admiration for Byron had turned sour, and the novel contains two negative Byronic characters, Van Pahlen and Gray Galt, a kind of cynical Byron grown old. Another target of Paludan-Müller's irony is "little Jensen," Adam's faithful supporter and secretary. It is he who arranges the funeral and the inscription of the fine tombstone.

Alma's father, the old gardener, is completely in line with several other nineteenth-century idealized portraits of old, white-haired, noble representatives of the common or garden-variety man.

Throughout the book the views and the biases of a bourgeois mid-nineteenth-century Christian moralist predominate, a man who condemned the times in which he lived in Denmark—and as far as *Adam Homo* is concerned, the period is roughly 1835–48. He condemned the times on artistic grounds (as in the Prologue) as well as on political, religious and human grounds generally.

There are many topical references in the book, e.g. to the new rationalistic theology of David Friedrich Strauss (*c.* 1835), to M. Goldschmidt's Danish radical satirical weekly *Corsaren* ("The Corsair," 1840–46), to the founding of political societies and debating clubs (it is in one such debating club that Adam's lecture is a total failure), and to the faint beginning of a proletarian revolutionary movement (of which Paludan-Müller of course disapproved strongly). It is worth remembering that *Adam Homo* was completed in the year that the French February Revolution took place, and that same year the *Communist Manifesto* was published. At the end of Canto Nine we hear about Adam taking up the cause of charity, but to his annoyance a young worker refuses to accept alms humbly and gratefully from the rich:

> *"Yes, look at me! And if you can't stay cool,*
> *Go sling your cloak politely round your coat!*
> *But we have newspapers in evening school*
> *And our teacher knows just what's afloat.*
> *A storm is blotting out the sun—I quote!—*
> *And lightning soon will strike where rich men rule.*
> *We little people know our catechism;*
> *Be careful—and make way for pauperism!"*

"Pauperism" was the word Paludan-Müller used for a conspiracy he feared, a new revolutionary movement whose real name he did not yet know: socialism. He was able to see it only as a dangerous threat to all the values he so firmly believed in.

Though essays have been published in English about Frederik Paludan-Müller (by Edmund Gosse in the chapter "Four Danish Poets" in his *Studies in the Literature of Northern*

Europe, London, 1879, and by Georg Brandes in his book *Eminent Authors of the Nineteenth Century*, London, 1880),* only extracts of his main work have been printed in English translation previously. Professor Stephen Klass's translation of *Adam Homo* is the first complete one in English. I have had the opportunity of scrutinizing it carefully, and I was able to express my great admiration for this excellent and faithful translation, which has achieved the almost miraculous result of keeping the original meter and rhymes while at the same time rendering the contents of both the narrative and the lyrical parts with complete fidelity to the Danish original. It must indeed have been a labor of love for Professor Klass, and though it is true that every translation loses something, Stephen Klass has lost less than I thought was possible.

A great literary work which belongs not only to Danish or to Scandinavian literature, but to world literature, has at long last been made available in English.

* Reprinted in Georg Brandes's *Creative Spirits of the Nineteenth Century*, London, 1924.

T R A N S L A T O R ' S
N O T E

The chief task for the translator of a work so grave in its vision and so frolicsome in its episodes and vignettes is to keep as close as possible to the author's magisterial control of tone, his sardonic distance from the sins and follies he records. Paludan-Müller's generous sentiment quickly and deliberately crusts over into frigid clarity, and it is the translator's duty to choose the words and phrases in his own language which come as close as possible to what is being said and, above all, how it is being said.

Contributory to the tone's cool gravity is, of course, the *ottava rima* stanza, keeping the thought within fixed bounds of rhyme and line-length and acting as a gentle brake upon the narrative's exuberance. The stanza form, then, had to be kept: it is a crucial part of the work's equipoise. Since, however, English lacks many feminine rhymes with any tonal dignity, I have not attempted to reproduce Paludan-Müller's alternation of masculine and feminine rhymes in the sestina of each stanza. Also, since he regularly shifts the rhyme scheme of the sestina (between, say, ABABBA and ABBAAB), I have felt at liberty to alter the rhyme scheme of any given stanza so long as the English scheme is identical to one Paludan-Müller uses in Danish. In those rare cases in which he himself has violated the rhyme scheme (as in Canto X, p. 430) or the line-length (as in Canto V, p. 148), I have reproduced the violation when it would not render the English awkward.

Some Danish words and titles have been left untranslated,

such as *posteier, Geheimeraad, konditori;* explanations of them
are given in the Notes along with explanations of other un-
common terms found in the text. For the reader who may have
some uncertainty about Danish pronunciation, the information
that follows may be useful. Danish consonants have roughly
the same value as English consonants, save for the *j* (pronounced like the *y* in *young*); the *d* (pronounced after a
vowel like the *th* in *they* and not pronounced at all after *l, n, r*
or before *s;* the *th* (pronounced like the *t* in *too*); and the *g*
(pronounced like *y* between two vowels). The final *g* in *Galtenborg* is so weakly sounded that I have felt free to rhyme it with
door and *before* (p. 242). The only diphthongs occurring in
the text are *eg, ei, ej* (all of them pronounced like the pronoun
I). Danish vowels have approximately these values:

   a as in *cat*
   e as in *men*
   i as in *gasoline*
   o as in *bold*
   u as in *glue*
   æ like the vowel-sound in *air*
   ø like the vowel-sound in *her*
   aa or *å* like the vowel-sound in *flaw*

The unaccented *e* is pronounced like the *e* in *oven.*

Punctuation has been normalized to meet the expectations
of a twentieth-century English-speaking reader.

I should like to express my gratitude for the great help and
encouragement extended to me by Dr. Elias Bredsdorff, for the
kindness and confidence in my work shown me by Dr. Leif
Sjöberg, and for the aid rendered me on several difficult points
by Dr. P. M. Mitchell.

                                              S. I. K.

Part One

P R O L O G U E

Long vanished from us is that ancient past
When bardic harp would peal to clashing shield
And stir the heroes to the battlefield
And sing to solace those by fate downcast.
The ancient champions' souls lie bounden fast
Within a sleep that cannot be unsealed:
Who now would tell in song of derring-do
But fills old leathern flasks with wine yet new.

So too are vanished now the golden days
When to the knightly halls the bard was brought
And, as his eye among the ladies sought,
Of Roland and Sir Lancelot sang lays.
As one the hero and the poet wrought
To win themselves their countrymen's high praise!
Chivalric times—ah, but they were poetic;
Our times are at the very most aesthetic.

Every man's his own best friend, it's said,
A saying just as true of every time;
That music pleases most whose echoing chime
Reveals our own hearts full-interpreted.
Therefore the Muse will blaze new paths to tread
In the illimitable land of rhyme;
Therefore, in forms that answer to our day,
Unto us now she will her world display.

Since every poet has this new advice,
At long last from Illusion's bonds set free,
More and more we see pure history,
As poetic matter, drop in price.
Out from Fancy's brilliant paradise
The bald exploits, far-famed though they may be,
The unclad heroes, bare of throat and limb,
Are driven by the critic cherubim.

From Scylla to Charybdis, though, we fall,
From eiderdown to straw, as hereabout
Such falls into Charybdis Northmen call.
The truth in that old saying still holds out:
He who once doubted it can no more doubt
On seeing this age, prosier than them all,
Set naked into genre illustrations
Issued as poetical narrations.

And yet these pictures please; the rabble flocks
To see itself performing in the prints,
And few find aught amiss in mezzotints
Which show for soaring eagles strutting cocks,
For Amor's victories lewd leers and squints,
For swan songs only street-geese and their squawks.
What's to be done? What duty and command
May be as law to guide a poet's hand?

The Jews had ten commandments—an excess,
Found by the Jews themselves too hard to hold.
We Christians have but two, which merely stress
That we must keep our hearts from growing cold.
Yet, these two give us much uneasiness
And cause the whole world troubles manifold,
So that we've now reduced the sum of these
From ten and two to one: Seek ye to please!

To that commandment this world's reconciled:
It stands engraved in gold on each man's gate.
The father wise confides it to his child
That he might grow up to be something great.
Please all, my son! Then happy is your state.
From such advice the son is not beguiled:
He grows up, with a beard to shave and tweeze,
Then out he goes into the world, to please.

41

And, as he goes, he sees his lesson right
And no delusion, no false theorem;
As rings from costly diamonds set in them,
So from that lesson all of life's made bright.
Tartuffe will please, as any tart at night;
Fools and heroes, for crowns-brummagem;
So too the diva, screeching on all stages;
And, yes, the priest, whose unction so assuages.

The old will please no less than will the young,
Please any which way so their end's effected,
For to their end no means can be rejected:
A will please by dint of his sharp tongue,
B's heart has open wounds to be inspected,
C has an ailing liver or a lung
As, languishing, he comes with pallid face
To cough himself into his lady's grace.

Then that word "Please!" is just the right reply
To what I've racked my brain to understand;
For what to all the world is a command
Is not for any poet to defy.
But *whom* to please? That question comes to hand.
Oneself, one's neighbor, or one's God on high?
That mighty question I'll dare ponder through,
I will not simply chop its knot in two.

I've chosen stuff that's rather ordinary,
With coloring that's national in stain;
Its hero, mind and mold and speech a Dane,
Is in his daily life to move round free.
He's kept apart from ideality,
His course is unromantic, prosy-plain,
Attempting all, not once for all his labor
Choosing right—he'll surely please my neighbor.

But, as I let him sail on his own ocean
And let him age until his hair grows gray,
You'll see my poem's overarching notion
Mirrored in his life ere we're midway.
May this avowal not prove braggadocian
And my veracity stand the assay;
Then I would hope—if not to win the throng—
To please high Heaven with my moral song.

5l

My own approval does not come with ease
And, let there be no doubt, that's yet to come.
To garner that and my own self to please
With stuff by nature rather troublesome,
I'll have my work expand its boundaries
In hopes to rescue it from tedium;
Thus, as my pen pursues my hero's strides,
I'll have a look about me on all sides.

And here the Prologue well might reach its close—
My weak design, I fear, is all too plain—
Lest one should say these cantos don't contain
One whit of what he'd been led to suppose.
Should he ask whence this poverty arose,
The author and his times he can arraign;
Should he charge just the author for their flaws,
The author answers: "My times are the cause!"

I should have ended; but when one *begins*
It happens that to *end* is rather hard.
Just think about the young, as yet unscarred,
Who take life's open road like paladins,
And see if soon life forfeits their regard;
Think even (if I may) of one who sins
And whom the voice of conscience cries to, "Halt!"
And see if soon its master mends his fault.

Each beginning—ah! so rich, so grand,
As though the splendor of it had no end!
See all things gilded by the red dawn's brand
As though all Heaven's riches would descend;
See spring blooms teeming on the loamy land;
See joyful children playing, friend with friend;
See eyes their first love-glances shyly cast
And to that instant bind Eternity fast.

Nor can a singer take a different course,
The seed of poetry roused in his breast;
He hears the future's voice before the rest
Demanding from him its expressive force.
Hope and love, joy, grief, scorn, and remorse,
Bitter sorrow and delight twice-blest,
Before their time they seize on his heartstrings
So they ring strong, and long their echoings.

6/

C A N T O I

On Jutland's coast, not far from Vejle town,
The Jutish Eden, by general accord,
Along the sweep of lovely Vejle Fjord
Which gentle, ever-mirrored hillsides crown
And on which ships and boats race up and down
And scarce a shimmering trace of wake afford:
A village and white church stand at the spot
Where on the map one sees a double dot.

It is the winter: frozen is the land
And roundabout, far as the eye can go,
The fields and woods are as though sown with snow;
Thick ice has nearly all the inlet spanned.
Gray, faithful as the North by which their band
Has always stood throughout its winter woe,
The nimble sparrows on the farm roofs wake
And beg some bits of farmstead Christmas-cake.

For it is Christmas Eve: when winter-bright
The sprightly wreaths of festive stars have shed
Upon the snow's chill gleam a silvery white
Such as we sometimes may see overspread
The cold and pallid faces of the dead
When bursts the Infinite upon their sight.
All is so still—the winds are all but dumb;
But from the fjord the sounds of footsteps come.

It is Herr Peter Homo, country priest,
As toward the shore across the ice he goes;
Though somewhat short and though his girth's increased,
He's much more nimble than you might suppose.
A greatcoat, jacket, waistcoat are his clothes,
For which gray woollens his own sheep were fleeced;
He has just gone to check his fishing ground,
And now he's tramping briskly, homeward bound.

And as he strides across the field for home
Along a trail now scarce to be descried,
His eyes go up to where the stars abide,
But swift go down again from Heaven's dome
As to his parsonage windows now they glide,
Then seek once more that starry honeycomb.
It's clear, so split 'twixt earth and heaven is he,
His thoughts are more than apt to make him dizzy.

And little wonder: Christmas's starlight
Reminds him that his sermon, scarce begun,
Is on his desk at home, its pages white,
And straight on that his thoughts begin to run.
Therefore, as ancient shepherds once had done,
He stares at Heaven, till with the blinding sight
Of an angelic figure, all light ends—
Before his eyes a veil at once descends.

No wonder: for the gentle candlelight
Gleaming through the parsonage windowpanes,
Betokening the joys that home contains
Whose roof grows ever closer in his sight,
His busy mind to new and lesser gods constrains:
To Christmas porridge and his wife this night.
In the cheerful parlor of the parsonage,
With both of them at once he will engage.

There too his little son he will behold,
Born Martinmas, and next day he will bear
The lad to be baptized, when he will wear
A christening gown and green cap trimmed with gold.
Already he can hear the boy scream bold
Against the sprinkling and the drawn-out prayer.
Then he looks up—again his thoughts alight
Upon the Christ-child, born this very night.

Our priest, in his divided reverie,
Walks through the snow, but meanwhile I will guide
The reader to his parlor. There we see
A narrow room, above which low beams ride;
Tile oven with a cheerful flame inside;
Six chairs and also one outworn settee;
A cradle by the clock against the wall,
Over which a bird sits, caged and small.

And before the cradle, to it bending,
The priest's young wife sits, delicate and fair,
Warmth and joy in her expression blending
To contemplate her first-born lying there.
Now a smile her mild, clear glances bear,
Now they cloud, some somber thought portending,
Until her joyful gaze again breaks through
In thoughts which, verbally, I thus construe:

"O little child, to whom I've given birth,
How you refresh my eyes as well as heart!
If I were offered all the gold of earth,
With not your smallest finger would I part.
No one can ever know what you are worth,
You little angel, and you great upstart!
With all your smiles and all your rogueries,
The priest and ev'n the dean himself you please.

"All rosy-cheeked I see you sweetly sleeping,
The pillow clutched within your pudgy fists;
I feel your gentle breath, just like the mists
Of warm, enlivening winds when Spring is peeping;
Your voice reveals what Time has in its keeping,
Which to a mother's mind alone exists:
Your future gladness and your future fear—
Ah, let me rock you until they appear."

Just then there comes a chiming from the clock;
Its striking wakes her from her dreams, and she
Rises up and lays the crockery
As from the stove the cat decides to stalk
And, softly purring, stretches lazily.
It hears quick footsteps coming up the walk
And, finished feeding, out it lightly leaps
As through the open door the pastor sweeps.

The Christmas porridge is set out and steaming.
When he has finished, Homo puffs a while
Upon his pipe and casts a loving smile
Toward his son, swaddled up and dreaming.
Then to the study, where he'd left his pile
Of sermon notes; while, busy with the seaming
Of new ribbons for a baby bonnet,
His wife stays back to finish working on it.

The ribbons lying on her lap outspread,
Once again she sits there quietly
And has a look as if her eyes had read
Deep into the baby's destiny.
What can't a mother know! But prophecy
Is tricksome even in a mother's head;
The future man lies back a heavy curtain,
And mother-love's desires all too certain.

Those tears of joy before the cradle shed
At some heroic future for one's child
Might consecrate a tailor's life instead,
Some bungler on whom fate will ne'er have smiled.
And mothers' smiles on life still to be led—
Salt of the earth, 'neath cradle blankets piled,
Light whose beams the world has yet to mark—
Those smiles may fall upon a child of dark.

The parson's wife was deeply moved inside,
In prayer commending unto God her son,
And, glancing out the window when she'd done,
The lamps of night in heaven she espied.
A star shot down and, then, before it died,
A new and greater starfall had begun.
She took that as a sign of his success
And, as it came, prayed for his happiness.

And here I wish to let the cover fall
On Christmas Eve, till scenes more bright and gay
Can greet the reader upon Christmas Day
When it shall dawn upon the sunbeams' call.
But there's one question I must pose to all:
What better shows the Danish mind and way,
What so delightful, what so sanctified,
As parson's Christmas in the countryside?

Such crowds of friends from miles and miles around
Come 'neath the parson's roof a-visiting
That heart's space must provide them quartering
When there's no house-space, as is often found.
Six to one room—so ends the evening—
Two to one bed—now, not another sound!
Let them, thinks the priest's wife, stay the night,
I only hope they find the beds all right.

10/

Among the guests awaited above all
Is very like to be the parson's son,
With five, six students from the capital
He's brought along to share the Christmas fun.
Tense expectation has the house in thrall—
The priest's young daughters more than anyone;
Whenever one of them a carriage hears,
They all begin to blush up to their ears.

And when at last the guests have all arrived
To share the season's hospitality,
The walls resound with such cacophony
You'd think that Babylon had been revived.
Through clouds of pipe smoke you might get to see
Some flash of wit, regrettably short-lived;
But oftenest, when laughter rolls and thunders,
It's just a roar at overweening blunders.

Each gets the floor with his one gift, a tongue,
And as he speaks he turns from cold to bold:
Each notion heard before is once more sprung,
Each anecdote remembered is retold;
The field of politics is well patrolled,
The sheltering tents of art are walked among;
Discussion swoops up to the mystagogic,
Then takes a header down to tapster's logic.

So on it goes, till the assembled swarm
Relieve their souls by taking morning tea.
Once breakfast has restored their energy,
To spend the day in parties they re-form.
Some take their hats and sticks to ramble free,
And some to hopes of learnèd discourse warm,
While others slip upstairs before they're missed
To use the loft-room for a day of whist.

Downstairs, several students have remained,
Each one of them extremely energetic
In showing off his grasp of things aesthetic
And keeping the young daughters entertained.
Each word that serves the cause of the poetic
The young girls take to heart with so unfeigned
A zeal that, ere the holiday is through,
They taste what life's own poetry can do.

While inside matters are so well in hand,
Outside the day is equally well sped:
Dogs, horses, boys and girls high-spirited
And fed on all the bounty of the land.
For every age has come to understand
Not only that man can't live just on bread,
But that contentment is proportionate
To just how much is in one's glass and plate.

And so, what bustling cellars, sculleries,
What drawings off and, too, what pourings in,
What squanderings of spices have there been,
What crowds of wildfowl suffer casualties!
In cooking, girls must learn the art to please,
And mother duly watches them begin;
And then a flood pours down on each guest's head
Of crullers, Christmas-loaves, and gingerbread.

In such ways do the mind and body glory
As each day passes like a festival;
At night they dance in the conservatory
Or else they pay a nearby priest a call.
Such parish visits only start the story—
East, west, and everywhere the visits fall—
Each cleric with a fatted calf to slaughter,
Each genteel miller, and each cultured cotter.

One visit brings another in return,
Only New Year's Day will end the rite;
And, in time's fullness, one girl may incite
A student's heart, as oft is so, to yearn.
Most like, two hands are all that they can plight,
And two young hearts that for each other burn;
But how, with all this plenty, could the pair
Suppose a future where the cupboard's bare?

The joy is all the greater on that head,
And when the holiday at last must end,
And handclasps go around from friend to friend,
Two will exchange a loving kiss instead.
In two open carriages, with sled,
The dogs all barking, home the houseguests wend.
Down to the road the household will come too:
The gate must not too soon cut off the view.

And there once more they all must say farewell
And thank you for the splendid holidays,
And once again the happy couple tell
Their two hearts' rapture in their loving gaze—
Then hats are swung as they are swung always
And all the guests their "Take good care, now" yell,
While shouts accompany the parting throng,
"Farewell, farewell! Don't stay away too long!"

'Twas but an episode; for, else, it's still
Out in the country with its days serene.
The sun makes no noise as his mild rays spill
Their light on life in that secluded scene.
The moon makes not a sound when, late at e'en,
Her beams slant in across the windowsill;
And grove and garden, field and verdant lea
Diffuse a deep, though gentle, melody.

The wave of life monotonously flows,
And all its savage roaring is here stilled;
But, if it rise, immediately it's killed
In toil by day and by the night's repose.
With hope and thought a rural life is filled,
And strong the fancy in these small homes grows;
It is as if so softly flowed time's stream
That men get lost inside themselves and dream.

But in our clay contrary urges reign,
And ev'n the cozy cottager is stirred
To brave the outside like a hardy bird
And try his wings against life's hurricane;
While he who has its violence incurred
And learned the hollow taste of fruit profane
Will yearn to take his staff and seek the road
That leads back to his little, calm abode.

But to the text now! Homo's grand salon,
Illumined by the winter sun's bright glare,
Is opened for this Christmas day's affair.
Into a circle an assembly's drawn.
Dean Matthias Holm and wife we come upon,
Homo's in-laws, sitting by his chair:
He, orthodox and strict of word and life;
She, quiet, sweet, the model of a wife.

Beside them, Reverend Jeremias Top
Together with his helpmeet, Amalie,
Who both would fain be known for piety,
Though of their spirit there seems scarce a drop
Their massive fleshy bodies failed to sop.
Of Top I must report this mystery:
That, while he thinks himself a child of light,
His curses oft invoke the Prince of Night.

Next, Reverend Henrik Flint and sister come,
She a chaste maid, straight and proud of bearing,
And her brother, heart-cold, ever airing
His deep and perspicacious cerebrum.
He cocks his ear to each new theorem,
By Doctor Strauss particularly swearing,
As, super-wise and skeptic, it's his stance
That Scripture is but legend and romance.

Aside from them, there's only left to name
Our Peter Homo, he the rationalist,
Who'll shave a text, but will, however, claim
He keeps the faith, a good religionist.
By such procedure did the egoist
(For such was Homo) hope to 'scape Hell's flame;
According to his method, what he now
Explains away he next will re-allow.

So gathered in a circle are the dear
And loving friends, who on that day would stand
Godparents for the parson's baby here
And now are sitting with some snacks in hand.
The new-made Christmas-cakes soon disappear,
While drinks are served around upon demand,
Until the two church bells begin to ring
The parish to its Yuletide worshipping.

Just at that time the parlor door swings wide;
From her cold room to join the well-warmed rest,
In snow-white gown, and ribbons at her chest,
Faint rose upon her lips and cheeks, for pride,
Baptismal candidate upon her breast
And Ambush, sturdy pointer, at her side,
The priest's young wife steps lightly, to enhance
The joy of all with her mild countenance.

Into her mother's arms she gently lays
Her little son, whose fine baptismal dress
That her own hands had put in readiness
Brings to her all the company's high praise.
Fru Holm then gives her godson a caress
And promises, according to the phrase
We use at christenings when babies wail:
"He'll be an opera singer, without fail."

But Dean Holm's voice is raised above the rest:
"Let's go on to church! You heard the carillon!
Up! We're warm enough now to move on
And sing the hymns out from a faithful breast!
Up, up, my friends! The priest's already gone;
Let's follow where he leads us, as is best!"
He takes his hat—to church the guests all wind,
And only the child's mother stays behind.

But in the little church, within all lit
With gold that streamed from Christmas day's bright sun,
The farmers and their wives already sit
With young townspeople in their plain homespun.
The Baron's stall creaks open to admit
Him and his wife, observed by everyone;
And, as their godchild sleeps on unawares,
His sponsors take the stall just under theirs.

The services begin. From his podium
The deacon, in the open choir, speaks out
The first prayer, twirling absently one thumb
And then the other round and round about.
His voice lends wings unto the song devout,
And though the straining turns him soon quite dumb,
So perfectly his congregation took him
They caught his music just as it forsook him.

Two hymns are sung. The third had just been chanted
When, with the deacon, ready for the day,
His hands deep down inside his gown firm-planted,
The Reverend Peter Homo made his way,
Sunlit, from sacristy to pulpit bay.
He squeezes up the stairs, in breadth much scanted;
His goal achieved, he lifts the cross and sighs,
And then bows low before the Baron's eyes.

Does he forget something? His head's a-nod,
As if he spoke but to himself alone.
His opening prayer is in an undertone,
But then his voice swells, powerful and broad,
To read the gospel of the Son of God,
That in the farthest pews it might be known.
Then to the volume of his normal speech
He drops, as at that point he starts to preach.

With this transition, he put text aside:
As all held strongly by this festival,
He chose to leave the theme unamplified,
And a related matter he would call
To the consideration of them all,
For in his sermon he'd be occupied
"With fear and hope commingled on the earth
Whenever a child of dust is given birth."

"A child is born!" he shouted joyfully,
And his right hand upon the pulpit fell.
"But what's called into life—O who can tell?—
In this life venturing on infancy?
First tears, for it begins with misery;
Then laughter, for it smiles to find all well;
Then all earth's hopes and sorrows thousandfold,
For—know—the child has earth in copyhold.

"Earth's copyholder!—Just what does that mean?
My Christian brothers! Do you rightly know?
It means a soul that from its Empyrean
Home descends upon the earth below
And goes to school and from school back does go
Into its mansions glorious and serene;
A soul that will with worthless dust unite
Although it knows itself a child of light.

"Not souls alone, but bodies, too, are we:
World-copyholders, that's the epithet
For men of clay, now happy, now beset,
Who wived to yield the race more progeny,
Who fell to lust and gross cupidity
And ate their bread in their own foreheads' sweat,
Who finally, when God would have it so,
Against their will, their death must undergo.

"This phrase, then, clearly has a double sense,
Though many a life is lived in only one,
For this assertion hardly needs defence:
When a being comes forth beneath the sun,
Both fearfulness and hope together run
In the hearts which made that life commence,
In those who, may we say it, must make good
Through that same child their choice of parenthood.

"For what will this child take himself to be?
Should he, a mystic, think himself all soul,
Disdaining life and its activity?
Or leave all spiritual mastery
And root about the earth like any mole?
Does he, in other words, make it his goal
To pay his debt to God or Caesar here?
To such questions are the answers clear?

"O, seeing how the world about him stood,
The apostle says: In every house we see
Bowls used for honor and indignity,
Not silver only, but of earth and wood.
Who fears not lest a shameful vessel be
The silver one hope sees in babyhood—
A joyous hope that heeds the Nazarene
In Matthew, chapters eighteen and nineteen?"

Homo kept on this exalted bent
And often brought his two hands down with force
Upon the pulpit, by which blows he meant
To wake attention to his high discourse.
Reaching down into a pocket vent
For a pouch, he paused in middle course
To take a pinch of snuff, in sight of all;
Then once more to his sermon did he fall:

"My talk of hope and joy has been abstract:
Now I shall turn to life in the concrete,
At whose hard hands we are forever thwacked,
Life far from ideal in the balance sheet:
To life, such life as we in Denmark meet,
To life which goes askew and comes out cracked—
And here, my Christian friends, I'd like to know:
At our child's birth should we feel joy or woe?

"For look about you, all you who have eyes!
And use your ears, those of you who have ears!
And tell me if this land, in former years,
Saw such a ferment, saw such troubles rise.
Faith, science, government some would revise;
In lands, flocks, folk, a meaning new inheres:
Anyone can tear down. —Who builds up?
See, brothers, that's the bitter in our cup!

"And what a thought to have: my child I cast
Upon the deep, the furious-raging flood.
How can that little dinghy safely scud
When founder mighty ships of many a mast?
Can faith and hope and courage still hold fast
Amidst a world with vice for its lifeblood?
Can infant virtue anywhere find grace
Throughout this feeble, this perverted race?

"So speaks Morality. But no less grim
Is Reason as she makes this declaration:
Our Denmark is a poor and tiny nation,
Where each man crowds the man who's next to him.
But, as a jar can't be filled past the brim,
It is the same with every state and station:
If no class can keep many people fed,
Whom shall we look to for our children's bread?

"The lad can till the land, you may maintain;
But where's his meadow, farmhouse, field, and plot?
I'd like to know where land can now be got
When all's been ploughed up in the King's domain.
Then he can be a merchant! Still my brain
Is puzzled by my Christian friend's kind thought:
For one who buys, there will be ten who'll sell;
Where shall our merchant find his clientele?

"Officialdom has failed to comfort me.
My pleas for daily bread get this reply:
A has it now; and after A comes B;
Next, C has claims that we must satisfy.
If I but mention university,
'Student-glut' is everybody's cry.
And, more or less as one, they all concur—
Each artist, artisan, and officer.

"What's to be done? The child must earn his bread.
When I ask that, and no one pays me heed,
Then in my Bible once again I read
What in the ancient days Our Lord had said:
Behold the lilies growing in the mead!
Behold the birds of Heaven overhead!
With birds and lilies safe beneath God's sight,
Why should finances cause you all this fright?"

Here Homo feels right in his element—
For fear of poverty is the hell-hound
That, day and night, has held his soul fast-bound
And by the name of Old Debt kept him bent.
He lists the woes of being indigent,
The ways in which the poor man can be ground,
Until, returning from his long digression,
He ends his sermon with a last profession:

"The child as type had been my theme before;
Now it's my own son I am coming to,
For it was he I really had in view
When I considered what life holds in store.
And it's my hope no heart will here deplore
My speaking of my own child as I do.
For as a priest I owe it everyone
To tell how I myself shall raise a son.

"So know it now, beloved congregation,
That here today I'll have my son baptized,
So that his right to grace is solemnized
In time to save him from abomination.
His name, by which his race is recognized,
Is oldest of all names: with the Creation,
As we know, it is coincident:
To call my first-born Adam's my intent.

"I shall rear my boy in godly ways,
As I scarce need give you assurance for,
But let me say a few words on that score:
He shall be toughened from his early days
In mind and body; when he disobeys
He'll taste the rod, till he's a child no more;
And if to tell a lie he'll but begin,
He'll quickly feel just what it is to sin.

19/

"Of that truth I'll never be negligent
Which, though it's near forgot by one and all,
Parents ought especially recall:
When the branch is young, it may be bent.
But with mere bending I won't be content;
As twigs are grafted onto trees when small,
So early on my son I shall impress
Each principle which I have learned to bless.

"Thus, for example, I have no ambition
To teach too much trust in humanity,
But neither would I foster his suspicion
Of wickedness in everything he'll see.
No! From illusions he must be kept free,
Nor shall he break from civilized tradition,
But toward what's old and good remain devout
Until he sees the modern drive it out.

"In good works done his honor he shall find,
And through the rifts, the heavings of this age,
And while temptations round about him rage,
He'll win a vantage and a strength of mind
Whereby he'll not let pleasure make him blind
And, out of reason's light, at will rampage.
Through earthly fogs her brilliant beams will steer
Him forth, if he'll but keep his vision clear.

"See, Christian friend, the course on which I've hit
For this child's tender, inexperienced feet;
I know the danger flesh and blood will meet
On life's wide road, but I don't fear for it.
If I add my own knowledge to his wit
And my experience to his youthful heat,
Then, when together hope and fear I weigh,
In my heart it's hope that wins the day.

"But whether outward circumstances bless him
Once he's braved his struggles and his woe,
In what direction then his life will go,
If the wicked of the world oppress him,
If fortune with her laurel wreath should dress him
And he achieve life's most revered plateau—
Well, such things we'll not speak of *in extenso*,
Since everything remains yet *in suspenso*.

"Therefore, my child I only will commend
To all assembled and to everyone
Who, in the parson, loves the parson's son,
And here I'll bring my sermon to an end.
This Christmas Day I sought to comprehend
How Christian fathers' duties should be done;
And now—commending every citizen
To Heaven's safekeeping—I shall say Amen."

As Homo wiped the sweat beads from his face
And mumbled thereupon his closing prayer,
The congregation's eyes stole to his heir
To search for any future glory's trace.
But, though it shyly kept its hiding place,
They found the sermon quite beyond compare!
Not once from the strait pathway had it wandered:
The priest and his new son was all it pondered.

But there were some not quite so overawed,
Like Pastor Flint, a man who without fail
Took pleasure with his sister to assail
Everything with satire's chastening rod.
Old Holm, ice-cold, bit on his fingernail
And, through the sermon, sat and never thawed.
Beneath his breath he twice was heard to say:
"No, from his text a priest must never stray."

What else took place in church that Christmas Day
Will take me but a little time to tell:
The count of offerings from the altar tray
Did not make Homo's household coffer swell.
If here a mark, and there four shillings, fell,
The pastor nodded in a friendly way;
To see four shillings Homo sighed aloud,
To see a mark he delicately bowed.

In the baptismal act itself, they swore
The man was simply too enthusiastic,
For, were it fatherly devotion, or
Eruption of caprice ecclesiastic,
When to the font Fru Holm her grandson bore,
His dousing of the baby was so drastic
That, unable to endure his bath,
He screamed to Heaven to mitigate its wrath.

And Heaven showed its mercy; and I pray
The gentle reader note this show of mine,
For I'll no longer have him stay and pine
Within the church's chilly walls this day.
Home to the parsonage my song's design
Will have him wander on the snow-packed way,
While, as on Time's own rapid-beating wing,
Ahead five hours I will have him spring.

So! to the parsonage's tableside,
Where, after toasting Adam, all arose
With souls refreshed and bodies fortified.
Deep into the glass all worry goes;
With pipes all lit, with coffee well-supplied,
They form a circle. Conversation flows:
The gentle ladies, knitting on and clucking,
The gentle priests, upon their pipestems sucking.

And, as they sit partaking of the cool
And bracing coffee, and the white smoke sprawls,
They seem like gods in cloudy Olympian halls.
Then the learnèd clerics come to pool
Their thoughts about the meaning of the rule
That reads: "Whoever Christ his Savior calls
And is baptized, is blest"—a sure foundation—
"But who believeth not shall have damnation."

About these words the company was split.
Hr. Jeremias Top maintained that all
Who to baptismal rites would not submit,
Despite their faith, would to damnation fall.
"For," said he—and here his eyes alit
On Pastor Flint, who often roused his gall—
"Since baptized folk are oft to hell consigned,
What salvation can unbaptized find?"

"That point"—Flint smiled—"I cannot comprehend,
The logic of it's far above my head.
But even if the doctrine's warranted
Which Germany's philosophers commend:
That dead is dead, nor worth a candle's end
The soul, when once in crepe we're laid to bed—
Then—as to whether it is false or true—
Then, my dear Top, I've my opinion too.

"Here's what I think—as many others hold—
The message can't to just some men apply,
But points the path we all must travel by
When once our bodies in the earth lie cold.
I think we're all cut from the selfsame mold—
You, good Pastor Top, as well as I,
My sister, just as is Fru Amalie:
We all, I think, shall share that destiny."

"I can't believe in that!" retorted Top,
As Mistress Top abruptly tossed her head.
"Why, such a Heaven is well forfeited
That gathers to it such a motley crop.
No one unbaptized can be blessed." "Stop!"
Cried Flint. "By Reason let our talk be led.
Do you think David damned? Say yes or no!"
"No," sighed Top, "but blest? I say, not so."

Some time they kept up this confabulation,
With Holm and Homo hanging on each word,
Until the heated battle was transferred
From holy water to the faith's foundation.
Here Top exceeded every expectation:
He talked until his innards hotly stirred,
He talked as if alight with sacred fire,
But 'gainst a Flint what logic could aspire?

"My view," said Flint, "is simply this, that science
Trumps all faith, brimful though it may be;
For, frankly, there's but little faith in me
If Christian faith on myths must place reliance.
All's solved by science—modern prophecy—
But faith's bald puzzles set it at defiance.
I live by science; but the cow that fed
On faith in grass still underground dropped dead."

Here Homo entered: "Please, dear Flint, do find
For faith a different measuring stick!
In your conclusion you are much too quick!
This simile should make you of our mind:
As at a mill they take in wheat to grind
Into a flour which is so soft and slick
It can be used for bread to feed humanity,
Interpreting refines on Christianity.

"But when its contents are well sifted through,
Cleansed by Criticism's keen inspection
Of passages of dubious complexion,
More and more of which, I fear, accrue,
Then faith is purified and clear and true,
A lodestar to give life its right direction.
A faith which will no honest man betray,
Such is the faith which shows to me my way."

Then up arose Dean Holm; though elderly,
He'd dare to stake his priesthood in a brawl,
For he was up to any of them all
In fine mind, ardor, and sonority.
The cloud of wrath that on his brow we see
Gathering all this time, like storms in fall,
Broke forth in speech with all its might and main,
And down upon the clergymen did rain.

"I've long been listening in indignation!
Are these fit thoughts for clergy to propound?
Your dean, by law diaconal, has found
Not one thing Christian in this conversation.
Hr. Top, who's perfect in his estimation,
Reveals himself a Pharisee hidebound,
Who sees himself alone as Heaven's man,
Though in Herr Flint I see no publican.

"But when he talks, he seems quite close to sinning,
Just as close, dear son-in-law, as you!
For wisdom rotted dry is no more winning
Than intellect that still is parvenu.
I do declare you both are now beginning
To find in worldly science heady brew,
And—to speak plain—all I can do is spit
At myths and your interpretative wit.

"Among the orthodox let me be classed:
I will not take away or add a whit,
And never stretch upon the modern last
My Christian faith and, no less, Holy Writ.
And, though I'll fight when zeal is pushed to it,
Like any priest, I hold peace unsurpassed.
And—if this protest can bring some surcease—
I'll have this Christmas kept to rites of peace."

24/

So our Dean Holm concluded in this vein,
And with his words my canto too shall end.
I felt it right my readers comprehend
What sponsors my song's hero did obtain.
One favorite byword of the south-coast Dane
(A byword with which this work must contend)
Is that each boy—oh, how they prattle on, sir—
Takes after both his father and his sponsor.

C A N T O   I I

O distant childhood, from us you departed
As we from you, and in our memory sleep.
Where is the joy that from your root once darted,
'Neath time's thick sediment now buried deep?
A hope you are that Paradise we'll reap,
You move our feet to tread the ways you've charted
With promises no man can let alone:
"All will be given, once you are full grown."

We do grow up, and forth we wander blind,
Relying constantly upon hope's word;
In time, the glory hope had once conferred
On earth is but to memory consigned.
We stand stock-still, and thoughts run through our mind.
Back along its traces hope has spurred
And now, behind us, comes the muted call:
"Paradise was yours—when you were small!"

Still we are wanderers—and our avenue
Slopes downward from the start, beneath our feet,
And the flowers on it are but few.
But, under our day's burden, our day's heat,
Still the prize delusive we pursue
To seize it ere our losses are complete.
We search about—and yon lie death and night;
But where is childhood and the dawn's rose light?

As one example of a childhood sprout,
Before my reader Adam Homo here
I bring, who's entered now on his sixth year.
His gold hair rings his ruddy cheeks about;
In coat and trousers he sweeps in and out
The house like a bird in full career;
And, while about in infant-shoes he plies,
He eats, he drinks, he sings and laughs and cries.

Already he has learnt both love and fear,
One at his mother's, one his father's side;
For, from the cradle on, the priest applied
Much strictness to his son, to prove sincere
His pedagogic call, which was his pride.
Thus, rarely would he show his son good cheer,
And very, very rarely his profile
Would break, in Adam's sight, into a smile.

But very differently exhibited
Was his mother's love, all sweet and mild:
Her songs at morn would soothe the feckless child;
At night she kissed and carried him to bed;
They'd potter in the garden and the shed,
And in the meadow green glad hours beguiled;
She shared in all, his mirth and his distress,
And always watched to see his life progress.

One lovely summer morning, bright and warming,
The boy sat on his bench with book in hand
Beside her in the garden, his lips forming
Silently the letters that he scanned.
Down upon the book his tears were swarming;
Though he read well, he could not understand
A thing about the auxiliary *to be*,
Which father set him to learn thoroughly.

The pastor did not want mere repetition,
But full accounting for each last detail,
For he'd paid dearly for his recognition
That clear ideas in all things should prevail;
And so these lessons aimed not to regale
The lad, but urge him to a strict rendition
Of every point in the grammarians' codex;
And if he failed—then woe betide his podex!

"Oh, mother," Adam sobs, "I just don't see!"
Saying this, from where he sat he threw
A look to her with eyes wide-open, blue.
"Please, mother! What's the meaning of *to be*?
I cannot make it out! What shall I do?
And father said to learn it thoroughly.
I've read my lesson, every point and letter,
But what it means to *be* I know no better."

"To *be*?" asked Dean Holm's daughter, so entreated,
As, smiling gently and in deep thought cast,
Along her young son's cheek her hands she passed.
"Is that the word that has you so defeated?
Well, we can't have those tears of yours repeated!
Crying too much can turn us blind at last.
Now dry your eyes! And you shall learn from me
The proper meaning of the verb *to be*."

She spoke and, rising from her bench, she brought
The boy such comfort that he clapped and cast
His book aside with happiness as hot
As any slave's whose chains are off at last.
"Come!" said his mother, after she had thought,
And into her hand his hand gladly passed.
"Come, Adam! You and I will take a walk
And all about your lesson we shall talk."

Down the garden pathway go the two
And, full of fire, with mischief in his eyes,
In and out of bushes Adam flies
And calls out from his shelter: "Peek-a-boo!"
As they turned down a little avenue
And saw the meadow spread beneath the skies,
A bird flew past them on a downward swing
From heaven's blue upon its supple wing.

"Look, see the little bird!" his mother said,
As Adam stared at it while it progressed
Along the sky. "It's dipping to its nest
Over in the meadow just ahead.
Just hear it sing while its prepares a bed
For all its young, so tiny and so blest.
To sing, to fly, to feed their family,
That, Adam, is what birds would call to *be*.

"And can you see that big snail slip away
Along the path there, very fat and black,
Who sends you with his long horns a 'Good day'
And who you think is such a nasty jack?
When he is taking food and feeling gay,
With sunshine pouring on his wavy back,
He says, though he's not heard by anyone,
'To *be* is to be stirring in the sun.'

"And if the trees had mouths, like leaves and flowers,
So they could tell you about everything,
And if you asked *them*, they'd be answering:
'To *be*, oh, it's to stand in verdant bowers
And send forth, pair by pair, our blossom-showers,
And round like great long waving arms to swing
Our boughs, and then to have enough of heat,
Enough of rain, to make our lives complete.' "

As, in this fashion, from her heart's fresh spring
Her gentle speech flows on in one smooth stream,
Adam stood and stared as in a dream,
In earnest silence, hearing everything.
When she had ceased, he started fidgeting
And begged her to continue on that theme,
His voice so plaintive: "Mother, please tell me
Again just what it means, that word, to *be*."

"Do I know that?" she whispered half aloud,
And then with mother-love did her heart beat,
And, lifting her small son from off his feet,
She held him tight against her breast, and vowed:
"When you are in my arms, my little sweet,
And, in those moments, when my head is bowed
In prayer for you and all our family,
I feel most strongly what it is to *be*.

"But come now, father has these things in hand,
And he'll explain to us that weighty word;
Perhaps we must find out from one so grand
What to us little folk can't have occurred.
Today Herr Peter's by Herr Adam heard
And to us both he'll answer on demand
And both of us shall kiss him lovingly
If he can tell us what it is to *be*."

We do not know the Reverend's reply;
But it is certain that, from that day on,
His logic-course was dropped, as too were gone
Construings of such words as *you* and *I*.
On theory he no longer could rely,
And to a new, more useful organon
He set the boy, whereby the course grammatic
He had him change for training acrobatic.

But on this too his stamp must be applied,
Of fervor, strictness, and of constancy;
And hours on end did Adam spend astride
His vaulting-horse, 'midst Nature's majesty.
Homo even served as his son's guide
In leaps and climbs, perspiring copiously;
So son and father tourneyed, not by halves,
With much good done for their respective calves.

As to their fervor and the method which
Homo used, just one example need be conned:
His son and he stood near the garden ditch,
As deep and muddy as a village pond.
Each with a vaulting pole in hand, they hitch
Their knees and raise their heads to leap beyond
The trench upon the signal One-Two-Three,
From Lars the coachman, there to oversee.

"One!" yelled Lars, and they began the dash.
"Two!" he yelled: into the ground they threw
The one end of their poles quick as a flash,
And their torsos slightly backward drew.
"Three!" cried Lars; and with no more ado
You saw straight up in air their four legs thrash,
While, aided by their poles, a daring sweep
Sent them aloft in one grand master-leap.

But whether it was some defect in vision
So that the distance was not gauged aright,
Or that they did not reckon with precision
The force required to keep them on their flight,
Well, like two Icaruses' was their plight:
Neck-deep they fell from air into collision
With the muck-heap in the ditch, with Lars
In horror yelling: "Jiminy! My stars!"

In this way Adam's infancy progressed
In leaps and bounds; and all the hours remaining
From gymnastics, with unfailing zest
His mother occupied with her own training.
In every sense, her little son's attaining
Heaven was her consuming interest.
And she, so good, pursued, as did her man,
A settled method and specific plan.

Thus, for example, so as to prepare
Him for a humble and a steadfast mind,
She daily set him on the floor to find
The threads and fibers that had fallen there.
And early he had his own place assigned
To keep his things from lying everywhere;
And each day, as his special task, he fed
The bird its water and the dog its bread.

And, too, she taught him many a favorite song,
With words set to a simple melody;
Herself poetic, she could see no wrong
In teaching him a little poetry.
And it was fine to hear when, frequently,
She and little Adam sang along
To catches, in the most melodious strains,
In praise of Denmark and the noble Danes.

Every morning verses she'd recite
From Holy Scripture, and their words explain,
And she would call him to the windowpane
And show to him the starry choir at night.
Then she'd explain God's greatness and His might
And how this universe He did ordain,
Till both her son, who heard her with devotion,
And she herself were stirred with like emotion.

She had some notion of what rearing meant,
An art that to adults is hardly known:
They'd have their minds seem so intelligent
That children must think poorly of their own.
But every parent must make a descent
And, 'spite his wisdom, be as if half grown—
A novel method God Himself began
When He sent down to us His son as man.

And to her method, with avidity,
The young wife of the country pastor clung;
Adam and she were as two souls that hung
Upon the scene of life in company.
While *her* soul gave to thought both form and tongue,
His stood alert and heard attentively;
And, in that tongue, so childlike to his ear,
It was his own thought that he seemed to hear.

So Adam grew, a handsome little man,
Sweet, complex, with talents manifold,
Though not so splendid or so pure as gold.
He was an earth through which two fountains ran:
His reason, formed to Father Homo's plan,
Was cut and polished in the worldly mold;
His feelings, quick to brighten and to smart,
Came from the fullness of his mother's heart.

Her features his own features did repeat,
But his broad hands his father did bequeath,
As well as his thick hair and his sharp teeth
That cut through bone as handily as meat.
But these belied the character beneath;
For rarely would he be so indiscreet
As bare those teeth, much less let down that hair:
He'd sooner cry when life became unfair.

Still, by heart-pangs he was little tried,
For all the farmstead had him in their care:
At watering time, if Lars would take a ride,
He'd gladly lift him up astride the mare.
Niels Gardener carved the little rake he plied,
And oft he got the thresher's flail to share
When he'd come to the barn from morning-groats
And feel a sudden urge to thresh the oats.

The maids would let him work the butter-churn
And do some milking for the minister;
And glad he was if he should ever earn
A drop or two for his own porringer.
He ran along when they, on some concern,
Went to the franklin or the almoner.
He was indeed—nor did he mind at all—
The pastor's son, on whom all eyes would fall.

31/

Thus, it was early that ambition stirred
(Like a little snake) within his breast;
And, little wonder, when each day he heard
What in paternal voice would be expressed:
That honor, honor on our lives conferred,
Honor builds the temple of the blessed;
That he must first attain a worthy state,
For then alone could he achieve the great.

But now he is content to do the small.
Of these activities I'll only speak
Of how in summertime he would play ball
With boys from town, despite his frail physique;
How he forgave, and would not ever seek
Revenge for wrongs done in some free-for-all;
How many journeys son and mother made
To pick the blooms or berries in the glade.

How busily at harvest home he'd fall
To sharpening the scythes upon a strop
For Hans and Christen when they cut the crop;
And when, in from the fields they'd haul
The grain or hay, he'd ride along atop
The load, proud but afraid to sit so tall;
How, next, he'd help them when they tossed the rye
Up from the wagon through the hayloft eye.

How, finally, about the house he'd patter,
All dressed up in the homespun that he wore,
A household elf who could all calm restore;
For every time a washing-tub would shatter
And every time a maid would let a platter
Drop from her hand onto the kitchen floor
Or Lars would drive the cart so hard it broke,
Adam always turned it to a joke.

But of the travels of his infancy
It's only of his Sunday jaunts I'd speak,
When he'd go riding every other week
To see grandfather at the deanery.
And this the grandson waits for eagerly,
For here he knows his freedom's at its peak;
What fun to have the run of everything—
Our Adam here is happy as a king.

32/

But, after such a Sunday, on the whole
The boy seemed lazy and much out of sorts,
Attesting to a truth near every soul,
Ev'n Adam, father of us all, supports:
If round a man the sun of Eden roll,
Not till its last rays will he end his sports.
For this is Nemesis: that Paradise
Necessitates the rhyme of Pay-the-Price.

Thus Adam grew, and in that neighborhood
No brighter child than he had ever been seen;
And he, to do his mind still greater good,
Went to the deacon once a week to glean
Such writing, drawing, counting as he could
From him, who long a Dannebrog Man had been
For having upon mutual teaching hit,
And many a farmer's child now slaved at it.

And to the system's praise you'd have been led,
To hear how Adam and the deacon's child,
A girl named Hanne, with a clever head,
Into their mutual instruction piled.
Everyone would then be reconciled
To having one child by another bred
Were he to see those two, just like a brace
Of deacons, reckoning in each other's face.

For, sitting nose to nose, or practically,
No sooner Adam "Two times two!" would roar
Than Hanne yelled back: "Two times two is four!
Now you tell me how much is three times three!"
She got no chance to ask it one time more,
For, as a wolf may hap a lamb to see
And lunge upon its prey with eyes ashine,
So Adam screamed out: "Three times three is nine!"

They learned arithmetic as they learned art,
And so it went, too, when they learned to write;
But, when the deacon would feel kind at heart,
He'd leave one hour free, to their delight,
And out along the garden path they'd dart.
From there the country spread out to their sight
And, then, with eyes agleam, eagerly talking,
Arms round each other's neck, they would go walking.

33/

"Look!" his Hanne heard the boy once say.
"The Horsens road! —that white strip over there;
In three years I'll be going out that way
To Aarhus, to begin my school career.
I shall bid Vejle Fjord goodbye that day,
But you I won't forget, you needn't fear.
I'll come back as a pastor—" "Yes," she cried,
Interrupting, "and I'll be your bride!"

"Yes," the seven-year-old Adam said.
"And then we'll move into our rectory
And buy ourselves a fine four-poster bed."
"And don't forget a milk-tub," added she.
"You wouldn't want our cows to wander free
Out in the fields all day, uncomforted.
They must be milked! The butter and cheese-wheel
Must be laid out for the communion meal."

"You see to food and drink," Adam replied,
"While I tend to our children's upbringing
To make them worthy and well-qualified.
Nor from the girls will I keep anything
That I have learned out in the world so wide."
Again she broke in, eyes all glittering:
"I'll teach them how to read and sew and knit;
For daughters of a deacon that is fit."

"But I won't be a deacon," came his yell,
Flushed and angry, wishing honor done.
"I am already now a pastor's son,
And grandpa is a dean, as you know well."
Despite this taunt the girl did not rebel;
Of anger in her answer there was none:
"Well, deacon, pastor, what is in a name?
My father says it all comes out the same."

"No! A pastor can reach bishop's station;
A deacon always stays a deacon, though.
True! Your father's of the Dannebrog,
But he can never rise in his vocation."
"Humph!" Hanne proudly gave the boy to know:
"Well, as to that, there's one old observation
That deacons are best off, and it's true spoken:
Deacons just get damp when priests get soaken."

34/

With that, for now, they went off separately,
And on another path I now will bring
My hero, whom I would have travelling
A space of time amounting to years three.
Throughout them he'd scarce changed in anything
To do with day-to-day activity;
But in his mind, with more experience,
Of life and of himself he'd gained more sense.

So then, he's ten years old; but not, in fact,
Enrolled now in the deacon's grammar school,
Not that either head or heart he lacked,
But that his father took it for a rule
That Greek and Latin had much less impact
On life than any realistic tool,
And schools of useful science were the thing
To teach the child the art of managing.

While for such schools as these the pastor waited,
Our Adam lounged round in a vacuum,
Becoming day by day more addle-pated,
Roman in his taste for otium.
With slothfulness he now was permeated
Till fate's hand struck abruptly, meddlesome,
Laid the priest out sick upon his bed,
And stood the boy in good and happy stead.

For Adam's mother, who could not but rue it
To see him waste his golden years away,
Immediately determined to undo it:
She had them hitch the horses to the shay
And, late at night, as Homo slept all through it,
Had Adam pack his bags without delay.
They both climbed in the shay, and instantly
They made for Aarhus Boys' Academy.

Next day they went to see the Aarhus rector,
Who found the knowledge Adam then displayed
Fit him for low-boy in the bottom grade,
And sank his hope of top-man to a specter.
One tailor Brandt vowed he'd be his protector
And treat him like a son if Adam stayed.
They dined, then son and mother said farewell
With many a kiss, as many a teardrop fell.

351

And home went Madame Homo, to defy
(She knew it well) a fierce hullaballoo,
While Adam stayed at Aarhus, with an eye
That swam in tears, alas, the whole day through.
Toward night Brandt led him up the stairs so high
To the attic story and withdrew.
And there he saw his bed, his little room,
And there was left alone with all his gloom.

He went and stared out through the windowpane,
And time, so slow before, how swift it hied.
Of course he missed the Vejle countryside,
For there his home and heart would ever remain.
At last, beyond the fog-hung woods, he spied
The place where Vejle must have lain:
Then, like a tyke of five, the ten-year-old
Sat on his bed and wept, wept uncontrolled.

"Oh," sobbed he, "it's forty miles from me,
So far to Vejle and its fjord from here;
Perhaps in this world I shall never see
Again my mother and my father dear.
At schooltime Hanne will think I'll appear,
But no more counting-lessons will there be;
And then my poor doves—what are they to do?
Was that the last time I shall see them too?

"From my home I have been snatched outright!
And grandpa, grandma, neither of them knew
Last Sunday evening was our last adieu,
The last last time I bid them both good night.
They all of them want me out of their sight,
And all alone I'll live my whole life through
In this dark room that we have found to rent
From that repulsive, horrid tailor Brandt.

"Oh, to be back home now! The chestnut foal
Must now be leaping round upon her dance,
And Lars will give the mare's bit one quick glance
Before they all go to the wateringhole.
And Margaret with her milk pails on a pole;
The sheep all driven in by little Hans,
And Christen in the barn, sweeping away,
And mother —oh, she'd still be in the shay.

36/

"And see the moon rise! Look how huge and red!
At home its beauty was of a different kind.
That Vejle moon will never leave my mind,
The fjord agleam as it rode overhead.
The Great Bear's there; then north's not hard to find;
And there is—" down his voice dropped as he said:
"The harbor and the sea, where you can sail
Along the coast, and home to Vejle's dale."

Our hero, sobbing, moaning, to allay
His griefs, fell off to sleep in all his woe
And didn't waken till the following day,
When Brandt's apprentice sent his back a blow
To rouse him, for the tailor bade him know
He'd best come down to porridge right away:
It was seven now and getting late,
If he'd be going off to school by eight.

But when three quarter-hour chimes were sounding,
He had already grabbed his books and fled
And, with a heart now furiously pounding,
Down the streets to Latin School he sped.
"Oh, what awful boys!" went through his head
When, at the door, he heard a shout resounding
To the top-boy's loud command, which ran:
"Come, comrades, and let's greet the bottom-man!"

Upon him instantly his classmates leapt
And at him, for their welcome, whaled away
So hard, one boy gave him a sobriquet
Which, till long after that first day, he kept;
For when our Adam begged them for fair play,
And hung his head down and most sorely wept,
One Søren Jensen cried out: "*Homo flens!*
O monstrum hominis! Indigna mens!"

And Søren's witticism could not fall
On better ground; for from that very date
Monstrum Homo's Adam Homo's fate,
A name that hung upon him like a pall.
But can the small prevail against the great,
And how can one prevail against them all?
Long they battered the poor Monster's frame
Till—like a dog—he answered to the name.

37*/*

My reader! if at any time you were
A schoolboy—worse, one of the smaller set—
Those early schooldays you cannot forget,
With all those pains and sorrows to incur,
Such pains whose memory only time can blur;
From hearth and home, alas, where you were pet,
Where sweetness could be felt but not be kept,
Out onto a hard schoolbench you were swept.

And with life's earnest you were then confronted,
Embodied in each Latin conjugation,
And by it all your golden dreams were stunted;
And by your fellow students' flagellation
Your childhood sensitivity was blunted.
Your tearful eyes and bitter trepidation
Each time the teacher fetched out his rattan
Inured you to the blows fate deals to man.

You quickly turned ingenious, smooth, and wise;
And you who once had only scamped, at worst,
The share of wisdom you could utilize:
You little sinner, from your youth accursed!
In only half your lesson you were versed;
The other half you used to plagiarize
Out of a book held in your lap well-hidden,
With fears and tremblings of a heart guilt-ridden.

O say, if you, from days when you were small
Till now, when you are probably full grown,
Have seen so deep a change as this befall
Of all the twists and turns your life has known?
No doubt, time's seen you come into your own,
From sergeant, say, to major general,
From judge to statesman; but still life's wide range
Can scarce afford someone this great a change.

So put yourself in Adam Homo's place,
And, incidentally, make my task more light;
For, then, his work and progress and disgrace
Will take a very short time to recite.
Nor will we feel obliged then to retrace
Each instance of his doing wrong or right,
Each time his diligence is praised, his sin
Imprinted deep upon his tender skin.

38/

And neither shall we need to be deterred
By following his schoolboy's daily round,
Where, as a frisky foal might leap and bound,
Along the paths of knowledge he is spurred;
How sometimes he is bored and sometimes stirred
By songs from Danish or from Roman ground;
How moved he is by history's epos
And how he thrills to read Cornelius Nepos.

And therefore I can also let alone
(For of such things my reader knows enough)
His frequent scuffles when the games got rough
And many skinnings at the knucklebone;
And how, in every case, he'd always shown
The highest sense of noble schoolboy stuff
And never sinned 'gainst honor's cardinal rule
By telling tales to those in charge at school.

Then I can also easily pass by
How he put forth the claims of his own ego
In haughty airs put on for smaller fry
When, as the top-boy, he could tell them, "*Rego*";
How often he was heard to whisper, "*Nego*,"
And hardly kept from letting laughter fly
When Adjunkt Stæhr, a churchman most pathetic,
Made miracles more strange by exegetic.

But what I absolutely must report
(For every author's duty-bound to do it,
No matter if the reader's been all through it)
Is this: that with a schooling of this sort,
The feats and fruits of mind pertaining to it,
Soon a swelled head did our hero sport,
And he who'd been a shy young introvert
Became, by twelve, both proud and malapert.

This most of all was seen when his vacation
Took him home; for loudly he'd preside
Among adults and keep them edified
With home-truths of perfervid intonation.
But not contented with such scintillation,
He visited the farmboys to confide
To them his wisdom and his whole life story,
Standing in their midst in his full glory.

For, as on him with jaws agape they gazed
And thought they listened to new prophecy,
He gave a full account, with eyes that blazed,
Of every wonder in his history.
Then he'd use words which left them all bedazed,
Like "rhombus," "paradox," "intensity";
And taught that Earth was round and told them, truly,
Our Denmark's name more properly was Thule.

He lectured on celestial rotation,
Explained with ease by laws of gravity,
And all objections met with fulmination
Against the brain-rot in the yokelry
And country wits gone into dormancy
While souls athirst found full alleviation
In knowledge, offered like a beverage cooling,
Once they'd embarked upon their grammar-schooling.

We see that Adam thought himself a prize
And that he now had gone quite far astray,
That, having passed the stage of popinjay,
An egoist was now upon the rise.
Exactly how the boy learned otherwise,
And came not just to think a different way
But let his human heart find voice again,
The gentle reader now shall ascertain.

Upon the fourteenth birthday in the life
Of this our hero, matters then so lay
That Tailor Brandt upon that very day
Took Stine Hansen for his second wife.
Now, though Brandt's whiskers were completely gray,
Scarce twenty summers had come Stine's way,
And for her sweet and innocent demeanor
The town referred to her as "lovely Stine."

How had this beauty ever been persuaded
To join in matrimony with old Brandt,
Whose bristly hair time had already faded
And who was no more pleasing than *galant*?
Was it his kindness that could so enchant?
Was it her gratitude on which Brandt traded?
Or was the honor of the name *patronne*
The reason that she did what she had done?

Oh no, she only changed her maiden-name,
For you must change it sometime, after all;
The reason Stine old Brandt's wife became
Was just that marriage was a young girl's call.
No gust of longing fluttered Amor's flame
When as his bride she stood in Hymen's hall;
With no elation did her arms enclose him;
She must be wed—and that is why she chose him.

I too find her behavior rather poor,
But I deny she sinned in any way,
Unlike someone caught 'twixt yea and nay
Till of her suitor's sacks she can be sure,
His manorhouse plus meadow, wood, and moor,
His foothold on the official *escalier*,
His rank among the peerage of the nation,
His probable quick death, her widow's station.

No, Stine's action I won't celebrate,
And yet I'd say that she no worse had sped
Than one who comes into the bridal bed
Because her last hope left her desperate,
Than one whose love is given its proper head
Because her youth came sixty years too late,
Than one who once at eighteen found too dirty
The crow she found delectable at thirty.

So Stine Hansen changed to Stine Brandt
And got her matron-duties, matron-right,
And as a maiden disappeared from sight,
But as a wife was very much extant.
And every day now Adam saw her, bright
With youth and beauty that might well enchant
Both older gentleman and youthful stripling
With consequences which they'd both find crippling.

Yes, beauty's power Adam came to feel
With feeling so extremely feverish
That nothing soothed his stricken heart's anguish.
As if off in a dream, he'd take his meal
At table; minute after minute would he wheel
His spoon about the soup in his full dish.
And should his eye and Stine's ever meet,
He could no longer bring himself to eat.

41/

His young breast by a force was mesmerized,
Like some weak planet by the mighty sun;
For day and night his heart was tyrannized
By the enchantment Stine Brandt had spun.
But only in a sleep had he surmised
The nature of the wonder on him done,
When, like an angel brushing by his lips,
Past him in a dream her image slips.

Why, even in school—who could have thought it so?—
Not seldom he would see her charming head
Before him when he read old Cicero;
And oft with Virgil's Dido his heart bled,
And often one of Ovid's lines he read
That struck his restive heart so fierce a blow
That it must arm itself like some new Hector
Lest it cry out its sorrows to the rector.

But, ah, the color of his lips seemed dead now,
And many times, for reasons none could name,
Up through his cheeks a crimson overspread now
And vanished on the instant that it came;
And all his former cheerfulness had fled now,
And gloomy solitude was all his aim,
As dark he gazed upon the rolling seas
Before the shelter of the leaf-thick trees.

But, like all desperate lovers, in his plight
Our hero sought the balm of poetry
And wandered round beneath the moon's pale light
And sang his passion and his misery.
When he beheld the clouds upon their flight,
And nightingales poured out their sympathy,
Our Adam could no more hold back his fire:
He sang—and here's a sample from his lyre!

When in woodlands shadowy
Hunting dogs aprowl I see,
And hear rifle shots resound,
And hear trumpets echo round,
Ah, when stricken creatures lie
Gasping out 'neath heaven's sky
Their poor lives in deaths unkind—
Stine comes to mind.

When I stand by this deep sea
Where many sailors buried be
Of whose deaths the waves yet tell;
When on the ocean's shining swell
I see the agèd fisher hook
A fish with pale and bloody look
And on his line behold it wind,
Stine comes to mind.

When I walk alone, ill-starred,
Round about the old churchyard
In the night black as a raven,
Wishing I lay in that haven:
Up from where the dead are lying
Rises wild and hidden sighing
While the whistling night-winds wind—
Stine comes to mind.

No one knows my grief at all;
Even in my lecture hall
I never gave my love a voice;
But when birds in song rejoice
Deep in nature's sanctuary
For their loves, all sweet and merry,
Calls, ah, meltingly combined—
Stine comes to mind.

Thus Adam in his sorrow would lament,
And dark as shadows his fair boyhood days
Fled by him in heartsickness and malaise.
"But," says the reader, "but that Stine Brandt—
Could any match the blindness she displays,
Finding no key to his discontent?"
I do not say she never found the key,
But I would say she had propriety.

For when sometimes she'd sit and rack her brain
To understand why Adam felt so bad,
This thought would come: "Why, really, am I mad?
That like the boy I too should act inane?"
With that she took some sewing that she had
To sew away sighs she could not contain.
So some time passed—till an event arose
That brought their little novel to a close.

One evening, just as Tailor Brandt stood making
Small talk with Herr Fine the clothier
By the seaside where the gardens were,
A little while, because her head was aching,
Fair Stine lay upon the sofa, taking
Rest which quickly brought relief to her.
To her cheek fresh roses she'd applied;
The window to the garden was thrown wide.

And while indoors at anchor Stine lay,
Outdoors, that haven for all solitaries,
On the path that led past the strawberries,
Adam paced, the young lad's thoughts distrait.
My reader knows, and I don't need to say,
Who it was that caused all these vagaries;
He walked and stopped and walked—and then stood still
When Stine's sighs came over the windowsill.

Astonished, Adam came close to the wall,
And, leaning through the open window frame,
He sees Dame Nature's wonder of them all
Illumined by the evening sun's red flame.
To see that figure exquisitely loll
That so bewitched his senses, all his claim
To reason vanishes—he'll dare all crimes,
And through the window noiselessly he climbs.

Now in the room he stood atremble,
While lovely Stine on the sofa lay
In slumber deep—for how could she dissemble?
As one transfixed, he stared at the display
Of gentle charms that might a dove's resemble,
Of lily cheek against its rose-bouquet,
Of swanlike breast, now fluttering so high,
Of lips that opened once again to sigh.

What conflict in our hero's youthful breast!
How must there now have raged within his heart,
Already full of passionate unrest,
Fear that she might waken with a start,
Terror for the kiss he would impart,
And, with it, deep desire that it be pressed.
He struggles with the thought that tempts his soul—
Alas, it vanquishes his self-control.

44/

On tiptoe he draws near the beauty—hush!
His very breathing he suspends for this;
He bends his head and brings his lips now flush
To Stine's, oh so lightly, in a kiss.
But scarce some nectar 'gainst his mouth can brush,
Scarce came the news of Paradise's bliss,
When, terrified, he's sent off in a spin
With crimson on his forehead, cheek, and chin.

The window had slammed shut, although no breeze
On that calm evening was to be perceived,
The moment that a tailor-voice had cleaved
Like thunder through his sensibilities.
Stine blushed—O who would have believed?—
At once; and, losing all her memories
Of being asleep, she leaped from her settee,
As Adam looked at her remorsefully.

Of hearing, trial, and sentence I won't tell:
They pulverized that heart once so robust;
For, in the end, out of the house he's thrust
And forced to find another place to dwell.
Thus, for the first time, Adam Homo fell
On passion's steep road down into the dust,
And learned the tenth commandment from the life:
"Thou shan't go coveting thy neighbor's wife."

You fathers wise and mothers wise, reflect
Upon yourselves, who all too often set
Your precious sons within a siren's net,
Though she's a Danish lady you respect.
For think, if Stine'd been a true coquette,
Much more experienced and much less correct,
Why, Adam might have had a real comeuppance:
Perhaps his life would not have been worth tuppence.

Reflect here, too, you lovely womankind,
Who'd have it that a boy of but fourteen
Who may at times in your eyes favor find
Has no conception of what love might mean.
A fourteen-year-old heart, please call to mind,
Till sixteen beats but two years in between.
So treat those fourteen years quite gingerly:
When boys turn sixteen, you're in jeopardy.

45/

And, finally, do some reflecting here,
You schoolboys, who upon life's road soon spy
The god of love's red banner drawing nigh
And, from your schooldays, hold that color dear.
No, Eros loves to gossip and to jeer,
And rectors are the first to hear his cry,
And they'll make you stay on after your classes
For being lovesick, sluggardly, he-asses.

Such was our hero Adam's situation.
So heavy on him did his sorrows mass
It was all the boy could do to pass
His comprehensive term examination.
This time he did not even make Fourth Class;
For industry he got no approbation;
The thing in which he proved himself quite handy
Was this and nothing more: the *ars amandi*.

God knows how much of Adam's industry,
In such a foggy bank of love's perfume,
Might actually have gone down to its doom
And brought him to perpetual truancy,
If, in time, his rationality
Had not been fully able to resume,
Through two events which cut him to the quick
And sent his love off packing to Old Nick.

The first was that his ailing mother sent
A letter on his confirmation day,
Exhorting him to be obedient:
Thus caught within a crossfire Adam lay.
The second was that once, by accident,
He saw his Stine on a public way,
Not floating by, as once, youthful, affecting,
But wobbling as she walked, as if expecting.

At such a sight he flushed red as a beet
And, while he turned away his head and glance,
He wheeled around and rushed down a side street,
Then dashed into a forested expanse.
Here bitter tears fell, never to repeat,
And with them his pain found deliverance;
For when he made his way back into town,
His mind, he felt, no longer was weighed down.

From that time forth into his books he threw
Himself with ardor—not, as once, for show;
And now, with zeal, he hastened to accrue
The knowledge that for months he had let go.
No more did Cupid's arrow lay him low,
And, though his heart beat soft as hitherto,
He never more in all his Aarhus days
Experienced a sighing, moon-struck phase.

From Cicero, the dry-as-dust, he drained
Pure stoic wisdom, and within his glass
Saw one more hero of the *Ilias*.
All but fundamentals he disdained,
Piercing through history's obscure morass
To glimpse the laws by which all was explained;
He wanted philosophic poetry
And sought for geometric cogency.

He solved his problems with great industry
By means of algebraic x and y;
He pondered axioms of philosophy
And earned his fellows' high acclaim thereby.
He built small systems, rickety
Like most new systems meant to edify;
For Time's strong gusts blew round them, shaking them
While Adam kept on reading books and making them.

Thus three years passed; and knowledge which had sent
Its root deep in him now brought forth some shoots:
The rector found he had the attributes
Needed for his Student's Document.
At eighteen then he pulled on his new boots
And, having turned his old black clothes, he went
One fine morning, with his traveling pack
Slung round his neck, to sail off in the smack.

His passport still exists. Its last lines said:
"Stud. Adam Homo, Aarhus Academy,
Speaks Danish, born at Vejle rectory,
Is now—with a complexion white and red,
Blue eyes like two suns in resplendency,
Blond hair, in frock coat ready to be shed,
Quite tall—en route to Sjælland. No disease
Is raging here, at time of writing these."

47/

Once he had set his feet on Sjælland's ground,
Our hero took the Copenhagen road,
And there, upon his tests, such promise showed
He entered freshman with a joy profound.
The letter home to tell of praise bestowed
In no time found its answer come around;
For Homo Junior's strong encouragement,
This missive was what Homo Senior sent:

"My splendid boy! In college now at last!
You've come away with honors on your test
And commendations tucked inside your vest,
And our bedevilments have been outcast.
How glad you are I think I might have guessed,
For, once upon a time, my tests were passed;
But what I can't guess, what I've not been told,
Is the design for life to which you'll hold.

"For to some end a wise man undertakes
A life, a course of study, even a game,
Which otherwise becomes mere ducks and drakes,
Some piece of nonsense with no higher aim.
This truth one can't too many times proclaim,
Because a useful fingerpost it makes:
Man must have a plan for what's ahead,
Except—you'll understand the joke—when dead.

"Along your path I'll watch you hopefully;
With school behind, the world before you lies.
Now others' luster will impress your eyes,
As yours will others' to the same degree.
In many houses you'll be company,
But just so long as your behavior's wise;
Your peace, your calm, your fortune, your repute
Depend on leading with your strongest suit.

"But in the world's ways you are still quite green,
And lack the knowledge that experience brings
Of how a needy student, just eighteen,
Should come to terms with people and with things.
Let me explain then all the things I've seen
And just how I, when I first tried my wings,
Relied on reason to see all things through;
What I did then, you now can also do.

"About like yours now, then was my position:
To keep alive would cost us both some pains;
Dame Fortune did give me a small addition—
In *sano corpore*, one *sana mens*.
As for one shilling you will rack your brains,
So, many times, my purse knew such attrition.
Like you, my son, I also had been blest
In not quite ranking with the ugliest.

"Let my design for life do you some good!
In people and arrangements I, sharp-eyed,
Took notice of each weak and each strong side
And soon was known about the neighborhood.
I did as ancient missionaries would
To bring the Christian Gospel far and wide:
They changed their ways with each new situation,
To suit them to the manners of each nation.

"Thus—for example—to Etatsraad Zell
(A man whose favor was no empty phrase,
A formalist, though, without parallel)
I sent best wishes on his natal days.
Conversely, to the Kammerherre Bjeld,
Whose wife stood at the parting of youth's ways
And did not wish to know her years were fleeting,
I never offered any birthday greeting.

"One more example! With Professor Rether,
Who loved above all else a hot debate,
I gave my voice more volume and more weight,
And pitched into him just like Paul with Peter;
Conversely, with Conferensraad Gether,
Who had a passion to intimidate
And could abide none but his own discourse,
I sat there mute and let him ride his horse.

"Perhaps you'd call such matters pettiness?
Well, I don't say they're fraught with majesty;
I do say, so the world is and will be
And, if you know that, you will reap success.
I never would ascribe hypocrisy
To one who studied humankind's *faiblesses*;
To heed them is not only innocent
But, like true wisdom, always pertinent.

49/

"I almost daily added to the sum
Of rules we find among life's necessaries,
And I emerged soon *primus inter pares,*
Complaisant, true, but never overcome.
I'm pleased I never acted by contraries—
With wise men I was wise, with dumb ones, dumb;
With serious scholars I was scholarly;
With jovial sorts, all wit and gaiety.

"With older ladies, those times I'd recall
When they had had some plumage fit to preen;
With young girls I would wave hope's banner green;
With men, debating was my all-in-all,
But I'd not let one contradiction fall.
On fixed opinions I was never keen,
For such conviction is a perfect waste:
It harms me, and it's viewed with great distaste.

"Reforming others was not my disease,
For I believed that it was their affair,
While I took pleasure in good everywhere,
To make the most of their good qualities.
I never talked ill of one who wasn't there,
Nor did my praise stir up antipathies.
Always uncensorious and subdued,
The world approved my speech and attitude.

"Thus I became the favorite of all,
And, although poor, I quickly got about;
For nearly every evening I dined out,
And many a purse was at my beck and call.
The world and I were never in a brawl;
Life and I were on good terms throughout;
And had I gone on for a law degree,
The doors would soon have opened wide for me.

"But that's enough! I hope that you can see
Just what I meant by what I've written here.
Some people poison every atmosphere
By speaking out the truth relentlessly.
Though nothing's gained by brutal honesty,
Though their stake in the case is quite unclear,
They always must upset the applecart
And ram right on to drive good friends apart.

"Item, some perpetually descend,
To their own hurt, to foolish self-conceit,
Who cry, 'We must stand on our own two feet,
In this life we're our best and only friend,'
While, actually, no one can pretend
He got, unaided, so much as a sheet.
So shun those fools pride turns into transgressors,
And shun as well that crowd of truth-professors.

"Trust me, who've seen the world and now am wise
In what life on this earth turns out to be.
The young man preaching truth and decency
Is not averse, when old, to telling lies,
And, almost always, as a fraud he dies
Who proudly trusts his own capacity.
For we do nothing great without the lever
Frenchmen give the name of *savoir vivre*.

"Take my advice, you won't come out the worse:
Conduct your life with strength and common sense;
For if a youth will use intelligence,
He'll quickly learn its value from his purse.
Beyond this, I have no more to dispense
Of wisdom you can to yourself rehearse:
No need to say you must act virtuously
And heed your God, your King, your faculty.

"One more thing! Of the new philosophy
With which the brains of all the learned spin,
Take a good swig, that's wise policy:
For, though you don't hit learning's every pin,
All nine can't be left standing as they'd been.
A vogue should not be taken casually:
Its terminology must be attended to—
With that one's work's begun and with that ended, too.

"Should you discover a compendium
Explaining that philosophy in brief,
Which, in a pinch, might give a man relief,
You'd have my gratitude for such a plum.
To Copenhagen I think I might come,
Unless my purse should say: 'Take in your reef!'
And should I make a visit to the place,
I wouldn't want to suffer a disgrace.

"Well, I've used up this sheet—I'll say adieu;
I see your mother's letter's at an end.
And now, in closing, I am pleased to send
Your old grandfather's best regards to you.
Farewell, my son! I only wish you knew
How much I wish always to be your friend.
Nothing new has happened out our way.
A marten got two doves the other day."

So closed the letter, and as Adam read
He felt a heavy duty on him thrust
To lead a life intelligent and just,
To scale the heights of happiness ahead,
And bend like rushes in a riverbed.
He unsealed mother's letter with great gust,
Which first extended her congratulation
And went on thus in the continuation:

"You still recall the line of poplar trees
That last year father had them carry through
From past the garden gate out to our leas
Along which all the fjord comes into view.
Now that I am cured of my disease,
I go as often as I'm able to
And walk along the alley, up and back,
And let my thoughts go off on any track.

"Whom would you say I think the most about?
On him who's in my mind both day and night,
On him whose love makes mine the more devout,
On him I loved before he came in sight,
On him I cannot bear to live without,
To whom I'd gladly fly with all my might,
Between whom and myself there's now a sea,
Whom time will distance more and more from me.

"Ah yes, my Adam, farther will you stray
The farther on along life's path you go,
For every kindness fate has to bestow
Will lead from home into the world away.
When roses come, but you don't come as they,
What happiness next summer shall I know?
Whom shall I then, beneath the pink night skies,
Search down the road for with such eager eyes?

52/

"Yesterday my thoughts were swept aside;
A hen that keeps a duckling in her care
Was running by the pondside, terrified.
She stared aghast out on the water, where
The duckling swam, its down, though, still quite spare.
The hen's distress to mine was close allied:
You flee afar now on a sea unknown,
I stay behind as you go forth alone.

"But that's enough about myself! For I
Shall evermore rejoice deep in my heart
For all successes falling to your part,
For all the joys your fair youth may supply,
For all life's roses that may please your eye,
Just so their thorns don't cause you any smart.
Once more, if not in this world, then the other,
I know we'll be together, son and mother.

"Now, there is just one more thing I must say.
Two days ago I sent by Vejle mail,
With Skipper Poulsen, who today will sail,
So they will reach you by this Saturday:
Six pairs of socks, so your supply won't fail
(Three pairs of white, and three pairs of the gray);
Your collars with the edging that inverts;
And finally the four new formal shirts.

"With the same you also will receive
Two crates of apples of the very best,
But, eaten all at once, hard to digest
(They'll keep well over many a winter eve),
Sausage and smoked salmon, by your leave,
And what beef jerky there was in our chest.
I've packed in with them, ready to be shipped,
Six pounds of candles by my own hand dipped.

"This time I won't send you currency,
I dare say you will know the reason why;
But calm! Once father finds someone to buy
His grain—which should be momentarily—
Then, if I have to move the earth and sky,
No matter what's left in our treasury,
You'll have the forty dalers in short shrift
We promised to you for your Christmas gift.

"And now farewell! And promise to be true—
Be true and promise every month you'll write
To tell me all that's happening to you,
And don't be guilty of an oversight.
That way we'll clasp each other's hands despite
The land and sea that separate us two.
Let us not vanish from each other's ken.
To that I say a most heartfelt Amen."

And so she closed—and like day's candle burning
In farewell through clouds of deepest red,
Her letter, once he'd read through what she said,
Left in his bosom strong sensations churning.
He felt the joy of hope and pain of yearning,
And flung the window wide and craned his head,
And long and silently he gazed afar—
Far over Jutland there had burst a star.

C A N T O   I I I

In earthly matters one law's manifest
In all that is, that was, and that will be,
In everything that lies north, south, east, west,
That has the least spark of vitality.
In all within the cosmos, outwardly
Or inwardly, which form and shape invest,
The law is simple and of great renown
(For all great things are simple): *Up* and *Down*.

Up flies the bird into a higher zone
To swoop down suddenly upon the strand;
Up thrusts the spire to where the clouds are blown
To tumble down in ruins and in sand;
Up for the laurel gropes the hero's hand
Till his appointed victory has flown;
For up and down goes fate, go men of mark:
What's brilliant going up, goes down in dark.

54/

Yes, up and down indeed in this world go
Not just the sun and moon, the eye of night,
Not just the golden stars at heaven's height,
Not just the sea, whose ebb succeeds its flow:
But every heart that beats on earth below,
That heaves, sometimes for woe, sometimes delight;
Our joy, pain, fear and hope and peace, they all
Rise like the swelling waves, and like them fall.

And up the prayers of dust ascend; the Word
Comes down with heavenly voice from overhead,
And sorrow, in the breast long closeted
Until such time that voice at last is heard,
Bursts from the heart and leaves joy in its stead.
All we have hoped for, loved, all we've incurred,
May well sink to the bottom of time's sea,
But will float up into Eternity.

And yet of all that rises and descends
And in this world of ours goes up and down,
There's nothing more deserving of the crown
Than life upon its outset, when it blends
Its bright ideals with dreams of happy ends,
All golden with bright visions of renown.
If I but set the hour of death aside,
In youth alone do force and fire abide.

Deep well of hope, what riches you possess!
Far at your bottom, where life's fountains stream,
The youth finds every fair fantastic dream
In which his thoughts, from childhood, incandesce.
When he looks down in you, at once, agleam,
There comes to him the face of happiness;
But should he stretch to seize the vision, then
Like fog at once it vanishes again.

And filled with youthful hope, our Adam tried
Himself through all the paces of life's dance,
And, like a student, everything he eyed
With open mind and penetrating glance.
To all his life a rose dye he applied,
Not stinting on its depth or radiance,
And, as he took all things, at that same rate
All things reflected back his own portrait.

Should he be sitting in the lecture hall,
Imbibing what of wisdom was his mite,
And hearing his professor there recite
And demonstrate until he saw it all,
Fancy's brush would in a twinkling fall
To paint a life among the erudite;
Up to the lectern he beheld his path
And saw himself there, turned a polymath.

And if, on Sunday mornings, he should walk
In black, with hat and cane, the promenades,
And see the pretty misses in that flock
Which, if there's sun, the capital parades
To see and be seen on each city block
And which, though large, could always use more maids;
Our hero saw—and few are so clear-eyed—
In every lovely lass his future bride.

Were he in church, among a numerous crowd
Devoutly listening as its pastor spoke,
Then, to unlock life's puzzles for his folk
And turn a preacher of the Word he vowed.
If at the theater, and he chanced to smoke
A player with the slightest art endowed,
The poet in him did not quite back down:
In dreams he's beckoned by a laurel crown.

Now, as for how he used his liberty
And how life's inextinguishable streams
Poured out into his heart abundantly
And bred exuberant sentiments and dreams
Upon which, as on waves, he floated free,
My reader best can judge of all these themes
By reading the first letter home he penned
When Christmas holidays were at an end.

"Sweet Mother dear"—it opened on that note—
"First let me wish a good New Year to you,
Then thank you for the letter you last wrote
And for the filthy lucre you sent, too.
My stipend, though, still helps keep me afloat,
I live as royally as I used to do;
And, with the aid of patrons, in addition
I've been permitted now to give tuition.

"From this you see that everything is grand
And you've been overly concerned for me:
For I scarce lack for one necessity
And one must learn to lend himself a hand.
I stopped in to a tailor recently
To ask if I had credit to command,
And he said yes—dear Mother, call to mind
Your son dressed in a Russian coat, silk-lined.

"But you will want to know the way I live,
And in your latest letter bade me say
In great detail how things go day by day.
Instead of writing a long narrative,
There's one all-purpose answer I can give
For every circumstance, like trumps in play.
These words can sum it all up in a trice:
Copenhagen is my Paradise.

"But how I spend my day you now shall learn:
When six strokes from the church's clock tower sound,
Then I wake up and out of bed I bound
Lest longer sleep should tempt me to return.
My bread I must myself spread butter round
And fill my milk cup from the landlord's urn;
Once I have drunk, I take my books in hand
And read some hours until I understand.

"Then to my lecture hall I make my way,
Where all my friends make up a jolly corps.
I really hate to leave there every day,
For we've professors full of wit and lore
Welling out of every single pore,
As with men of genius such as they.
In everything they always keep in sight
The students' profit and, too, their delight.

"At one o'clock, though, your son leaves the wise,
For with a family, as you know, he eats
The finest luncheons that they can devise—
On Sundays, sago soup and roast and beets.
Miss Lise and I have adjacent seats,
And her attentiveness I dearly prize;
For she—no less than all the family—
Will often scant herself in serving me.

"No sooner is the table cleared than I'll
Be dashing off to the Sodality,
Where, with the Muses' sons I stay a while
To read and do some chatting, splendidly.
Now that's high living, when the Muses smile
Through mouths of students who have years on me
But still stay on and, although their endeavor
May be questioned, are extremely clever.

"When I have let some hours' time go by—
I say 'go by,' but this would be more fit:
When I have lived some hours' time in wit—
Back home in greatest haste they see me fly.
Then to the book my mind I reapply
And what, that morning, I wrote down from it
With rushing pen, and oft too rushed a brain,
I work hard to absorb and to retain.

"Comes evening. Time should not be thrown away;
I tell myself that time and time again;
I might drop in on other college men
Or, if I can afford it, see a play,
For which my taste increases every day.
I'm pleased above all by the tragic pen,
And one tragedienne now lights the stage
For whom fit praise would take page after page.

"Conceive a figure of an average height,
Her soul triumphant and her flesh subdued;
Conceive an azure eye, soulful and bright,
A voice to bring the heart to quietude,
An art which does with nature so unite
In every gracious movement, every mood,
In smiles and sighs, in joy or mournful strains,
Conceive all this! and more yet still remains.

"Among the other pleasures I have here
I ought to mention evening dancing class,
At which, on Saturdays, I now appear.
There I was set a test I had to pass
Which pleased the ladies, but not me, alas!
As my left leg was acting up quite queer.
What's more, the dancing-master kept on whooping:
'Herr Homo! Watch your head! It's always drooping.'

"But the young ladies there could not be better,
And how their taste can be relied upon!
Especially I must name young Miss Jette,
Who is the leader of the whole salon.
Why, once you've seen her waltz, you can't forget her,
And her good sense makes her a paragon!
When, in the dance, her brilliant eyes go glancing,
I think I see one of the Graces dancing.

"Besides these exercises, whose intent
Is just amusement and some social cheer,
There is another company I frequent,
A group that takes all knowledge for its sphere,
A brotherhood for talk and argument
Wherein it's only Latin that you'll hear.
Each Wednesday morning there we join debate,
In mental war our powers to demonstrate.

"I'll mention here as well our army drill,
For you know soldiering's a student's lot:
In my old frock coat I'm dressed fit to kill,
My shako's borrowed from a fellow swot.
By turns and close-formations I've been taught
To shield our state and people with a will.
But it would take more powers than I claim
If all the highjinks of it I should name.

"You see, my life is busy as a bee;
For, when I add to what I've just now said,
And what, in my last letter, you'll have read—
That I don't even have one Sunday free—
You must admit these days are full for me.
But I'm so thrilled with how my life is led,
I often feel I'm blessed a thousandfold
And I must take the air, up on the Vold!

"Up there I go with springing step, the wind,
Which often blows in storming from the east,
Streaming past my cheek with wings unpinned
And puffing so the fire in me's increased;
Thus, by it in and out I'm disciplined;
I rush down to the coast, my mind released,
And stand there, sunk in reverie,
And look out long and silent to the sea.

"Loud its roar and loudly beats my breast,
And full my heart for every enterprise;
Yes, every deed that lies at life's behest
I've seen performed before my very eyes.
I've seen my future there materialize
In gleaming clouds by sunlight opalesced,
And that bright afterglow on shore and sea
Has seemed the nation's memory of me.

"But now where has my pen gone bolting to?
Best that I lay it down and keep my peace,
So that these daydreams, visions of caprice,
Do not wash over your poor son anew.
—The clock says eight upon the mantelpiece,
And still I haven't got this letter through.
I've yet to dress and wash and comb my hair,
For I'm invited out tonight somewhere.

"It's to the home of a big city squire,
Known on Exchange and in the world of trade—
One Etatsraad and wholesaler named Hr. Dreyer,
Whose name in print you must have seen displayed.
His son's acquaintance last school term I made
And now and then we meet, if we desire,
By dint of which I have an invitation
To Fru Dreyer's birthday celebration.

"So let me break this letter at this line
And use the little time that still remains
To brush and brush again these clothes of mine
And use some alcohol on any stains.
Yes, elegance repays us for our pains:
With silken vest and ascot superfine,
One's figure will send critics' arrows glancing.
Rumor has it that there will be dancing."

Thus did his letter back to Jutland read,
And, as my hero gets himself well dressed,
My reader off to Dreyer's house I'll lead,
Where Madam's bid *bonjour* to each new guest.
There's nothing in the house that is at rest
As loud well-wishes more well-wishes breed,
And soon a various assembly booms
In three splendiferously lit large rooms.

The one in which the host began card-play
Had eight mahogany tables, all brand new,
To sit at which no others might essay
Save men in coats with crosses in plain view
Who bore at least a Justitsraad's cachet
(One Kammerraad, though, was among the crew).
It was agreed 'mongst Dreyer's dilettanti
That two rigsdalers was the proper ante.

If round the room a man's gaze were inclined,
He'd see such crosses, sashes, stars as shone,
If not to turn all other persons blind,
At least to blind the man they hung upon.
For, now and then, when with a smile he'd con
The honors all along his breast aligned,
He'd then look up again, stunned by the glare,
His eyes half closed, his nose high in the air.

The observer's eyes were here as much engrossed
As when they would, upon a brilliant night,
Seek in vain to catch a single light
Which had been drowned within the entire host.
Though he knew many great men were in sight
And saw they could the highest merits boast,
With greatness in a sum so unbelievable
Each single greatness was near inconceivable.

And in room number two, where they served tea,
And where a group of older women sat,
A table bore the gifts, a panoply
Of clocks, rings, chains, shawls, gowns, and many a hat,
Of gloves and collars, ribbons plait on plait,
Below all which, in cramped hand, one could see
A sheet where each gift was enumerated
And every donor's name in full was stated.

"Oh, what profusion!" Fru von Pappe cried,
Sending Fru Dreyer a beguiling glance:
"I have a feeling that I cannot hide:
I'd filch some things here if I had the chance,
That cape, for instance, ah! such elegance!
Your daughter's workmanship can't be denied,
Such excellence! It just gives me the chills,
All that embroidering and all those frills!"

61/

"And see the shawl!" Von Pappe's sister squealed,
Who, though new-married, still found cause to moan.
"From head to foot the thought of being sealed
In such a shawl! It thrills me to the bone!
In garb like that all gloom would be overthrown!
To you, Fru Dreyer, what more can fortune yield?
Dreyer clothes you in the Persian vein
And gives you love and worship like a Dane!"

"Oh, what a ring!" "Oh, what a splendid chain!"
"Look, what an armlet!" "What a pretty stone!"
Thus each vied with the other in this vein
And gave Fru Dreyer happiness full blown.
Some people to the floor were nearly thrown
And there was pushing, strangely inurbane,
As, tightly crammed around the table, each
In turn delivered her excited speech.

In room number three, which for the young
Was meant to serve as gathering place tonight,
And where games would be played and songs be sung
To a clavier the door near hid from sight,
Along the wall sat ladies, faces tight,
And hardly dared to move a hand or tongue,
While the young gentlemen stood panicky
Off to one side and eyed them furtively.

High expectation showed in every face,
But no one there had any sort of knack
To overcome the stiffness of the place
And let the loaded guns of gladness crack.
Heaven would have had to pour down grace,
And to the door they longingly looked back
In hopes a spirit would appear to loose
The party from its strangulating noose.

There was a single figure there who moved
About that anxious crowd with confidence,
Some thirty-odd or fifty-odd years old,
Of either age he gave an equal sense.
Some gray hairs witnessed time's slight influence,
But, like a youth, self-satisfied and bold,
About the room he made his graceful way,
Known by the name Van Pahlen, *rentier*.

He was a cavalier, *galant*, smooth-faced,
Whose stream of riches had not yet been dried,
Whose days and body were unoccupied,
Whose mind found younger friends much to his taste.
He had a little goose now by his side,
Drawing her out (for so the thing is graced);
The goose was stammering some words of her own
When, at that instant, wide the doors were thrown.

Behold our Adam Homo stepping in;
And to him swiftly all the glances went
While his own shining deep-blue eyes he sent
Around the room, open and genuine.
His two cheeks burned a crimson on his skin,
His locks flowed down like waves the winds foment,
His clothes, tight-fit, a fabric-saving feature,
Splendidly revealed the healthy creature.

But, as a conquering hero strides through fire,
Briskly Adam crossed the carpeting
And paid his compliments unto Fru Dreyer
With those congratulations birthdays bring.
Our lady curtsies, her fan fluttering,
Nods graciously and smiles to the young squire,
At which she puts her hand up to her heart,
Half jesting, half in earnest to impart:

"So long a time, Hr. Homo, you'd not dare
To let us ladies wait for you in vain,
Were you not sure our favor could not wane.
We're so hard-pressed for people with *your* flair;
The youngsters here are near asleep, I swear,
And won't be roused save by your clever brain.
Now go to work! The ladies must comply!
Rentier Van Pahlen will be your ally."

What good those words of hers to Adam brought!
How strong he felt his heart beat in his breast
At this so-flattering and splendid thought,
That all the lady's hopes upon him rest.
A doubled brightness his glad eyes expressed,
A tiny smile across his lips was caught
As, in his inmost mind, he made a vow
To live up to the faith she'd shown just now.

63/

On being introduced to his ally,
He studied him. Each thought, "Could he serve me?"
Admiration could be read in Adam's eye
For Pahlen's frame and bearing, blithe and free,
His elegance of dress, and for the high
Stiff collar of the new variety.
And, as he took in Adam, Pahlen thought
This young recruit was just the friend he sought.

But, by the lady's wish, the youngsters group
Into two companies and so divide
That one part gravitates to Pahlen's side,
The other forms itself as Adam's troupe.
And in charades they all are cock-a-hoop,
Dressed up from top to toe in youthful pride;
Each byword is presented to the view
In turns by *jeune premier* and *ingénue*.

In this the greatest honor did reflect
On Adam Homo, who outshone them all;
Such striking sayings could he recollect,
Upon such genius could the young man call.
His fancy and his spirit rose unchecked,
Before no knotty problems did they fall;
The others' wits, alas, fell off their fettle
Each time he guessed their bywords with such mettle.

The games now ended. It was time to eat
And everybody's eyes were shining bright;
The questions and the answers grew forthright
And had more life—the belly is life's seat.
The lifting of the barriers was complete
As all the party did as one unite,
For every eye was fixed upon Fru Dreyer
Who herself brought round the small *posteier.*

When now they were to skoal, they all arose
As if much stirred and, though half in dismay,
In each face flags of happiness did play
In honor of the birthday at its close.
With thanks and curtsies—now this, now that way—
The lady, moved, amid the circle glows
As round each lifts his voice with all his soul:
"And let this now stand as our lady's skoal!"

Loud rang the song, but no voice louder rose
Than did our hero's in his exultation;
Why, it befell him, due to his elation,
To stamp hard on one miss's tender toes.
She shed grim tears on suffering such woes
While he grew doubly loud through his libation.
But when his and Fru Dreyer's glasses clinked,
In utter sympathy his moist eyes blinked.

That's all? my reader says, as if to chide.
Dear reader, yes! There is no more for you;
No worse a fate to you do I provide
Than to the guests who now have bid adieu.
But, since I pushed you 'mongst that retinue,
I'll see to it that you're indemnified:
We'll trail the guests upon their homeward strolls,
And both of us shall peek into their souls.

"Oh, Lord be praised! We're back out on the street!"
Exclaimed Etatsraad Hatch, audibly sighing.
"The saying's true, there's more to life than meat,
And staying snug at home's most satisfying."
"The next affair will be our turn to treat!"
His wife broke in with eager prophesying.
"*Bon ton* requires that one must not partake
Of others' food if no return he'd make."

"Did you see what eyes Von Pappe made
When she was talking with that Captain Wals?
Her look said: 'Were it not for protocols,
These arms would round your neck have surely strayed.'
Such brazenness should end up being flayed:
To every wealthy man her virtue falls—"
So thundered forth the virginal Miss Stengel,
Attended home by one Lieutenant Engel.

"How large a loss did you take at the game?"
To *frère* Conf'rensraad whispered Kam'raad Franz.
"Near thirty dalers," answered brother Hans.
"I swear, those stakes were what put me to shame.
Who thought he'd have such high debts to his name?
Eight dalers at each table—two, each man's!
They'll soon demand—but who'd accept the squeeze?—
Teacup-, flatware-, glass-, and bottle-fees."

"O, dear Emily!" Thus young Miss Fine
On her friend's arm decided to give vent.
"If only my poor head were competent
To know what makes the heart so grandly pine,
What makes that melancholy, doleful scent
(Which your look vouches for as well as mine)
That comes upon me after reveling
And leaves a sad, lorn, empty everything!"

Not finding emptiness in anything,
Our Adam Homo, while the bright stars flash,
Walks back to where he lives, remembering
The vanished evening's richness and panache,
Making sure his heady thoughts don't crash
'Gainst matters not worth any worrying;
He lives the evening over from the start,
Not leaving out even the smallest part.

Upon his taking leave, the lady said:
"Why, to be plain, Hr. Homo, and exact,
I've never met your like upon the head
Of liveliness and wit, of taste and tact."
Van Pahlen pumped his hand, and in the act
Said: "Let the occasion not be forfeited!
I hope our talks are not now at an end:
Consider me from this day forth your friend."

Thus home he hurried, with his star ascending,
And, once the lamp upon his desk was lit,
His mother's letter got a proper ending,
Indeed near five new sheets tacked on to it:
About the evening he had just been spending,
About the guests and how his talk had hit,
The hand Van Pahlen offered in farewell,
The lady's mouth and what it had to tell.

O reader! should my hero seem to you
A little poor, a little mean of mind,
Then search, I beg of you, your own heart through
Before you judge of Adam's humankind.
Did you, in youth's bright summer, not pursue
Perfervid all the trifles you might find?
Did you not send up bravos for a thing
Which now you think not worth a piece of string?

It all depends upon the eye that sees
And on the mirror in which all is read;
Scenes now that raise your risibilities
You may view later, bathed in tears instead;
The fair and good who earns your rhapsodies
You soon may find a lump, all beauty fled;
For life is growth, and from its kernel's rind
Contrary fruit oft springs up in one mind.

The one fruit, soft and sweet, does so invite
Just to be near it makes the lips bedewed
And appetite needs hardly to be wooed.
One need not even pluck it from its height;
It falls all by itself, our eyes shut tight,
Into the open lap of hebetude.
We merely shake the tree—and down there comes
Into our lap a shower of soft sweet plums.

The other fruit is contrary in kind;
For only through experience we win it
And, even when it's won, we quickly find
That there is something hard and sour in it.
It brings the hardy winter-fruit to mind—
Once plucked, it can't be eaten that same minute:
Some time out in the cold it must have spent
If it's to reach full sweetness and rare scent.

But when the summer's vanished, and the fall,
And life's own winter dampens the blood's fire,
We sit, grown old, unto the hearth in thrall,
And count those treasures living can acquire.
The fruit we hard and sour were wont to call
Is fresh as spring now, mild as we desire,
Both to the tongue, the eye, and to the mind,
In Irony's gay lamplight new defined.

—But to our Adam! who not long ago
At Dreyer's did his wit and charms display
And now appears, that following Saturday,
At dancing lessons held in Aabenraa.
Here his figure will more plainly show;
But ere my reader cast an eye his way,
The hall, with every glowing chandelier,
Of dancing-master Friis I'll open here.

67/

There's old Friis tuning up his violin
As seven lasses, give or take a lass,
Who've just arrived from town for dancing class,
Find space to put their boots and mantles in;
Then, each foot squeezed into a moccasin,
And swirling round the dancing floor en masse,
They ask Herr Friis, did he expect to see
All six men from the University?

"Alas, young ladies!" old Friis must insist,
His foot stretched out in attitude precise,
And filling up his pipe bowl with small twist.
"We find today Fate's not been very nice.
Hr. Holm, Hr. Steen, Hr. Øst, Hr. Mehl, Hr. Grist,
Have all caught colds from walking on the ice.
Tonight it's just Hr. Homo who will come;
His plenitude must fill the vacuum."

"He's coming!" they all shouted their halloo,
And, truly, at those words in came the chap
Straight through the door, and doffed his shaggy cap,
While to him instantly the ladies flew.
His cheeks glowed red at such a warm to-do,
But these words struck him like a thunderclap:
"Hr. Homo, think! Today you must exist
As you, Øst, Steen, Holm, Mehl, and also Grist!"

"How's that, young ladies?" Adam starts and blinks;
But when the girls behold him so nonplussed,
They break into loud laughter, fit to bust,
For girls were born the same time as highjinks.
Then, as in this confusion back he shrinks,
Old Friis calls out to him: "You surely must
Have gathered from the welcome of this flock
That, in this party, you're cock of the walk."

These words worked on them all like sorcery!
At once the young girls read the words aright,
That they were hens and that there shone most bright
'Mongst hens one virtue, which was modesty,
For every one of them shut her beak tight.
But on his cock-a-doodle excellency
Our youthful hero pondered that same while,
Then launched into a speech in merry style.

These were his words: "Your sentence you have passed,
And ladies' sentences have no appeal;
Therefore to serve my ladies' common weal,
I shall my self into six selves recast,
Six partners round in waltzes shall I reel,
Six hearts in my heart shall be locked up fast,
And, if sextuple love be your dictate,
I'll dance sextuply, speak sextuplicate."

And scrupulously he fulfilled his vow,
As all the ladies quickly came to find:
He danced with each of them, as he'd designed,
Led reels and waltzes with a full dry brow,
Conversed incessantly, ne'er fell behind;
He paid all court, with many a pretty bow;
He used his feet and mouth with equal ease,
And proved unflagging in these ministries.

His ardor led to only one mischance:
Those thin-soled shoes could scarce withstand the blows,
So at the end he had to tread the dance,
To general laughter, half shod, half in hose.
But, sitting down at last for some repose,
Upon him the whole flock of girls advance
To peer more closely at his soles and heels
And, at each hole they find, their laughter peals.

The evening flew by with the greatest zest,
But, ere they separated, homeward bound,
Each sat down by the other in a round,
To comfortably cool the cheek and breast.
"Sing!" little Alexandra did request
Of Jomfru Bine, whose voice was renowned;
And Bine, urged on by them all, agreeing,
She sang, the violin accompanying:

Now it is cold winter's time,
Short and dark and sad the day;
Stormwinds beat and storm-wings flay,
Snows like quiltings overlap
Meadows tight and white with rime.
O, but dost recall the time
When the forest trees had budded,
When with flowers the fields were studded,

Warm days, nights in brightness flooded,
Summer air so sweet with lime!

See, back walls of brick and stone,
Close in wire cages bound,
Hangs a bird without a sound,
Shedding no more song around,
Prisoner left all alone!
Call to mind its varied tone
When it sang in woodland pride,
When, like wave upon the tide,
Down from heaven it did glide,
Freedom's child to freedom grown!

Oh, what harvests rich years wrest!
Silver does my hair now shine.
You are old, O lady mine,
And we live on days lang syne,
Half in joy and half distressed.
But that time yet makes me blessed
When I could the hart outrace,
When the rose blushed in your face,
When your curls like winds did chase
Round your white and swanlike breast.

Golden days, fled to your end,
Which, called from the grave by woe,
Like a mourners' choir turn slow
With your wreaths of long ago
To your old, forgotten friend:
Let my eyes on you attend!
They would see you where they are!
All your life is like a star:
Rays of daylight drive you far,
Night comes and you reascend.

Here ended both the words and melody;
Old Friis, who felt that longing and chagrin,
Sighed softly and put down his violin,
As soul and body shook with memory.
The sorrow of the song was graven in
The faces of the silent company
As though time's changes all could now perceive—
When chimes remind the ladies they must leave.

Our hero saw them home, still fresh and bright,
And at each lady's home his eyes would glow,
As gallantly he let the fair one know
Of escort's firm and customary right.
She half accepts, and half attempts to go,
As on her cheek he plants a kiss so light;
To all the selfsame courtesy was shown,
And, full of kisses, now he stood alone.

(Apologies in these parentheses
For Adam, who does lack a modern ring,
Who finds great pleasure in affairs like these
And scarcely seems to criticize a thing.
Whatever in his mind was happening,
Poor wretch! he'll have to bear the mockeries
Of those who let themselves and all go hang
To have a chance at critical harangue:

Of those who see and hear and feel just for
The sake of training trenchant critic lights
On those same feelings, those same sounds and sights;
Of those who dread disaster on the score
Of taking fool's gold for the choicest ore
And fly from all gold in their own despites;
Of those who, ere they dare the least enjoyment
Must give the Ogre-Critic full employment.

Cared for by everyone, the Ogre thrives,
And wanders wild and hungry on the land;
Torn to shreds are laurels, crowns, and wives,
No work, no book can his fell tooth withstand;
Promise in its crib dies at his hand,
Nor spares he those who've parted with their lives;
Our Lord Himself, if He could be attempted,
From critics' hunger would not be exempted.

But when his work concludes—as well it may—
When all is savaged, trod into the dust,
When telling black from white leaves us nonplussed,
And all things are a general shade of gray,
When to one level all things shall decay
And sweet's the same as sour, unjust just,
Then criticism must—or else eat stones—
At last chew off the flesh from its own bones.

71/

There lies the hope of our deliverance.
Take comfort, kings and bards and mighty men!
Ye richest magnates! Comfort, mendicants!
You too are no friends of the critic pen.
Once off his clean-picked bones his fierce teeth glance
And no meat's left for him to eat again,
It's sure he lives but minutes after this
—This comfort closes my parenthesis.)

Next morning late our Adam, in his chair
By the corner window of his room,
Mulled his Sunday thoughts, all brave and fair.
From there he could behold the Rampart loom
And winter's bright sun beaming gently there
On rows of trees now naked, reft of bloom,
While on the roof above he heard the sound
Of tiny, blithesome sparrows hopping round.

Then, from the distant tower, bells were tolled,
And that sound borne upon the winter air
Seemed a command from Heaven to make bold
And to accord his life its proper care.
The deeper their clear-knelling music rolled,
The louder did his heart sing out in prayer;
By means of those mild sounds was Adam wooed
From worldly din to thoughtful solitude.

"See," he sighs, "see, earth is lying dead,
And bare the boughs upon the chestnut tree.
The hope I bear comes not alone from me,
But up from deepest earth one prayer is bred,
From every tree to Heaven, to that Godhead
That hears all things that cry in misery.
He from His kingdom lets the spring appear
To fill full all things comfortless and drear.

"Yon lies His home out in the Infinite!
Yon in the brilliant sun I see His gaze,
Whence comes the light whereby the world is lit.
But in my littleness I yet give praise
To find God's kingdom in this bosom sit
And wings to lift me upward to His rays.
Yes, here too, in this close bed-sitting-room,
A still flame on His altar breaks the gloom!

"Now every faculty must be exerted
And rooted firm in full activity;
Now it is time to put out on life's sea
With head held high and will boldly asserted;
I must not rest, by nothing be diverted,
Till spirit turns to flesh and blood in me,
Till I myself am one with the Ideal
And show its splendor forth within the Real."

Filled with his purpose, he sat deeply stirred,
And, when his concentrated thoughts had flown
To whether love's own leaf and flower alone
Might be the measure most to be preferred,
Some forceful knocking at his door he heard,
To which he called "Come in" in courteous tone.
The door was opened—in Van Pahlen came,
At which sight Adam had to blush for shame.

For all his thoughts ran to his small abode
And to the shabby clothing that he wore,
To Pahlen's finery a contrast sore.
But of his blush the man no notice showed
As toward him, hat in hand, he calmly strode,
And, smiling merrily, thus took the floor:
"Young friend, you live high up just like the hawk,
But, bird of prey or not, I thought I'd knock.

"Some tending-to our new acquaintance bears;
My family and friends have left of late,
Gone to the countryside to shoot some hares,
And I'm left here half in a hermit state.
Now, like with like, they say, will congregate:
You're safe inside this cell so far upstairs,
And far from all the world near lost from sight,
You're just the company for an eremite."

To enter in upon that easy tone,
As much as his befuddlement allowed,
Our Adam tried; but totally uncowed
In this first banter he by no means shone.
Soon, though, his brief embarrassment had flown
And both tongues ran to do themselves up proud;
And, while Van Pahlen's wit gave him the cue,
It was no verbal short straw Adam drew.

73/

A full hour thus slipped by most pleasantly,
And, as each with himself proved quite content,
He found the other's wit his cup of tea.
Adam's smiles made Pahlen confident,
Nodding comfortably in charmed assent,
Although his laughs might be derisory.
But Adam noticed nothing: both ears cocked,
He kept his chair, to hear how his friend talked.

His friend now rose—glanced at his watch's face—
"But," said he, "one thing I'd not forget!
If on the morrow you may here be met,
You'll find me sitting in my coachman's place
To 'sconce you all day in my landaulet
And ride you round upon a merry chase.
First we'll look in upon my sister's seat,
Then out to Bellevue for some oyster meat."

Delighted, Adam promised he would go,
And Pahlen went on: "You're the man for me!
The people I choose must be *comme il faut*,
For oyster-eating takes urbanity.
If folks were oysters, we'd eat company,
But in these times such meals won't do, you know."
He left—and there's our hero, much elated,
Staring off as if intoxicated.

How wonderful! A parish priest's poor son,
His hopes of fortune in their diapers yet,
Had made a friendship in the leisured set,
With one whose every wish Fortune saw done,
Whose sense of Fortune was no abstract one
(For Adam had that with his ears still wet),
But who'd the key—like Peter's keys of gold—
To Paradise's glories thousandfold.

Thus out he went upon his ride next day,
And all the greater was his gratitude
To find his friendship all the more pursued
When Pahlen took him to that evening's play.
From that time on his whole heart was subdued
To Pahlen's generous and charming sway,
In whose company other people faded
As daily through the streets they promenaded.

74/

However, ere I paint him here as friend,
I would, O Friendship, dwell a while on Thee;
Aye, at Thine altar's foot, my knee I'd bend
And think upon a friend once dear to me
And offer up a mite, though small it be,
If Thou beest worth what offering I extend;
Oft only withered shoots dost Thou possess,
In sorest need of loving tenderness.

Yes, where now for such friendship can we go
As in Patroclus and Achilles shone?
That comradeship in all, in weal and woe,
When gladness beckoned and when death drew on?
That noble force, the highest good to grow,
Perhaps, in that old pagan dawn,
Which to its strength and force may reascend
But when it meets its own fire in a friend?

How high it blazed in heroes of old Greece,
When one friend for the other his life dared!
At night he anxious to his tent repaired
And, thinking of his friend, could find no peace!
For his friend's shade high vengeance he declared
And sprang wild from his pallet to release
His rage, to drag three times around the grave
The hero who his friend the deathblow gave!

O Friendship! hardly doth Thy face remain.
All traits of passion Thou hast now laid by
And only forms of virtue dost retain.
In place of one friend, scores now multiply,
But friends impartial and of such a dye
That their friend's good repute is snapped in twain.
The sentence, though, is passed with rectitude
And always as strict justice is construed.

And there are friends, steadfast, compassionate,
Who oftener than on birthdays manifest
Their wish that their loved friend have all the best
And in his sorrows will commiserate;
Yes, even when the storm clouds congregate,
When great things and small weigh on his breast,
And he is crushed by worldly misery,
They've still a sigh of Christian charity.

75/

And friends there are, so shrewd and oh! so wise,
Endowed with so acute an inner sense
They smell the wind before it ev'n commence
Whereby they'll have their dearest friend capsize;
And some friends, tolerant, who gourmandize
At dinner at their friend's foe's great expense.
What else? For if a friend you'd undermine,
You must drown the vexation with some wine.

Yes, friends we have, more than we want, perhaps,
Whose mills of friendship turn by wind and wave
And oft in sunshine utterly collapse
And are too busy when the wild storms rave.
But friendship pure? Why, that goes to its grave!
The ague's set deep hollows in its chaps,
And here it would have died, completely cold,
Had Adam not, his arm in Pahlen's, strolled.

But what was Adam's happiness! For find
He did the true Thou for his very I:
The soul which brought the first peace to his mind,
The brother-spirit toward whom he'd drawn nigh!
Till now, his life seemed but a lullaby,
But now he woke, in friendship's arms entwined;
For, by two hearts aglow, he had a view
Of comradeship to last life and death through.

And what was Pahlen's happiness! The time
So burdensome that patience nearly cracked
Could be made over to his friend intact,
Who bore the burden with a smile sublime.
Those fancies which had long since passed their prime,
Despite their author's work to hide the fact,
Those phrases others cared no more to hear,
How lively did they ring in Adam's ear!

For he clung to him fast as any burr,
And Adam felt such earnest gratitude
His heart near burst in his ecstatic mood.
But what rewards such loyalties confer!
At Pahlen's side his tree of life's renewed,
It greens at once into a blossomer:
Drives, billiards, horses, cafés, pantomime,
Are given him—and all he gives is time.

Seldom was he seen with his books more;
For, almost every day, when, full resigned,
He would sit down to read the books assigned,
Presto! came Van Pahlen in the door
With thousands of adventures on his mind.
Then out they tramped in sunshine or downpour
To straggle here and there along their walk
And gaggle after pastimes on each block.

Once on such a walk our hero thought
To penetrate and gain the very key
To that profound, that wondrous mystery
With which the bosom of his friend was fraught
And which would oft break forth peculiarly
In rueful tones, profound and overwrought,
Aye, etched itself in clouds upon his brow
That hatred of the world seemed to avow.

"If you'll permit it," Adam then began,
As Pahlen's brow formed furrows row on row
And, sighing, he abruptly laughed, "Ho, ho!"
"If you'll permit it, if another can
Ask questions of things touching you, the man,
For motives that you must not think are low,
Then I would ask, in friendship, please believe,
How is it possible that you should grieve?

"How is it possible that hid away
In you so large a store of pain can lie?
For oft deep melancholy you convey
Though, like a man, your sorrows you defy.
Are you unhappy? You who for each day
Have plans in hand to keep its spirit high—
But for some time now I have sensed some smart:
Confide in me and open up your heart!"

Great gravity was etched on Pahlen's cheek;
He looks at Adam very long and hard.
"My friend," he says, "some memories are so bleak
That, to our pain, they leave us ever scarred.
All round we find the world with baseness marred
And narrow hearts." With laughter dark with pique,
Gesticulating wildly, this one shibboleth,
"Misunderstood," he mutters 'neath his breath.

Moved, Adam answers him: "What if recall
Should cast a shadow over your life's way,
Your peace of mind it never can betray,
And you are not misunderstood by all.
Surely this your sorrow can allay,
That I know you down deep—whate'er befall,
Beside you like a hope I'll gladly fight
Whenever you confront the beast of fright."

Thus Adam sought to soothe his friend's chagrin;
But Pahlen answers, laughing scornfully:
"Those baby-shoes we had our feet pinched in,
I soon wore those things out, as you can see.
This hope and fright, they make my poor head spin!
The two of them mean nothing more to me.
I hold, as do the tragic dramatists,
By Fate, which slays all high protagonists.

"Be merry, my young friend. What should life be?
Ask of the poet. Here's all he'll concede:
All life is but a gust against a reed,
All flesh is grass, to put it biblically.
Builders at the grave's edge, such are we,
And to us but one moment is decreed.
Deep in earth's vale of tears in wretchedness,
Let's live for life, then, with a fine excess!"

While this speech struck our Adam deep with fear,
Swift reassuming its habitual air,
His friend's wildly disordered mind grew clear.
Van Pahlen hurried him across the square,
Found a *konditori* and sat him there,
Handing him a toddy with a sneer;
It took two glassfuls for his own libation,
Poured down his throat amid his desperation.

The waitress came and brought them both some tea,
And Pahlen cried: "O pearl of womankind!
Might you be waiting for a tip from me?
Sweet Lise, if your cheek would be inclined,
One mark in hand for every kiss you'd find—
Now, let's be quick! That's one—and two—and three.
There's four—five, six—one daler I'll not miss!
What say, Hr. Homo? We pay dear to kiss!"

78/

He jumped up—and, as onward they went faring,
He slung his cloak around him, laughing loud,
But all that evening Adam's head was bowed
In thinking of his friend's life and his bearing.
The thoughts descended on him in a crowd
Until he summed Van Pahlen up, declaring:
"A rare mind! Brave, deep, dark with turbulence,
The home of genius and improvidence!"

Around this time he wrote home to his mother,
Describing his affection for his friend,
Depicting Pahlen as like to no other
On each page of a letter slow to end.
"Once every wind would cause my mind to bend,
My course was set now one way, now another;
But now my thoughts in Pahlen find a prop,
My ship now has an anchor I can drop.

"I won't maintain that my views harmonize
With my new friend's in every circumstance;
However, by that very variance,
What one lacks the other well supplies.
He the cause of reason will advance,
I the heart's cause; he would satirize
And is my master for sheer eloquence,
But I win over him for moral sense.

"One thing already I observe I've won,
One real gain that my friendship's given me:
I've now seen life in fullest clarity,
No longer by so many mists o'errun.
My days of bending like a reed are done,
Always obsequious and mannerly;
I know now what I owe Tom, Dick, and Harry."
His mother wrote back: "You had best be wary!"

In just this fashion, gloriously content,
For some months Adam's life remained the same,
And Pahlen found his warmth as permanent
As pictures fitted tight inside their frame;
Like adjutant and colonel, they became
The best of friends by mutual consent
And equals, though the evidence was scant:
For Colonel Pahlen ruled his adjutant.

79/

The adjutant by Colonel Pahlen swore,
But, strange to say, the more his dedication
To serving him, the more his liberation
From his awe, which was so great before.
From time to time—as I must not ignore—
His words attested to some irritation;
But, nonetheless, transported by some brew
(That is, the brew of friendship), they were *du.*

They regularly go off on a spree
And are seen taking turns to make a coup
In competitions to find something new
To be the source of their hilarity.
One certain circumstance I have in view
Of which I feel I must give a précis:
One evening they had seats in the parquet
To see the premiere of a new ballet.

The ballerina they found nonpareil,
A little fool, but one who did know how
To run on tiptoe and did very well
(To Art's disgust and viewer's knitted brow)
In stretching upward for a forward bow
And, shoulders, calf, and foot all parallel,
In skimpy costume, making circles sweeping,
The house applauding and the Graces weeping.

The laughter of the two friends knew no bound,
But when, at last, the ballet reached its end,
Van Pahlen said to Adam: "Let's extend
Our compliments for all her twisting round.
For such a one I need close vantage ground—
She'll fuss and strut, on that you can depend.
The flattery just pours down such a throat,
Not the Deuce himself could make her bloat."

In the foyer they asked the manager
To notify the lady they were there,
And faster than a minute hand could stir,
She stood before them, smiling at the pair.
Since Flora was the goddess danced by her,
Her arms and feet were still completely bare;
Her shoulders sported wings, and still her tulle
Clung round the well-rouged lady in a spool.

And as the members of that evening's cast
Rushed out into the lobby for a view
Of what the dancer had been running to—
Her ears pricked up for praises to be passed,
Her lips into a grateful smile set fast—
Van Pahlen came and by the hand he drew
His now, for once, intensely shy young friend,
Who wished for wings to take him to land's end.

For, truly, he was mightily impressed
By this young ballerina in full splendor;
To see her as the wingèd Flora dressed,
She almost seemed beyond her human gender.
Had they been out of view of all the rest,
He would have knelt before her in surrender,
Such power has whatever may be near
On those just setting out on life's career.

But to the fair one, with an irony
So patent it escaped no one but her,
Van Pahlen said: "O pardon us that we
Disturb your rest amidst this lobby's stir!
But from us we have seen our own peace flee,
Your graceful leg has been its conqueror.
Our admiration you cannot begrudge!"
He stopped—and gave our hero's back a nudge.

And Adam, boldened, in poetic style
Took up the thread: "O, pray, be not irate
That we have furiously stormed your gate
To bathe our eyes for just this little while
Beholding one who could each Grace exile
And Cupid's dart, by twirling, confiscate.
Now we the taken see what 'twas that took:
With Flora's litheness, you've fair Hebe's look."

"To know your Hebe I've not had the pleasure!"
Replied the lady, and did sweetly add:
"Your warm approval I must greatly treasure,
For, with your praise, who'd dare say something bad?
We dancers must bear hatred beyond measure,
Since we're the ones for whom the public's mad;
You take my word, but ask no proof from me—"
She eyed the actresses in victory.

"Where is the greatness envy does not meet?"
Van Pahlen asked. "But we'll give evidence
Of our two hearts' new turbulence
If you'll permit tonight, while you sleep sweet,
That at your house, below you on the street
We loudly sing of your preëminence.
In Spain they call suchlike a serenade—"
"I know," she answered. "Let your songs be played."

With thanks and bows away the two men went,
But at eleven, when the stars of night
Far in the eastern sky were twinkling bright
And down the crescent moon its soft beams sent,
Then by the fair one's door, where lantern light
Fell on a greengrocer's establishment,
Wrapped up in capes, with their guitar to hand,
Beneath the open window they both stand.

Van Pahlen strums the chords as Adam sings:
"Would Thou Wert Mine," so touching and commended,
Then "Pretty Minka" and, when Minka ended,
"Rejoice In Life" to the guitar then rings.
From time to time, though, as the song ascended,
The *danseuse* felt a tug at her heartstrings
And moved up to her window, triumph-crowned,
For those below parading on the ground.

When once the music ceased its resonance,
She loudly cleared her throat and sweetly told
Her singers, who'd cast many an upward glance:
"Might I invite you, sirs, if it's not bold,
To have a warm and bracing drink, perchance,
Since you have been so long out in the cold?"
"What's this? We thought you'd nested long ago.
Thank you so much!" the word came from below.

No sooner did the friends come in the door
Than they beheld a table fully spread
And, round it, ladies with hands slightly red,
The dazzling extras of the ballet corps.
The ballerina dazzled even more
When, smiling graciously, she kindly said
They should be seated and then portioned out
Roast goose along with prunes and sauerkraut.

Van Pahlen felt right in his element,
And Adam was completely at his ease.
Both felt they could permit themselves to tease,
Which quickly makes all form inconsequent.
Down on the kind ones' laps by turns they sent
A shower of pleasant ambiguities;
But she at whom their freest jests were fired
Was the fair herself, the much-admired.

Midnight was long past when she arose
Out of her chair, her glass held in her hand,
Her voice a little quavery, to propose:
"To those whose lively wit and humor grand
As was their music wafting to our band
Have tied us all in happiness's bows,
To them a toast!" —And so the bowl was drained
And all went home to sleep where sweet dreams reigned.

One sees with just what sort of jests and fun
Herr Pahlen-Pylades and his Oreste,
Whose young wits after his friend's tend to run,
Were passing time the way that they knew best.
I'll add no more examples to this one,
Which can, as model and as last, attest
To what tame expeditions these two made
Now that the grounds of friendship were firm-laid.

They could be seen to tipple every day
At some *konditori* till well past three.
And every evening they played *écarté*,
Drank punch, and lashed the world unmercifully.
And more and more our hero would give way
To Pahlen in that high art—showing glee
When earth or heaven, they themselves or neighbors,
Were graced to feel their epigrams' keen sabers.

But when their intimacy reached its height,
And Pahlen on a lady paid a call
Whose reputation was not quite snow-white,
Who was, almost, disposable to all,
Then, in true friendship, Adam held the light
When, on their merry troupe, the night would fall.
And, though the lady's signals weren't returned,
Of many nasty matters Adam learned.

83/

Thus, there followed a great alteration
Not only in his manner, but his mind—
No wonder! for, upon our road, we find
It's step by step we near our destination.
Storms swell up from a gentle wind's foundation
And swiftly ships to sea floors are consigned—
A reader may feel all's too hurried here,
But poets turn a page into a year.

Gone was summer and the autumn came—
It was a sunny mid-September day;
The friends, on mounts, like knights of ancient fame,
Rode off, the open country to survey.
Through Nørreport's arched gate their steeds they aim,
Van Pahlen keeping his from breaking 'way,
While Adam spurred his on, and fairly flew
Off in a gallop, quickly lost from view.

Though Pahlen had to follow at that pace,
When he caught up with him, his mien was grave:
His bile was up; and, crimson in the face,
He set about indignantly to rave.
"Damn! my horse is frothing like a wave.
Recall, Hr. Homo, that I own this brace.
Get down, and go on foot like your old stock,
If you still think my orders are just talk."

At these words Adam felt his brow grow hot,
And, blood-red color rising in his cheek,
He answered with a smile: "Kind words you speak!
Damned if I care about what goods you've got.
Go buy another horse if that one's shot,
Else follow me, unless you are too weak."
With these words, once again the spurs were used
And Pahlen laughed, as if those words amused.

They rode a while, and their relations grew
As brotherly as they had always been.
Toward evening they dismounted at an inn,
Where Pahlen ordered punch brought in for two.
He deftly mixed some well-aged rum therein
And toward our hero pushed the bowl of brew;
And he, from his long ride now overheated,
Drank till the bowl was nearly half depleted.

They both gave their cigar ends a good bite
And, for a while, in tandem puffed and smoked,
And of the fair sex somewhat coarsely joked
When the proprietress brought them fresh light.
Van Pahlen whispered: "Though you're not provoked
To fear the Devil and his realm of night,
I still would bet"—he dropped his voice for this—
"You dare not give our host's fair wife a kiss."

Our hero took such doubts in the worst light;
And then his pride received still further shocks
When Pahlen added: "That man is an ox,
Watch out! He's built like some Teutonic Knight
And as hot-tempered as the orthodox."
In scornful answer Adam cried: "All right!
Tomorrow your champagne cork's going to pop;
If I don't do it, call your friend milksop."

Upon that very shout, the host walked in,
And, conscience sparing him the slightest tweak,
Our youthful hero on the lady's cheek
Impressed a kiss, and more where that had been.
"If we don't want a well-thrashed-over skin,
More favors of that sort we'd best not seek!"
So roared the angry host, for action braced;
But Adam's arm slipped round the lady's waist.

The innkeeper's complexion changed its hue.
But Adam's wooing still continued warm
Toward the hostess's delightful form,
And Pahlen smiled to see him bill and coo.
Then down on Adam's ears the host's hand flew
With all the violence of a sudden storm;
The host and Adam fought, the hostess squealed,
And, from his chair, Van Pahlen's laughter pealed.

He suddenly got up and said: "As you,
I see, still have some business, and my ride
Back into town is really overdue,
With your permission I'll no longer bide.
What strength you have! A brisk chop to the side!
Don't spare your challenger! A good one-two!
As for the horse, you'll find someone to loan one,
Since you don't care about which people own one."

85/

Van Pahlen left, both horses in his tow;
And out into the night, with bloody eye
And tattered jacket, pride in short supply,
Back to town on foot did Adam go.
His heart was stung as if by arrows, though,
And O what grief to eat that humble pie!
And how, once home, he bore the yoke of wrath
While sleep would not so much as cross his path.

To Pahlen, soon as daylight dawned, a note,
In which he let his raging heart speak free
And then break off their friendship, Adam wrote.
He first rebuked him for his treachery,
Next of a deep contempt spoke openly,
And on the final page to bits he smote
Their friendship's temple with much din and clatter—
Pahlen shrugged on reading of this matter.

For Adam (to his honor, be it said)
Perceived the case as far from light in weight;
He'd sought and entered Paradise's gate
And with that Heaven was not surfeited.
His letter done, those were real tears he shed;
With all his soul he'd yearned to find its mate,
A fellow-soul, as his long-sought Ideal,
And his heart hadn't yet turned into steel.

For to that happy age he could lay claim
When shattered hopes have built the heart no shield,
When, near and far, the eye of fancy's peeled
For that rare bloom we "lasting friendship" name,
When ostrich-hearts charge all things in the field
And eat up stone and steel—it's all the same;
When we are drunk with inner revelation
That sorely lacks external confirmation.

All that day he kept to his retreat
In hopes to get a letter from his friend
That might bring this misfortune to an end.
The next day Adam even took the street
Past Pahlen's door, but white as any sheet
Back up to his own room had to ascend;
For he had seen his friend, coming right to him,
But Pahlen made believe he never knew him.

Adam's heart was seized with indignation,
And out forever from a wounded breast
He tore the false friend with a savage zest,
Yes, doused the last flame of his veneration.
In this affair, though painfully distressed,
His pride could take as well some consolation:
To fawn was foul, and to defy was good;
He stood alone, but as a man he stood.

Thus up in smoke this fervent friendship flew.
To Adam's great good fortune it accrues,
Since now he has a full eight weeks to use
Before examination number two.
He buckles down to what he has to do,
And by a stroke of luck success ensues.
And Vejle of his *laude* he alerts,
And gets high praise, though not his just deserts.

His father sent a letter, which advised
Studies that would lead to a vocation.
To these he gave his strong recommendation,
Though study was a plague that he despised.
It was a long epistle. I've excised
A goodly chunk to spare you consternation;
Its essence only will be here conferred.
This is the close. I give it word for word:

"Your answer, my fine son, pray expedite;
Say whether, when this intersession's through,
You will the priesthood's sour apple bite
Or split the hairs that all attorneys do;
If, as a doctor, you'll use others' plight
To let the cream of life all come to you;
If, as a classicist, you would be drunk
On agèd wine in which your future's sunk.

"I counsel but in jest, but you decide!
Perhaps you'll guess right which shell hides the pea;
They might sell pokes in which real pigs are tied,
But buyers should beware, it seems to me.
In soft pods hard peas oft are found to hide,
And light decisions oft weigh heavily.
Try and decide! And then don't cast about
And complicate yourself and life with doubt."

There was a letter, too, his mother sent,
Which made him feel at once both large and small,
For in it he could hear the old voice call
That from one heart unto the other went.
As he read on, his tears began to fall,
And in his soul he felt embarrassment
On folding up the letter, in which he
Was counseled to pursue theology.

For in that study he had tried his hand,
Though his attempts at it were rather slight;
Its contents he had never more than scanned
Before his vision failed and all was night.
What cloud could darken so—you demand—
His clear eyes that the book was dropped outright,
And he a youth in but his twentieth year?
My hero, reader, stands at a frontier.

C A N T O   I V

Forbearance—O if I could inculcate
That glowing virtue in my reader's mind,
So that with his forbearance he might wait
Till my book's hero is of hero's kind;
Till he, whose cheek with down is not yet lined,
Too young much interest to stimulate,
Is in Time's mold a little more perfected
And gets himself and me the more respected.

Can there be question that an author must
Attend to what forbearance will allow,
Since, step by step, he too is forced to plow
Life's prosy road, however thick the dust?
When (though it may well cloud the Muse's brow)
Of all ills, large or small, upon him thrust,
He must keep up a careful ledger book
Lest any crucial thing he overlook?

In life itself you'll find that nothing's truer!
Forbearance in it all things do require!
The maiden who is waiting for a wooer,
The soldier facing his lieutenant's ire,
The teacher with a child who won't aspire,
A beggar off to see what he can skewer,
An agèd copyist for the corporation,
Ill-paid for faithful drudging for the nation.

And let us pause a little at this last;
For many his life stands as paradigm.
In Danish legal ranks he's held down fast;
And, sadly, he is now well past that prime
When in new fields he might his fortunes cast.
And so to have his bread in wintertime
And keep from falling into fierce distress,
He banks upon his law and business.

For he's devoted to the corporation.
Day in, day out, he sits upon his chair
Behind his little desk and shelf, and there
He copies duteously for the nation,
His back turned on the sunlight's golden glare,
Divers reports—the naturalization
Of Jewish Nathan, which the guild denies;
The police post for which Bertel Brask applies;

Or Fru von Kuhl, who would divorce her spouse
Since he has been abroad now seven years;
Or Madam Juul who cannot stop her tears
Because she lost her husband *and* her house;
Or moneys filched by tax-collector Maus,
Still undelivered to the town cashiers;
In short, the thousand bits of business
About which he himself could not care less.

He's at his office with the sun's first ray;
Straight to his desk he races, nothing slack,
Removes his frock coat from his spindly back,
Lest it be spoiled, though it's worn through halfway.
He takes a fully worn one from the rack
And sits in it, his hue a sparrow-gray.
His cheeks have paled now through the years and days;
His hair is thin, and trained back so it stays.

89/

He sits and copies for the aldermen
Day in, day out, for weeks, for months, for years,
And never something new comes into ken,
Save when the point of some new pen he shears
Or when he fills his inkhorn up again.
Each day along the same street he appears,
Each day, from morn till far into the night,
He sits hunched over, with his lips sealed tight.

And sometimes he looks up and deeply sighs
When sudden flashes of life's splendor fill
His mind's eye with a world far otherwise
Than that in which he's spent long years so ill.
But, in a moment, dazed in nerves and eyes,
He bows his head, and bows it lower still,
And on his chair shifts round against the light,
For it is painful when the sun shines bright.

He sits there, writing on until he dies;
And at his grave alone he will arrive,
A poor old bachelor still, at his demise,
Since he could barely keep himself alive.
His overriding need was to survive!
He did his duty, though but small his prize;
For sad reward he toiled, one in the mass;
May Heaven bring a great reward to pass!

To learn forbearance, let the reader mull
From time to time that faithful copyist
(A copyist can teach an original),
And he will learn the art if he persist.
And now I have the task congenial
To bring you back to our protagonist,
Who was a youth upon his twentieth year
And stood, like many more, at a frontier.

For at a crossroads in his life once stood
Not just the ancient Hercules, and not
Alone the mighty Caesar, when he would
Upon that fateful river cast his lot;
Not just Napoleon, when blood and shot
In Russia turned his clouded vision good:
We all confront some situation where I
Sense the question: "Dare I not or dare I?"

It's strange that such a question's not passé,
Since it is often found to be the fact
That in the heart it's long been put away
Before the hand is ever raised to act.
And yet we've heard it every single day,
As if our liberty were kept intact
By simply asking: Do I dare? Not dare?
When all the time the answer is right there.

To such remarks I now must set a seal,
For it is time that I resume my tale;
And there is much I have yet to reveal
Before our hero's freed from his travail.
He's now set out upon the selfsame trail
All take who will not listen, but must feel.
He's living high, has debts, pursues his fun,
And devil he cares if he gets a dun.

"His purse, though?" asks the reader.—Yes, the purse,
I need not say, before long empty hung;
The dirge for his fine stipend had been sung,
And now his credit could not be much worse.
He lived by pawning things, helped by his tongue,
And as a hired tutor would traverse
The city end to end, in hope to scour
Money, giving lessons by the hour.

At this time he found a situation
With the Count de Fix, whose young sons two
Our hero, showing much appreciation,
Is to give a thorough overview
Based on method sound and science true.
What's more, the Count will give rich compensation
If, when he delves into history,
His daughter swells the student-list to three.

It was a Friday when our hero first
Set foot inside the Count's imposing home
And through the long, wide corridor did roam,
In black garb, while his method he rehearsed.
A servant, done up *à la mode*, with great aplomb
Threw wide the door, and with a sudden burst
Of voices talking in the sitting room
There came to him a sweet, discreet perfume.

Impressed with such a scent, he stepped inside
Onto a carpet richly sewn, red-hued.
At a center table Adam viewed
Two young boys who were much preoccupied
And who, when Adam was identified,
Slammed shut the maps on which their eyes were glued.
To that the tutor paid but scant attention:
He'd found a looking glass of large dimension.

He looks about—the brilliance of the place!
Gilt furniture he'd never seen before.
But hush! At one wall opens a side door,
And through it steps the Count's good wife, Her Grace,
In silken gown, and at her throat some lace.
He bows low like a reed upon the shore.
He looks up, and again the door swings wide:
The Countess, her young daughter, comes inside.

As she approached the table from the door,
He could but look—he could not hear at all,
Her feet seemed to him not to touch the floor.
Down round her shoulders her dark hair did fall,
And, slim and straight, great dignity she bore
As she surveyed the room from wall to wall.
What eyes! so very glistening and clear,
With pride and mildness gleaming in each sphere.

O form of Hebe! Juno's stately pace!
What cheeks, and with the fairest red overlaid,
And tresses curling round them with what grace!
Just as the Ideal is so oft portrayed!
Her skirts leave her foot's beauty undisplayed;
A shawl gives her shy throat a hiding place—
So fair, so noble, and so young in years:
See with what thoughts our Adam's mind careers.

But her mother's talking to our friend:
"Hr. Homo! would you, if I might entreat,
Come to the table and please take a seat
While I explain to you what we intend.
My children: Count Franz, may his health soon mend,
My youngest boy. And now you have to meet
Count Herman, he's my oldest. And here sits
Countess Clara—all three have quick wits."

The young instructor, with a smile, averred,
Uncomfortably turning in his chair,
That, as for wits, there could be no doubt there—
And coughed, once his opinion was conferred.
He broached then, with that periphrastic flair
And pregnant speech from teachers often heard
(Awaiting *her* opinion of the whole),
His thoughts on how best to attain their goal.

Her Grace opined his plans were quite, quite sound;
And Adam went straight to the work at hand,
Declaring with some justice he had found
That history, before it can be scanned,
Some geographic knowledge will demand:
The former's foot must have the latter's ground.
The older Countess put in, "That's quite true,"
But over Clara's cheek a faint smile flew.

Our hero saw it, and he did not doubt
It was his speech that was the cause of it;
He gravely pursed his lips into a pout
And, sore discomfited, his eyebrows knit,
The map that lay before him he held out,
Repeating: "Just the groundwork, I admit."
"I'm sure you're right," Her Grace said as before,
But Countess Clara only smiled the more.

This, luckily, our teacher did not see,
Else he would surely have been quite confounded;
But he was launched upon Antiquity,
The facts of which he eagerly expounded.
Some questions were allowed occasionally;
Her Grace desired some points more deeply sounded,
Though he much doubted he could do his duty
To geography with such a beauty.

He spurned the method of Hr. Jacotot,
And that of Lancaster was not the way;
He sought a method best for day-to-day:
First deep in thought for something apropos,
He gives so masterful a résumé
That no one's mind succumbed to vertigo.
And on he sat, glued to his chair, in talk,
Till one was sounded on the mantel clock.

93/

He then arose and, bowing, said farewell,
Delighted with his visit and what passed;
He kept the vision of that *demoiselle*
Whose tender cheeks took on a crimson cast
When on the map she let her soft eyes dwell;
And he recalled that heavenly look at last
From her to him, when from Illyria
He traced for her the high road to Assyria.

There was another of a cheerful mind
Who afterwards went to her looking glass
And thought, as it revealed a pretty lass,
"So young a teacher surely can't be blind,"
Then whispered, as she let her fingers pass
Among her tresses, which she tugged and twined,
"And history's not really such a bore!
You rest at ease while going in for war."

And truly! in the course of just one week,
Once Adam plumbed the depths of history
And reached the Roman, having done the Greek,
With her sharp vision Clara came to see
That 'gainst the Cimbri Marius's technique
Was: postpone contact with the enemy.
Thus more and more she kept on drawing back,
As if she would retreat from the attack.

While she sat pensive now and much withdrawn,
Across the table Adam's passion grew
Till he became the nations' champion,
Striding to battle, utterly made new.
To speak herself was more than she could do,
Until her mother gently urged her on,
"My dear sweet Clara! Do give some reply
To what your teacher's asked you. Don't be shy."

When she talked, it was with lowered eyes;
And, when a word like Vestals she must speak,
A blushing red at once suffused her cheek,
So that it seemed some anger made it rise.
The sight of this made Adam hot and weak,
Though what it was he could not analyze.
But still the thought kept running through his head:
"Was this dear creature hurt by what I said?"

94/

With *him* now faint of heart, there came a gleam
Into Clara's beautiful bright eyes;
She called to mind some points in Adam's theme
Which she would have Hr. Homo summarize.
She dwelt on matters small in the extreme,
Nor were the large too large to utilize
As bellows for a flame still more intense
Than that of which his cheeks gave evidence.

He was the teacher, his disciple she!
What did the lady's mother think of this
When she stopped in so unsuspectingly?
He, tender youth—and she, a lovely miss!
And could the Count permit such things to be
And let them move on toward a precipice?
I think that both Their Graces stood too high
To feel a wind or use a weather-eye.

But Adam felt that wind with all its might,
For, though it blew from off a gracious lip,
It nearly blew him over with its whip.
And whether he were in or out at night,
Being meditative or just being flip,
The face of Clara came to haunt his sight.
However far his thoughts went traveling,
It kept on binding him within a ring.

It seemed to him he'd not seen anyone
So marvelous, a creature from romance;
The curtain rose to let hope's brilliant sun
Beam bright on life's least circumstance;
A flower bloomed of fairest countenance,
A treasure beckoned where there had been none;
And there was no one in all womankind
To match the noble Clara in his mind.

For one month now their lessons had been read,
And all the closer he and Clara grew
The more they from the tree of knowledge fed.
It often happened, sad to say, but true,
That Her Grace, before the hour was through,
Sometimes as soon as Adam showed his head,
Would leave the room to tend to her household
(Her duties in the house were manifold).

One day our hero chose to represent
With much excitement Cleopatra's story,
A tale from Clio of such ravishment
He worshipped that enchantress amatory.
You saw her on the throne in all her glory
And then all meek in Caesar's arms and tent.
What he had sown was Antony's to reap;
At last an asp-sting brought her final sleep.

And while majestically, as of yore,
The Egyptian queen stood forth, beyond compare,
Young Clara sat, reclining in her chair,
Quite pretty in the white dress that she wore.
With finger to her chin to underscore
Her concentration on this whole affair,
Her other hand plucks at her bodice bow
And, like bright stars, her eyes are all aglow.

She paid close heed to everything that passed
In that extraordinary life, and now
When Adam broke off, by her charms held fast,
She lowered, in all modesty, her brow.
Half to herself she spoke: "I'd be aghast
If snakes had lain upon this heart, I vow,"
And her breast heaved as if in agony,
Her hand pressed to her heart quite tenderly.

Our hero had completely lost his head;
His pulse was furiously hammering
As he envisioned, with its garment shed,
That lovely breast that bore the serpent's sting.
His wits were nearly so discomfited
As to forget the two sons' questioning.
With Clara, Cleopatra, sorely muddled,
Poor Adam's mind was wandering befuddled.

He had to weather even more upheaval
When treating intellectual history;
Among the authors of celebrity
Who were at work in ages medieval,
Adam, in his discourse rambling free,
Called upon their learnèd French coeval,
Whose fate so many hearts have taken hard:
That lofty lover-cleric Abelard.

On hearing that name Clara grew alert
—Her mood had been exceptionally mild—
And question upon question she then piled
On matters in which he was not expert.
The question that bade fair to drive him wild
And in a tone half modest and half pert
Was proffered of a sudden by the creature:
"Was Abelard not Heloise's teacher?"

He had to answer yes, though all the while
Envisioning himself as Abelard;
For Clara turned on him the same regard
With which fair Heloise would once beguile.
"One can't be clear," she went on with a smile,
"About just why their love was so ill-starred.
Would you, Hr. Homo, have the kindness, please,
To tell me something about Heloise?"

What was the young instructor then to do?
A fish upon a hook, he'd been pinned tight;
And let him turn and twist with all his might,
The hook that held him never broke in two.
He quickly did his best to tell aright
What parts were worth the telling, in his view,
Describing Heloise's growing love
(Her uncle's misdeed was not spoken of).

How quietly the Countess sat to hear!
How fixed upon her teacher was her eye!
What feeling did her features signify
When both the lovers found their fate so drear!
But soon they changed: she seemed near fit to cry
When they both chose a cloistered life austere;
Yes, her lips whispered softly an Amen
When in one grave the two were met again.

My reader has, I trust, had quite enough,
For Adam long has had much more than that
And would have hanged himself right where he sat
If Clara's locks had made the noose's stuff.
But crowds of darts remained to Venus's brat
Which Adam's groaning heart could not rebuff.
If there was danger when she was pathetic,
When gay, if possible, she's more magnetic.

For anything would serve her for wordplay,
In which her whimsy always called the tunes,
When—holding to her lips a rose bouquet—
She asks to know if Adam can read runes
And over Nero's many merits swoons,
While Cato barely gets the time of day.
Catiline she thinks *bravissimo*,
And gently rallies the old Cicero.

But when, by all her merriment transported,
At last our hero got his mouth in action,
And, with elation and deep satisfaction,
He held his own against her, nothing thwarted,
She'd cut poor Adam short with a distraction,
As to her noble lineage she resorted
In these words: "We must cut the matter short!
I have no time! Today I go to court."

Down into nullity our hero flew.
He closed the hour, his heart much agitated.
When he looked up, out on the avenue,
His face blushed hotly as he contemplated
Clara and her birth so elevated
That he, the low-born, knew not what to do.
He was of common stock, and she *noblesse*,
He was a pastor's son, she the *comtesse*.

In his young blood a fever had been started;
At night, when in his alcove he would lie,
He rarely slept, for in the day gone by
Were thoughts that from him never had departed.
He, once so blithe, had now grown so downhearted
That he would not so much as heave a sigh—
He, once so bold and anything but meek,
Now felt most often sick at heart and weak.

He needed but to pass the Count's front gate
To turn all pale and shake with apprehension:
Inside, did *torment* or did *kindness* wait?
His fate each day was hanging in suspension.
On leaving, if he'd reaped the condescension
Of a smile, how did his hope grow great!
He held his head up, and he brushed his clothes;
His cheeks once more would glow a feverish rose.

When oftentimes he took a horse for hire
And galloped off into the countryside,
Into his sweet thoughts he would soon retire
And dream the golden dreams they could provide.
But at the flowering of his heart's desire
A sharp blast from the head would come to chide
With lucid home-truths, counsels of despair,
And snuffed like fogs his castles in the air.

I can't expect her ever to be mine!
(Deep in his horse's flanks both spurs he pressed.)
She is a flower for me too proud and fine!
(He buttoned up his riding coat and vest.)
Her beauty leaves me to a fate malign!
It is already here, I might protest.
He loosened both the reins till they were slack
And, at an amble, took the highway back.

Does she care for me? (Again he's lost.)
Where is the oracle can answer me?
In truth I can declare that I've a lot
Of proof of her especial amity,
And yet (his gaze again grew shadowy)
At times I feel that she must love me not.
O that the certain sign might be displayed
And my high hope might be in full repaid.

But such repayment would be hard come by,
For Clara, I believe, was not too straight
About the nature of her present state
And what her heart's alarms might signify.
Her sense of her own dignity was high,
And others' pain she fixed at lower rate;
I do believe, though, Cupid had a part
In all her toyings with poor Adam's heart.

The crucial moment now was close at hand,
Which, however, let in no new light
But spread a new scene to our hero's sight
Which he had never had to understand.
The history of Rome had now been scanned,
And each reviewed it all alone at night,
So as to be quite sure to get down pat
The very crucial moments of all that.

It was a gloomy February day
When Adam came at three as specified.
In the room Her Grace was occupied
In work of some sort she had under way,
While Clara sat there waiting, still as clay,
Her fine hand to her lovely cheek applied;
And to his eye she looked a bit put out,
For that day the two boys were not about.

He feels his heart already start to burn
And hastens to the table, panicky;
But his approach she scarce looks up to see,
And over him his fever chills return.
Her mother now must leave their company,
For Baron Aster comes on some concern.
Alone, on history the two begin,
The hero Adam and his heroine.

The Romans now had come to that transition
At which the Lex Canuleia was carried,
So that at last plebeian and patrician
Might pass beneath the yoke of being married.
In praise of this law long our Adam tarried,
For (so he says), by everyone's admission,
The Romans' greatness only can be recked
From that time when this law took full effect.

Naive he was, that no man can deny;
He wasn't thinking of his own affairs.
His thesis he went on to justify
Till Clara verbal war on him declares,
Asserting his conclusions were but snares.
"The opposite effects, I think, apply;
I would contend that Rome was plainly wrecked
When all such intermarriage went unchecked."

At these words Adam turned a crimson red,
But quickly his cheek takes a different hue
As she goes on: "Its case might well be pled
In chapbooks or in tales of derring-do.
The princess and the slave might well be wed
And she be faithful till his life be through;
But in the real world, there is no debate:
Like will seek out like to be his mate."

"The truth of what you say I can't ignore"
(So Adam jumped in, voice transformed by passion)
"If it were Danes who married in that fashion
And not a nation on the Italian shore.
Yet" (here his color seemed to turn quite ashen,
His voice much weaker than it was before)
"Yet even in the North, as many own,
Occasional exceptions aren't unknown."

"Indeed, the fools among us are not rare,"
The Countess answered, very cold and stern,
And tossed her head in lofty unconcern
To let her glances wander in the air.
The young instructor could no longer bear
The pains in which his heart was left to burn.
He laid his book and map of Rome aside
And, raising himself to his feet, replied:

"I think I'll say good-bye now for today.
Some other day we will pick up the thread.
The history of Rome we'll put away;
It's high time we did something else instead."
He bowed and left. But what he chose to say
And how he said it stayed in Clara's head;
She wished she'd called to him to turn about
And, by a word, a smile, had smoothed things out.

Now haven't I been in a frightful mood!
(So she began her mute soliloquy.)
But why should mother have forbidden me
To wear a shawl because it was red-hued?
I didn't mean that he should come unglued,
He's just as charming now as formerly!
Next Friday I shall clear the atmosphere,
And only kind words will he get to hear.

So Clara mused—but wholly otherwise
We find our hero's agitated state
As through the city streets he all but flies,
His heart's blood pounding at a furious rate.
At times the passers-by would remonstrate
With him, with "Ho! Why don't you use your eyes?"
For, blind with love, by Clara quite undone,
He's nearly knocked down every second one.

He came to his own door. And up the stair
He bolted loud, nay, thunderingly.
Not even in his room could he breathe free;
His lips burned, grinning his despair.
To and fro he paced and clutched his hair
And often stopped in useless hope that he
Could fetch one sigh on which there might depart
This pain that would burst open his whole heart.

Disjointed phrases from his lips now flew,
Reflecting his unsettled state of mind:
"False hope, your horrid lies have proved untrue!
The star that shone so fair has now declined!
O tenfold darkness that has left me blind!
O headlong fall from high in heaven's blue!
What is a smile, a look? Why that reply
So cold and harsh? O Clara! Clara! Why?"

The darkness fell, but up and down he paced,
Just as before, his little chamber's floor;
Suddenly a flame blazed at the door
As, with a candle in her hand, he faced
The maid, who blurted out in haste:
Would not the gentle student, as before,
Have fire and lights, for sure he must require
By now, she would have thought, a little fire.

"It's almost hot enough here to be Hell!"
"Hr. Homo, no! It's bitter cold in here.
And outside snow's been coming down pell-mell
For a good hour, and the wind's severe!"
"Then leave the light, and, yes, you might as well
Bring up the fire, to keep your conscience clear."
Down on his sofa he proceeds to sit
And Lotte's back to get the fire lit.

She knelt before the oven and set to,
Piling it near full with wood for burning;
And Adam kept her figure in full view,
Her prettiness for the first time discerning.
The rounded legs, enclosed in hose of blue,
Are visible upon her every turning;
And as she bent down to her task so dearly,
He glimpsed her splendid bosom very clearly.

Her face all flushed, she rises, stands up straight,
But when she starts to go, she is embraced
By Adam, with his arm around her waist,
Who calls out to the frightened maid: "Oh, wait!"
The tender Lotte's nearly insensate,
A spinning top within his arms enlaced,
Until she says, with great anxiety,
"I must go down, there's no one home but me."

But Adam whispers: "Lotte, please stay here!
I've never been so miserable before.
Ah, such afflictions down upon me pour,
A bit of graciousness would bring much cheer!
I've often thought how kind you are, how dear.
You'd not deny the solace I implore:
I need a gentle soul who'll understand,
And tender are your eyes, and soft your hand."

But Lotte answered, obviously stirred,
For she had liked the student all along:
"Has somebody, Hr. Homo, done you wrong?
I know I thought that something had occurred.
I'd gladly stay, but duty's call is strong,
And nobody's downstairs, as you have heard.
—Let go, let go! Don't tempt me! Don't be bold!
A poor girl still has honor to uphold!"

But Adam heard no more of honor's case,
Deafened by the storm within his breast;
A fevered crimson spread along his face,
And quick his lips and Lotte's coalesced.
"O Lotte, could you really love me best?"
His arm came round her in a firm embrace;
Unable to resist more, though she tried,
He pulled her to the sofa by his side.

"Oh, no, Hr. Homo! Where will all this lead?
You must know that I hold you very dear.
If you like me a little, please take heed:
You mustn't touch me, mustn't come so near!"
But such a preachment fell on a deaf ear;
He liked his sport, and he would not concede.
Lotte was the mistress of his choosing,
And she could only sigh, past all refusing.

103/

Remarkable is man's mentality!
Can any sage its mysteries impart?
He who for petty doings lacks all heart
Will often tackle large ones thoughtlessly.
He who quakes if any fistfight start
Is not, in battle, even panicky.
He who a Clara hardly dares to touch
Fears not a Lotte's honor to besmutch.

And curious the labyrinth of fate!
Because the lady's shawl was not bright red,
Her deep resentment gave her pride its head,
Which down on Adam fell with all its weight.
And so a fog round Adam's vision spread
So thick that honor could not penetrate;
And thus and therefore rose the Evil One
And—wretched Lotte had to be undone.

Rejected by a countess and coquette,
Whom he still loved deep down within his heart,
He took a girl to play a mistress part
Who never would have thought of traps to set.
In this miasma, which grew deeper yet,
He'd gone on nearly one month since the start,
Deceiving her and by himself deceived—
Till of his blindfold he was swift relieved.

What is a passion? It's a cresting wave
That tosses up the heart into the sky
And hurls it, like a ship no one can save,
Down to the deeps in agony to lie!
It's lightning, like a candle flaming high
Beneath the clouds wherein the thunders rave;
It is the rose whose thorn has made us blanch,
The sunlight on a hurtling avalanche!

What is a passion? A forbidden word!
A sacrifice that's fit for bards to flay,
A scapegoat which all wise men swore to slay!
And yet a teacher certain to be heard
Whose teaching, harshly paid for, will repay,
Such the enrichment on the heart conferred.
For as the mind has knowledge for its dame,
So for the heart will passion act the same.

104/

With such assurance we go down life's way,
And each of us in no time falls asleep:
One because he hones his wits all day,
And one because he has no wits to keep.
How dully we two, you and I, do creep,
With blindfolds on, and scales more dark than they,
And find that all is right, whate'er it be,
And never think of what we do not see.

Then comes the warning of a storm, and roused
From lethargy we rush to meet the threat.
The storm grows to a hurricane: upset
Are props that held us while we drowsed;
The thunder rolls above us, now unhoused
And feeble in the wildness and the wet;
Deep in the gloom of night the lightning hisses
And we catch sight of deepest Hell's abysses.

Into ourselves we look then, and we sigh,
Finding now the world completely new,
And, shuddering, we open up our eye
To heaven, hell, in cheerfulness and rue.
The mind can no more sing its lullaby,
The bubble of heart's ease has burst in two,
And yet we have awakened, though we quake
At what it costs to learn and be awake.

And Adam wakened. "—Oh, where have I been?"
Thus on one morning to himself he said,
Bolt upright on the corner of his bed,
No longer by his passion taken in,
The fire within his blood at long last dead.
"Oh, in what fogs did my poor reason spin!
What darkness did my eyesight overtake!
Too late, oh much too late, am I awake!

"How was it possible from day to day
To lull myself with hope's false fantasy
And keep my eyes from the discovery
That Clara's frigid heart could only play?
How possible that in the soul of me
I never heard the groans of my dismay,
But her caprices for true love I took,
Self-betrayed because I would not look?

"If it were but myself I had betrayed!
O, if, though blind in these debaucheries,
I had not ruined someone else's ease!"
Here, deep inside, the pain so heavy weighed
That in a flash (all dressed and toilet made)
He rushed outside to still his agonies;
But though he wandered round all over town,
He could not keep his apprehension down.

For wheresoever he'd direct his feet,
He ran into companions of his woe:
None but fellow-sufferers walked the street,
The crosses on whose shoulders bent them low;
None but those whose hearts bled as they beat,
Whose eyes had naught but misery to show,
Who all were dragging round the weight of life,
In hope of balm, of solace, for their strife.

So many people, sick and halt and blind,
So grim, so poor as he'd not seen before;
And when no signs of wretchedness they bore
He guessed that in their hearts it was confined.
Among them all he came upon a whore
Whose red lips sent a smile to him and signed,
But, looking through the smile, he saw expressed
The fear and unease nagging at her breast.

"And has the world at last slipped from its frame?"
He whispers nervously while looking round.
"I don't recall this new life that I've found;
All here is changed, and nothing is the same.
No eyes with any gaiety abound,
And all the wings of hope are drooping lame.
And bowing under sin's and sorrow's weight,
The whole race heads for death and to its fate."

Then through his heart he felt a fierce pain grow,
Which everyone who has been born of dust
By mere experience must come to know
While feelings yet remain warm and robust;
How often people have upon them thrust
Not just their own, but other people's woe;
How, Atlas-like, the world and all its wrack
Each one must often bear on his own back.

For sometimes in that circle grand we're found
Wherein we each form links upon one chain,
Whether made of gladness or of pain;
And when a flash electric finds its ground
In one, it spreads to all the circle round
A stroke of lightning nothing can restrain.
Its power is diffused throughout its course,
And ev'n the smallest link feels all its force.

With heart intent on finding consolation,
Our hero thus continued on his way;
But in most things it seemed a poison lay
And nearly every sight brought new vexation.
In heaven's vault did Luna's taper play
When he regained in haste his habitation
And, wrapped in his cloak, back up the staircase swept—
There on the top step Lotte sat and wept.

But Adam made believe he saw her not;
How could he to another be of use?
He who, in sore distress, much overwrought,
Had all that weight to bear as his excuse?
Some pangs, though, Lotte's sobbing did produce
In Adam's heart as past the girl he shot,
And in his room his own hot tears he cried
Once he had safely locked himself inside.

"How strange a thing is time!" he mused once more,
As he took up his seat before the stove
And gazed into the fire, whose dull flame strove
To cast a glimmer on the chamber floor.
"Who understands what it has been before
When from the present it will always rove?
That it is here, and in that instant goes,
Is known but by the shadow that it throws.

"To think that it was scarce a month ago
When Lotte at this very oven knelt,
And at the time I actually felt
I could on her my yearning heart bestow!
How could I think I'd ever have so dealt
Were it not for her weeping and her woe,
Were it not for my sobs, my own self-blame,
That constantly remind me of my shame?

"And don't I know that I have now grown old?
Is not my youth with all its pleasures past?
Has not my lover's garland been off-cast
And friendship's flower withered into mold?
What is this life, harassed and unconsoled,
When every breath the panting soul does blast,
When everywhere one looks he sees travail
And earth itself becomes a dismal jail!"

Once more in thought our hero was engrossed.
And there he was now in his youth's bright spring:
When all is haste and speed is uppermost;
When, whether it be bliss or suffering,
It must be had past all imagining
And be the greatest feeling man can boast;
When mediums will never do at all,
And pistol-shot sounds like a cannonball.

But, added to these stingings from within,
Were thorns that struck from outside, sharp and keen:
At countless classes he had not been seen,
And at some few of those which he had been
Accustomed to get highest honors in
A boom had fallen like a guillotine.
The near-death of his purse cut like a knife
Just as his creditors all sprang to life.

From Count de Fix, from whom he'd stayed away
One month already, claiming to be ill—
Since seeing Clara would have turned him gray
And it was far beyond his strength of will
To break relations with that domicile—
From Count de Fix a letter came one day
In which that Eminence with thanks now graced him
And then described the tutor who'd replaced him.

Adam, having now read everything
And found enclosed the full sum he was due
As wages for his former tutoring,
Smiled bitterly, exclaiming, "It's not true
That all the gains and losses we accrue
Near balance on the day of reckoning.
The truth of that old saw can't be sustained:
My heart's ease has been lost—and what's been gained?

"But all that will be different now! Indeed,
I still can feel the blood course through my veins;
Meek desperation is for scatterbrains—
Just let me be a man and I'll succeed!
No more with me shall Lotte's teardrops plead.
I must get out, be set free from these chains.
A haven from life's storms will get me by;
Now only on myself will I rely."

Such our proud hero's thoughts, on paying rent
For lodgings at the city's other end,
On which the bustling world did not descend;
To Lotte, in a letter, he then sent
(Less five rigsdalers he on logs must spend)
His total hoard, of thirty coins' extent.
As always, he blamed fate and not himself
For having put his love up on the shelf.

The letter once sent off, how calmed he felt!
But that same day he had received one, too,
That shook him like a thunder through and through.
From Jutland came this blow his father dealt:
That debts had made him tighten in his belt,
And, with a future vague and dark of hue,
He was compelled to scrimp and save: in short,
He could no longer be his son's support.

"You won't," he wrote, "therefore be in receipt
Of fifteen dalers monthly as before
Until I can get back upon my feet.
I would be deeply grieved upon this score
Had your bright star gone into a retreat
And not been leading upward more and more;
But you yourself recount such victories
That, in regard to this, I feel at ease."

That was the end of Adam's whole existence!
Those fifteen dalers were the solid pile,
The firm foundation, which he'd kept the while
His tutoring provided but subsistence.
Now clouds were gathering darkly in the distance,
His hopes were pale and his finances vile;
And now the only means he had in reach
To keep himself alive and well was: teach.

Heroically, he took himself in hand.
Ten hours he toiled each day, with all his might,
To learn of patience and of self-command,
From sunny morning to the dark of night.
All this the meanest wages must requite,
In such a bad way did his credit stand;
Rewards are small in an instructor's post,
And he earned six marks daily at the most.

But this amount, how could it satisfy
The creditors who now were at his door
Both day and night with triumph in each eye,
While he, ashamed, must beg a few weeks more?
And if, on hearing him, one man forbore,
Right on the spot another man came by,
Waving proofs of his indebtedness
And threatening to send them to the press.

Still, Adam would not let his courage fail;
He did whatever any man could do:
He put his books and fob-watch up for sale,
And all his finest clothes went with them too,
Leaving but one vest of narrow wale
He'd worn, alas, upon that interview
When Clara's face had made its deep impression
And when was sown the seed of his obsession.

But that was gone now; in his looking glass
He saw himself in an old pair of pants
And threadbare shirt, all one dark gray expanse,
Like castle thralls or dunces in a class:
Upon his forehead clouds of misery mass
And o'er his heart grief near gains dominance.
Of course he'd vowed to bear up like a man;
With such a burden, though, he barely can.

Still, he *did* bear up, but went to school
No longer by the major thoroughfares,
Avoiding all the busy city squares,
And keeping from the sun became his rule.
It would have certainly exposed the tears
And bleach-marks on his shirt to ridicule.
Oft in the shadows, hands behind his waist
(Where he'd a button off), he sneaked, shamefaced.

When from far off he saw someone he knew
He pulled his hat still lower on his brow,
And on the sidewalk he would fix his view
Although the other man had passed him now.
But if a lovely lady chose somehow
To glance his way, one of the sidewalk crew
That hover round in silks from top to toe,
His heart in a deep sigh would overflow.

For him sheer loneliness was all he had,
For him his pleasures now were at an end,
And school became a jail where he was penned
To slave for bread in days no longer glad.
Each day the same lament would keep him sad
As down the customary streets he'd wend.
Enough lamenting! There's the institution,
There's his jailhouse and his persecution!

And truly! here he sits as in a jail
From morning until evening every day,
Instructing for long hours in that lycée
Young boys who'd gladly save him his travail.
A thousand times he hears himself purvey
The same idea in just the same detail;
With one class and the next he's closeted
And lectures till there's nothing in his head.

Hour by hour here, unremittingly,
He harped and harped upon the same old strings,
And gave out work to fill the evenings
Of which, come morning, he took custody.
Here terribly he yearned for liberty
From all the burdens weighting down his wings;
Here, in his labors, he had quickly found
That without joy all labor was unsound.

When day was gone and lessons at an end,
And on came night when all things take their rest,
Then homeward in the darkness he would wend
To study for his civil service test.
But ere he could one word of it digest,
His mind went blank; he could not comprehend.
And in this way months flew by aimlessly,
And freedom still remained a quandary.

111/

—To what can we compare a soul which leaves
The Paradise that it had thought its own,
Far from the joys to which it fast had grown
Because at last real sorrows it receives?
It's like the people of a plain well-sown
Who lived in peace and plenty 'mongst their sheaves
But suddenly, when foes lay waste their crops,
Must flee for refuge to the mountaintops.

There they bear the winds that howl and crack
And, as the wild cascades go crashing past,
They move along the narrow mountain track
And through the dark pines find their way at last.
There they the beetling summit must attack
Or be into the gaping chasm cast,
Must grow at ease with the stupendous view,
For they now see a world they never knew.

But by Necessity they are well-taught,
And—though with sighs—each one constructs his hut,
Which for protection mountain walls abut
To ward off landslides and the storms' onslaught.
The wood, not into spades but pikes, is cut
And in its wilderness wild game is sought;
And up life goes, along the snow-packed peaks
Where battle threatens and where peril shrieks.

It's then that hidden powers are revealed
Which had been slumbering in the tender breast;
It's then the once lethargic glance is steeled
As soul and arm are hardened at each test;
Then to the storm's voice is the ear kept peeled
As down it rumbles from the mountain crest;
And by these chill and bracing breezes blown,
The heart feels it has come into its own.

When sometimes from the mountain's barren crown,
Half ecstatic, and compassionate,
They gaze into the valley's lap and down
Upon those happy fields they left of late,
Where hopes would smile but fear would ever frown,
Where comfort dwells but thralldom lies in wait;
Then—on the very rim of an abyss—
Their sense of freedom lifts them into bliss.

So goes it too with him whom sorrow takes,
When into his own self he draws apart,
Although the soul's dark regions make him start
And at its endless depths he stands and shakes:
In time he's drawn into its secret heart
And there within his home and refuge makes,
While he who faints with cares is idly tossed,
An exile, pondering the life he's lost.

Faint of heart was Adam, though at last
He seized his Bible and his Testament
In hope that from it comfort might be lent
Unto his soul so anxious and aghast.
But how to find it? None seemed evident;
It seemed to him he'd been by God outcast;
The candle of his promise now had guttered,
And Heaven's gates against him had been shuttered.

It was as if his heart had no more notion
(For it was long since he had knelt to pray)
Of how, in boyhood, he had done devotion.
To him the Word no meaning did convey,
He found in it no sturdy hope to stay
His mind against his thoughts' commotion.
He shuts the Bible, and for comfort looks
To philosophical and famous books.

Here, he thinks, I'm certain to be aided,
For so their prefaces all guarantee.
When he wound out the fine threads that they braided
And brocaded so ingeniously,
Undoing all their knotted mystery,
He found a system's bones, unfleshed and faded:
Concept, without substance, was his gleaning.
The idea was there, but not its meaning.

He shut those far-famed books that failed his need,
That glossed a comfort they could not impart,
And back into himself he sought to read—
Into the springs of life within his heart.
But though he sowed still further mental seed,
Still scant the crop he drew home in his cart;
However loud his soul cried out for gladness,
It's answered, note for note, in songs of sadness.

—From his window he, in fascination,
Stared down one Sunday at the passers-by
In carriages or walking, low and high,
Hastening to the woods in high elation.
They sang and piped beneath the morning sky,
Off to the Deer Park for their recreation.
Such life a-plenty in that joyous throng
But made his aching sorrows doubly strong.

By afternoon the streets were mute and still,
And home, though low and in no proper mood,
He thought he'd write, while he'd some solitude.
Just then beyond his attic's windowsill,
The tall, blond, pallid clerk next door renewed
His fluting with a melancholy trill,
The same who every Sunday tried the souls
Of neighbors who endured his scales and rolls.

What reason is there that this flautist keeps
Each blessèd Sunday free for music drills,
For practising short runs and drawn-out trills?
Is it a pleasure playing all these cheeps?
Does he expect that someday soon he reaps
A sweetheart who's enraptured with his skills?
What's in him that he plagues his fellowmen
And, nothing daunted, sets to work again?

Would he, since these are Sunday mysteries,
Release his soul from that week's slavery?
Into his prosy life must poetry
Be breathed with these entrancing melodies,
With these impassionated fantasies
Which sorely tax his lungs' capacity?
Would he, by variations on a theme,
Give some variety to life's fixed scheme?

Would he in his potpourri bring air
Around the bird confined inside of him,
The bird of paradise, who's yet aware
It dwelt once with sweet flowers and cherubim?
Or are his soft legatos meant to spare
His heart and reason from a battle grim?
Would he by that nostalgic waltz express
His hope of love, his loss of happiness?

Who knows what such a flautist might intend!
(You know it, you who've scraped a fiddle-bow!)
I do know this: that solace is his end,
And he is moved—what by he does not know.
He will grow old and to his flute still bend
In hopes to play precisely *comme il faut*;
He won't go very far for all his drill,
But will remain his neighbors' bitter pill.

Just now a sad adagio he was playing,
And played it over after it was through;
And with each note that to our hero flew
He felt foul nuisances were on him preying.
His own handwriting he no longer knew
But on he wrote, against his state inveighing;
And, while the other tooted, wrote two pages
Good as one of Jeremiah's rages.

Just as the fluting stopped, he signed his name,
And blackly now he read the letter through;
But when to the concluding lines he came,
He picked it up and ripped the sheets in two,
And there they lay, a day's work's residue.
A new epistle he sat down to frame,
In which he wrote home just a simple line
To say he was alive and feeling fine.

With the post his missive winged its way;
And Pastor Homo was most pleased at knowing
How very well his Adam's life was going,
Although the brevity did seem outré.
But that's the world! In dole, in disarray,
You still must keep your outside fresh and glowing.
If ever we turned *out* what had been *in,*
Would anybody know who we had been?

C A N T O   V

Which fate is worst? —If people should respond,
The headstrong chorus of replies would run:
To be forever bored; a simpleton;
No, coldness from someone of whom you're fond;
No, when your wife has passed to the beyond;
No, when her days on earth are not yet done;
No, children-trouble; trouble from old sin;
No, money-trouble, once it's dug deep in!

I'd better answer this myself; these frays,
Interminable, hardly worth the price,
I'll end them, tyrant-fashion, in a trice.
The worst of fates—the least of them these days
In which small faith's a mark of minds worth praise
And hearts are fired up when doubt's the spice—
Is when the soul is plunged in viewless night
And knows no longer if it travels right.

For from the grave will suddenly emerge
With iron scepter and a heavy tread
The fearful Fate, the ancient demiurge
That sank below when heathendom was dead.
Then its gloomy kingdom will resurge,
By cold despair alone inhabited;
Then miracles are over. All that's known
Will be to bow beneath the yoke and groan.

But yet the circle's open. There endures
A stirring heart within the earth's broad breast.
The strong physician still exists and cures,
The mighty preacher comforts the distressed.
The hand stays open still that reassures,
The sharp ear hearkens when it is addressed,
An eye looks down. And miracles are wrought
To aid mankind and comfort the distraught.

Burst are the chains, those hundredweights that pressed
Upon the soul which forged them in despair.
Then gloriously it swung its sword in air
And killed the tyrant Fate as its first geste.
Yet Fate is ever with us, ours to bear,
And it resides within our very breast.
Its home is inside, whence it walks abroad;
It is our creature, we ourselves its god.

But this god's no god; no more than the root's
The root of life when once the plant's in bloom;
Our Fate but lies there licking at our boots
That we might raise it from its dusty doom.
It grows on, endless changes executes,
And yet no perfect shape can it assume.
First one hue, then another it will try,
For it's the grub to Psyche's butterfly.

And as a grub it comes at last to die
When soul and its Idea are as one;
For fortune, joy, and woe beneath the sun
The first rough draft will only clarify
To set their image clearly in our eye.
That made, so that its outlines do not run
(As pain and struggle can cause them to do),
Then Freedom soars upon its wings—Fate's life is through.

To that belief our hero had not come.
He stood then at the parting of life's ways,
Where 'gainst him Fate its scepter did upraise
To stymie him and leave him lost and numb.
Already he heard fall upon his days
The blood-red sentence of opprobrium
Which said that Adam Homo shall be lost;
To death and to corruption has he crossed!

In the beginning he had shut his ear
Against this sinister and bitter word;
But when it came more clearly to be heard
And echoed back as in a choir drear,
Then to him suddenly a thought occurred:
The strings of Fate were his to commandeer;
He'd try if Providence had aught to say
That might at last dispatch him on his way.

With this new purpose hope burst forth alive:
"Yes," he exclaimed, "yes, I must have some air!
I must tear free from this unsound despair
If ever I expect myself to thrive.
A jammed wheel can be put in good repair,
And with a push my life too can revive.
The road that leads me out of woe I see,
And Providence has given it to me.

"My life has taken many a curious turn,
But good turns came to me with each defeat;
I feel now Heaven showed itself so stern
To make my knowledge of the world complete,
And feel too that its punishment was sweet,
And loud I praise it for its harsh concern.
Now happiness again spreads her arms wide
To melt this heart that once was petrified."

With these thoughts—reader, don't expect
That something wonderful will now occur
Of that sort that the novelists prefer,
Which widens eyes and boggles intellect.
No fairy-doings will we resurrect
For times when fairy tales mere laughter stir.
We lay before you only real-life lots:
To that end we present you with these thoughts—

With these thoughts Adam sat down in his chair
And wrote in telling phrases, full of dash,
To five men he had long known, for some cash
To rid himself at last of his despair.
He'd seen them at their homes and everywhere,
They were so kind they wouldn't think it brash,
And they would not be throwing bills away—
Upon his word of honor he'd repay.

He wrote sincerely, he wrote movingly,
And even borrowed out of Holy Writ
So that his correspondent must admit
That charity meant giving charity.
His style in closing was so exquisite
He felt at once what the result must be,
Especially when he ensured success
By writing off to more than one address.

Then, with the letters posted, plans he drew
For his future and a better day.
First all his many debts he would repay
To the last shilling, with the interest due.
Then he'd buy good clothing, all brand new,
Such as no longer would wear thin and fray.
And he would ease his teaching drudgery
To plunge himself into theology.

Such was his will—but more than will did wrought
The power of wishful thinking in his brain.
The promptings of good sense he set at naught
And gave imagination freest rein,
Which to him all his golden future brought
While huge and huger swells his bubble vain.
Upon it and its iridescent hues,
Bedazzled he would stare out long and muse.

Not only will he be, with money's aid
(That *nervus rerum* which undoes all wrong),
Back with his friends, whom he'd neglected long,
And acting out the part he once had played.
His wish will burst the bars that had held strong
And kept his Clara safe from ambuscade.
'Neath Time impossibility must totter—
Has no priest ever married a count's daughter?

One evening he had come back home from class
And on his table spied five envelopes,
And, as by lightning, changed were all his hopes
To fears that they contained his coup de grâce.
They looked the very work of misanthropes
Who had but adverse sentences to pass.
A long time back and forth he paced the floor
Till fear changed into hope as once before.

To himself he spoke (completely free
He is not found to be, in this effusion,
From a not-uncommon self-delusion):
"I'll shape myself a happy destiny!
I don't foresee a favorable conclusion
In Fortune's glance. She does not stop for me.
The old faith, though, has this fine rule of thumb:
The least expected is the soonest come."

He then unsealed the letters one by one,
And swiftly scanned the first one, two, three, four,
About which there was nothing to be done,
And threw them down—and rested from his chore.
Then with a sigh that made his spirit soar,
And with a hot look burning like the sun,
He gazed to Heaven, seizing number five
—But of those four the reader I deprive.

The first one read: He too in need did stand,
Weighted down beneath severe taxation.
The second: That the cash he'd had on hand
Regrettably was out in circulation.
The third: That he'd be forced into starvation
If such a sum were drawn out on demand.
The fourth: That orphanages took what pelf
He did not spend on wife and child and self.

The fifth note, on which Adam's bleary eye
Was hanging now as if this were a dream,
Did sound a sweet and philosophic theme,
The closing words of which I here supply:
"You know, Hr. Homo, it would ill beseem
To heed the heart and yet the head deny;
The justice of this principle you'll own,
By which I must not let out cash on loan."

The devil take such principles as these!
And that's the only thing that I can say,
For Adam cannot speak in his dismay.
May those whose own sweet words can give heart's ease
While neighbors' ribs the tempest's fierce winds flay,
May they depart their dry Hesperides
And in the depths of ocean sink from view!
I'll wager then their preaching would be through.

May those who to their neighbors will not spread
The least part of their superfluity
Lose every bit of it, soon as can be!
May those who butter only their own bread,
With not a crust to those who must be fed,
Go hungry fast and turn more brotherly!
May those who would do good, but in right measure,
Learn what it is to live at others' pleasure!

Now, these are wishes of a Christian sort!
But I did not intend a reference
That could in any manner give offence
To those just men of whom I've made report.
In their refusals there was much good sense,
In which his applications fell far short:
Since no pledge or security was offered
When his mere word of honor Adam proffered.

For if a word of honor should be sold,
There's rarely much in it to realize
By either party, he who sells or buys.
More like than not, that honor soon will fold,
And creditors who this "estate" now hold
(The word of honor) lay claim to no prize.
For what are promises sworn to before us?
Mere wind and sound! *O tempora, O mores!*

But once more to our hero! His soul knows
The dizziness we feel in dreaming, when
We seem to stand on crumbling mountain snows
And our foot fails to find safe ground again.
A faintness spreads in us from head to toes,
Sure we'll plunge down the steep walls of this glen;
But from our lips there's no cry 'gainst our death,
Though we can hear our tired and heavy breath.

One thing he felt: that every hope was gone;
The bow of hope had been stretched all too taut,
No farther could its springy arch be drawn,
And by its recoil he was soundly caught.
His mental life had been so overwrought,
So lofty were the hopes he'd floated on,
That down he came, refusing every aid,
And gravity increased the speed he made.

The first thing that he did was to resign
From most of his school duties, save a few
By which he earned the wherewithal to dine
And give his body what to it was due.
Why should he branch out into ventures new
When diligence's fruits stayed on the vine?
And—if on all sides it be leaking—why
Fill up a jug like the Danaidae?

The next effect was, since he almost had
All day to sit around and deeply think,
That he was free to let his thoughts go sink
To bottomless abysses, black and sad.
And there they formed a chain, to which they add
In time himself and all else, link on link,
Whose loops day after day become more tight
Till they prevent all movement by their bite.

Across the world he sees the chariot
Of triumph roll and thereupon stands Fate,
Both its hands with tender seedlings fraught
To sow in men's lives, there to foliate.
It knits its brow—all's dark and desolate;
It smiles—and out the sun comes, bright and hot.
It harrows nations like a thunderpeal,
And every heart is crushed beneath its wheel.

Now in his own life Adam could make sense
Of paradoxes it had never been
Permitted him to find the wisdom in;
And how profound now was his confidence
That Life not only breaks the soul's defence,
Not only puts the reason in a spin
(For Life's effects on lives can be but grave),
But makes the will into its utter slave.

No doubt, my will still rules within my breast,
But when there's aught to do, it can no more,
So very cold the comfort on that score.
'Gainst Fate, by whom all mankind is oppressed,
It's useless in my weakness to contest;
What chances and mischances on me pour,
Whatever state of things Fate next propound,
They're bound to turn me and my heart around.

When pressed by need my spirits sink, but glide
Aloft they must when buoyed by happiness;
My courage withers under dark distress,
And, bathed by hope, it is new fortified;
My heart is captive to the least caress,
And turns to hatred when it is denied.
And so my will is at Fate's beck and call:
My grave once dug, then into it I'll fall!

Such were his thoughts, but hotter, more intense,
Than can in this account of them be shared,
For he saw his existence in suspense
And his own failure being now prepared.
For every thought which in his hot brain flared
There rose more bitterness at being cheated,
And all he did not know was one detail—
The hour when by Fate's will he was to fail.

—One August eve, as day began to fade
And, like a net slung high above the town,
The twilight spread its veil of dusky brown,
Among the throngs that strolled the Promenade
Near desperate he wandered up and down
As gentle breezes of the evening played
And sounds of happy voices could be heard,
Till more and more he found his heart was stirred.

"Hear them enjoy themselves, the purblind dupes!"
Beneath his breath, as he walked on, he said.
"They do not see the dart that likely swoops
On them tomorrow, leaving them all dead.
Behind the show of laughter tears are bred;
And, as with all us human nincompoops,
They don't reveal their real selves in their eyes,
For equally they serve both truth and lies."

When once he'd got his strictures under way,
He spared nor earth nor heaven from his rod.
For, looking up, he found some fault with God,
Who lived in bliss, while all men must obey
And drain their bitter drink day after day.
And, looking down, found earth a mirror broad
Wherein the inner man stood unconcealed,
His coldness, fraud, and falsehood all revealed.

From such remarks the poison he extracts
As from a gall-besodden bitter herb;
And there he was, just pausing at a curb
And taking measures of his life's bleak acts
With thoughts to sting his heart and to disturb
His peace of mind with facts on woeful facts
(For when one thought was finished, came one colder)
When someone from behind him tapped his shoulder.

123/

He turns—. A painted miss, demimondaine,
Is standing there with her right hand extended,
Which she immediately takes back again,
And whispers if he'd like to be befriended:
"All loneliness, my dear love, can be mended
And you do seem a lonely specimen:
What if we oddments chased away our blues,
Pooled forces to find something to amuse?"

"We oddments, yes! that is the very word;
You've pricked the center of the abscess there!"
He answered, being instantly aware
Of just what sort of creature he had stirred
With finery so shabby and threadbare.
The nymph's arm went through his arm undeterred,
And through the city streets the two now stray,
Changing their direction as they may.

The lady strove at first with lively jest
To laugh him from his melancholy mind;
But when to such she found him disinclined,
She thought her beauty's power might serve best.
When at a lamppost they would stop to rest,
Her brown eyes cast a look that intertwined
With his great blue ones, staring as in dreams
At hers, which sent him ever softer beams.

"What view of Destiny, dear lady, do you hold?"
Our hero cried, a grim smile on his face,
When to a certain house the two had strolled.
"*Him* I sent off on a wild-goose chase
Every time he asked, Was this the place
Where dwelt a maid with love dart tipped with gold?
And so he never won me to his will."
She burst out with a laughter loud and shrill.

"But really, if it please my lovely boy,
I'd gladly see Fate snap the whole world's throat,
For there is nothing here but *hoi polloi*
Save you, my dear, for you're not in their boat.
There's something in you that I do enjoy.
Just thank me for my love; don't pay a groat.
I see that thanks is all that you can leave me,
Unless your build and that frock coat deceive me."

124/

Saying this, she slipped inside the door
And Adam, quite prepared to stay behind,
Seemed to hear a voice within his mind
That said to him: "Go in! Delay no more!"
And when it was repeated as before,
He saw in it something his Fate designed.
Fate's hand reached out, a hand he gladly gripped,
And up the staircase one-two-three he tripped.

Once in her room he finds a double prize:
Not only was Black Trine living there
(A name for which she had to thank her hair),
But Pretty Line, who with Trine vies
In that fine talent which fell to their share
Of jabbering and shrieking to the skies
And gaping to the full span of her jaws
When for her laughter there was slightest cause.

Now in their free and easy company
Our hero soon warms to their merry game.
Need we say, the jests were very free,
The last thing ever thought of being shame.
Enticing songs and dances were their aim,
For both the beauties practised gallantry
On Adam with a like licentiousness,
And neither had a conscience to suppress.

But as they say in novels: "I omit,
By choice, to give this scene in full detail"—
Or else: "Allow me here to draw a veil
While angels weep that know what's under it"—
Two sentences which crop up without fail.
And I will use these words, most apposite:
In need, our hero found what friends he could,
And was accepted, if not understood.

And let nobody marvel that he found
Such company equipped to soothe his pain;
For in the things they said all thoughts were drowned
And time, till then stopped dead, ran on amain.
For these were human beings, to speak plain,
Living people whom he was around,
And—if they'd neither purity nor tone—
They did have hearts, and he was not alone.

125/

To Pretty Line and Black Trine, as well,
Unused to such a sight as they saw here,
Our hero grew day after day more dear,
And in their parlance he was called The Swell.
They very often found The Swell most queer,
Moping round their rooms, locked in his shell;
But still they felt it a great dignity
For them to have the student's company.

Especially was Line captivated.
In her intense, somewhat distorted mind
This thought was irremovably enshrined:
That to his heart her gaze had penetrated,
To her his life and fortunes were resigned,
To her his flesh and feeling subjugated.
Her own unfaithfulness she quite forgot,
While with Black Trine now she loudly fought.

The two friends formed a kind of lawless state
Along with Adam, and they wildly hurled,
All three, their imprecations at the world
As at a wicked, hostile potentate.
He heard them give, until his hair near curled
(For other pastimes this stood surrogate),
A strict accounting of their dissipation,
Of lives whose stories made a grim narration.

But when the voice of sympathy was stirred
At such descriptions, deep within his breast,
A sudden laughter from the two he heard
And he in soothing them lost interest.
Then in their hats and shawls was Adam dressed
And, in thick voices, they in deed and word
Showed him how, when evening's hours came,
The swells would speak their mind and show no shame.

"And that's the way that you should talk, you swell!"
They added. "Don't just sit there in the murk
And sulk like any heathen or a Turk
Whose head and stomach doesn't feel quite well.
You have the bottle! Put the thing to work,
You'll see how fast you come out of your shell!
You are a student, right? Then show us you
Aren't just a preacher, but a kisser too!"

126/

That's how they spoke—no doubt, to finer sound
And other tones his ear had once been tuned;
But when at dusk he sat at home and mooned
And nets of somber thoughts about him wound,
He could recall, so that he nearly swooned,
The wells of life still running all around.
He yearned to break free into fresher air
And felt he had to go out, anywhere.

But once he stood out on the street and saw,
Besides remarks and glances on him bent,
The whole world looking cold as on it went,
It seemed to him those tones that fell so raw
Upon his ear before had no such flaw,
But gentle charm and warm encouragement.
And so he cancelled out all recollection,
Returning to his two new friends' affection.

No doubt, this fantasy was dissipated
As soon as he had set foot back inside;
No doubt, upon his ear those tones still grated
And harsh the sounds which he'd just glorified.
But what led him to be conciliated
Was not just habit, no, not just the tide
Of time, but that his every injury
Found Line in the warmest sympathy.

In company like this our hero mooned
Three months or four, half stupefied,
Half mortified, and all the while the wound
Deep in his heart bled on and on inside.
It is an autumn day at eventide
When my kind reader will be importuned
To view him in the two young ladies' rooms,
Where tapers flicker and the oven booms.

On everything a drowsy light is shed,
Along the walls there hang in disarray,
As if to decorate each lady's bed,
Blouses, hose, silk scarves to dance till day,
Swirls of collars, hats in colors gay
Which brushing up might well have profited.
A mirror with its panel split in two
Will serve to keep this setting in our view.

127/

The table's in the middle of the floor
And, huddled over it, in wine far gone,
Are Adam with a hollow cheek and wan,
Black Trine, color high with paint galore,
And Line, in the Greek coiffure she wore,
Eyes a-twinkle as the firelight shone.
In everybody's reach a punch bowl stands,
And all three sit with cards held in their hands.

To Line, Trine says: "That suit's misplayed!"
"No, miss. That's your fault, you have been misled
Because you've stained that yellow card all red."
"I'm through if these mistakes keep being made,"
Black Trine answers, stung by what she said,
And screams to Adam with this fusillade:
"Well, did you ever see so dim a wit?
She's got *pique-dame!* Much good she'll get from it."

"Now, tell the truth. I've got you on my side?"
To Adam Line turns in confidence.
"I find," says he, when asked so to preside,
"This whole affair not worth such truculence."
"But *I* do! All this is at *my* expense!
My play would force her queen and turn the tide!"
Again Black Trine hollers to the sky,
And with her answer Line is not shy.

Things turned dead earnest. Adam must decide;
For both demand his judgment in this case
In words that gushed out in a mighty tide,
Each raging fit to scratch the other's face.
He seems to listen from some far-off place,
Not caring much whose claims were justified.
He leans back in his chair and takes small sips,
In silence, from the glass he firmly grips.

But to him, half upbraiding, Line turned,
Still thinking it was she whom he loved more:
"Well, Adam, speak! What are you waiting for?
You're my sweetheart, that you've surely learned.
You must come to my aid, for that I earned
When solemnly my love for you I swore."
While she talks on, her own glass Trine drains;
Once Line stops, she breaks forth in these strains:

"Your sweetheart! Really, now, that's hard to beat!
Who went and filled your head with all those lies?
Just listen to the foolishness you bleat!
He's *my* sweetheart! Adam is *my* prize;
It's long been plain to anybody's eyes.
Besides, it's me who found him on the street.
Hey! Answer, Adam! It's me you prefer!"
And Adam mumbles, "No, not you or her."

"What? Not my sweetheart? No sweetheart for you?
And when you've been the apple of my eye,
My heart's delight, in whom my young hopes lie!"
Thus Line's lamentations grew and grew
Till on his neck she fell, to kiss and sigh
And then implore him: "Say it isn't true!
Don't crush the hope on which my prospects ride!"
But he just shook his head from side to side.

When to her love for him she then referred
In terms as kind as she knew how to speak,
And still in giving answer he demurred,
She heaved a sigh; teardrops began to streak
In little rivulets along each cheek,
Until his heart with pangs of pity stirred.
"Just look," she says, as still more tears she spilt,
"Look what grief you bring on me, you jilt!"

While Line pours her heart out in her tears,
Black Trine stands, not relishing the scene,
And, bridling at the sentiments she hears
Off by herself, she finds the business mean.
She laughs aloud, or else her throat she clears,
And takes great gulps of liquor in between
Till she is good and ready to let loose.
Then comes an idea worthy of her use.

"How's this for something that can scald a sow?"
She bursts out, hot with anger and beet-red,
Picks up the bowl, still full of drink ev'n now,
And pours the whole thing over Line's head.
But Line, who'd been pressing Adam's brow
Against her breast, thrust him aside, and said
In fury, clenching both her fists: "You cad, you!
Why don't you speak up for me, as I bade you?"

129/

Screams and furious curses did she spew
At Trine, who stood smiling in sheer spite.
She seemed a maenad in a frenzied rite,
For all her well-coiffed hair about her flew
And fell down on her shoulders all askew,
While cheek and eyes blazed out in war's red light.
High her proud heart rose, and anger hung
In clouds around her brow, as her hand swung.

The ladies came to combat hand to hand
And tumbled, these two warriors thoroughbred,
First onto one and then the other bed.
Our hero tried to part them on command
And used a voice that sounded harsh and grand
In hope that shame would get them quieted.
Then hurriedly he came between the twain,
But over him, for this, what rough words rain!

"Just listen to him! Oh, how brave he rants
As if he always gave the orders here,
This beggar who can't make the price of beer
And barely owns suspenders for his pants,"
Black Trine shouts out to her fair compeer.
But Line's rage exceeds her confidante's:
She grabs the knife that on the table lay
And with it makes for Adam straightaway.

She screams: "Deceiver, it is time you died,
You who shamefully my love betrayed!
With your heart's blood I will be satisfied!"
Once more she rushed upon him with the blade,
And, shielding himself with his coat, he tried
A dash around the table to evade
Both persecuting Furies—but he found,
Just as he reached the door, things turned around.

While Trine still continued her loud fit,
Fair Line hurled the knife across the floor
And threw herself upon his breast once more
As if her pain had forced her to submit.
"Alas," she sighed. "Let mercy carry it!
Don't leave me! Let's remain friends as before!
I always thought, in spite of all our rancor,
That in my hour of need you'd be my anchor.

"True," she went on, "if ever you should flee
To someone else, my peace too would be fled.
I think I'd throw myself into the sea,
For sometimes I would rather I were dead.
Sometimes I almost go out of my head,
I feel a kind of Hell inside of me,
As if there were a spike piercing my heart."
And once again the floods of teardrops start.

"You know the way we've been, you can't forget!"
She spoke again with an imploring look,
Her sobbing voice so passionate it shook.
"Forgive me this one time. I meant no threat.
I will be good, and nothing you'll regret;
I'm not as bad and mean as you mistook!"
A sigh rose audibly from Adam's breast,
But her arms round him all the tighter pressed.

"Don't leave me in my need! Don't leave me here!
Don't dash the hope I've built on you alone!"
And in her eyes such an expression shone
As made her seem to be in mortal fear.
Adam felt his heart pricked by a spear,
But left the woman lying there to moan,
As suddenly free from her arms he tears
And, flying out the door, runs down the stairs.

He stood there, hatless, out upon the street
But did not mind November's frosty bite.
The wind, he thought, might cool the raging heat
That burned into his heart with all its might.
He wandered round, delaying his retreat,
Although it now was practically night.
The soul of him was shaken to the core,
And in the gale his heart swelled all the more.

He roamed the streets and alleyways around,
Imagining himself a ship offshore
That on the rocks at night had gone aground;
He knew he'd sink now to the ocean floor,
He heard what seemed his final hour sound.
While changing his direction evermore
As he trudged on, all restlessness and woe,
At last he reached the head of Langebro.

Across its wooden planks he slowly went
As through the night and up into the sky,
Which to him not a gleam of comfort sent,
In sheer despair he lifted up his eye.
"Yes," he exclaimed, no longer gazing high
As over the railing of the bridge he bent:
"I know it now—I've heard my own death knell!
And Life has bidden me a last farewell.

"On me she built her hopes! —Unhappy girl!
You built your hopes not merely on soft sand;
On yielding waters did you build, not land,
The pilings borne off in the current's swirl.
What woes does this world down upon us hurl!
Who can conceive it! Who can understand?
This earth's too small for all its misery;
That's why there is the deep and endless sea.

"I hear its voice—out there its arms are spread;
Its yielding coverlet is open wide
And, when I've taken one last step ahead,
Will softly take and wrap me deep inside.
And then no day will wake me from my bed,
No morning light I've stared at terrified:
A star of calm—I know that I am right—
Will shimmer through the blackness into sight.

"Why do I wait? —The way ahead is clear;
A little while and then I can be free.
In my mind's eye it is my death I see:
I feel it, yes, my final hour is near!
I hear the storm winds howling, judging me,
And ever higher how the waves uprear:
They want their victim— Well, away with woe!
Ahead is peace, behind me death shall go!"

Up onto the guardrail he then hurled
Himself, and clapped his hands against his eyes
Lest he be roused by looking at the world.
Then, suddenly, behind him someone cries;
A hand comes round his elbow like a vise
And, backwards, as in dreams, his body's twirled.
Once more upon the bridge he stands; the other
Shouts to him: "Have you gone mad there, brother?"

132/

Deep in his breast he felt his heart a-quake
Beneath the stranger's penetrating stare,
And hit on an evasion then and there.
But, as the fellow's doubt proves hard to shake,
The reader will perhaps this query make:
Would Adam have been drowned without a prayer
If this man had not cried out on the spot?
Who knows? What's certain is, he talked a lot.

He hurried home, the man still keeping pace,
Who, each time Adam turned his head around,
Was still in view, and, only when he'd found
His door, slipped off to go some other place.
"Was it my genius who, before I drowned,
Took shape to save me from the sea's embrace?"
Our hero whispered, frozen and half dead,
Dropping, in his own room, on his bed.

Nor did he get up on the following day;
His life was injured to the very root.
A fever raged within him to pollute
Each drop of his young blood; it sapped away
The strength and spirit that once in him lay.
He let himself be led, with no dispute,
To his perdition, as if by a giant
With whose fury he remained compliant.

It seemed to him his head had turned to stone,
And all his humors turbid in their flow;
The marrow seemed to drain out from each bone;
And nothing seemed to bring the fire low
That blazed within his veins from head to toe.
He seemed to feel his reason overthrown
And, in wild ferment, just as if they hated,
Soul and body burst and separated.

And while his body suffered tyranny,
His soul sat much afraid, but self-possessed
In deep seclusion far inside its nest,
Beyond the threats of life's brute enemy.
Upon the strife it peered out cautiously,
And if the foe some new advantage pressed
And closed in on it, hoping for the kill,
Contracted all the tighter, scared and still.

133/

But when, sore pressed, the soul would dash out blind,
As if stark raving mad, to strike a blow,
It was unable to tell friend from foe
And thought them one in its unsettled mind.
It strove with fancies, shapes from long ago,
With dreams in that dark home it was assigned;
It quickly caught itself; chagrined, but steady,
It regained its nest, on guard and ready.

'Twixt life and death for nearly thirty days
Lay Adam on his sickbed in this case.
Sometimes he thought he saw a well-known face
And sometimes seemed to hear a pitying phrase.
But each impression vanished in short space
And every glimpse was muffled in a haze,
Until one morn, with consciousness new-found,
He raised his eyes and slowly looked around.

He gave a start, and only with great strain
Recognized his room, where splendidly
The sun came pouring through the windowpane.
Then he gave his hands close scrutiny—
Did the haze still make it hard to see?
Of both of them but skin and bone remain.
Then over to the chair his glances glide—
His mother sits, unmoving, at his side.

Is all of this a dream? A dream it's not!
She stretches out to him her gentle hand;
Upon him are those tender glances brought
Wherein her very soul does clearly stand;
She lays her heart by his upon his cot,
Her arm, wrapped round him, holds him like a band:
O! what a warmth into his breast does race!
In silent tears he weeps in her embrace.

"You here! But how!" —Oh, need it be explained?
For some time now she had seen through the veil
That had been cast o'er each piece of his mail,
And knew enough to tell the real from feigned.
But, caring for a life about to fail
To which she owed her own, she'd been detained.
Not till the old dear rested in his grave
Could she rush off in hopes her son to save.

"But—" She broke off his question with a smile:
"This talking will not help your strength one mite."
And with those words his pillow she sets right,
Adding: "Now just rest your head a while!"
The wings of Adam's soul felt oh, so light!
He shut his eyes without the slightest guile
And drifted on soft fancy's tender beams
Through rosy-colored clouds and golden dreams.

Oh, reader! Had you ever once been near
Your ruin, then you also would have known,
When, saved, you woke again to find Death flown,
That life upon this earth is very dear.
And if the memory stayed ever clear
Of how that hope's new morning brightly shone,
You know then how the hearts in us exult
To regain childhood with a mind adult.

In truth, you have then had an early taste
Of how the soul delights, when from the grave
Where dust will have whatever it might crave,
It wakes once more, to be in glory graced;
When over death its path to life it's traced
And shed each burden that had kept it slave;
And, like a bird, borne up on weightless wing,
It feels itself at home once more in spring.

Against this freedom what was earth's dark cell?
Or what against joy's morrow sorrow's night?
What heart's desires and fearsome appetite
Against a prize of bliss in which to dwell?
What were the long road's struggles and our plight
Against its end, the house where all is well?
What was—as proof, won't hope itself suffice?—
A Purgatory-earth to Paradise?

Down from this Paradise there fell a gleam
On Adam's soul as he grew more acute,
As, sparingly, life fed him with its fruit,
And, once again, he sucked of its fresh stream.
His sense and taste new-born, all things did brim
With sustenance, no matter how minute;
He felt refreshed by all he saw and heard,
By all things gently moved and softly stirred.

135/

For hours on end he kept still in a seat
Beside the window, feeling no whit dry,
While eyeing avidly the busy street
Or gazing at a cloud up in the sky.
When lamps were lit, when in a house nearby
The lights came on at dusk, they seemed to greet
Him kindly with their beaming, like a star
Whose lucid gleam the eye would follow far.

This Creation seemed so open-handed,
So inexhaustible life's treasury,
He felt a brother to humanity,
And mightily the heart in him expanded.
His mother's voice, so gracious and so candid,
Seemed to him as an angel's voice would be,
And like a dream his past appeared to fade
From him, who sat in Peace's quiet glade.

For round his bosom like a guardian sprite
His mother moved about him, calm and true.
She read to him, her voice both sweet and bright,
And when he would prefer to be talked to
His ear imbibed the comfort and delight
Which welled up in her words forever new.
Each day there rose from deep in his mind's roots
His shattered hope, in ever higher shoots.

When day sank low, they oft with arms entwined
Walked back and forth together on the floor,
And much pure truth she could be heard to pour
Into his heart, her voice to him still kind.
She used religion not to fright his mind,
But as a cure, to heal his breast the more;
She sought to set the inner Adam free
And ease his sighs with Christian sympathy.

And when the lamps were lit, the night come on,
She loved to take a seat at the clavier
And weave a wreath of music round his ear
Whose echo from his deepest soul was drawn.
They'd sing a hymn or songs from the salon
Of an idyllic cast, for much to fear
Had he from those of a romantic bent;
One quiet evening here's how their songs went:

Fly from me, O hectic world!
Far from me thy levity!
Better flowers than bloom in thee
In this bosom have uncurled.
Thy sweet roses I have picked,
But one rainstorm spoiled their hue;
By thy thorns I have been pricked,
And my gladness quickly flew.

On my breast a winter fell,
Pressing so that I did smart,
And the storm so took my heart
That I shivered in its swell.
Down upon the earth it bowed
My head low as 'twould a reed,
Oft my soul would sigh aloud
In its longing to be freed.

What hope vows she will supply,
Earth conceals the shoots of spring;
For I heard the glad birds sing
Mounting upward to the sky.
And, as life they loudly praised
And the buds that moment spread,
Then so silently my head
Upward from the dust I raised.

———•———

Alone, the soul's irresolute!
It is a plant without a root,
A bough cut from the bole.
On this earth 'tis good withal,
In life and death, in great and small,
To keep steadfast and whole!

I traced the bee as it flew home,
I saw within the honeycomb
The shared work of its walls;
I followed on the ants' calm trail
And one the other did not fail
Within their hill's dark halls.

To Heaven's vault I turned my gaze
Where all the stars are ranged ablaze
And to their courses stay.

137/

On each the world's full weight is cast,
They hold to one another fast
And light each other's way.

Then do not seal away your mind!
Be bound to God and humankind
In seasons rich or dry.
You stand among the counted droves
Round which perpetually roves
The blessèd Shepherd's eye.

———•———

I tore myself from soft embraces
And to the forest I went out,
But once more I must see those faces
And toward home I turned about.

The roof tiles gleamed beneath the sun,
The chimney smoke did calmly climb;
Beside the door they waved, each one,
Farewell to me for one last time.

But far out in the world I ranged,
And went on lonely in a daze;
And life repatterned and exchanged
Its hues forever in my gaze.

Through surging storms at sea I plowed
And stood 'midst clouds on mountains' crowns,
And time and want my neck low bowed
In foreign lands and far-off towns.

There came a morning—one more time
I saw my home beside the wood;
The smoke curled gently on the climb,
The sun upon the roof shone good.

And to the door they came and beamed,
Old witnesses to what befell;
Then said I to the dreams I dreamed,
The worlds of wonderment, farewell.

Farewell's the thorn that pricks and spears,
Farewell's the flower for us distressed:

The selfsame word, how rich in tears,
How full of comfort for our breast.

———•———

In this world no hope comes to its full greening,
No sowing will repay itself at gleaning;
Every soul must struggle, sink dismayed.
Beside life's often desiccated springs,
Man drags his burden with no mutterings,
By his brief dreams of happiness betrayed.

Where's comfort, if from earth it has been thrust?
In faith raise your eyes upward from the dust!
God's holy; there is comfort of great worth.
From deep within Him power streams and streams,
A font of holiness that ever teems,
Vast enough for Heaven and an earth.

But when the mighty Festival arises,
When the fullness which God's heart comprises
Pours, through the valves of every heart, abroad,
Then up the fountains of all joy shall well!
All souls, the highest with the low, shall swell
In holy jubilation, filled with God!

———•———

How daily converse acts like freshest air!
We take it in and, as we breathe it, meet,
Breathtaken by it, heart and reason there.
Now mild and warm, it makes our lives more sweet
With scents that joyous harmonies do bear;
Now cold and harsh, it makes our griefs complete.
Through everything its unseen way it winds,
Ev'n to the farthest corner of our minds.

When it is easy, how we freely swing
Through common efforts upward to life's fruit;
When it is hard, how crippled the soul's wing,
So darkly sadness can its strength confute.
How small souls find life to be destitute!
How noble spirits find it a grand thing!
For everywhere within perception's bounds
A quiet echo of our converse sounds.

139/

In Adam's soul it summoned forth a peace
Which at long last was in him now resumed;
The flower of his faith, which therewith bloomed,
Did daily, by its gentle breath, increase.
His bitter doubt down to its root consumed,
He finds that Fate has granted him release,
Replaced within his mind by Providence:
That miracles are in him he can sense.

They'd lived together thus for half a year,
He and his mother, in a comity
Of hearts, a single, simple you-and-me.
The stream of Adam's life again ran clear;
As in the past, hope's voice now found his ear
And, laved with it, he regained energy.
Now struck the parting hour—again they parted;
But memories would make them less downhearted.

For, though his mother had left him behind,
Her memory had left a kindly sense
Of life set fast within his heart and mind.
He often would reflect with confidence
That his fate and the fate of all mankind
Lay in avoiding this life's turbulence:
While keeping oneself quietly aside,
One let himself be carried on time's tide.

In this belief he kept on quietly;
He did his tasks and duties every day,
Intent on bettering his acuity
With books which close attention would repay.
By wellsprings of religion he would stray,
In waters turbid with theology.
On priestly orders he'd not set his course;
He merely wished to drink at life's true source.

In such pursuits near three years had gone by.
Through all that time so calmly beat his breast
That all his former health he now possessed
And, though still thoughtful, clear too was his eye.
A storm had come on him, one could descry—
Its stamp upon his brow had been impressed—
But by the peaceful set his lips now form,
One saw as well that vanished was the storm.

Across three years, then, I will swiftly stride,
Producing Adam Homo at their end
Back in his rooms one evening, where a friend,
The student Jensen, stands now at his side.
To no great height this Jensen could pretend,
But his eyes swept all life up, gratified.
Now, through his persuasive utterance,
His friend was coming to that evening's dance.

"You won't believe," says Adam, just as he
Was putting on his coal-black evening cape,
Which fell on his firm frame in one smooth drape:
"You won't believe it, with your gaiety,
That going to a ball near frightens me.
Just dancing puts my mind in horrid shape,
And my frail heart sinks underneath a cloud
When I bethink myself in such a crowd."

"Because," the little Jensen makes reply,
"You've moped for such a long time here upstairs.
I should have been as timorous as hares
If I were not forever on the fly.
The less experience a man comes by,
The more he's overwhelmed by life's affairs;
When we but see the world through jalousies,
We might well take mere men for deities."

"I know you're right," our hero must agree,
"But still my heart is booming just as deep."
"I'll bet," says Jensen, laughing gleefully,
"That once you're at the ball your fears won't keep.
When we see one of Eve's dear progeny,
What do we see? A lamb! At most, a sheep!
I know of things more apt to make hair curl
Than simply waltzing with a little girl."

They left, and quickly to the club they came;
Adam, with his heart much disconcerted,
Climbed the stairs up to the candle flame
That marked the entry, huge and quite deserted.
Small Jensen would not honor Adam's claim
To one brief respite; he'd not be diverted
From pushing on into the anteroom
Wherefrom on Adam's ear the voices boom.

141/

Here sit the faithful regular clubmen,
Who, 'spite the nearness of the dance, insist
On getting games of ombre up, or whist.
Professor and attorney come in ken,
And actor, doctor, broker, pensionist
Sit face to face as in a gambling den,
And after their day's work will now relax
In easy chat, as each his cards attacks.

One hears the news from town and local marts
And, while the daily papers are rehashed,
Everyone would see all kings well lashed,
Save those of spades, clubs, diamonds, and hearts.
At talking politics no one's abashed,
They'll solve its puzzles, all these men of parts;
While, in there, on the surface people dance,
Out here they're deep in taxes and finance.

"Come with me!" Jensen says to Adam now.
"A few steps only, to that table there!
I'll point you out a man who will not bow
To any man on earth in savoir-faire.
He has almost more prudence to his share
Than definitions of it would allow.
He's an original, although you find
So many lesser models of his kind."

They walked off to the table, where, at play,
They saw the prudent hero aforesaid.
He was a man of years, his hair now gray,
His stature tall, his look instantly read.
Deep worry graved itself on his forehead;
He looked about him in an anxious way,
And, lest the doorway drafts should grow severe,
He'd stuck a clump of cotton in each ear.

"Look," whispered Jensen, "isn't that pain grand?
Just let us move a little closer in;
I see he's got a fine trump in his hand,
And that's the thing that gives him such chagrin.
Watch for the stratagem his brain will spin
Now that his good cards call for self-command."
That very moment, glancing through his brass,
The man said with a sigh: "Ah, well, I'll pass!"

"You see!" said Jensen still in whispers low.
"I didn't think he'd go on the offense:
His guiding principle is diffidence;
That's why he's one for strict punctilio.
See there! He gets up for His Excellence
And bows so low you'd think his spine were dough.
He'd scare himself, I think, into his grave
If in that presence he should misbehave.

"See how gingerly he takes his seat!
He feels about the four legs of his chair
In case they'd suddenly required repair.
Poor man! In death alone is his retreat.
To guess why he's not married is no feat:
A henpecked life would be a vile affair.
His housekeeper must be his bugaboo—
For visiting the club's all *he* can do."

As he and Adam walked from where they'd been,
He said aloud, as if to make report:
"Our police tonight released a bulletin:
There's cholera at one place of resort."
One ombre-player shouted: "There's fine sport!"
But the prudential one, who started in
Imagining the worst, white as a sheet,
Took out a peppermint pastille to eat.

The friends went off to look in on the ball.
The sconce lights cast their beams on every hand,
And, just as they stepped in, the rousing band
And waltzing stopped. There along one wall,
Beneath the lights, sat matrons, well-dressed all,
With younger ladies flushed of cheek and grand.
And those who'd had the first waltz of the night
Puffed out their chests and gabbed with all their might.

Up and down the floor went cavaliers
With hats in hand, their foreheads hot and bare,
Some by themselves, some walking as a pair,
And Adam joined the rounds of his compeers
With smiling eyes, though inwardly all fears,
While Jensen made report of who was there.
This friend was useful, now that Adam came,
For every woman there he knew by name.

"Who's that one there," our hero softly said,
"Sitting there half hidden by the door,
The farthest from us in the young girls' corps—
Gold tresses and a wreath around her head?
She darts her eyes round like a bird in dread—
I'll bet she's never left the nest before.
She keeps herself so shyly out of view,
As if she saw a world completely new."

"Yes, her," he heard. "That's someone I don't know."
And, saying this, the little Jensen leapt
Off to a man whose arm in his he swept,
Returning with some news *prestissimo.*
"Her name is Alma and you're right, she's kept
At home until tonight, just lying low;
She lives way out in Vesterbro, quite far;
Her father is a gardener, name of Star."

"The star, I think, deserves a closer view,"
Said Adam, smiling to his counterpart,
Who, as if shot out from a bowstring, flew
Across the floor straight as a dart.
But Adam, disapproving this brash start,
His arm from Jensen's instantly withdrew
And, leaning on a pillar at the wall,
Observed the star that would not speak at all.

For like the clock, whose hands so silently
Move slow across each number on its face,
Although the works within its case
Each second puts to hard activity:
So change in Alma's physiognomy
Reflects her nature in its quiet grace,
Although her heart, which knows for hope no bounds,
With sweet activity and yearning pounds.

She sat in dreams of what might come along,
And mightn't *that* arrive for Alma too
Toward which all human hearts, when young, must throng—
The great illusion, never lost from view;
The great completion, making all things new;
The cadence to that most mysterious song
That makes the hearts of young girls leap on high
On hearing flutes and violin strings cry?

She sat there—then again the music welled,
And through her cheeks she felt a blush ascend;
In her mind she saw herself compelled
Once more to sit a dance out to the end.
But her strong fears by hope are swiftly quelled:
Approaching with an easy gait, our friend
Bows low. Might he be honored with the chance
To be her partner for the coming dance?

She tears herself from her aunt's company
And, wearing on her cheek a newborn rose,
Led out by Adam, she goes hurriedly
To join the crowded lines before they close.
A charming smile upon her small mouth grows,
Her shining eyes can't hide their gaiety,
Her very heartbeat Adam plainly feels
Along the arm her modest glove conceals.

Now it's their turn to start—may it go well!
She follows all his steps around the floor;
Her hair (in which sweet violets she wore)
Around her face, like garlands, rose and fell.
Her moleskin gown now shows its folds no more,
But swings round in a brilliant, snow-white swell,
And as she turns her string of pearls spins too;
But then the spinning stops—the dance is through.

Another came, and vanished all too fast;
And after still another dance they shared,
Back to her seat the two of them repaired
While she a grateful look on Adam cast.
Might he bring refreshment, if she cared?
Oh, no, she'd had it in the dance just past.
Might she in the cotillion acquiesce?
With barely hidden joy, she tells him yes.

But here he's hit upon a ruse of war;
For when, as mere civility demands,
He speaks some to the aunt, who, with both hands,
Grasps the chance to be more than decor,
Adam's luck increases. For he stands
Near Alma till there's naught to talk of more.
Then with a double bow and one last stare
At her who'd captured him, he leaves them there.

They parted, yes, but stayed together still,
In thought, that is. Our hero's fantasy,
While his intelligence stopped utterly,
Had with this rich material its will.
He often struck his brow, amazed that he
Saw images of Alma round him mill;
And, hoping that a rest would break his trance,
He thought he'd best not go back to the dance.

Alma had the time to think as well.
She did not have the gift that most acquire
To turn herself out like a proper belle
And coolly make the gentlemen admire.
She blithely sat the dance out for a spell;
She thought—and her thoughts never seemed to tire—
Of her past and future cavalier,
So earnest in this giddy atmosphere.

Cotillion call! The ladies are addressed.
Now Alma stands with Adam in the ring,
To dance with him again at his request
While flutes pipe up and all the fiddles sing.
This brief connection both find maddening;
The conversation flies, intense, compressed:
Like slight acquaintances, 'mid strangers lost,
Between the two the ball of talk is tossed.

And talk they did! But lo! another came
To claim the waltz the band would next provide;
And Adam, who had yielded to the claim,
Had time to judge, while standing to one side,
The graceful sylphlike form which set aflame
The glances of all those who saw her glide.
She suddenly is seen to catch the eye,
A very pearl, of all who'd passed her by.

Now she's come home from her brief truancy,
He asks, "You like to be out on the floor?"
"Oh, there is almost nothing I like more!"
She says in answer, somewhat breathlessly.
"And yet you've not been to a ball before!
To do so well at your terpsichore,
You must have had the loan of Zephyr's wings!"
"My wings," she laughs, "are just those lovely strings."

146/

Another dancing-partner!—How they chase!
As earlier, she left our hero's side;
As earlier, he stood alone and spied
The gladness playing finely on her face,
As she appeared and disappeared, all grace
And swaying lithely with her new-found guide.
Again she's back. "Your debt of constancy,"
He now remarks, "you have not paid to me."

This observation left the girl nonplussed,
Though round her mouth a smile began to play.
But he went on: "Well, bear my cross I must;
A cross is quite an honor, so they say."
"If I might have the honor!" in there thrust
Another man to waltz the girl away.
Then came the whispers, as the music caught her:
"Well, look at her, the gardener's little daughter!"

The cuttings-in have all at last been checked,
To Adam's happiness. And now there's found
Some different music for the next time round.
But Alma's still the pearl all eyes inspect!
It almost seemed these strains themselves had bound
These suitors to make up for their neglect!
She often had to go back to her chair,
Disturbed and pleased to be this lady fair.

There was a dance well worth the mentioning:
A couple with two flower baskets brought
Them to the rest, who all had formed a ring.
With eyes closed, each of them must draw a lot,
And those who picked a flower not varying
In kind to one which someone else had got
Must walk out on the floor, exchange the chance
They'd drawn, and take each other for the dance.

Now was there not a clamoring and shout!
Their nettles, myrtles, violets they cried,
And from the circle's edge they all stormed out
Onto the floor, with hope or doubt for guide.
Each held his token up, with arms spread wide,
To catch his partner as all milled about.
They're pushed, they're shoved, they laugh, at last they find
The soulmate with the flower of their kind.

147/

Each found his partner; there were only two
Left back—our hero and his lady. She
Was holding one round rose, deep red in hue,
But for his sprig of thorn no mate found *he.*
"Will you, for your rose, take thorn from me?"
He asks imploringly. "For, though it's true
You lose thereby, the rose and thorn are kin,
As both do have a common origin."

They exchanged their tokens; and Fate demonstrated
Again to him at last its charity
As off into the dance they flew, new-mated
By the charms of sound and melody.
It seemed a thousand birds sang merrily
And all the hall's lights in a wreath were plaited
To constitute an aureole that graced
The brow agleam before him, candid, chaste.

It was the last dance; such, alas, the speed
With which this grand cotillion reached its end.
The couples separate and homeward wend,
And now his lady Adam's seen to lead
Back to her seat, which he knew well indeed.
Her aunt remarks: "Our coach and horse attend.
Your shawl! Be quick! The driver's let me know
Three times now that the time was going slow."

They left at once. And up the gallants storm
To offer arms to Alma on her way;
But she, at Adam's side, strolls from the swarm
And, with great joy, he sees that there still lay,
Pinned against her bosom, his thorn spray.
The flock of gentlemen, their heads a-spin,
As in a triumph, tend the aunt instead,
Who glowed with all this favor on her shed.

The carriage rolled away—and far behind
The swarm, our hero went back up the stairs.
But what an empty look the packed hall wears!
Although the place is full of humankind
And still that clamoring and shouting blares,
The huge space seemed quite deathly to his mind.
Off in a corner, stirred, he went to stand
And stare at Alma's rose, which he still had in hand.

Soon someone's voice aroused him with a start;
The voice had little Jensen's special sound:
"It doesn't take a spyglass finely ground
To see a star's arisen in your heart;
A little god has speared you on his dart
And twiddles you and twirls you round and round."
"Aren't you sharp, then!" Adam's voice was gruff:
Of little Jensen he had had enough.

He took his hat and left—drawn back by Fate
Into the game of life so cleverly,
Such wiles it knows whereby to fascinate
Ev'n those who've sunk down in despondency.
Inside its urn the lots of all men wait,
And only they may pluck their destiny;
The means, though, by which one may win his lot
Are in Fate's tight-clenched fingers to be sought.

And, oh! what means that power has in store!
One it will elevate by casting down;
One it will help to peace by means of war;
One it leads to light through shadows brown;
One it brings to truth through fraud's own door;
But him whose life gains earth's most lovely crown
It ties unto a woman's leading-string,
That through the heart the soul may rise and sing.

For many a man this doctrine goes to waste
Whose heart and, more, whose soul is lost to him,
Who thirsts beside a well filled to the brim,
Whose life, though rich, is wretched and debased.
And is our hero's lot to be this grim?
My reader might request reply posthaste—
His wait, I fear, I must a while prolong,
For ended, if not finished, is my song.

149/

CANTO VI

The spring is come! And yet again have I
Heard the merry lark, the bird of spring;
Up it swung upon its sturdy wing,
All twittering with music, to the sky.
The work of those warm beams one can descry
On city, country, earth, sea, air on high;
The power of white winter swiftly wanes;
It dies—and with its death come loose its chains.

The wholesome spring presents itself as heir;
The treasure which the old man sat upon
And covered, so no eye could see it there,
Now flies about and blinds those who look on.
Young hopes arise which ancient memories spawn,
The dark skies glisten azure-blue and fair,
'Neath coverlets of grass the earth lies curled,
And day with all its sunshine gilds the world.

Old winter on the instant is forgot,
Save by the other old ones, whose minds run
On how in it they wrought and wove and spun,
How oft its stars set them to earnest thought.
But these sighs by rejoicing are undone,
By youthful hope which rises now full hot:
"The sun's come back! What can we now not dream
Beneath this new, this golden-bright regime?"

And it is true! On high and down below
All bespeaks delight and loveliness;
Untamed the billows rush and iridesce
And, in rich crimson, clouds above them flow.
Bright Flora through the forest does progress
And binds her hair with garlands row on row;
The voices of the birds love's ardor tell,
And shepherdesses tremble in its spell.

The town life too now changes regimen.
Young ladies cast their heavy coats away
And go abroad with parasols again,
While gallants wear their frock coats night and day.
All talk of politics is now passé;
Instead, possessed of paper and a pen,
A host of nincompoops send their regards:
"Now do we feel the urge to sing, we bards!"

What shall become of all this loveliness?
Of all these thousand hopes, of this great hoard
Of feelings which is suddenly outpoured,
Of these warm rays which all the world caress?
How can one ask? The storms soon will have roared
Down on each flower, each leaf—night will distress
(Though inconceivable it seem to some)
The earth again, when once its cold winds come.

How quick the songs of summer are suppressed!
How joy and loss do every heart divide.
How many times have winters come and died,
How many times the spring, in every breast!
O time when we have languished, we have sighed!
O time when we let nothing give us rest.
In never-ending circles our life ranges,
Returning on itself ev'n as it changes.

Again in Adam Homo it was spring.
The only clouds he knew had hope's pink stain;
He felt that he and everything had lain
For many years profoundly languishing.
Up from its grave his youth came triumphing
And set its mark upon his talk and brain.
He hardly could conceive this amplitude
Which to his heart had suddenly accrued.

At last he had become a proper man!
All that he had seen and taken in,
All that he'd once done and lived and been,
Appeared to him a mad, mistaken plan.
The wild life in which all too long he ran,
The mild life—both of them weren't worth a pin.
There was but one goal worthy of his care,
And only one road that could lead him there.

This was the road he was about to take;
For, that same morn, half glad, half full of glooms,
Dressed in his summer coat he left his rooms
To walk through Nørreport, and round the lake,
Where Alma's image followed in his wake
And hovered up and down on memory's plumes
And, having flown away, came ever back
As he kept walking on along his track.

He chanced to wonder in these morning hours
(The brilliant sun of spring now turned that chance
To certainty beneath its ripening powers),
Dare he go—and one month since the dance
Cannot be judged to be precipitance—
And look in on the lady and her flowers?
But lest his interest show too plain to her eye,
Some bulbs of hyacinth he'll say he'd buy.

All went as hoped. Behind the garden trees
He came upon the father, daughter, aunt,
Whose greetings were so little hesitant
He knew they were not mere civilities.
He must come round and see the way they plant,
And either Alma did the courtesies
Or else he was escorted by all three
To view the flowers and the nursery.

While out of doors Dame Flora half dozed still,
How fresh the scents that he had come into!
Amongst the crocus violets did spill,
'Midst all the coxcomb, white and red and blue,
Bear's-ear, anemone, and daffodil.
The year's first hyacinth had broken through,
And, in the sun's goodwill, half opened up
Is the golden Easter lily's cup.

A Paradise the garden seemed to him;
The little house that stood out there thick-vined
With ivy running all around as trim,
Appeared a fane where peace had been enshrined.
While with a thousand scents the ground did brim,
Beside an open garret window twined
A rose, which in a window pot was kept;
There was the little room where Alma slept.

From there, he thought, she sees the sun arise
And there, on quiet nights, alone she stands
To watch the moon proceed across the skies
And peers into imaginary lands.
She bids the clouds goodnight there with her eyes,
And in the wood the nightingale expands
Its song, while, drinking in the pure night air,
She could dream Paradise spread round her there.

His soul enlarged itself—his gaze and tone
Reflected what it was that filled his mind;
In lively talk none cared what time had flown,
Save Aunt, who at such liberties repined.
Then Adam's struck: his books he can't postpone;
He shook the gardener's hand, who then combined
His farewell to him with this warm addition:
"Come see us often. Don't wait for permission."

Back to the city did our hero wind,
And on his walk these thoughts he entertains:
"I once was wrapped in arrogance's chains
And to the world about me stony-blind;
For years and years I sealed away my mind.
But gladness comes no less from peace than pains;
A little maid at one stroke makes me wise:
There always must be two in Paradise.

"All things must come together, great and small;
This doctrine is what Nature teaches men.
Man in the world should be its citizen
And act, not simply contemplate it all.
One makes his home, his sphere, in it, and then
Sees to it good on him and others fall;
The goal of life, whatever its detail be,
Is to be happy and live usefully."

And in these times how usefully he wrought!
For, though exams were not too far away,
Nonetheless, when he had closed his day
And finished all his studies as he ought,
Then he could give his happiness fair play.
Then in the evening to his feet he got
And walked out to the garden, oh so far,
To watch behind the leaves his shining star.

Yet I shall leave my hero in the lurch,
His exegetics having been traversed,
Though he still hears the Fathers of the Church,
As deeply in dogmatics he's immersed.
Now, while he gets his Augustine rehearsed,
Round Vesterbro I'll do my own research;
Though they'd no final for which to prepare,
The breath of life draws just as deeply there.

—It is a lively morning hour in June;
Over the gardener's fields the day had rolled
With myriad beams and mouth aglow with gold.
Fine webs of gossamer the trees festoon;
Each leaf and tender blade of grass is strewn
With bright, round morning dewdrops, trembling-cold,
As, fresh and pink, and white-clad like a bride,
Steps Alma through the garden door, outside.

Why should she be so formally bedight?
What could today have made it apropos
For her to don, of all her frocks, the white
And on her bodice green to fix a bow?
All very natural, if read aright!
Today is, as the reader now may know,
The birthday of her father, and she dressed
Accordingly, all in her Sunday best.

The final touches to the embroidered braces
(Which she hadn't breathed a word upon)
Up in her attic room she'd just put on;
And, as the sun the morning mists now chases
And all still sleep, her way she softly traces
To where the silent trees keep watch this dawn.
Upon her face expectancy is read;
Off she rushes to the potting shed.

On a ladder rung she stands and cocks
Her head to listen at the dovecote door.
Hark! Inside there's a cooing—she unlocks
The door halfway, and listens as before.
The white dove peeps its head out of the box;
The preening red is busy at her chore.
No sooner is she seen than they take flight,
Retiring to a nook far from the light.

This reception hardly satisfied;
Nor did she understand why fear went through them.
She started speaking in sweet tones to them,
And even whistling to the birds she tried
In hope that it would make their fright subside.
She deftly used this method to subdue them:
She threw to them a little morning food,
And in short time the little doves were wooed.

Next time, when nearer her the food she lay,
Upon the grain the little white did seize;
She reached her hand in toward it, full of peas,
But timidly it quickly backed away.
Then came the red one, happy to essay
This eye-bedazzling heap of savories.
Stretching toward her hand, it bowed its head,
And Alma dared not breathe the while it fed.

She spoke but with her eyes—but with what eyes!
The dove itself, now being put at ease,
Already had begun to peck the peas.
Then once again, in fear, its feathers rise—
It turns around—and then no longer shies,
But comes back closer, near as you could please.
Now it stood still—and Alma found it grand
To have it nibbling breakfast from her hand.

In this fine sport an hour's time slips away,
Until the sun, now blazing in the east,
Reminds her of her duties for this day,
And so the birds are left alone to feast.
'Twas in the garden that her duties lay,
And there she roams, her joy the more increased,
Where all the pathways, new-combed by the rake,
The prints of her light, skipping footsteps take.

Those paths had known those prints from long ago,
From days in which that foot was still quite small
Till now, when it would never larger grow,
Although no one could call it large at all.
She'd always lived in peace behind this wall
Among these trees, these flowers row on row,
Snug in the home her aunt and father made
Since Death had drawn her mother to his shade.

She left the house with girlfriends only rarely;
And, as to what one might excitement call,
Her life was furnished out with it so sparely
I know not what to point to save that ball.
What she had come to learn, she learned quite fairly,
But there was much she did not know at all,
A thousand things which are the pabulum
That girls must down at their Gymnasium.

Enclosed in her own world, here she remained,
Far from the great one, where she had no part.
And free she was, although with roots well-trained;
For what it was most deeply stirred her heart
Could nowhere in the troubled world be gained,
Nor could its absence cause her tears to start.
She'd fixed her hopes since she was very small
On winter, spring, the summer, and the fall.

Thus from within her she was fitted out,
By isolation schooled, for contemplation;
She'd found herself—a case of turnabout—
By losing herself in her homely station.
She comes, as fresh as any springtime sprout;
Her white frock flutters in the wind's flirtation,
As up and down she strolls the garden plots,
Filled with the joy of youth and full of thoughts.

But every instant she must look around,
For each time she extends her hand, it brings
To mind, as on she strolls, a thousand things.
Sometimes she finds a new weed in the ground,
Sometimes into a little side-path swings
Where she ties back a branch that came unbound;
She frees some myrtle from a cobweb's mazes,
And over there the fallen rosebush raises.

Now, to my lady reader, bear in mind:
If you'd feel rich, though back at home located,
Like Alma's your life must be intertwined
With those to live amongst whom you've been fated.
And for your heart you must the sustenance find
In life as it is daily cultivated:
Do not, like her or her—perhaps I'm wrong—
Just sit there till a suitor comes along.

156/

He comes the quickest who arrives unsought;
But even if he shouldn't come, your breast,
When once its treasures to the light you've brought,
Has seeds to make the later harvest blest.
Thou shalt love, be that commandment stressed;
But only where there's life are such joys wrought.
Will you just sit and on your sewing pore?
Your heart and you yourself were made for more!

You've seen how Alma on this morning glowed,
But from her let your vision now turn back;
For out the garden door her aunt just strode
And now approaches Alma down the track.
She's dressed with taste today, quite in the mode,
But yet with an imaginative knack:
Her artificial curls prop up a cap
From which pink ribbons dangle down and flap.

The nice old aunt, though decent through and through,
Did have a certain quirk: it made her ill,
While time took giant steps, to stand stock-still
And not sail out when lusty breezes blew.
Though up in years, with cheeks of faded hue,
Her feeling for the world had yet to chill;
In Vesterbro no gossip she'd ignore
Of Østergade and Amalienborg.

Alma saw at once, as she came nigh,
That round her brow there hung a cloud of gray,
And when she raised her hand to say good day
There was still more discomfort in her eye.
When Alma gently asked the reason why,
Evasively her aunt would only say
That, though she'd tried and tried with all her might,
She could not get her cap to sit quite right.

"Why," answered Alma, "that's soon rectified;
That is, Aunt, if you'll take my poor advice:
The bow should have been shifted to the side,
Close to the ribbons. Then it would look nice.
I'll move it so! We'll have it in a trice!
—There, look! Now! And to make sure it won't slide,
A pin! —Now, that I call a first-class change!"
But Aunt by then had wandered out of range.

Back to her room and looking glass she rushed
To see the happy change upon her pate;
And, looking in the glass at her portrait,
Content with cap and self, she smiled and blushed.
All her heart's anxieties were hushed,
And from the glass she strode with regal gait
Down to the garden, did that good old aunt,
Forgotten by the world—but still *galante!*

She beckons Alma, and the two festoon
The small green arbor, setting for the fête.
And next they lay the tablecloth and set
Upon it cup and jug and serving spoon.
The gifts they cover with a serviette,
Lest father should discover them too soon.
Already he's arrived—his hair, all shocks
Of white, comes down his ruddy cheeks in locks.

How gentle are his eyes! Heart's ease expands
Upon his brow and in the smile he shows.
He walks a little slow, but don't suppose
He needs the cane he carries in his hands.
He's wearing knickers, buckles on their bands,
And buckles on the shoes in which he goes
Along the path beneath the pink dawn sky,
Still full of life, although he soon must die.

His flowers he'd tended to, his God no less,
And so he has a double harvest's cheer;
Already given a seventieth year,
Another now's about to effloresce.
His garden's fairest shoot, his Alma's here,
Her arm about his waist in tenderness,
Her young mouth pressed upon his ancient hand:
O how the warmth that filled his soul was grand!

Now to him his sister gives (the treasure)
Best wishes prim as any ladyship's.
He gaily cries: "Now, come! Let's have your lips!
A hearty kiss is what would give me pleasure!"
Of what he wants he takes his proper measure,
Though Aunt looks down upon such social slips.
Into the arbor then they go, all three,
And take their seats for the festivity.

Once all the drinks by Aunt were ladled round,
No more did Alma hide her offering
As round his shoulders she the braces wound
And begged him not to be disparaging
Of presents for which good use could be found.
"Well," says he, his eyes fast moistening,
"Now that's a present I would never trade!
That's what I call a busy little maid!"

Her aunt speaks up: "How kind is destiny,
How fortunate you are to get those braces!
This supplement won't cause you to make faces,
For, Brother, you've not been forgot by me.
You know, time brings new fashions in its traces—
That tyrant will exact conformity.
There's no use trying to turn back the page;
The wise man should move forward with the age."

The agèd gardener asks, "What do you mean?"
And takes for answer: "My dear brother! You
Must be the only man still to be seen
Who wears short breeches, with his calves on view!
Knee-breeches strike the eye now as taboo;
Good taste's at war against a leg so lean.
Don't grumble at this gift, it's smart and smashin':
A pair of summer trousers, quite in fashion."

She took the trousers without more ado
And held them up before her brother's eyes.
Struck by the morning sun, their brilliant hue
Flashed all the more beneath the gracious skies.
The old man laughed: "You'd better take my prize
Back home! I have a well-earned kiss for you,
But give the pants to someone else, I pray.
I want to keep my legs the same old way."

"You must, you must!" his sister then makes bold.
"You must adjust to what the age thinks fit."
"No," he replies, "I think the opposite:
The old should take their stand upon the old."
"No," answers she, "they should have done with it,
Not stick to notions which were once extolled."
"Rot," says he. "It's an old fool who goes
To children for the proper thoughts and clothes."

To Alma's grief, the battle gathers heat
When on the following question they engage:
How far should oldsters imitate the age?
The gardener's words are sharp and indiscreet,
Nor is the aunt unable to compete.
At last the old man bursts out in a rage:
"Go wear the pants yourself if you've a care,
But on my legs you'll never see a pair."

A sob from Aunt calls Alma to the attack:
"May I take charge here, if I'm not too brash?"
And when permission's granted in a flash,
She gently makes her father turn his back
And, with her scissors, makes so deep a slash
Along the trousers Auntie's heart did crack.
They lay there now, cut clean off at the knee,
The pant-legs lying by them, like debris.

The old man's laughter pealed out merrily,
But Alma says: "Now, so much for that fray.
Aunt's gift can still do honor to the day,
And father still escape modernity.
The legs may make the child of our trainee
A pair of gloves, perhaps. And, in this way,
My aunt will have two beneficiaries."
"Yes, let her have the gloves!" her aunt agrees.

They went their separate ways—for everyone
The work-hours calmly passed among the flowers.
At dinner time the gardener's lively fun
All memory of the squabble overpowers.
The beams shot ever dimmer from the sun
As five was struck upon the town's church towers.
Then Alma, taking up the watering-pot,
Goes to her chore of sprinkling every plot.

Her summer shawl around her neck she's worn,
A hat of yellow straw sits on her brow,
That brow behind which many thoughts are born,
A recent one of which comes forward now:
How is it, when such garments now adorn
The earth and sky and every flower and bough,
That here, when waits a welcome this sublime,
We've not seen Adam Homo all this time?

He'd gotten on with all of them so well,
And he had often visited before,
She mused; but at this point I must dispel
The notion that she worried on this score.
Her heart was still a place for peace to dwell,
All passions lay at rest within its core;
She knew too little of the old world's game
To go in search of romance ere it came.

Now that her patch of herbs was good and wet,
She stopped near to the gate on heading back,
When suddenly she heard the gate latch clack—
Why!—It was Adam Homo her eyes met.
High on his hat he had a flower set,
And head to toe he was attired in black;
With eyes in which his hope and longing glowed
He waved at her and rushed on down the road.

She stood stock-still; a marveling smile did part
Her lips; her pot she still held in her hand
As he flew up the pathway like a dart
And high above his head his hat he fanned.
Now very near each other do they stand:
"Exams are done!" he shouts with all his heart.
So many things at once her mind confuse,
And soon she sees she's watering his shoes.

She stammers out, "I'm sorry!" "I would swear
You're seeing flowers, and not shoes, on me,"
Remarks our hero, laughing merrily.
She smilingly regrets the whole affair,
But he won't hear of an apology,
And adds, while gulping in a draft of air,
"When I went out, a bird predicted this:
Upon that hand I would plant my first kiss."

Her cheeks a lovely crimson beautified.
Before she knew how it was happening,
She saw her hand up to his warm lips glide,
Her joy so great that it was dizzying.
"Now go and greet my father. He's inside,"
Her voice is shy, but still encouraging:
"His birthday celebration goes on still."
And he says: "Soon! One moment, then I will.

"There's one more favor you must grant to me,
For, even though I've just now left a test,
My studies never give me any rest,
And student I continue now to be.
I long have wished to learn to some degree
That lovely language of which you're possessed.
Teach me some flower-language, only some;
I only ask the barest minimum."

"That language," she laughed, "is not meet for you."
"But," Adam says, his voice now twice as sweet,
And holds her with a soft look, to entreat:
"If for your hand and heart I were to sue
And tell you, without them, my life were through,
Say, would that language also not be meet?"
They pressed each other's hands, love in their eyes;
Then, in a burst of joy, off Adam flies.

How long he stays with father, all the same!
As for herself, she'll go down to the copse
To put her churning thoughts in proper frame;
But into view her breathless old aunt pops.
"Well!" she shouts to Alma, who now stops.
"That I should meet you here won't spoil the game.
I've just been round the parlor for a turn,
Where they're discussing things of great concern!"

"You've seen Hr. Homo?" "Draw your ribbon string
A little tighter!" "He's a Candidate!
Now he can serve his country, king, and state—"
"This limp hair of yours needs managing.
Push up these curls. I'll fix this collar-wing—"
"Now he's all ready for a pastorate.
A pastor would be no disgrace to wed."
"He's coming! Now, young lady, lift your head!"

Her eyes alone she raised—but from afar,
Coming ever nearer, she espies
Our youthful hero and old gardener Star,
With merriment a-twinkle in his eyes.
Though Alma would have fled with no good-byes,
Her feet felt heavier than if stuck in tar.
She does not find a smile at her command
When, with her now, her father takes her hand.

"You poor thing! You look downright mortified!
It almost makes one feel that you're afraid.
One might think you'd been sent to the stockade,
Did not your air proclaim you as a bride.
But let that be—let God's will be obeyed!
We ought not look for more than He'll provide.
Cupid is a hunter—deft at snares
To catch a fair young maiden unawares.

"There stands the worthy Candidate! Consent
To wish him well 'gainst that great day;
And, if you have a heart you would present,
I know he will not turn that heart away.
My little Alma, happy be and stay!
And may this world bring you your heart's content!
You two are of one mind. I say Amen;
Aunt, come along! They'd be alone again."

They left the two alone, without ado,
But how two people can be called alone
Whose hearts contain a whole world of their own,
And how, alone, they still come out to two,
But never think they're three, I wish I knew.
Of such things those philosophers have known
Who, by the Idea, grasped with clarity,
Reduce the dual to singularity.

It seemed to Alma she'd been fast asleep,
As if to life she'd wakened from a dream
That held her still within its mild regime;
But at the truth of it she dared not leap,
Such wondrous visions floated on its stream.
That she should be engaged, all of a heap,
That she would really be a bride—oh no!
It was beyond her, it could not be so.

And as with Alma, so with everyone;
For who's in fact prepared to understand
How premises can alter, all unplanned,
And bring on consequences dreamt by none?
But, as time passed, she found her doubts were done
And, as time passed, her faith took bold command;
And arm in arm with Adam Alma treads
Along the walks beside the flower beds.

163/

But if *she* kept silence, not so he;
Up to his lips his bursting heart would swell
And, gushing like cool water from a well,
In massive waves his feelings poured forth free.
Now into dreams of what was past he fell,
Now his thoughts rushed to countries yet to be;
And Alma's soul, though folded were its wings,
Kept faithful pace with his mind's wanderings.

Their hearts resounded to the same plucked string
As, from the walks, they stepped out on the grass
To listen first to sweet birds caroling;
Then over to the blue pond did they pass
That lay amid the meadows, clear as glass.
There Adam saw a vision ravishing,
For in the water's shining glass he spied
The form of Alma standing by his side.

"Look there," he said, his eyes agleam and warm.
"All our days to come are there to view,
Reflected in that quiet silver-blue,
Imperiled by no rocks and by no storm.
I see the two of us forever true;
But I see even more things that inform
Those clear depths, showing us what will befall—
Just look! The looking glass contains it all.

"Yes, I can see a little rectory
Outside a country town, against a slope,
Its side wall likely held in place by hope—
Beginners, though, cannot be finicky.
I see our sheep and cattle; there they lope
Back to their stalls from browsing on the lea.
And there's the milkmaid coming with her pail,
The sheep dog up ahead, wagging his tail."

Alma smiles and cranes her head to spy
A little of this splendid circumstance,
And to his visions brings her own supply:
"Those are the parsonage's grounds, perchance;
There linden trees in long dark rows advance,
Where one can walk at ease when winds are high.
There's the garden; there a summer bower
Of lilac bushes twined in thickest flower."

164/

"Why, yes, it's there quite plainly," Adam said.
"The image of the two of us I see:
We're sitting at the table, drinking tea;
Behind the wood the sun's last light is spread.
A star's already risen overhead;
The moon is out, and white as snow is she,
Reminding me to work among my people,
For look! beyond the town, my church's steeple!

"I'll raise myself up with the others there;
There, in undefiled and fertile sod,
I'll year-long sow the fruitful Word of God,
Cut, plant, manure, weed, water it with care.
I'll live my life as an example fair
So that the flock may follow where I've trod,
And you shall be a paragon displayed
For every village wife and parish maid."

No less than him the notion made her glow,
And long they stood there, silent, arms entwined,
Although their eyes revealed their inmost mind.
They looked off to the sun, which had sunk low
Beneath a purple sea and left behind
A blush upon the clouds' breasts, white as snow.
"As lovely," he explains, "will death come on,
When all the light we walked amid is gone!"

His words found echo in her deepest heart.
Half in Heaven, earth they quite forgot
While bird songs in that silent wooded spot
Rehearsed the joys now fallen to their part.
From far away her aunt gave them a start,
Calling them to supper while it's hot.
Holding hands and smiling all the way,
They took the path to where the arbor lay.

How splendidly the arbor had been dressed!
A lamp was lit for the festivity,
The kitchen of the house produced its best,
And Alma's aunt had braided garlands three.
They knew for whom the myrtle wreath must be;
The balm was Adam's as the bridegroom-guest;
As for the gardener, of his work-hat shorn,
An oakleaf wreath did his white hair adorn.

Hr. Star was witty and ebullient,
The aunt was kindly, although overbearing;
Happily toward Alma Adam bent
And to the wreath of myrtle she was wearing
Added his of balm, so that their pairing
(On each side of her braided hair one leant)
Showed off her charming brow so fetchingly
Her loveliness was plain for all to see.

"Now, Aunt, let's hear the champagne cork pop free,"
The old man says. "First these two we shall skoal
With our best wine, then drink to you, good soul,
Then me, and then skoal all the company."
On saying this, his eyes to Alma stole,
Caught whispering in a sweet and tender key,
Though audible enough to Adam's love:
"Would chicken suit Hr. Homo or would dove?"

"What!" cries the gardener. "What do I hear there?
Is that how far you've gotten heretofore?
Say 'you' or 'Adam,' but don't call him 'Herr';
That jars the tender eardrums of Amor.
'You and I' and 'we' strike his soul fair,
And any ceremonials he'll abhor.
Arise, my children! Let us raise the cup!
The time for 'Herr' and suchlike's long been up."

Then each stood up at his allotted place.
And from their lips the one word "you" did pass,
Although it came in treble from the lass
While Adam's "you" was in a manly bass.
That evening they drank down full many a glass
To future joy and fortune's every grace;
It was past twelve they parted company,
And Alma—shy and anxious—first breathed free.

Why shy and anxious? I hear people say,
Insisting on the author's explanation,
Although the answer takes no penetration
If we've looked into life a little way.
Where has a soul been seen in all Creation
Who's not been such at start of a new day?
Who's kept his calm, kept perfect fortitude?
Whom have new fortunes not put in grave mood?

Why, can there be a creature anywhere
Whom novelty has not put to the rack?
From smallest tyke to Pope in his high chair?
Tell me, O Priest, when first you wore the black
(And knee-length, too) out in the thoroughfare:
Was not exuberance left somewhere back?
Was not your eye transfixed by that black stuff
And all your mind stuck fast upon your ruff?

And what became of your exuberance,
You lovely girl, when, by your mother led,
You left the quiet house where you were bred
And first stepped, flushed and warm, into a dance?
How should those furrows on your brow be read,
When bodice stays first had some relevance?
And you, when first called by your husband's name?
And you, the first time that a wet nurse came?

And you, young man! when in a gown of white
The first time in your life, at confirmation:
Your mind was fair divided—am I right?—
Between your gown's flaps and the priest's oblation.
And you, boy! cheeks flushed with vexation
When you tied your first neckerchief too tight:
I'd say you spent the whole day in a miff
About your collar and that neckerchief.

What wonder, therefore, that our heroine,
For whom betrothal was as yet so new,
Should act quite properly to outward view,
Although her mind was in a very spin?
And that anxiety she would be in
Until the next few days were gotten through;
But she soon put self-consciousness away
Once Eros set his master stroke in play.

For Echo doth in maidens' bosoms dwell.
Each note reverberating on their strings
Gives rise to kindred music's echoings,
Wherein the strains live long in ritornel.
Though full of trembling, full of joy as well;
Though it is rich in joy, like pain it stings
Into the deepest heart of womankind
And magically inspires her soul and mind.

167/

Then called to Life's a life of such sweet glow
As April's when 'twixt clouds, rain, sun it veers;
Then gladness often veils itself in tears,
While smiles convey anxiety and woe;
The sweetest healing in our bane inheres;
And hope soars like an arrow from the bow
Of memory, shot forth from its tautened strings
To penetrate a world of better things.

Imagination, which in days now past
Lay slumbering with pinions folded tight,
Now comes upon a field, so broad and vast!
Now it will sweep upon an eagle flight
To regions where the thunderclouds are massed,
Now gently on a flowered lea alight.
Now it must dip its brush in light and shade
Before life can be properly portrayed!

But very differently, we're satisfied,
Does this new life appear to different eyes;
And, though it may be called a paradise,
One takes its light- and one its shadow-side.
The whims of one unto its blisses glide;
One takes the rose with thorns as his full prize;
One leaves off drudging for its golden wings;
Another mopes with unsoothed languishings.

That such new life in Alma had been bred
Was plain both outwardly and inwardly.
For all the thoughts that spun round in her head,
Now hoping, now absorbed in memory,
Nothing smaller now was merited
Than boundless spaces of Eternity.
On wings her mind would ever higher climb
Into the Infinite beyond all Time.

But if the heights were high, the depths were not
Less deep which she commanded in these days.
If Adam's visage stood before her gaze
(And almost always it was in her thought),
Then down into its very depths she sought,
Like ocean divers who the sea floors graze,
To fetch up every pearl that she could see
In it and in its ideality.

And pearls she won, and those magnificent,
To gladden woman's heart and make it thrill;
To her each did a pledge of love fulfill
And, joined, composed life's loveliest ornament.
O, how she felt the sum of her content
Each time she found there in her lover still
The height of beauty, height of love transcendent,
Height of honor, and all things resplendent!

My reader, who has seen our hero grow,
May marvel that within the hero's head
Alma found such wealth as this outspread
And think, I would imagine, roughly so:
Young Cupid has had blindness patented
And blinds the eyes of others from his bow,
As there is hardly anyone to doubt
Who sees how matters in this world turn out.

Still one could argue that the blindness may
Derive from eyesight so superior,
That it can see beneath a man's exterior
And to his deepest soul first find the way.
What vision is there able to survey
(Love's vision surely cannot be inferior)
That wealth, those treasures without end,
Which all immortal souls must comprehend?

No less an alteration struck the eye
In the behavior of the future bride:
When questioned, she infrequently replied;
Oft questioning, she stayed for no reply.
"Distrait," the gardener hardly could deny;
"Confused," her aunt was more than satisfied;
And both of them, when they looked up, decided
That she no longer walked, but rather glided.

Whenever she would part her lips for talking,
They couldn't help exchanging smiles; for she
Would speak to them almost in melody,
As if the words upon her mouth were rocking.
She often sighed, which they found somewhat shocking,
And yet was very merry, blithe, and free;
And they could not conceive how her ears bore
With the garden gate such deep rapport.

For ere they'd caught the sound of Adam's tread,
She, her eyes aglow, cheeks crimsoning,
Already halfway down the path had fled
As blithe and fleet as breezes of the spring.
But sometimes thoughts would come into her head,
And round the linden tree her arms she'd fling
And watch with joy that figure make its way
Which she loved more than she could ever say.

Then how time hastened for them in its flight!
Around the garden arm in arm they fared,
And many a word and many a look they shared,
For opening their hearts was their delight.
He might begin from a didactic height,
But her esteem for him was unimpaired.
And he who thought her mind was his to hone
Began to grasp the dullness of his own.

A new conception of the world was framed
Within his mind (already in his breast
The idea was by Alma's name expressed).
That surface fortune at which he'd first aimed—
That gloomy fate for which he had been claimed—
That empty calm—that talent for unrest—
All fled like sunlit dew before life's majesty;
He saw that all lay under love's sole mastery.

It was the well from which the world was sprung,
At which each creature and each soul was nursed,
And love it was in every heart that rung
And would unite all that had been dispersed.
And love it was, by fates that joyed or stung,
That stormed each breast until its armor burst
And every eye was opened to acclaim
Itself and all things in its candid flame.

It was the charm whereby, out of the dark,
Life authentic was at long last freed;
It was for him as the electric spark
That changes gases to a water bead:
Combine them still inert and you'll remark
That your experiment did not succeed;
But let that wondrous flame be kindled in it,
The element is there that very minute.

This life that spread these blisses past compare
And with its beauty, ardor, warmth, and scent
Attracted both his sense and sentiment
He owed alone unto a lady fair.
Our hero then could call himself content
In Alma's company as in life's air;
If he is kept in town, your guess is true,
The air is wafted him in billets-doux.

But now it has arrived, the looked-for day,
When he'll be tested for his skill in preaching,
And he must call on all his arts and teaching
Before he can take up the priestly way;
When tastefulness and eloquence far-reaching
Must work enchantment on this first essay,
Which, that his sacred call be documented,
At Holy Spirit Church must be presented.

The gardener's household had been up since dawn;
When this day came, they were prepared for it,
For long ago it was decided on
That first they'd hear him preach on Holy Writ
And after that they'd hire a phaeton
Out to the Deer Park, which they would not quit
Till end of day. The moon must first come out
Before the driver turns their coach about.

To Alma's ears it clanged as for a squall
When, just at ten, to her aunt's arm she clung
As they walked past the Holy Spirit's wall
And entered while the tower bells were rung;
But soon the vaulting, high and broadly slung,
To higher thoughts her spirit did recall.
She took a corner pew and sat there prim,
And in her book turned to the posted hymn.

Fear and devotion vied within her breast,
For she felt both a solemn sympathy
And for Adam such anxiety
She almost shook, as if this were her test.
She'd often scan the church for all the rest,
But found, and that was sad, near vacancy;
Just seven or eight old men and women there
To sing the hymn the organ pipes now blare.

But hush! the pulpit steps begin to crack:
She lifts her gaze, unutterably shy,
And now the pounding of her heart comes back
As she beholds her dear friend up on high.
Then to her lap she lowers her meek eye
As Adam sets his papers in a stack.
Around his flock his shepherd eyes now sweep,
But where's the flock? —The shepherd has no sheep!

He stands—but does not stand there like a Paul
Who seeks for all a higher explanation,
Who makes the root of faith the source of all
And goes miles past the common observation
To see the world itself as revelation:
It was the moral law he would recall
And—was it chance that Fate's dice this way fell?—
He preached on good works to a faretheewell.

But that for his first sermon he had run
To good works as his subject of the day
Must have derived, at least I think that way,
From that good work he had just done, the one
Of finding for himself a fiancée.
What's more, he had a place now in the sun:
In such a case, one takes good works for text,
For faith's more suited to the sore perplexed.

On works he built his major argument,
That we can rest assured of blessedness;
But on his text his zeal laid so much stress
Its letter made a wreck of its intent.
He claimed that all save works was valueless,
And this is how his closing statement went:
"Your faith's shown in the works of all your days;
Your works shall seal your doom or bring you praise!"

Still, the sermon was quite good in spots,
Those where the temper of his mind shone through;
While, granted, he said little that was new,
Yet there was a grace to all his thoughts.
From this the deepest comfort Alma drew,
Who at the start was somewhat tied in knots:
She looked up, moved, those times when Adam spoke
And with his heart's brush added a bright stroke.

He rests now in the forecourt from his deed;
There Alma's little mouth sends him a smile
To thank him for the sermon; as agreed,
They thereupon must part a little while.
Homeward through the streets does Adam speed,
For, to enjoy the woods in proper style,
Where joyful zephyrs will about him sough,
He'll have to change his black suit for a blue.

But on his way he thinks: I'm standing here
At my life's apogee! For its dark ways
Lie bright before my eyes, and all is clear,
All its bounty in my breast it lays.
If I died now, those were not wasted days
I lived till this my five-and-twentieth year.
No farther does my learning time extend;
Were I a book, it's here I'd have to end.

As brisk he walked, pursuing many a thought,
His sights raised up to the Ideal on high,
Upon the street a vision passed close by
Which, half strange and half familiar, caught
The full attention of his mind and eye:
A female creature hovered round that spot,
So free and forward, prodigally painted,
He knew upon the instant she was tainted.

How her cloak swung! How her gait was lax
As boldly with a smile she went her ways,
Until on Adam she had fixed her gaze
And he and she stopped dead right in their tracks.
Astounded, he was all but turned to wax,
For it was little Lotte from old days,
Changed into a whore, adroit and wily.
She, once so shy, addresses him now dryly:

"Good day, Hr. Homo" (with a curtsey bow).
"I thought you'd left town long ago, true-blue!
I hope we can resume our friendship now:
The place is free that once belonged to you.
Your kindness I have often had to avow,
For, in my need, your money saw me through.
You'll find me in The Slip, at Number Four."
She left, and Adam's heart could breathe once more.

173/

But, without thinking, Adam turned around
And, with a sigh, he watched her as she walked
Along the street, poor wretched girl, and stalked
What prey her busy eyes could run to ground.
He saw her nod to gentlemen she found
And, by the world's opinion nothing balked,
Brush hard against an old beau's sleeve,
Whose weak sight, though, secured him a reprieve.

A heavy weight descended on his breast,
And in his heart there rose a bitter ache:
He felt a grief which could not be expressed
And which no solace and no aid could slake.
He knew the girl was wrecked through his mistake,
And to it his own voice did so attest:
"Your faith's shown by the works of all your days;
Your works shall seal your doom or bring you praise."

"Ah," he sighed, "how clouded was my sight
Indeed, as I stood preaching there today,
And in good works alone found true delight
And faith, salvation's anchor, cut away.
Without it, my affairs had gone astray
And she'd have no salvation from her plight."
He reached home, all contrition and regret,
And there a letter made him more upset.

It was his father writing him to say
That there was really not much time to waste
If he would see his mother one last day.
He had better leave for home posthaste.
For some time now she'd been in a bad way,
But now Death menaced, with his sickle braced;
From what the doctor said, all hope was through,
So Adam had to come, and quickly, too.

Then for the trip he settled each detail.
Next morning he would be off on his way,
Travelling swiftly by the fastest mail,
But must let Alma know this very day.
Along with this decision went a wail:
How soon my fair horizon's turned to gray!
From every side anxieties crowd round,
Just as my happiness was to abound.

Why, after all, should he feel *he* was free
When after liberty all people run
And overshoot their mark continually?
The Idea sends its light down like a sun,
But, though that light may dazzle everyone,
In single breasts alone burns liberty.
Yes, if another thousand years we wait,
It still would not be part of man's estate!

See how, like a snake, a chain is drawn
Round all the world, and hear on every side
The sigh for liberty that now is gone!
Of thought, which strong opinion sits astride;
Of speech, to which the lie is closely tied;
Of action, with a thousand checks thereon;
Of beasts and men, all whom the yoke has bent;
Of Nature, deep in thralldom and lament.

All would be free: the journalist's quill pen
That scorns the censor's stroke in politics;
The tradesmen who the prying excisemen,
Their fine friends, put off scent with business tricks;
The husband who, his verve come back again,
Leaves rosy-ribboned Hymen in a fix;
And lovers too, clamped by the kindest braces,
For freedom will, like foals, kick up the traces.

But even if the outward chains all gave,
Even those of gold, enough remains:
Sin, sorrow, greed, fierce passion and the pains
Of life uncertain by the certain grave.
Of past and future days are forged such chains,
Of instants' whims, of what for days we crave,
Of doubt and fear, of honor lost or sound,
So burdensome, and weighed by hundred-pound.

Have you in spring seen ice packs come asunder
And heard the ocean, as the storm's wings zoom,
Loudly forth in youthful vigor boom
And burst its winter burden with its thunder?
The waters tossing drunk with freedom's wonder,
And with each crashing wave the flying spume?
How proud a sight for mortal man to see!
But that is not the way the soul comes free.

175/

Have you traced down the brooklet from its source,
And seen it twist a thousand times or more,
Against its barriers waging endless war
As it pursued intent its forward course?
Now it flowed smoothly, though half still before;
Now it burst onward—with unceasing force
Until it reached its home, the mighty sea:
That too is how a soul wins liberty!

Just so the freedom of the soul is known
As love is and as faith is known as well:
Within constricting forms it cannot dwell,
For those are accidental, soon outgrown.
It has a passion in it naught can quell,
And in the tun of time can only groan.
By thousands to that tun we mortals pray—
The soul, though, has already gone its way!

Its freedom to myself I'll arrogate
And to my hero and the June woods deep
With green my reader I shall now translate.
The evening skies their last pink hour keep,
Through rustling leaves the birds their songs abate,
And beasts to rest among soft mosses creep.
The dark of night, the silent time, grows near,
The wellspring of all beauty and of fear.

The carriage still stands by the forest shed,
And into it the aunt and gardener nip
As Adam warmly gets his farewells said,
For he must leave next morning on his trip.
The carriage glides away, about to slip
Behind the foliage at the turn ahead.
To Alma, who had raised a sigh profound,
Our hero gave his arm to walk around.

How sorrowful and bleak the day had been!
He seemed withdrawn in somber reverie,
And Alma had become quite panicky
When told that he must travel to his kin
And when she saw the black mood he was in.
He had proposed that night that he and she
Should recommend themselves to the sea foam
And, from the forest, take a sailboat home.

Along the leafy walks, in thickening shade,
Toward the nearby shoreline on they pressed,
Where bobbed their sailboat on the ocean's breast.
Alma trembled as they walked, afraid,
As though her soul a prisoner were made,
And little comfort Adam's heart possessed.
But he, to hide what he had in his heart,
Burst out, as if he took it in good part:

"This world is very hard to understand!
We all must work against our own good luck,
We all must shuffle cards, that worthless truck,
And then complain about a losing hand.
Out through these forest shadows we have struck,
And we won't stop or linger on this land;
Why must our feet continue on so fast
When just these steps will part us at the last?"

"Oh," Alma said, in tones that showed her strain,
"To part is not the hardest business here;
Each farewell must a 'till we meet' contain
That makes the final moment still more dear.
What union is thus makes itself quite plain:
In all things it makes people draw more near.
That's why these lips cannot hold back this plea:
What's troubling you?—Don't keep it back from me!

"Our lives were only just about to start,
And suddenly it's time for you to go;
But if you leave with our minds far apart,
Before the clouds disperse that crowd so low,
Before we are united heart to heart,
Your farewell promises me only woe.
When doubt the flame of mutual trust can smother,
How can we through all trials stand by each other?

"For what is great? What small? In this world all
Is really life and death in urgency:
But two can oft resist adversity
Which, if it struck but one, would make him fall.
And even though your past tells things to me
Which seem to be a fountainhead of gall,
Through words the tears of sorrow can be blessed.
We part—but yet we still hope for the best."

To this appeal so sober and sincere
Adam was evasive in reply,
For Lotte's form and Clara's stood close by
And past them forms of others still appear.
He thought—but here his thinking was awry—
Why trouble someone whom I hold so dear?
It's up to me to make the best of things
And put to rest these dark rememberings.

And so, as reason for his state of mind,
He gave his mother's illness, as seemed true;
But though he had not rendered Alma blind,
And though with this her doubting was not through,
She knew that pressing further would not do.
They'd reached the road which round the forest twined,
Where night had spread its shining canopy
And waves beat on the coast melodiously.

They board the boat, where an old fisherman
At the helm unfurled the sails of white,
And took a place up at the steep prow's height
Where they could feel the cool fresh breezes fan.
Of earthly longings spoke the stars that night
As on the glassy waters their boat ran,
And, from the slice of moon hung o'er the glade,
A golden glimmer on the billows played.

So cradled in each other's arms and clapped
About with Adam's cloak, there at the prow
The two sat listening while the cold sea lapped,
Cleft by the keel, against the sailboat's bow
As on the night's pale glow they stared enrapt
And felt the pain of loneliness ev'n now.
It's present in the looks each gives to each
As to his dear one Adam makes this speech:

"You're sitting here so still, in reverie,
As though you heard the spirits of the air.
Have you no parting words to give to me
To take along when I go over there?
Don't shut the heart's cool springs, but let them bear
Relief to quench an earth's aridity!
Speak something that forever, come what may,
I'll carry as our watchword on my way."

178/

Out from Adam's cloak of darkest blue
Peered Alma earnestly with shining eyes
And warmly answered: "I'll not plead with you,
And for farewell you will not get my sighs.
From hope's beaker let us drink, we two,
And trustfully exchange these first good-byes.
Our longing, like a coin in two we'll split,
And take full joy when we've the whole of it.

"But until you return your half to me,
Upon my walks my eyes will never stray;
I won't ask which will be our writing-day,
For time would then pass far too tediously.
But when the spring and warmth return this way,
When hope calls with the birds' new melody,
Then every day I'll walk down to the strand
To see if there's a ship about to land.

"No matter where you travel—don't forget
The faithfulness of friends which you've seen here!
Though prospects darken, keep my memory near,
And know you've refuge here from every threat.
You'll find me still the same year after year,
No matter what has passed or will pass yet."
But Adam says: "God knows my heart is true!
We'll be together soon. I'll write to you.

"And do not think that far within me hides
A memory from which deep grief will sprout;
Though sometimes in my breast there sweep high tides,
From them your image ever shimmers out.
Wherever I roam you always are about,
For close beside you all my hope abides;
And there that quiet cottage I'll erect
Whose roof our common future shall protect."

So they exchanged upon this hour of night
Warm words by which all sorrows were fast bound,
And just as chords within each other sound,
From mouth to mouth their murmurs blended right.
Above, the stars sent greetings of soft light;
Below, the sea sang from its floor profound
As every breeze they felt above them play
Was heard in gentle sighs to die away.

179/

It was as though, in that clear summer night,
Nature all her glory had unpent
And at the same time sighed in its despite
Because her treasures are impermanent.
The waves leapt to the starry firmament,
But barely seized the beams ere from their height—
As when to joy the heart must bid farewell—
They toppled back into the pitch-dark swell.

But here it's sure to happen—it can't fail—
That one or other reader, while these two
Out in the Sound home from the forest sail,
Can't rest to get an answer overdue:
How can a journey on the Vejle mail
Be cause for such excitement and such rue?
How can so deep an ache, such consternation,
Issue from so small a complication?

My answer's Alma's: What is great? What small?
Is there for souls in love a little thing?
Does it but to tragic figures fall
To make farewells with tears as offerings?
Is not every heartstring formed to ring
On entering the love-god's temple hall,
When from within his sanctum sounds a strain
To gladden us and cause us bitter pain?

—Now to our hero! He was in his seat
Inside the coach which sped along the road
And, when at eve the coachman rested, strode
Ahead to where two highways came to meet.
Here from his breast he drew sheet after sheet
And heard again, as with a smile he glowed,
Alma's voice in notes of yesterday,
Which on his ears like sonnets seemed to play.

Through you alone I live as ne'er before,
Of all of mankind you and you alone!
Once in my mind I had dwelt all unknown,
A dolphin on the ocean's silent floor.

Then on an evening I heard your voice pour
When silence seemed to turn all things to stone,
And that voice lured me with its perfect tone
From ocean's deeps above the waves to soar.

The sound of you rang through the halls of air,
With music that before me life did lay,
And through your words this world belonged to me.

O, always speak to me as you did there!
You are my singer and I hear you play;
I am your dolphin, listening ceaselessly!

———•———

Often when these garden paths I take,
Where every tree stands decked in summer's ways,
Where every morning to our Author's praise
In song among the leaves the birds awake:

Then often comes a thought to make me quake;
It seems a Paradise on which I gaze,
And so complete in all things that to raze
Its loveliness I even have a snake.

The snake is that desire in me that woos
With promises of knowing your heart's core
If you would open your past life to me.

Say, might I then my Paradise well lose,
And might my loveliness then well be o'er,
Were I to pluck the knowledge from that tree?

I dreamt—how dreams, though, can be double-faced!
So lively had my dream exhibited
The world which ere you came was mild and dead
That from my days your name had been erased.

I felt that I an emptiness encased,
As if a cask whose contents all were shed,
As if its precious wine had all been bled,
And I, the dried-out wood, were left to waste.

Then I awakened—round about I gazed:
Your portrait did the young day newly gild
And with its beauty in my eyes it blazed.

With that the dried-out cask was once more filled!
Up to my heart there rose in swelling tides
That flood of joy which in your name abides.

———•———

I'm sitting here and writing. It is late,
The sun has set and left the sky behind;
And leaves and bushes, rocking in the wind,
Night's close-woven veil will cover straight.

The garden's wells of scent do now abate,
Within each folded petal-cup confined,
And every plant has now its head declined;
The violets' perfumes only penetrate.

Once, my Adam, when our day is run
And all its glory and refulgence done,
And life to us is as a sun that's set:

Then once again a dream shall stir our soul,
Then once again our love shall make us whole,
And send us fragrance like the violet.

———•———

You ask what can these little notes betide?
I could reply that letters which go on
Oft lead us not to read them but to yawn;
But there's another reason I'll provide.

You've seen a household on a woodland ride?
The infants, who to life are also drawn,
But left back on the doorstep woebegone,
Try pleading with Mama to take their side.

"Oh, don't leave in the carriage without us!
Oh, take us, too!" Mama replies thereto:
"You're still too little and too mischievous."

Likewise by toddler-notions I am pained:
They'd all join in each time I write to you,
But they must grow—they first have to be trained.

———•———

Tell me if my thinking is too odd
In how I've solved this weighty question here:
Why, of all those people who appear,
Above the rest our hearts should one applaud?

182/

And how are sight and feeling kept unflawed?
Why is the perfect one and, as is clear,
The handsomest not always the most dear?
I answer: "We are images of God."

He who our best happiness imparts
Is he to whom that Godlike trait does cleave
Which has the strongest pull upon our hearts.

Through that trait God shone gloriously above
And where it is reflected we perceive
His like, so very dear to us, or—love.

———•———

Amor and Psyche I have read straight through.
At last the happy pair together tread
On into kingdoms of the light ahead,
And I think I can tell you why they do.

When once hearts are united which were two,
It is as if their farewells must be said:
Out into life their two minds must be sped,
Out on the world they have to turn their view.

Once separate, they feel more incomplete,
Feel longing which reunion will abate,
And with a joy renewed once more they meet.

As o'er and o'er they meet and separate,
Love in its life at last becomes eternal,
And newborn always, as when it was vernal.

———•———

Herewith, the book sent yesterday to me
Which would to us that other life explain;
The author swears that we will meet again
But cannot live as one eternally.

My heart's long known a surer prophecy;
For, as our thoughts have life within the brain,
That life like birds' lives which quick wings sustain,
Whose flight has known and knows no boundary:

So there's no change our feeling undergoes,
But into other hearts its roots are pressed,
When, as for flight, the soul yearns for repose.

He who on us two natures has conferred
Has surely formed his Heaven to be best
For humankind—at once both plant and bird.

———•———

Each time I think about this life below,
Hope shines around me like a rosy dawn:
I see us glow with struggles undergone;
At times I see us harvest, at times sow.

Forward ever richer on we go,
From us life forever new is drawn;
So to fulfillment we two hasten on
To reach the blessedness we'll always know.

O, does not truth reside in hopes and dreams?
To triumph and increase we had to meet,
Else life had stayed a river without motion.

You drew me into your relentless streams,
And now united do our billows beat
With greater force upon the mighty ocean.

———•———

This morning in the garden I walked round,
Where on all things fresh roses brightness cast
And, under them, new-called to life, lay massed
Red strawberries that colored all the ground.

Then I thought of you, who sit desk-bound,
Upon your sermon laboring steadfast,
Which is to be the first, and not the last,
Which from your lips will God's Word purely sound.

This basketful of roses I send up,
And from each thorn to give you instant ease
I've hand-picked strawb'ries for you in a cup.

But more than they the cloudberries are sweet.
I wait upon your sermon to pluck these,
When you for earthly give me heavenly meat.

———•———

You gave me much to mull the other day.
You asked what would be the effect on me
If you should change your mind quite suddenly
And find yourself another fiancée;

If from your heart the love should go astray
And leave no drop of quickening property,
And with a heavy look I turned to see
My Eden with my Adam gone away—

Ah, if so low my head were ever bent,
If like an arrow, whining in its spin,
So sharp a pain my bosom ever found,

'Twould be with me as with a violin
That, shattered and restored with strong cement,
Gives a better tone, but weaker sound.

———•———

Your letter you regret as much untoward
In dwelling on the darker side of things,
Because from simple-souled meanderings
You caught me up with broodings now deplored.

May all your notes such honesty afford!
For me you're like the harp's resounding strings:
The sound that touches you forever sings
Deep in my heart, now made your sounding-board.

If you sound joy, with joy I'll answer you;
If you've left joy's notes for the strains of care,
Their somber echo shall in me ring true.

In all things I will haste to take your part;
A sounding-board responds to foul or fair;
But it can only answer—you must start.

———•———

That deep repentance, that indebtedness
To God and man you feel that you must clear,
Don't let your soul find that debt so severe
That it can frighten you from your success.

For it's no bagatelle that you possess;
As bankrupt you will never need appear.
You have one debtor left, my very dear!
A soul in need to whom you've shown largesse.

185/

What wreath of joy and bliss does life afford
That you've not given of your own accord!
What kingdom has your soul not shared with me!

If therefore an accounting one demand,
Then bring her forth who will your debtor stand.
With what you gave, she'll prove your solvency.

———•———

Here Adam had to let his reading go,
Although it caused the fellow great dismay,
For he had heard the coachman's cornet blow,
And, as its note their sad farewells convey,
In evening's silence now he drives away.
"Soon," he whispers, "soon once more I'll know
Your gaze, my Alma, and remove all doubt."
What's an intention?—We shall find that out!

Part Two

CANTO VII

Our hero at Korsør meets us once more,
Where, closer to his goal, he's much relieved
To be dropped off beside the posthouse door.
He found a letter waiting there, which bore
The news that he already was bereaved;
The news of mother, then, that he'd received
Ere from Copenhagen he broke free
Was not sent till her last extremity.

The new epistle ended with this thought:
"I walk round with a fog inside my brains;
Today, they still must take out her remains,
For it has been unusually hot.
Ere you arrive, with sand they'll fill her plot;
Ere you depart from Sjælland's verdant plains,
My tears will bathe the greensward o'er her tomb.
So hurry to your father sunk in gloom!"

As struck by lightning Adam speechless stood,
Imagining her in a coffin dead,
Till he was brought round by the clerk, who said:
"Twelve shillings, sir, for postage, if you would!"
He gathered up his wits, as Christian should,
Twelve shillings on the counter left, and fled
The posthouse for the room that he had rented,
And all his lamentation there he vented.

189/

But when his first lamentings were subdued
And in his loneliness he gazed around,
He called to mind in his grief-stricken mood
The now-dead face to every memory bound
Of those days which could never be renewed.
In all his recollections, there he found
That incorruptibility of soul
Which Holy Writ had taught him to extol.

"Yes!" he exclaimed, moved by his memory,
And folding his two hands, as these thoughts came:
"You were my guardian angel! Yours the flame
Which through my life has led and lighted me!
Through you I heard my call; and mine the shame
If I neglect the voice of sanctity
And veer from the direction which you gave,
If I break faith with you beyond the grave!"

His room was too confining—out he shot
To find the open, weed-strewn oceanside,
Where underneath the night sky's somber grot
The moonbeams on the shining waters glide.
A lonely path along the coast he sought
And, with the Belt's bright border for his guide,
He wandered silent, pensive and downcast,
And pondered on himself and on his past.

As purified did he from this bath rise;
A manful purpose proudly swelled his breast,
Demanding of himself the greatest, best,
And swearing hate eternal for all lies.
With such excitement was he now possessed
He seemed to see a parting of the skies:
His mother, as the moonlight round her spread,
Held out a garland for a life well-led.

Not till after midnight did he stir,
But when the semaphore first caught his eye
That from the church roof towered on the sky,
It seemed to him a wingèd messenger:
For now the face of Alma had come nigh
To bid that he back to his lodgings spur
So that, before he next day joined his boat,
He might delight her heart and send a note.

"My dearest one! My Alma!" (so he wrote
Once he had got his table lamp to light
And once the grievous news he found that night
Was shared as a preamble to that note)
"Don't think that this distress has crushed me quite;
The loss, although in two my soul it smote,
Has like a lightning bolt the darkness torn,
And in that brilliance I have been reborn.

"One other time—its memory comes to hand—
I also thought to seize on life's towrope.
Close beside the grave's edge did I stand
And sighted through the future's telescope
A peaceful home, enveloped in sweet hope;
But it proved not to be the promised land!
A new grief split my earth and firmament,
And on their healing all my strength I spent.

"I made a friend of you—the rift was filled,
And earth and heaven merged for me to one:
The selfsame golden beams on both were spilled;
Their meanings for me were together run.
All this by love's omnipotence was done,
For that it was that did my vision build
Which, in a world into two halves divided,
Let me perceive just where they coincided.

"But one thing I still lacked: the inner I
Had yet to find the power to break free;
Unused I left the powers of faith to lie
And sought outside myself a Deity.
Then on me the blow fell—within Death's eye
And from Death's lips came orders summary
That all faith's scattered sparks I must reclaim:
Then came a gust—and in me rose the flame.

"My inner self I barely know aright,
But as a soul reborn myself I prize.
My eye once more takes in the earth and skies,
But now I see them in a different light.
Amidst commotions always within sight
I see life from a single center rise,
And in that center I find a release
Near holy: faith is that same central peace.

191/

"But not repose alone does faith grant me,
Nor light alone when reason's light is bested;
What, in my mind, as faith is manifested
Will take the form of troth externally.
Faith, in the form of troth, to life's the key,
With good in good and soul in soul invested;
As troth it bids: Be steadfast and be true!
True to your calling, and to longing true!

"Yes, trust my longing! And how can I here
Make 'twixt earth and heaven a divorce?
The power that pulls me onward to life's source
Also makes my loved one doubly dear.
With that idea abate your longing's force
Until, before you know it, I am near.
A silent pilgrim I to the grave's lip,
And home to you I'll turn with staff and scrip."

He rose, and down hard on the wax he pressed
To seal his troth-epistle, at last ended,
And downstairs to the posthouse he descended
To frank the costly treasures of his breast.
Then he gave his worn-out limbs a rest
After so much energy expended
On daylong travel and his night-excursion
And his heart's most radical conversion.

He slept—but only found a brief repose;
The gleaming sun breaks through the windowpane,
And comes a tar-stained porter to obtain
The baggage he had taken and his clothes.
He, with a dreaming and beclouded brain,
Beside the porter to the harbor goes,
Where boarding passengers already swarm;
And soon the smack sets out into the storm.

He leans against the railing of the ship,
Pale and tired; for his intoxication
Of last night has turned to enervation,
His mind's confused, his spirits badly dip.
Then leaps to mind the object of this trip;
He sees his father's house in desolation,
Recalls the grave, and on grief's heavy wing
Again he struggles upward, fluttering.

But how his flight was low since yesterday's!
He felt it and allowed his wings to fall;
And long and silently he fixed his gaze
Upon the Belt waves, which did not recall,
As earlier, a cradle as it sways,
For all around the sea foamed in the squall,
The white waves rose and fell in loud travail
As over them the ship flew in full sail.

The boat was lurching; inside cattle roared,
And, somewhat sickened, with his cape wrapped fast,
He left the prow and went up to the mast,
Where he felt himself a bit restored.
Through his weak lungs the cooling breezes poured
And from his heart its burden they outcast;
With that, his youthful vigor proudly stirs,
As he surveys his fellow passengers.

It's then he sees—can he believe his eyes?—
On deck, far from the milling to and fro,
Some cushions serving as a bed—Lord, no!
Must his poor soul forever agonize?
Half hidden under travelling-cloaks he spies—
What was that nausea to this vertigo
That seized his soul with but one glance her way?—
He spies the Countess Clara plain as day!

But is it true? Is this sight witchery?
No! that same mouth and nose, refined and bold,
Same neck and shoulders, sloping gracefully,
Same lovely lines, though fuller in their mold.
But she was pale—in her infirmity
She lay still, frightened as the billows rolled,
And at that moment, as she shut her eyes,
"Oh, some water! Water, please!" she sighs.

Our hero does not budge upon her cry.
"Such things," he thinks, "are none of my affair!"
But as it seemed that no one heard her sigh,
He felt at last his duty was to care
And to her lips a glass of water bear.
She drank and suddenly raised up an eye:
"Hr. Homo, is it?" stammering, she exclaimed.
Hr. Homo blushed, as though somewhat ashamed.

193/

But Clara can sit up now all the way,
Restored by the cold water visibly;
Upon her lily cheeks rose highlights play
And round her lips a crimson tracery.
"Hr. Homo," Clara whispers—he's distrait—
"I thank you! I can't say what joy to me,
Our meeting in this way so unexpected;
You stand there like a dead man resurrected!"

Hr. Homo bows, and would have left, still dumb,
But Clara says: "Why do you rush away?
There was a time—I am much pleased to say—
You found my presence not so burdensome."
Her eyes' twin glittering stars began to play
And sent a merry look to bid him come
And sit upon a deck chair alongside.
Adam took a seat, half terrified.

"You're doing well?" once more the Countess started.
"Yes, very well . . . I meant to answer No!"
He stammered out his answer, heavy-hearted.
"I've been afflicted by a bitter woe."
He told of Mother, suddenly departed,
Spoke of her grave, to which he now must go;
And at his words, although they did not brood,
Her face showed more and more solicitude.

As soon as he had finished his confession,
He rose, his wits once more at his command;
But now he was to lose all self-possession
When Clara confidently grasped his hand.
"No!" she said, with timely indiscretion.
"You cannot leave a friend who'll understand.
You need some solace and some recreation;
Let me take charge of your recuperation!"

She hurriedly looked round through all the stir
And, just as Adam's farewell reached her ear,
Called half loud: "Hello! One word, my dear!"
A fat man turned around in search of her.
She beckoned him to come to where they were,
And, when the unknown gentleman drew near,
Her words to Adam made his heart near halt:
"This is my husband, Kammerherre Galt!"

194/

And there the fat man stood, upon her call,
And Adam stared, not knowing what to say.
He was a man fair-favored not at all,
With blond hair speckled through with gray;
With cheeks so fat they fairly pushed away
His melancholy eyes, half shut and small;
In green coat, hat with ribbon-fasteners,
And low-heeled boots got up with silver spurs.

"Permit"—a smile on Clara's lips now plays
As she turns to face the heavy gent—
"Will you permit me, dearest, to present
Herr . . . Herr Homo, from my former days.
Those Fate divides are joined by Accident.
It would please me—and you in many ways—
If for a short stay he might be invited."
"Oh," the fat man mumbled. "Be delighted!"

Making a slight bow, a smile he tested,
But still he was a melancholy sight;
His eyes beclouded, like a somber light,
He looked round, then went off, uninterested.
But Clara, with our hero once more, jested:
"You'll come with us, won't you? We shall just write
For leave your father will be sure to grant—"
"No," he stammered. "No, I really can't."

"You can't? You really dare to tell me this?"
The young seductress set to winningly:
"What's stopping you? Perhaps a much-loved miss?
Dear relatives? Or claims of bonhomie?
You shake your head. I am no prodigy
At dumb shows, but in my analysis
Your reasons for refusing are not strong.
Well, for a few days, then, you'll come along?"

"For a few days," Adam now repeated,
A phrase that he had meant to end with No;
Before his lips could make objection, though,
A nausea left his sentence uncompleted.
And truly he'd a touch of vertigo,
Whether in the Belt its cause was seated,
Which charged his heart with all its roilings vile,
Or in the lady's very lovely smile.

He quickly got away; but Clara's thanks
When he rushed off were hanging in his ear,
Yes, even in the waves he heard them clear,
Though seasick sighs were shivering his flanks.
Not long did his heart's moilings persevere;
The graceful smack slipped in toward Nyborg's banks;
A boat came out and, being rowed a way,
At last they found themselves upon the quay.

Here for the last time Adam made a flat
And fruitless effort for his liberty:
He must, now that they had reached Fyn, said he,
Go buy a band of black crepe for his hat.
But Clara killed that chance of truancy:
"You don't know where to buy a thing like that.
I'll go with you myself"—and off they hop;
He buys his band, she feathers in a shop.

At their hotel, the Kammerherr' they found
Absorbed in copies of the local press;
While he and Adam chatted, the *comtesse*
Onto her hat her ostrich feathers bound.
His hat she next with mourning-crepe tied round,
Declaring it an asset to his dress.
They joined their carriage—he, his black band streaming,
She in her white plumage grandly beaming.

From Nyborg off they rolled. Along the way
Through Funen's lovely country they were going,
With people in the wheatfields busy mowing
Amidst the fragrance of the new-cut hay;
With farmwives curtseying and girls helloing
And roguish maids who came 'neath their survey.
The sweets of love sang out from every tree;
The air was heavy with unchastity.

Westward they drove. The land's magnificence
Rolled out with valleys, hills, and woods,
The thick smoke from manorial neighborhoods
Where jovial yeomen thrive back earthen fence,
Where nobles dwell by age-old providence,
Where all is burnished, people and their goods;
For burnish Funen has, isle of my birth
I hold as dear as Jews hold Israel's earth.

Inside the landau Clara sat content,
And while her spouse slept through the scenery,
She kept amused, her fine head forward bent,
With Adam and each new locality.
But, as the two were sitting vis-à-vis,
She had to meet his gaze as on they went,
At which, of course, she did turn slightly red,
And he, in their discourse, oft lost the thread.

They travelled on. The sun, a golden plate
At evening, sank out of their view at last
As from the road they swung into the gate
And through a dark beech grove their carriage passed.
Here, with his hounds, a huntsman of the estate
Saluted with his cornet's merry blast,
As past him like the very wind they sped.
"We've reached our destination!" Clara said.

A-gallop down the avenue they drove,
And, as they passed the gateway, in an arc
That took them round the goodly fishing-park,
Into view a splendid building hove.
The ruddy roof shone past a poplar grove;
The staff stood on the staircase, on their mark.
Above the wide-flung doors, upon a field
One saw a hog be-crowned, the Galt clan's shield.

A servant led our hero up the stair
And to a suite of rooms; then entered too
Another to light lamps, which brought to view
A board laid out with gilded tableware;
Then came a little housemaid, very fair,
To fit his bed, its curtains silken blue,
With sheeting that as clean as white snow shone—
Whereupon all three left him alone.

And seating himself in an easy chair,
Against its back he rubbed his own around,
And twice he ran his fingers through his hair,
Upon which in his eyes his fists he ground.
He burst out: "Can it be my mind's unsound?
Who I am I'd be hard-pressed to swear.
Into what port have I now set my sail?
I feel like someone in a fairy tale!"

He jumped up, and uneasy to and fro
He paced, delivering this soliloquy:
"There I was on the Belt—it can't be so,
And yet it's happened in reality!
Me, Adam Homo, in her household! Me!
The one who on a pilgrimage would go
To plant a lily on the new-dug grave—
O, what is man with all his will so brave!

"And what is all this business?" pondered he.
"A fairy tale, but not so strange and new!
What does it matter for a day or two?
Once that is over I'll again be free.
I'm not required to deal in trickery;
I'll act in perfect truth, as all friends do—"
He stroked his hair, ran one hand through his locks,
Then, at the table, spooned tea from its box.

The food was splendid; for the appetite
Of heroes, even teatime ones, is great;
Once he'd eaten, he began to write
To Pastor Homo that he'd be home straight.
When that was done, he yielded to sleep's might;
And it so happened, startling to relate,
That point for point a dream arrived to show
What at that moment passed at Vesterbro.

Flung wide was Alma's little chamber door,
Whose threshold he was never to pass through,
And eyes aglow and cheeks a ruddy hue,
Lamp in hand, she walked across the floor.
Upon her head a bonnet gray she wore,
With veil of shoulder-length attached thereto;
Over to its stand the lamp she took,
And hung her hat and veil upon their hook.

The open casement in she gently drew
And pulled down back of it a dark green shade;
She watered then her myrtle, each sweet blade,
And with her breath she set a gentle dew
Upon an autumn rose of carmine hue,
Upon whose petals the night air had weighed;
She took a chair and set it at a place
Where her nightstand mirror could drink in her face.

Sitting down, she from her bodice took
A note still in its envelope, the note
Which from Korsør our hero to her wrote,
And on its cover cast a loving look.
She carefully removed the seal's wax coat,
But made a tear, and with a sigh she shook;
And then she trimmed the lampwick and prepared
To read the words upon the paper shared.

She sat there silent, her small hand, for shade
Against the glaring light, above her eyes—
In her chamber not a sound was made
Except for some few black and buzzing flies
That round her bed's white curtaining then played
And darted round the four walls zig-zagwise;
But these roused in our reader little pique:
She read along, a warm smile on her cheek.

Read and read again was every phrase.
She stood up and with quiet steps she paced
The floor; the music which her soul embraced
Now sounded forth in festive roundelays.
She stopped before the chest of drawers to gaze
At Adam's charcoal sketch, above it placed;
She fixed her eye on it—and doubly bright
And doubly sweet a look did it excite.

She stood there long—to his framed monochrome
She yields a sigh before she goes from there
To sit herself down and take up her comb
Before the mirror to arrange her hair.
With every braiding of her tresses fair,
Back to the letter Alma's eyes still roam,
So, when her nightcap 'neath her chin is bound,
She's read the letter through the third time round.

Hurriedly she put the letter down;
She took her tie-string, and her fingers spun
As all its knots were loosened, one by one,
Until she sat unclothed to her nightgown,
Charming from her ankles to her crown,
Bare-legged, in slippers yellow as the sun;
She let them drop and sighed out to the night,
Then jumped into her bed and snuffed the light.

It was a dream, but also verity;
And here the question calls for our attention
Of whether there's a proper comprehension
Of what's called truth and what mere reverie.
No wise man longer thinks dreams worth the mention,
The real has taken him in custody;
But is the gulf between the dreamt and actual,
Which our hands can seize on, really factual?

O childhood's dream, scarce known before it's fled!
O lovely dream of youth, gone instantly!
O dream of love, from out of which is bred
A whole life's pleasure and its poetry!
O dream of hope, the soul wound in its thread,
From which it never wholly is set free!
O joy's, O honor's, freedom's, golden dream!
Who'd drain your cup, from which enchantments stream?

As life's dream are its contents to us sent
And wells of truth up from its bottom teem,
So he who can't reach bottom in his dream
Knows not what truth in life is immanent.
Those souls but swim the surface of the stream
Who only toward reality are bent,
Which with the look of truth only misguides,
While true life in the depths of dreams abides.

For deep into our dreams we have to go,
Out like a rover of the night must stride
And must not look about on either side
Or listen to the calls from far below.
Nor should we trust in what luck may bestow,
As though we could retrieve a dream let slide
By merely dreaming it again some day:
It's lost forever once it's gone astray.

When to its end the great dream-play is brought,
With its enchantments and its poetry,
Who, when it's ended, will resolve the plot?
And, when the play is over, what will be?
Dare we hope a new dream will be wrought?
Or melt we in the sun of verity?
O, the belief has more grounds than a dream
That morning then will first begin to beam.

—The beaming morning bore in vividly
On Adam, who'd just risen out of bed
With that night's wreath of dreams still round his head
And oped the window as the sun poured free.
Looking out, he saw the far coast spread
And cresting waves upon the wind-tossed sea.
A little nearer were the park and wood;
The garden lay below where he now stood.

He finds the morning landscape ravishing
And can no longer stand there in one place.
Down the staircase with its porphyry vase
He runs out to the garden beckoning.
Within the arcade shadows entering,
He sighs: "O Alma, Alma! Only race
Into my arms as if a bird of air!"
He looks round—and sees Clara standing there.

She had approached him from a little lane,
Wearing a snow-white flowing negligée,
Round which a pleated shawl, the hue of hay,
Hung down to show her snowy throat more plain.
A hat of lace, with bows of deep red stain,
Showed off her brow and brown locks *à merveille,*
A pair of which were round her shoulders slung,
While in her hand a parasol she swung.

Up she tripped. Her glove, of Randers mold,
She waved to wish him sweetly a good day,
While saying: "How we Danes are right to say
That 'In the mouth of morning there is gold.'"
But Adam with that gold was swept away—
By that gold I mean Clara, be it told,
With whom he joined for one short promenade
And all about the golden morn parleyed.

One thing he did not grasp or understand:
That this fine girl, so womanly of form,
Who seemed to plead with him with looks so warm,
Was she who yesterday had him unmanned.
Where were those looks, where were those phrases grand,
That haughty beauty that took all by storm?
The smile upon her lips might be refined,
But yet her cheek told sweetly that she pined.

The shaded lane they now have walked beyond,
To where a broad and sunny meadow looms,
Speckled with the last of summer's blooms,
And, lying in the midst of it, a pond.
With double lightness in the white she'd donned
She races to the swans with their white plumes,
Whose home the pond was and whose breasts now ride
The limpid waters that reflect their pride.

At pondside stood a basketful of bread.
She picked it up, and, stretching out, she sought
To lure the swans—and to her they made head
To take the food her pretty hand had brought.
To Adam then she handed the last shred
With words that were like music, Adam thought:
"My guest just like my swans I have to feed
Lest he too soon to wanderlust accede."

Our hero, noting heat upon his face,
Looked round and said: "A garden like this one,
So bright and thriving in the shining sun,
Is what I'd call a heaven-blessèd place
For minds that can the hand of Nature trace
And know the God by Whom all this was done.
And your home there—how lovely, what a treasure!
O gracious lady! Life must be a pleasure."

"Whose pleasures do not die?" came the reply
The lovely wife then made him, with a stare
That pierced his soul, at which she dropped her eye
And got up from the two swans feeding there.
She asked again, "Whose pleasures do not die?"
And, pondering the fate she had to bear,
She eyed her figure with expression dour
And heaved a sigh: "*Ils sont passés ces jours!*"

In Adam's ear her sighing came to rest,
His mind goes stumbling wild from guess to guess,
But Clara now resumes her firm address
And, as before, she smiles her very best:
"Away with melancholy foolishness!"
Onward to a shady bench she pressed
And, as upon it he beheld her glide,
She motioned Adam to sit by her side.

"My friend," the silence suddenly she broke,
"When I see you assuming that position,
It does those youthful days of mine evoke
When I was privileged with your tuition.
It is as though I saw an apparition
Of the morning when we two first spoke,
I in my chair, a timid simpleton,
Set like a moon to take light from the sun.

"I still can hear you very clearly say
(It was the question you first asked of me),
Where would the Countess venture Sparta lay
And where sagacious Solon's polity?
—O, we went through the world so easily!
How we made peace and joined in every fray!
Like nomads we made visits to Cimmeria
And plucked the golden apples of Hesperia!

"Those were pleasure-filled and lovely days!
I know full well—the shame I feel ne'er ceases—
I then indulged a thousand childish ways
And paid your efforts ill with my caprices.
I often broke your train of thought in pieces
And went from merry into cross displays;
In short, I was obnoxious, and offended
Too often 'gainst the kindness you extended.

"But, trust me, I have also had to pay
For all my folly. First you disappeared,
And for me history long empty lay;
But from another quarter storm clouds reared.
Young into Fate's tourney I was steered,
I buckled under, though I won the day;
But I won't amplify my theme too much—
There are things one must only lightly touch."

A sigh—and she again took up the thread:
"Now I've confessed some part of what's occurred.
It's your turn now! What light have you to shed
On why your very name has gone unheard?
Of all the ways and measures I'd have word
Which life and all its powers have made you tread.
Have you found life a pleasure since we parted?
And, please, I do insist, be open-hearted."

203/

"Oh, Your Grace!" in answer Adam said.
"A student's life has little to reveal!
One lives alone, to all the world he's dead,
While he keeps company with the Ideal."
"Your Fates, though, I would not have you conceal,"
Her Grace immediately commented.
"You always stayed home with your books, alone?"
"Always," he replied with shaky tone.

"You mean you never met," she gave a smile,
"A little god with rosy wreaths for those—"
He broke in here, with reddening profile:
"Oh, Your Grace! Oh, how can you suppose—"
"No charming girl or widow all this while
To aim winged arrows at you from their bows?
You see it causes me no consternation—"
"Oh, Your Grace! Oh, stop from this temptation!"

"No, no, my friend! I'll challenge you no more.
Your answer must no longer be delayed.
But look! Who's coming. . . ?" Clara's chambermaid
Approached and ended the domestic war,
For from her husband a few words she bore.
She rose up from the bench to which they'd strayed.
Once Adam helped to get her shawl back on,
Charmingly she nodded and was gone.

He followed in a dream the lovely sight,
Standing still as if he'd been nailed fast;
But now beyond the terrace she had passed,
And he raised up his eyes to heaven's height.
While the sun dispersed the overcast,
A flash of thought pierced through his heart's dark night;
Off to the house he strode with confidence,
Talking to himself with great good sense.

"Whence comes this power, so silent and so grand,
That still remains in games of love long gone?
We're lured, though we no longer would be drawn;
It is as if again we'd have to hand
The sum of joy and pain the games demand,
The capital of hope we'd built upon.
That old complaint sounds forth from our heart's regions:
'Varus, give me back my fallen legions!' "

—He stopped inside. But outside I remain
With my reader, bathed in the reflection
Falling now upon my portrait's grain,
Which shows my hero in a new projection,
Who, as it seems, is running without rein,
His mind obeying many powers' direction.
How is it that the mind can be so pressed?
That 'gainst his will a man can be obsessed?

Could it lie in other people's might?
For that is, all too glibly, how it's glossed;
Or might, contrariwise, the knot pinch tight
Because a man has by himself been lost?
If he's himself, he's safe and not storm-tossed,
His mental balance keeps the truth in sight;
But when is he himself? Why, that would be
When he gives of himself unstintingly.

But he can give unstintingly alone
When to himself restored unstintedly;
Therefore, himself a man can only be
When in a sympathetic mirror shown.
Then he knows the clear, clean effigy
In which appears the I that is his own;
Then he gives of himself and is restored;
Then he lives life and by that life he's shored.

And as he wins himself upon that cast
And feels himself both doubled and alone,
So his heart feels a quiet unsurpassed,
Relieved of egoism's heavy stone.
All that was obsession's overthrown,
While his devotion rises pure and vast.
Though parted from his glass eventually,
He has himself in constant memory.

Among these souls a number far from small
Are to be found as well—it cannot fail—
Who without mirrors would fall in travail
At thinking they would lose themselves and all
And, like the ship that lost its rudder, sail
Which way the wind blew, with no inner call.
Did Adam fall among these good old chaps?
Hush now! On his door a servant raps.

Lunch was announced. And, down the stairs escorted,
Firm of foot into the room he trod
Where not the lady but her lord resorted.
There by the window, Adam watched him plod
Through papers and newsletters all assorted,
Each opened sheet of them near two feet broad.
Galt did not see our hero, who stayed put
And in amazement did not move one foot.

Indeed the sight was strange, one must allow:
Galt sat as though sharp needles lined his seat;
His cheek was burning, furrowed was his brow,
As he devoured his spiritual meat.
Like lightning through the columns did he plow,
Skipped something—halted—then turned back a sheet,
And with disdain he threw the thing aside
While to the next one eagerly he hied.

To one more he had just said how-d'ye-do
When in the lady came through a side door,
And from his vision all the mist withdrew
Before the breeze from the silk dress she wore.
He woke up, his complexion changing hue:
"Hr. Homo . . . Dear me . . . I was blind before.
Perhaps my wife will show you to your seat,
I'll be right along . . . Sit down and eat!"

So Adam went with Clara out the door.
With all his leaves Hr. Galt was left alone,
But not from any bough had these leaves grown
And for him neither fruit nor blossoms bore.
He new began the scene we have been shown
And from his pile another paper tore;
But only random peeks in it he took,
As to the next he threw an eager look.

What got into him? Ere I explain
The whole course of his life must be outlined.
At Galtenborg, heart of the Dane's domain,
Was Galt born, sound of body and of mind,
And there he grew up, quite without a brain,
Like many of the modern noble kind;
Nothing did his young pride more exalt
Than to be called the youngest noble Galt.

Like other junkers, hunting was his line,
And he could hit a hare upon the hop;
Like other junkers, the o'erflowing stein
He could drink down right to the final drop.
Like other junkers, he lent life a shine,
One monkeyshine that went on without stop;
Like other junkers, he knew German sounds
And spoke the language often with his hounds.

So far, so good; but then our young man wended
To the capital for recreation,
Where through kind friends he got an invitation
To a reading club much recommended.
Here, at long desks o'er which lamps were suspended,
Sat people with and without education,
Reading newspapers with folded hands
In such a hush as but the grave commands.

Then Satan whispered to him: "Galt! Suppose
You had some papers sent to you at home?
How nicely one could waste time on that prose
And on his sofa travel off to Rome.
Behold such cultivated folk as those,
Whose brains, ere they read papers, were like foam:
Behold them, stuffed now, how they rub their hands,
How out both ends of them the stuff expands!"

"Splendid!" said Galt. "If nothing more I got
Than spills, I'd take out my subscriptions straight."
With this intent he left for his estate,
The Tempter having taken the whole pot.
At first those columns struck him as sheer rot,
And reading lay upon him like dead weight;
But like tobacco, which at first's no pleasure,
Eventually he loves it past all measure.

The sickness got still worse; yet more and more
Newspapers did the wretched Galt digest;
What Danish and what German presses bore,
Quarto or folio, he downed all with zest.
So years ran by—all merriment was o'er,
And for a long time he was much depressed.
He darkly rushed past all that might amuse,
And only rested with the newest news.

207/

His friends found all this very much affrighting,
And when at last his doctor shared their dread,
They, at the first occasion, got him wed
To keep this fearful snake of his from biting.
For one year Galt in Hymen's chains was led,
But what is love to journalistic writing?
One stands there with its head so shyly hanging;
The other pushes to the fore, haranguing.

Day after day the latter called his tune;
Three times a day came papers to his seat—
At morning, German, and in the afternoon
And evening, Danish, ere he'd stop to eat.
Sunday brought near every Paris sheet,
With whose leaves he'd hungrily commune
Until to Clara for her curls he'd hand them;
For he, poor fellow, could not understand them.

At every post a fever seemed to seize him,
His whole face stiffened and his cheeks turned red;
Life's whole supply of riches seemed to tease him
Every time his mailbag hasps were spread.
Greedily upon the sheets he fed,
But once he'd fed, an apathy would seize him;
His strength succumbed to shams of novelty,
And in its wake came deathly vacancy.

All of life appeared to him as stinted,
It seemed to him his heart's blood ceased to flow;
He sees no sunshine and no sunset glow,
For, though it may be colored, it's not printed.
Only for fresh papers does he show
Emotion, using curses foully tinted
On the old ones he won't have about.
—Look! He gets up and he throws them out.

Wretched victim of such reading matter!
To the dining room his way he takes,
Where comes a servant with the meal's third platter,
Hart-kidneys and well-larded venison steaks.
Into the saddle a deep cut he makes,
While Adam's peace of mind is like to shatter,
Protecting himself from the lady's charm
Who for some hours had caused him much alarm.

Clad in that silk dress of heavenly blue
Whose pleatings half revealed her swan-white breast;
With bare and snowy arm—but it is best
I here make an apology long due
For making you at Galtenborg sit through
The dashing styles in which the lady dressed.
But from her clothing I can't break away:
In Adam's life it had a role to play.

Well, then, in her silk dress, whose drapery
For dinner-time could not be more judicious
But for another time too awfully free,
Sat Clara prideful and a bit officious,
Giving servants orders repetitious
To fill the glasses of the men; when she,
However, raised her own glass to her lip,
Adam saw Juno in her ladyship.

Involuntarily his eyes took leave
To trace the swell of arm that disappeared
Beneath the tight-laced puffing of her sleeve,
But re-emerged and from her shoulder veered
Down to where her lily breasts did heave.
Between them there a Cupid was upreared
Who called to him: "I'm warning you, forsake me!"
Then whispered: "If you really want me, take me!"

But for a deed so bold, so unashamed,
Our hero was, as we know well, too staid;
He by that beauty might have been inflamed,
But not so much to be a fool self-made.
Moreover, Clara'd raised a barricade:
She sat there cold, and short replies she framed,
With Spanish bearing, strict, nay pious, eye,
As different from that morn as earth from sky.

And so he sat there lost 'twixt fire and ice
As into them dessert the servants bear;
Of it the lady ate the sugar pear,
The gentlemen dividing its device.
Adam took his, and thanked them for his share,
Then read: "You've lost a pear, sir, of great price!"
Galt's read: "Fool, you've nothing to be scared of
Save too much pulp; for then your life's des*peared* of!"

209/

They shrugged at this confectionery wit,
Rose from the board and to the woods went out,
Where Adam's mind the reason tried to scout
For Clara's odd behavior, strangely split.
The change in that short time was infinite!
What, since the morning, caused this turnabout?
Had her whimsies of the past returned?
No, no! Those just that morning she had spurned.

"Extraordinary woman!" went his thought:
"Insisting now on form, strictly pedantic,
Now bold and free, her social class forgot,
And now again so movingly romantic!
With eyes sometimes so dreamy and bacchantic,
And sometimes roguish as a sea foam-shot.
Extraordinary creature! Amazon,
Yet witty, charming, lovely paragon!

"How proud a creature! What fine elegance!
And oh! what eyes, all glittering with light!
At once the picture of a water sprite
And of a Valkyrie at weapon-dance.
Semiramis had that same countenance,
Cleopatra that same power to excite,
And they wove wreaths for Ninon de Lenclos
For that same art of grooming *comme il faut.*

Our hero's life to fancy has been handed
As, in full sail and with a wind propitious,
He steered his course out toward the skerries vicious
On which so many a hero's ship was stranded.
He knew his feelings were most injudicious,
For Alma still his deepest mind commanded.
He just forgot what's plain enough to see,
Namely, that the types of love are three.

The first type has its life within the mind;
Upon the best blood of the heart it's fed,
Itself the sole protector it need find,
For, shy as children, it's heroic-bred.
Deep in fidelity its roots are twined,
But like a plant, when moved to a strange bed,
It dies bemoaning lost fidelity,
For in one earth it lives exclusively.

210/

The second type has fancy for its dame,
And only when it dreams does it feel free;
It likes to think its objects artistry
And sees to it they have a golden frame.
Fine ladies it as angels can proclaim,
Low prose as the sublimest poesy,
But if it's to make good on its vagaries
The world must aid it with auxiliaries.

Name, birth, position, honor, wealth, and class,
Praise and publicity are its reward
And always it looks out through colored glass
To feed emotion at illusion's board.
But much strength can this kind of love amass:
It does see whole the object that's adored,
Although, it's true, to splinters oft it smashes
And down into the final, third type crashes.

For number three, of senses born, is bred
On utter whimsy, lacking consequence;
It is a love composed of shred on shred
The heart has woven from the brain's nonsense.
An eye o'er which a few dark hairs are spread,
A waist of just the right circumference,
A skirt, a leg, a bosom, finger, arm,
A garter belt's ev'n counted as a charm.

It thrives, we know, especially at balls:
Gents take to table ladies they've selected,
Buried with loud laughter in their shawls
And only for cotillions resurrected.
With it the first type is as close connected
As kernels with the shells that form their walls;
A nut should lie within the shell that cased it,
But you can't smell it there—all right, then, taste it!

Our hero found out all three types to taste
As off at Galtenborg he chose to laze
Not two or three, but for a good eight days,
Though often wishing he might leave posthaste.
The thing was, his intentions were effaced
Whenever Clara whispered: "Go your ways?
So soon, my friend?—For my sake, one more day!"
And Adam thought: "For *your* sake, yes, I'll stay."

But once to his own solitude consigned,
His weakness and his promise made him smart;
He pictured his beloved in his mind
And oh! what tenderness suffused his heart.
A new determination then would start,
But then, half grown, it halted and declined.
Once more he suffered in uncertainty;
But next day he would leave, assuredly!

He swore an oath to shore up his intent;
At breakfast he announces it aloud
And, holding to it, keeps his head unbowed,
Although the lady stares in wonderment.
She quickly says, on finding him uncowed:
"You know best how your time is to be spent;
But as it's not today that you remove,
Let's go out riding, that's if you approve."

How glad he was to give his grateful vote
And lose the need for acting somber-faced!
He sought his chamber, where a redingote
He buttoned tightly round his slender waist.
Downstairs, an ostler in a stable coat
A supple reed whip in his fingers placed
And buckled heavy spurs to either heel,
Which rang out sharply with the voice of steel.

He walked round, savoring his victory;
But when he most feels freedom's mightiness,
The door swings in—and in her riding-dress,
Whose long train sweeps behind her billowy,
And toque from which a black plume flutters free,
And hair arranged into a double tress,
And with a little riding crop in hand,
The lady comes, in absolute command.

Our hero by that lovely sight was caught;
His blood ran alternately hot and cold;
With hat in hand he stammered out a thought,
Then ran to give her surer stirrup-hold.
She mounted, boldly pulling the reins taut,
So that her bay horse neighed and reared up bold.
Adam followed suit—away they race,
The groom behind, a smile upon his face.

It was a cloudless day; the winds were kind;
So warm did that September sunshine smile
That its bright beams almost turned Adam blind,
Who had not been on horseback a long while.
He let his vision roam round unconfined—
This was indeed an outing in high style!
He felt himself so light, so free of sorrow,
And he was free—he would be off tomorrow.

"Where shall we ride?" the question's sudden set
By Clara, in her saddle turned about.
"Close to the shore this forest path gives out,
But you've not seen the ancient castle yet,
And there's an owl up there you have not met
Who's made the castle tower his redoubt."
"And who might that be?" Adam interposes.
"The Kammerherre's uncle," she discloses.

"When he was young, he was uproarious,
And, rich as Croesus, flew off far and wide
Till, with wings clipped and by his age sore-tried,
He came back home here like a Lazarus.
A *philosophe* he calls himself to us;
Freethinker is the name the priest applied,
An atheist, to hear the parish clerk,
But as Gray Galt he's known around the park."

"Gray Galt?" he queried. Clara's laughter rang
As once more boldly out ahead she shot,
So that his many questions had to hang.
Now toward the woods they rode off at a trot,
Now through the greenery the hooves did clang
And only stopped when to the shore they'd got.
They spied the castle towers and walls of red,
Down whose pointed gables deep cracks spread.

At the tower's foot they stopped before
They made their way along the winding stair.
Clara, at the top, rapped on the door,
Which from the inside opened to the pair.
A man with large ears they saw standing there,
With large gray eyes that hosts of sparkles bore,
With thin and wizened mouth and pointed nose,
And gray from head to foot were all his clothes.

213/

"Aha!" he piped out, very like a rat.
"Aha, *ma belle cousine*—well met, well met!"
Into a tower chamber they were let,
Arched it was and rounded like a vat.
The only carpet was a horrid mat;
Around a table large armchairs were set;
In niches in the walls huge tomes they spied,
And windows opened out on every side.

Our hero was presented, and they sat.
"You see now, Uncle," Clara would begin,
"That I, despite your multifarious sin,
Haven't slapped your hand for all of that.
I've rushed to bring a friend here for a chat,
A friend who'll soon be lost" (sigh of chagrin)
"If you, dear Uncle, know not how to sway
The Fate severe that would take him away."

"The Fate severe!" piped up the little man,
Flinging himself backward in his chair:
"Fate always seems too much for you to bear.
Shame on you! Show some wisdom if you can.
To use a phrase like that you really dare?
You, so clever, hatching plan on plan,
You often seem to play the role of Fate—"
"Hush!" Clara threatened him. "Don't fulminate!"

"No fulmination! Sweet as pie, *cousine*!
And you, dear sir!" (Now, as his talk took fire,
He reached out with his hand, refined and lean.)
"I trust you too believe in Fate's empire?"
"No," Adam answered, with excited mien,
"My heart tells me that there is something higher;
That Fate, which once did me great violence,
At last has changed into a Providence."

"Good!" Galt smiled ironically. "Quite good!
By your belief you'll certainly reap glory;
You should wear heaven's azure, yes, you should.
But, niece, you are of Fate so laudatory
Royal purple would suit you, it really would.
My clothing, as you see, is gray and hoary,
My faith is colorless, but anchored right,
And lies precisely between black and white."

The argument grew warm; for Clara fought
Upon the side of Fate with words and eyes,
And, although Adam may have trimmed a jot,
On Providence he would not compromise.
Gray Galt just let the smoke of battle rise;
He knit together broken threads of thought,
Giving both his spiritual subvention.
But suddenly he claps for their attention.

"Lay down your weapon, lovely amazon!
Give ear, dear sir! Give ear to an old man
Who with a zeal that crowns are founded on
In search of Fate through many countries ran,
Who sought world over Providence's plan,
And from these tower walls did long time con
The landscape, and with glasses of some weight,
But could see neither Providence nor Fate.

"Just one thing did I see; but, all the worse,
It was, like me, a form in a gray pall;
For, young sir, though it's to your faith adverse,
Accident's the ruler over all!
Accident, which Happenstance some call,
Which to a system some folks may coerce,
But always will escape and walk abroad
And take its throne again like any god."

A low bow from the speaker closed this blast.
A chest below the table he unlocked.
To each of them a drinking cup he passed,
And well-aged Cyprus wine that he had stocked
He poured; and as they saw the wine decoct,
So clear and of a lovely ruby cast,
Excitedly he nods to both his guests,
Then raises up his own glass and protests:

"To Accident! Which in a skipper's shape
This summer carried to me this delight.
Though born among Greek boulders was the grape,
'Twas buried in my Danish cellar's night.
Drink up, young man! Drink ere the spirit 'scape!
Providence is nothing to its might;
It grips the heart, cajoles us to acknowledgment,
And bashes us a good one, just like Accident.

"And you, my pretty niece, so bright and pink!
Forget opinions so long over-crusted
That now they can't be busted or adjusted,
And come on, with your agèd uncle clink!
We'll see Fate drowned now in this very drink,
And to *your* will alone we'll be entrusted.
For once I drain the life out of that crone,
We'll place you in Fate's stead upon the throne."

"Then I'm supposed to stand for Accident,"
Came Clara's answer while the old man drank.
"No, my dear Uncle, you I will not thank!
To robes of gray I never would consent
Nor would I borrow your habiliment.
You yourself must take that noble rank,
For I have no more time to bide with you!"
"And I," our hero adds, "will ride with you."

Their visit's brevity made Galt's head hang.
He hoped next time they'd make a longer stay,
Whereon down to the gate he led the way,
And up onto their saddles they both sprang.
Clara tugged the reins upon her bay,
And off they rode through woods where wild birds sang.
Gray Galt returned up to his tower haunt,
Where he still bade them both, "Enjoy your jaunt!"

But this the young pair hardly could have heard,
For they were in the forest's leafy swell
Wherein the tops of beeches softly stirred
As through the mottled leaves the sunbeams fell
And sight and sense came 'neath the deep shades' spell.
In that quiet neither said a word;
They simply kept up with each other's pace
While, back of them, their groom left goodly space.

Our hero, though, was feeling very strange;
The potent wine was whirling in his head,
Its spirit working on his mind, which spread
By wondrous leaps across a startling range.
He thought he saw past into present change
And, in his fancy, almost thought he read
The granting of old wishes out of hand,
Like riding with his Clara on his land.

Suddenly his horse neighed—disappeared
Were land and dream, and he looked up awake.
His eyes met Clara's, and in them ensphered
He thought he could discern a lurking ache.
He half-turned round, not knowing what to make
Of this strange look of hers, and volunteered,
Desirous to discover how they stood:
"Your Grace spoke not a word all through the wood."

"Oh," she replied, and swept aside the hair
That had come down upon her cheek and brow:
"That silence comes when fall is in the air
And visits me in woods and groves, as now.
Look at these trees! At that tall beech's bough!
The crown of beauty it's been proud to wear
Will crumble down to wizened leaves and must—
What once had been a hope is soon but dust.

"Nature mocks at hope. The sounds of fall
Oft to me a tale of gloom devise.
But you, my friend, will not my hope despise,
Won't cast upon my happiness a pall."
And, as she spoke, out to him her hand flies:
"Don't go! Stay till the month is out, that's all!"
But Adam shook his head from side to side,
Although his heart already had complied.

No sooner had she seen him shake his head
Than angrily she bit down on her lip,
Then took hold of the reins she had let slip
And at the canter down the road she fled.
But Adam's spurs gave his horse too a nip:
He clearly saw the way that duty led—
He must not leave the lady in distress,
To her request his answer must be yes.

He rode on at a brisk pace—but in vain!
Into a gallop did the fair one shift,
And rising sylphlike to the saddle's lift,
Lithe and lovely was she at the rein.
Our hero, who must now be still more swift,
Gallops too, if ever he's to gain.
But Clara, to perfect her cavalier,
Bursts of a sudden into full career.

217/

"Ha!" Adam smiles. "She wants to break a lance!"
And off he dashes too in full career
As round his ears the dust and earth clumps dance
And only the wind's whipping can he hear.
"Beyond the gate she cannot well advance,
For it is closed, or so it would appear;
And vaulting that high rail she'd never dare—
Why, in one leap she's done it, I declare!"

He'd vault it, too! His honor had been pricked.
And though a voice might whisper: "Do not do it!"
With an arrow's speed he went right to it.
Then, as with his tongue his lips he licked,
His cheek turned ashen and his visage strict;
He crouched down low, determined not to rue it.
Only daring lands you in the clover—
One crack of the whip—the horse jumps over!

It jumps—but all at once the rider reins
The animal with such a violent force
That, suddenly arrested in its course,
It crashes to the ground for all his pains.
The full brunt of the fall Adam sustains,
For on him drops the body of the horse;
And hardly does he feel his right arm crack
When everything around him goes pitch black.

He lay there in a faint—an hour went by
Before, with greatest effort, he unwound
Dark swaddling in which he thought he'd been gowned,
And, fully conscious, up he cast his eye;
Above him Clara bent without a sound
There by the couch on which they'd had him lie;
Upon her cheek a glistening tear shone plain
Just as a doctor opened up a vein.

With finger to her mouth she moved away
And sent a look that he could not mistake,
While the doctor bandaged up the break.
But, as our fevered hero's forced to stay
Quite still, lest he an even worse wound take,
We will, my reader, who until this day
Have come to know him mostly through his heart,
From that heart and for his head depart.

For though there is a portion they both share
And each says it's a kingdom of its own,
There really is a fellowship, oft shown
To rouse them into working as a pair.
For in the brain the thoughts are often sown
That keep the steps of passion from a snare;
Or else, the heart may render feeling hot
Enough to hone the stinger of a thought.

Why, this alliance can be so complete
That each allows the other in its space,
And, where one thinks he hears his heart to beat,
It is his head he hears, judging the case;
And, likewise, marks emotion run apace
And loud, where logic he had thought to meet
And sober thinking had been credited—
Well, that's why we must plumb the hero's head!

He had too bright a head that such a blow
As had come down with fearful force on him
Should not have caused the many fogs to go
Which hitherto had kept his vision dim.
And since he must lie sick this interim,
While honest thinking has the time to grow,
And since he has been born to meditate,
He must well ponder on his present state.

What by his tumble Providence designed,
Which brought his travel plans to ruination,
Was the great theme that absorbed his mind
In very near continuous variation.
Providence—which always had been kind—
Did not direct without premeditation.
His broken arm some higher purpose bore;
What purpose, though?—But he could think no more.

—And then one morning a dream vision sent
Old Gray Galt's face to hang before his eyes,
When clear and quick as lightning in the skies
Forth burst the concept of sheer Accident
Upon his brain, complete and eloquent.
Just as he awakens with surprise,
He whispers, "Gray Galt cannot be gainsaid;
It's Accident that put me in this bed."

In thought, back to the past he then referred
As his Belt passage came at once to mind
(The first occasion for what since occurred),
Causing him discomfort undefined.
"What!" he exclaimed. "And have I then been blind?
Accident to me was just a word!
That I met Clara accidentally
Alone explains my present state to me."

He now was in full swing. The past's long chain
He link by link traversed in utmost haste,
And in his soul a great awe was emplaced.
Life, as without swaddling, was made plain,
As the true cause of things stood forth bold-faced
Which once had crept round hidden in Fate's skein:
Accident befell him everywhere;
With every step he took pure Chance was there.

Was it not Chance to which his thanks were due
For having met with Trine, fair and black;
Not Chance that by his throat he'd been held back
When he was seeking in the billows blue
That ran 'neath Langebro for Charon's smack?
Was it not Chance, then, which he ran into
That evening when the Tempter did entice,
When he led Lotte out upon thin ice?

Remarkable! A new means to make sense
Of all the mysteries of life was here;
And it seemed particularly queer
That it should tally with experience.
But this is naught but sheer coincidence!
For he has seen a Providence full near,
He's long been harbored within Christendom.
How to Nemesis can he succumb?

No sooner, though, was this decision out
Than with his broken arm his eye connected,
And once again appeared the imp of doubt.
However much his mind might have objected,
The might of Accident must be respected.
He saw himself a ball Chance kicked about,
Into whose somber game his eye now read
And for whose lawlessness his heart felt dread.

For if capricious power can order all,
How is it possible to think one's free?
And when a person loses liberty
The edifice of faith must also fall,
On which depends as well life's constancy.
Oh, but the hope and comfort's much more small
In that shifty power whose game he's learnt
Than in the Fate by which he once was burnt!

He felt his source of comfort had been drained.
He lay uneasy, underneath his sheet,
And all day long with no rest could he meet,
And all that week his restlessness remained.
Accident, sole thought he entertained,
Fought his Christian faith with so much heat
And put his brains into so fast a spin
That soon he knew no longer out from in.

He cursed Gray Galt—and yet it might just be
That doubts he raised he could as well allay!
With this thought in his mind, he's cheered one day
When old Galt came to keep him company.
He pressed the hand extended amiably,
Admitting he was in a fearful way,
And as he opened up his sack of doubt,
His faith in a confession he poured out.

Gray Galt smiled a merry smile and sniffed
A pinch of snuff, and stretched out in a chair,
Listening very briefly to his drift
Before he burst out: "Now, that's logic rare!
To Accident you seem to give short shrift,
But its existence you find hard to bear;
You welcome golden freedom eagerly,
But want to slave in Christianity!

"I feel that if there's going to be a feast,
It ought to be all-out—no paltering!
We can't from sense and instinct be released;
We must admit we don't know anything
More about such things than does a beast.
My faith thus has one hot and one cold spring:
In outward things pure Epicureanism,
In inward things decided skepticism.

"It's Epicurus whom I emulate,
And him I thank for having been converted
From empty dreams to Nature's healthy state.
It was by his help I was first alerted
To Chance, whose force on all things is exerted
And which lies everywhere, as if in wait;
It is the bull in all our china shops,
It comes to knock out all our underprops.

"I grasped the doctrine of felicity
When I first understood that hedonist
Who differences 'twixt beasts and men dismissed,
Who from vain fears of death has set us free,
Who from our doorsteps drives hypocrisy
And finds life's goal in doing as we list,
Commanding: 'Take your joys and so employ them
That ever afterwards you can enjoy them.'

"But, though revering him, as I have said,
For all of that it still is my position
There must be skepticism in addition
If he's to get our hearts well quieted;
While sense and instincts, all without omission,
Are 'neath the Epicurean scepter spread,
On the transcendental Pyrrho founded
A realm which by nor time nor space is bounded.

"And when he orders us: Doubt everything!
I too have done my utmost to adhere
To this great doctrine in the moral sphere,
What zeros for deportment this might bring,
For with them I make whole worlds disappear;
Down into Nothing freedom's chains I fling,
Conscience is devoured in Nothing's trap
And, filled with just myself, I fill the gap.

"And that's my faith *in nuce*, my dear friend!
And never think I ever doubt these rules
Because a half a score of half-read fools
Say they're but outworn rules none now defend.
Where are these miracles from Sunday schools
That teach another world at this one's end?
When they slice men in half as well as life
And cut the choicest piece off with their knife?"

The old man stopped, while Adam sought support
For his beliefs and Christianity;
But little Galt made Adam's words his sport
And treated every new proof mockingly.
"You preach as if there were no contrary;
But, since you give the faith such good report,
Let's take a true believer thoroughbred
And see how he conforms to what you've said.

"Our Christian is a sinner—that we know.
With good intentions out of bed he pops,
But before evening these good works he drops,
On which account his head hangs very low.
He clambers up again; and down he flops
Again at virtue, same as his last go,
And just as then he's heartsick at reneging;
But, as time passes, this life gets fatiguing.

"Our Christian cares not for the shams of flesh,
His mind is fixed on Heaven, so he'll say;
But put him face to face with life that's fresh
And sensuous, and see which he'll obey.
That's when he sees his heaven straightaway,
Beside that earth he once found in sin's mesh,
Lose its color like the pallid moon
That in the gay light of the sun must swoon.

"Our Christian sometimes falls in ecstasy,
Imagining he shall become new-born;
We see him hold his very flesh in scorn
And flee himself as from an enemy;
But follow him in his new liberty,
You'll see Old Adam, all his fears forsworn,
Up to his old tricks—with his Oremus
Thus reborn *justement* like Nicodemus.

"Our Christian knows that death comes to his aid!
That, as in triumph, angels take him in;
But why does death, then, leave him so dismayed,
As if he'd bit the sour apple's skin?
So that he'd rather see his life decayed
Through many years of suffering and sin,
So that he'd kiss the rod in but a trice
If it would drive him home from Paradise.

223/

"Our Christian—oh, but you yourself complete
This silly, pitiable counterfeit.
My hand will have no more to do with it;
Besides, it's time that I were on my feet."
He leapt up, saying: "May I just submit
My judgment on this chap? It's short and sweet.
I do declare a sinner of this class
A cross between a hypocrite and ass."

He pitched out of the door he'd burst in by,
And home directly to his tower sped,
While thoughts filled Adam's overheated head:
"Did he mean me? Was this bad Christian I?
Was I attacked?" He was discomfited.
But that description just did not apply;
And why by Gray Galt should he be attacked?
No doubt he meant it all in the abstract.

One thing is sure, whatever else may be,
With all his other sins he'd ne'er amass
An ugly burden of hypocrisy.
With that his heavy mood began to pass;
It won't be he that people call an ass,
For at first glance he can see instantly
His mind once had a hole of ignorance
Which can be darned but by the idea of Chance.

But from his faith he will not therefore veer!
He still maintains that there's a Providence,
Though to him the connection's not quite clear
'Twixt it and Chance's busy influence.
He is secure in this one inference,
That if a Providence won't interfere
With Accident's encroachments—patently
It shrinks each man's responsibility.

This was the major outcome, roughly stated,
Produced by what was thought about and said,
As well as by the long time spent in bed
While very slowly he recuperated.
For two whole months our hero was prostrated,
And that long time a close acquaintance bred
With Clara, who looked after him each day,
And with Gray Galt, who often made a stay.

One grim November morn—his arm had knitted—
He stood before a mirror, finally,
And shaved, as sad at leaving as could be,
For now no new delay could be permitted.
Duty urges Galtenborg be quitted
And he has not the heart to disagree.
In the town he'll hire a coach and hack
And on the house next morning turn his back.

He packs his articles in his valise,
But on the top he lays black formal clothes,
For in the evening he's to dress in these
When out into the wider world he goes
To mix with gentry in festivities
For the Prince who's touring their chateaux;
And, with this Prince now haunting all his thoughts,
Over to the nearby town he trots.

About the coach he soon reached an accord,
And by a longing for the forest drawn
That at the far horizon darkly soared,
Along the meadow path he hurries on.
To his soft heart it seemed hard to be gone,
Leaving all those places he'd explored
And which he'd never more, assuredly,
Get to see in Clara's company.

At the forest edge he deeply sighed:
"It was here—at this same gate, all right—
That at the fair one's feet I lost my sight,
And this is where she must have stood and cried
Her quiet tears upon me in my plight
When I was carried off still stupefied.
Why must near-fatal weakness be sustained
In order that such precious pearls be gained?

"This sacrifice is costly," he went on,
"Which to you, Alma, your beloved brings,
To tear himself from such a place anon,
Where loveliness and splendor lend life wings;
A sob of pain sounds through this orison
To which the heart adds melancholy strings,
But willingly my offering I give,
For I shall keep my vow long as I live."

He walked on, moved by words so eloquent,
And solitary roved the woodland park
Till, with his mind made up, when all was dark,
As from victorious battle home he went.
There he was greeted by the dog's fierce bark;
Five landaus were drawn up, magnificent;
And servants up and down the stairs were streaming,
While from the vestibule bright light came beaming.

"Well," he thought, "there is no time to spare!"
He rushed upstairs and quickly changed his clothes;
But when, pale, stiff, and all in black, he goes
Back down the splendid staircase at a tear,
Heart pounding at what might await him there,
A letter just arrived his progress slows.
He saw his name there, in his father's hand,
And, once he'd broke the seal, the letter scanned.

His father wrote about his own condition,
But, since he said that he was right as rain,
He dwelt on Adam's late indisposition,
Which Galt had kindly written to explain.
In jest he chid him, in paternal vein,
For crashing through the gates of a patrician;
And with great earnestness he was exhorted
To use the access which no more was thwarted.

"Just make sure," he wrote, "that you don't catch
The thread that linked you to bright destiny;
No, this fair occasion you must snatch
So that your fall can lead to victory.
To Galt *jus proponendi* does attach
And he's obliged for life to his grantee;
Therefore, hang in, don't lose the man before
He shows you to a living *and* his door!"

Adam found this utterly appalling;
At such a project he turned up his nose,
That *here* he should pursue his priestly calling.
Clara seeing him in priestly clothes!
He blushed just at the thought, it was too galling.
But meanwhile what was he to do? Oppose
His father's wishes, see his journey through?
Who was there to advise him here?—Yes, who?

Still pondering, he opened the hall door,
And now he joined the splendid celebration
Where lights and mirrors polished conversation.
Some stood in groups, some couples walked the floor:
Barons, courtiers, generals of the nation,
Royal foresters, counts, junkers by the score
Exchanging every last civility—
But Adam thought: "They're all nobility!"

Slowly he slipped in, with blushing cheek,
To where the ladies perched in velvet dresses
Like noble birds together on one peak,
Countesses, church ladies, baronesses,
While round Their Graces stood a little clique
Of twenty maidens, all with well-curled tresses;
But suddenly their little circle stirred
As in the courtyard carriages were heard.

Our hero stumbled backward to a chair,
For with uncustomary energy,
In uniform, and with official key,
Kammerherre Galt passed at a tear,
His wife behind, a sun in radiancy,
Who wore a jeweled tiara in her hair.
This lovely sight he'd hardly seized upon
Before, just like a shooting star, 'twas gone.

He'd lost it at the farthermost hall door;
But instantly both doors were opened wide
And, like a glorious comet, tail and core,
There came that shooting star in all its pride.
The noble Prince appeared at Clara's side,
Behind them officers with braid galore,
Who formed the long tail to the comet's head
And dazzled in their uniforms of red.

The comet slowly moved in from the door;
And both the Prince, be-ribboned and be-starred,
And Countess Clara formed the comet's core
For Adam, who was staring at them hard.
The thoughts within his brain had been so jarred
He was transported to the Olympian tor
And saw the forms of Venus and of Mars
As all the others made them their devoirs.

Great gentlemen and ladies form a row;
His Highness walks around, and he's top-hole;
His every word entrances, makes them glow;
His every smile wins to himself a soul;
For princes, they are magnets, by whose flow
Of force electric we found life's top pole
And which, moreover, loosen from their threads
The screws that hold on men's and women's heads.

A screw came loose inside our hero's head:
He saw an opening and got in place,
But when His Highness wished to know the race
And family in which the lad was bred,
He gave this answer with a trusting face:
"The race of Homo!" To which the Prince said:
"I don't know that line. Is it from Holland?"
"No," he stammered. "Our stock comes from Lolland!"

With that the audience was at an end;
The Prince was pleased to leave this last transaction
And, freed of his magnetical attraction,
Adam to a window niche did wend.
From there to this unique dramatic action
He could in all its poetry attend,
By which he was transfixed against his wall
Until the Prince was through with protocol.

In all the rooms high spirits had revived,
And Adam thought: "It's high time that I hurled
Myself still harder into this great world!
The soul from which this grandeur has derived,
By which its power has far and wide been furled,
I'd learn the secret by which it has thrived!"
With that he mustered all his self-possession
To keep him from the shame of indiscretion.

He took the measure of the things he knew:
The benefits from his examination
And what his life had taught him hitherto,
Artistic, scientific information,
He gave them all their proper valuation;
And *then* he sought, well-armed, his rendezvous.
At the doorframe, which the fat Count hoards,
He wanders up against the great world's lords.

228/

His ears catch Hector mentioned by these men.
He thinks, this will be Homer, without fail;
But no! the talk here is of Hector's tail,
Of Hector tracking down some poor grouse hen,
And added thereto, many a "Blow me pale!"
And other phrases quite beyond his ken;
For they're discussing hunting grouse and duck,
Of which he doesn't know a thing, worse luck.

Off in the distance he heard Moses' name,
To charm an ear trained by the orthodox;
He gathers little bits as each one talks,
But for the prophet's sake turns red for shame.
They argued Moses' legs and Moses' socks,
About the blood that Moses' veins could claim,
And finally—the reason this was done—
The coming race that Moses was to run.

This time his knowledge also was confounded!
But he's well-pleased to leave it unadvanced
When music, ever graspable, entranced
Him to the neighboring room from which it sounded.
Into the chandelier-lit room he bounded
Where leaping officers and ladies danced;
The flute made merry with the fiddle's tunes,
And joy was in the wind of the bassoons.

He found a corner and stood staring there,
His ears enchanted and his sense of sight
Lost in the youthful noblemen's delight.
Then Clara, with her jewels in her hair,
The Prince's waltzing-partner for that night,
Rushed past him, light and velvet on the air.
No! Nothing so miraculously high,
So mystically lovely, had passed by!

A princess—Princess? No, a goddess clear!
And even "goddess" gave faint indication
Of the creature causing this sensation
Which made his common sense quite disappear,
Made him reject all rational explanation
For her ignoring that he still was here.
One does not find a goddess so unkind—
And yet how well he understood her mind!

He'd join the dancing! Over there a small
But utterly distinguished lady sat;
For she has kept her distance from them all
With her expression—and with more than that.
She'd sat alone there, quiet as a cat,
But when he'd asked her, at the polka-call,
She smiled politely and without ado
She joined him in the polka, and they flew.

Here his luck at last cooperated:
He changed her with a court magnifico,
And he and Clara did a *dos-à-dos*
(The Prince's role, then, could be delegated).
Upon the lady's name he speculated
When, just then, came the Countess Bärenklo
While they still danced together, just to glance in:
"You dance quite prettily, good Mamselle Jansen."

"What's this? A Mamselle Jansen!" Adam thought.
"Then this is nothing but a governess."
And all the luster vanished on the spot.
That she is somewhat common in address
He plainly sees. For at the band's recess
She curtseys thanks ere to her seat she's brought.
That bird he let fly; no more content
With music, to a side room Adam went.

There they'd just risen from the gaming board,
Church ladies, generals, keepers of great seals,
Who, with a Kammerjunker at their heels,
Left Adam all alone and quite ignored.
There at the table where they'd talked of deals
Alone, of trumps, of losses they had scored,
He gathered up the cards they'd left outspread,
And, lost in thinking, to himself he said:

"There still are many things I must be learning!
Just when I must set forth, I come in here
Into life's higher and much grander sphere.
What wonder is it that my mind is churning?
I see what I was born not to come near,
A life round which a golden glow is burning;
I see a race whose luck smooths all their ways,
All Christians, who give Epicurus praise.

230/

"What shall I do? A hard choice with no guide!
If I go home, what will my father say?
And when will I be off if I should stay?
Well," he exclaimed, "I'll just let Chance decide!
I'll pick a card. If black should come my way,
Then, with no more ado, for home I'll ride."
He mixed the cards and cut them with some dread,
Then stood as if struck dumb—the card was red!

He had no time for further meditation;
For through the room swept ladies from the ball,
And he saw (turning round to face the hall)
The Prince, with Clara, go to the collation.
Though couples followed, he just watched them all,
Still considering his situation.
There was one person left, an old Miss Thott,
So in to dinner it was she he brought.

As last man, he was given the last chair,
Far from that Paradise as he could be
Where Clara reigned between the silverware
And His Monopolist Serenity.
The table lamp shone with the sun's own glare;
The guests spoke German, laughed, smirked mincingly;
Their manners were refined and animated.
So this is life among the celebrated!

Their tone he thought he had already caught
And to his lady this remark directed:
Could the gentlewoman be connected
With Denmark's much admired Hr. Otto Thott?
She, with a look or two, Adam inspected
And answered: "Yes, and more than that, I wot!
But here, amongst the kingdom's patriots,
You see the last of all the ancient Thotts."

With that her fingers fumbled in her hair,
Till proudly she resumed her omelet;
But every look and every last lorgnette
Turned on him, who, confused by the affair,
Beet-red, upon his plate could only stare
And squeeze hard as he could his serviette.
He strained to hear the whisper growing wider:
"And is that the unlucky horseback-rider?"

231/

"It's me!" he thought as the full horror hit;
And then he thought: "Now I am prostituted!
In front of the great world I've been polluted
Just when I've been introduced to it!"
He held on with the toughness requisite,
But now the table's joys no longer suited;
Not till, with noise, they rose from their repast
Did his heart cease from pounding very fast.

And that was that. But not in Adam's case.
Once again held back by circumstance,
When now at liberty to leave the place,
Accident again must lead his dance.
Each invitation of Galt's issuance
He could not well refuse with any grace.
The season had begun, and round the land
All sorts of noble gatherings were planned.

From manor house to manor house he went.
Three months he drove about as in a ring,
The guest of counts and barons, trafficking
Among the great for several miles' extent.
Clara brought him to each revelment;
A protégé of hers, from Not a Thing
He rose in many eyes to be Someone,
And soon his life was sparkling in their sun.

He learned the great art now of pleasure-taking,
Although for him this new art was confined
To chasing off reflection and forsaking
Memories which lay deep in his mind
And putting off a future full of aching,
To all things but the present moment blind.
Indeed, he made especially his own
The negative side of that art alone.

Did he forget his Alma? In no way!
At the escritoire he'd often sit
And write her of his doings day by day
And of the reasons she could trust to it
That his emotions had not changed one whit.
But in the middle down his pen he'd lay,
Exclaiming to himself: "No, no, not me!
I can't be guilty of hypocrisy!"

The name of hypocrite stuck in his throat,
And that name, leagued of course with Chance,
Had been the reason that he never wrote;
As for his journey's discontinuance,
No matter what the plans he might advance,
Hypocrisy and Chance cast final vote:
By this he was to Galtenborg secured;
By that all his professions were abjured.

Thus, gradually, the dream became corroded
In which for so long now he had existed:
The dream which, if by feeling unassisted,
Finds its seeds deep in the mind exploded.
He's now by his imagination goaded;
It keeps his soul perpetually misted,
Save that, from day to day, came an intrusion
Of seven-colored rainbows of Illusion.

Always to the soul a veil first cleaves
On which external life projects its shows
When, like the colored bow that Iris weaves,
On a mind Illusion would impose.
A veil like this a tender soul receives
The moment when into this world it goes;
And, let that veil of mist upon it swoop,
At once it's turned into Illusion's dupe.

For at the moment when life bursts the sheath
Of mist about the soul in its full light,
The shining changes to a colored wreath
That widens and extends before the sight.
And on it hangs a babe ere it's cut teeth;
Up to it looks a boy, his eyes all bright;
As for a girl, it melts that heart of hers
Which soon finds heroes in mere officers.

By that shining we're caught in a spell
And see ourselves as great in others' eyes;
With that shining our heads often swell,
We think we're Dalai Lamas in disguise;
In that shining all our greatness lies,
Let it vanish and we're Pulcinell';
Not just in others' eyes do we sink deep,
But, gone that shining, hold our own selves cheap.

To serve that shining how the tailor sews,
For without it we're but *sans-culottes*;
By that shining we know men by clothes,
Know which kettle's blacker than which pot;
In that shining often steps a sot
To play the hero to enrapt back rows.
Put briefly: in that shining flares a sun
That warms us not, but blinds us every one.

Once the dream-life of the heart enlists
This fancied life, not all remains veneer:
Some part, with time, grows strong; in form comes clear;
And, gone the shows, that residue persists.
For all these borrowed splendors disappear,
And torn at last the soul's old veil of mists;
But when it bursts, worn thin by time that's passed,
We hold on to the tatters to the last.

In vain! They flutter one by one away;
Light mists, with mournful noises they are blown,
And one by one have life's illusions flown
With them, far off to regions of decay.
Clear, cold, and bare, a life dried out and gray
Stalks through their ruins to assume its throne.
And if one found that satisfactory,
The soul would be forced into bankruptcy!

It matters whether out of secret dreams
It's built itself an ocean-worthy ark
To sail like Noah, safe within its beams,
When the illusions of the world go dark.
It matters that, amid the rapid streams,
It nears the Ararat which was its mark,
Where flies the dove, the olive leaf retrieved,
And life's reborn, washed clean, and so reprieved.

—But to our hero in Illusion's maze!
Christmas passed and Shrovetide was quite near,
When over Adam's heretofore bright days
On Clara's side the weather turned from clear.
She seemed to go back to her moody ways
With sarcasms directed to his ear,
All the time commingling sour and sweet,
One moment cold, the next one full of heat.

234/

What was the reason? Were her nerves distraught?
Was it the effect of winter's cold?
Had her passions grown so blazing hot
They burnt the love her deep heart used to hold?
Had her feelings now been all forgot?
But nowhere could he find the answer told!
Quite understandable! Where's bottom found
When art upon sheer instinct runs aground?

How he put Clara's patience in a pet!
The lovely fruit just hung before her eyes.
She did so yearn to bite into that prize
For, in her desert, she'd not been filled yet;
And, since the fruit had not dropped in her net,
Up to the bough she'd naturally rise:
She shook it and she rocked it and she fiddled,
And by her Adam's wits were sorely diddled.

But how these tricks into his soul had bit
Can only be experienced, not related.
To bloody deeds he was by pain oft baited;
For with his rifle to the woods he lit,
And, while he was by thorn shrubs lacerated,
Many rabbit hearts did Adam split.
From day to day he grew a better shot,
But never learned to hit the lady's thought.

The balance it had taken all his might
To keep could now no longer persevere:
Clara's voice alone rang in his ear
And she absorbed his eyes both day and night.
His mind was soaking in her atmosphere,
Her image made him soar to height on height,
Until he heard his former passion call
And back into its open gulf did fall.

He lay there till again he was lent wings
Thanks to an important accident
Which to an issue brought his sufferings.
One evening, as he roamed about, intent
On sorting out his own predicament,
He found the forest after many swings;
And there a while he wandered all about
Till on the shore he finally came out.

2357

On the ancient castle moonbeams played.
Through Gray Galt's windows he saw lamplight pouring
Down on the scrub along the palisade
'Gainst which the coastline's breaking waves were roaring.
He stood a while, watching the waves cascade,
Then to the tower sent his eyes exploring:
"Yes," he says, "he'll know just what to say!
Things can't go on like this day after day."

He climbed the tower, groping as he came
Up through the darkness, like a midnight rook;
But only when he'd loudly called his name
And knocked some time did Galt lift up the hook.
Hardly had the old man time to look
When Adam rushed upon his little frame,
Pouring out his suffering, his smart,
As to him he revealed his inmost heart.

He told him of how Clara would torment him,
Of burnings and of yearnings night and day.
He sobbed at how unfeelingly she'd rent him
By rousing hope which she'd as quickly slay.
He swore that to despair the girl had sent him,
He hardly knew what he should do or say;
Sign cancelled sign, and if her uncle knew
No way to help, his heart would break in two.

Now, little Galt, with Adam in the door,
Had met him with a brow profoundly lined,
As if there were real anger in his mind,
And now cried, half distrait: "Here's some uproar!
You nearly lost your reason once before,
And now it is your heart that you can't find.
So, here you come by moonlight, youth to age,
To fetch auxiliaries and counsel sage.

"And what help can the old man offer you
When your strength's gone and your heart but a hole?
How can I speed you onward to your goal,
Which you've done everything not to pursue?
It takes brave hearts to see their pleasures through!
The reason I near lost my self-control
Was that you broke in on my holy hour.
Come here! Perhaps it might revive your power."

236/

Behind the hangings he unlocked a door
Which led into a darkened gallery
Where through cracked panes the owl sighed heavily.
With Adam at his back, he strode before,
His candle dying as a gust blew free
And casements back of them slammed with a roar.
"Keep on!" cried old Gray Galt. "I've lost the candle,
But here's the door—I have hold of the handle."

They stepped inside, where glowing lamps were slung,
And in the light which leapt up dazzlingly
An ancient banquet hall could Adam see
Around the walls of which portraits were hung.
But no knights menaced in armed panoply
And his lance no bearded hero swung:
The only subjects which could there be conned
Were smiling women, both brunette and blonde.

There hung, in garb a bit too wide of mesh
(So that their lovely forms were plain to view),
Dames galantes and beggar girls quite fresh,
And dark-brown pupils interspersed with blue.
One had leaned down, her garter to undo,
Another at her mirror saw much flesh,
A third slept in a forest on the grass,
A fourth was lifting up a champagne glass.

As if he too'd partaken of the vine,
Our hero stood enchanted by such grace.
The old man, meanwhile, like a host benign
Went round and started up the fireplace,
And brought forth glasses and a flask of wine.
He lastly took a fiddle from its case
(A real Cremona) with the utmost care
And spoke out while his strumming filled the air:

"My young friend! lost in admiration
At what, no doubt, a weak brain can amaze,
These bright stars of my long-gone former days
Shine down cures which are my heart's salvation.
Here you see happiness which never strays,
A brief joy turned to endless delectation!
Here are the fruits I managed to collect
When, as a young man, round the world I trekked.

237/

"O lovely times, saved from oblivion!"
He went on, his excitement not subsiding.
"O host of memories beyond me gliding,
Which draw my soul and vision ever on:
O Spanish donna, on your mule still riding!
O Swiss maid, 'midst your thyme and tarragon!
O Roman lady, glittering coquette!
Who shall upon my list be foremost set?"

He went back to the table, where he drained
A beakerful of wine, strong and well-spiced,
And from the violin strings he enticed
A sea of music where lust dreamed unchained.
Now damned and now again imparadised,
It waxed in joy and in a moan it waned
Until a perfect chord brought it to rest,
At which he turned and Adam readdressed:

"My sanctuary," he said, "you now have seen.
You know these mystical divinities
Whose lover and whose votary I've been,
Whom still I worship with sweet memories.
Once a week I come to visit these
When earth is veiled beneath the black night's screen,
And in the depths of night my heaven swarms
With all these lovely visages and forms."

He looked around with an expression fond
And bowed the violin to set it ringing,
Whereupon he strode up to a blonde,
A tambourine-girl, dancing there and singing.
"Rosina, weaver of a magic bond,
Where are the days when round *we two* went swinging,
When my arm curved about your slender waist
And I could feel the warmth as your heart raced!"

Wild across the strings his bow he drew,
His little foot was tapping now in time,
From his eyes a mighty fire there flew
And, carried off as by a power sublime,
Far into a dream he seemed to climb
And with his guest had nothing more to do.
Like someone drunk he eyed the Spanish maid
While his bolero once again he played.

Our hero stood amazed, without a word,
Sore tempted by the beauties in this vault,
Not certain that a dream had not occurred,
So odd his blood leapt to the bow's assault.
He went up to the old man, just as Galt
A farewell bow on his *danseuse* conferred;
He wished to paint his own dream's aspiration,
But Galt was past conducting conversation.

By another portrait he was won,
A pallid figure, kneeling down in prayer,
Who represented a repentant nun,
The wind dishevelling her unbound hair.
Galt heaved a sigh, while a chorale he spun,
To which he chanted with a psalmist's air:
"My prayers once moved you, lovely Magdalen,
But your prayers could move stones to say Amen.

"You were so proud and Spanish—long the wait
Before you let yourself to sweet words yield.
I wandered round, as monks walk in a field,
Swearing myself hoarse before your grate.
At your cell window my guitar-strings pealed
With pain and pining—triumph came, though late!
Ah, great was my reward!" A hymn he played,
Then over to the next portrait he strayed.

This one revealed, in a less holy pose,
Her mouth all smiles and looking more than willing,
A fair young beggar maid in ragged clothes,
The lap of whom a little cat was filling.
She had her hand outstretched to beg a shilling.
"Ha!" cried Galt. "Though tattered, you ne'er froze!
Your blood was hot! I'd hardly spread my arms
Before you warmed my bosom with your charms."

The fever to his fiddle seemed to spread
And long before that portrait did he stand
While he caressed the little kitten's head;
He then walked round to view more of his band,
His joy by lovely sounds inspirited,
And always found new strains at his command.
"This is exhausting!" all at once he mumbled,
And down into an armchair, drained, he tumbled.

239/

Our hero, who had just put down his glass,
Dashed over for what aid he could provide
And sat himself down at the old man's side.
Galt spoke up, once his weakness seemed to pass:
"You see me pay the price for sins *en masse*;
All too ecstatic, I was like to have died.
I fell in vertigo against my will,
And here I lie like some crushed daffodil.

"Enough of me! for whom it's been one week
Since last I came here where my joys survive;
And now that I've regained my senses five
And breathing does not tax my poor physique,
To you just like a father I shall speak.
What was it now? Advice must I contrive?
Eh bien! But my advice won't be donated
Until our tongues are somewhat lubricated!"

Galt led him over to the serving board,
Put the wine before him, and said, "Drink!
Drink up, friend! Only through a drunkard's blink
Can Paradise's splendors be explored.
Wine and pleasure have an age-old link,
For Bacchus goes with Venus as her lord,
And excitation when one's dry as sand
Is not a thing to make the heart expand."

He set the bottles out symmetrically;
And, while Adam reached his own cup's lees,
Galt tried eight or nine varieties
And then exclaimed: "With what temerity
Philosophers explain our century!
That talk of Unity—it's a disease!
And what is Unity? It just won't do
When Multiplicity is in plain view.

"Unity is Spirit? Pshaw! The notion's
Too pure to stand up to alcohol;
If on the Unity of wine they'd call,
I'll bet they'd find just water in these potions.
No, life has no such pretty folderol;
It does have Multiplicity's commotions:
With hundreds of good wines it's bounteous,
And women, yes, not Woman, gives to us.

240/

"This is the first point which I would confide:
Heart's ease dwells but in Multiplicity.
With pleasure next we must be occupied,
For pleasure is the prize which we foresee.
But when we ask where pleasure then might be,
Experience's wise voice has replied:
True pleasure memory alone enshrines,
And it's lured out by music and fine wines.

"Now, there, my young friend, is my theory,
My practice of which you may surely guess;
Surrounded by this host of loveliness,
I set my mood first with a melody
That leads me back to memory's recess;
Next, wakened by the wine, my fantasy
Of every single portrait takes control
And what was only half revealed makes whole.

"Now you will ask what's this to do with you.
Just imagine this your christening!
You are a handsome young man, yes, it's true,
And in this world you could have everything.
'Gainst fair maids' hearts your weapons you must bring,
And all the memories you can, accrue:
In spring's the time to salt the winter's herring,
And he who sows in autumn's sadly erring.

"It would be nice if you could get a *bischen*
Of the good things Fortune can supply,
And, first and foremost, a secure position,
For otherwise your goal will stay too high.
Go find a wife who's put some shillings by
If otherwise you can't complete your mission;
With her gold you'll soar on golden wing,
And like the phoenix you'll arise and sing.

"And now" (with this he casts a roguish eye
On Adam, who is listening thoughtfully)
"And now my powers have returned to me,
We'll empty out a beaker of good-bye.
Just skoal me back, I want no more reply!
Fair Clara's favor calls for gravity:
Skoal to the hero, triumph and be blessed;
Skoal to the bosom on which he shall rest!"

241/

Our hero turned bright crimson, but he clinked
His cup with Galt's, who filled it up once more,
And at his portraits sweetly bowed and winked,
Swinging his cup, excited as before.
"Skoal, all my nymphs!" he cried, and his eyes blinked
To stop the tears that were about to pour.
"May you while I'm alive keep my flame tall,
And at my death one grave shall claim us all!"

Here he stopped, and in bewilderment
Adam left him in his bright repair
As down the tower hurriedly he went
Along the dark steps of the winding stair.
He stood once more beneath the moon, which sent
Its beams down from among the branches spare;
And, keeping to the coast, as breakers crashed,
Homeward on the empty road he dashed.

As he ran, hot from the stimulant,
A new illumination then began:
For, though, when on Gray Galt his thinking ran,
His ways struck Adam as extravagant,
And though he even smiled at the old man,
There was some truth, he really had to grant,
Behind that talk of Multiplicity
That could make life quite satisfactory.

His own past life caused him discomfiture,
Practically bereft of poesy
In contrast to the old man's gallery
Where paramour hung next to paramour.
It seemed a splendid lot, so to secure
So many hearts and nonetheless be free;
It seemed a most poetical projection
To make himself a similar collection.

In this mood, drowned, his shipwreck now completed,
At last he reached the steps of Galtenborg,
Where they had had their supper long before.
With this news by a servant he was greeted,
By whom he was attended to the door
Of Clara's parlor, where the fair was seated
By a glowing lamp, as he came in,
At cards, with one hand underneath her chin.

She sat there in those tasteful clothes she'd wear,
Lost in thought and with a look intent,
All alone and playing solitaire,
At which her evenings frequently were spent.
She had just yawned aloud, when her eye went
To Adam; but, not turning ev'n a hair,
She jumped up from the chair she sat upon
And made a smile of what had been a yawn.

Still smiling, toward the lad she softly strode,
But suddenly she slackened in her stride,
For he, who'd been respect personified,
Looked upon her now with eyes that glowed;
And he, upon whose lips words often died,
With intimacies fairly overflowed;
And he, who once was shy as any miss,
Presses on her hand a fervid kiss.

In her astonishment she starts to shrink,
And looks at him as though she were aghast;
But, since he still is holding her hand fast,
The rushing blood her lily cheek turns pink,
And, turning to the board quick as a wink,
She points to all the cards that she had cast:
"Piquet's a charming game, wouldn't you say?
If you would like to, let's sit down and play."

"With pleasure!" says he, without faltering,
And at the parlor table takes a seat.
But Clara, whose mind thinks of everything,
Quickly makes into a bundle neat
The papers which had come that evening;
She rings, and tells the servant he's to greet
The Kammerherre with this fine bouquet
And say it's from the last post of the day.

Once that is done, she sits down at her place
And, eyeing him as with a measuring stick,
She turns the lamp up and adjusts the wick
So that the light won't fall on either's face.
As may be guessed, our hero, in this space,
Has mixed the cards and dealt them double quick;
And to the great game he now bends his head,
For the lady has already led:

243/

"I've seven diamonds—and my good sir, you,
How big a run do you have, without bluff?"
"Alas!" he answers boldly. "You play rough!
That run of yours undoes me. It is true,
I fear, the cards I have are not enough.
Just four hearts, and that bid would never do.
But—if Your Grace won't think me very bad—
My own heart, as the fifth, I'll gladly add."

It's plain, our hero, freed from every fear,
Drunk, and keen to try audacity,
With his head full of the gallery,
Began the game like its gay cavalier.
But Clara knew the same game perfectly;
She shows a brow beclouded and severe,
Remarking shortly: "Rules here do not stop;
We don't let bulls into this china shop."

It worked. The drunkenness was quickly past;
His brave heart fell with such humiliation
He hardly dares a timid look to cast
Upon that bristling lady of high station.
The beauty's won by Adam's subjugation;
She smiles a smile which has a meaning vast:
"Combat me with your doughtiest attacks,
For in my hand I'm holding fourteen jacks."

"Oh," he thinks, "she could make up fifteen
If she would only add me to them all."
Aloud he says: "Your jacks have stripped me clean,
Into the dust they've made my tens all fall."
As if triumphant she went on to glean
Kings and lays of fours, threes, large and small,
Until at last she sat back in her chair
And, laughing, said: "Well, that's my ninety there.

"Now," she cried, "now that I've made my score,
You're dumb? My blow has left you high and dry!"
"Indeed I'm lost," he stammers in reply,
As from his cards he looks at her once more.
He looks upon a blazing cheek and eye,
Sees carmine lips that laugh and yet implore,
While from her shoulders she flings off her shawl,
Declaring: "It is hot here, after all!"

244/

This was too much! He lost to see who'd lead,
Although the first time it was she who'd led.
"Skoal to the bosom!" rang out in his head;
To rest upon it was his only need.
Everything, save Clara's image, fled!
He dropped his card, got to his feet with speed,
And like a tree whose roots had just been lopped,
At Clara's feet with these words Adam dropped.

"O forgive me! O forgive, Your Grace!
But for my pain send down a remedy!"
"What?" she asks, both sweet and out of face.
"What's wrong with you? You are a mystery
That, in all truth, is much too deep for me."
"Ah," he stammers, "love explains my case!
It's *you* I love! *You* are my heart's compulsion!"
And grasps her hands as if in a convulsion.

"So it is I you bear this great love for?"
She slowly says, but briefly adds thereto:
"Now there you tell me something that's brand new.
Ouch! Let go my hand! You make it sore.
Hr. Homo—I must beg of you! Let go now, or—"
She stands and pushes off with some ado
Her kneeling guest; but he gets to his feet
And, voice a-quiver, speaks, all flushed with heat:

"Enchanting one! With every grace bedight!
My idol! To whom I'm a slave fast bound!
O, Clara! Clara! Grant that joy profound
Of which alone I've dreamt both day and night,
Just once against this breast to press you tight—"
Now firm and tenderly his arm he wound
About her waist and, though he feared her look,
Burning kisses from her mouth he took.

"Hr. Homo!" Clara lisped. "Why act like this?"
"Oh," he replies, "I've just now told you why."
"Hr. Homo! What misfortune!" comes her cry,
But it is smothered by another kiss.
"Hr. Homo! Must I scream to heaven on high?"
But, blanching, he bids silence with a hiss:
The door creaks and a voice is heard to mumble,
"There was a paper missing in that jumble!"

245/

"Be off!" she cries to Adam, whom she knocks
Aside. Our hero turns himself around
To face her husband, who is dressing-gowned
And, candle in his hand, still closer walks.
He thinks he sees an eye where vengeance stalks,
Fiery letters which his doom expound,
And, paralyzed in every limb and sense,
Meets Galt's Medusa-head with no defense.

He stood rigid in this frightful scene,
And there the lady stood, her arm extended,
The stance of noble womanhood defended,
With such an excellence in look and mien
That excellence it actually transcended.
But utterly unmoved, like a machine,
Phlegmatic Galt stared coldly at the sight
And, uncomplaining, stood in his own light.

Suddenly to his fair spouse he signed,
And in a little side room went the twain:
She to cleanse herself of every stain,
And he in part to have her turn him blind,
In part the missing newspaper to find
By searching out a place it might have lain.
But hardly was the couple gone before
Our hero flew out by the other door.

Up the staircase to his room he raced
And clothing, linen, boots, this odd, this end,
He packed together in the greatest haste,
For no more time in this house would he spend.
And, though his heavy suitcase made him bend
And groan, off to the market-town he chased,
Turned up coach and coachman for his flight,
And drove off in the middle of the night.

The coachman held the reins, but he the whip,
Which on the horses was so brisk bestowed
That all that night they ran at furious clip.
It was not long before a rooster crowed,
But on and on to Middelfart they rode
And there, before noon, finished off their trip.
A smack lay in the port, tarred recently.
He boarded it—at last he could breathe free.

246/

He heaved a sigh when they pushed off from land,
And, shaking from the cold, a dark survey
He made of Funen's coast, a foggy band
Of winter coldness and of solid gray.
Down through his cloak the hard rain made its way,
Upon his legs he felt he scarce could stand,
He felt his soul had been whipped through and through,
By faith forsaken, with hope lost from view.

He could recall when things were otherwise,
When he had sailed across the Belt last year;
And now—the smack was swiftly drawing near
The Jutland coast, spread out before his eyes—
He thought of what the future might comprise.
Long our hero stood in doubt and fear,
Then sighed, as struck by the significance:
"What's man, if not the product of pure Chance?"

CANTO VIII

My reader! you who've reached the episode
Which ends my latest song, though not my last,
And would still forge beyond those pages past
To follow on my hero's crooked road,
But, as a thoughtful reader, feel you're owed
A full accounting of his mental cast:
Let me ask if ever you've surveyed
A young apprentice on a promenade.

His bundle round his neck, down through the street
He strode, the merry chap, as to a dance!
His oilcloth hat, round which sat flowers sweet,
Was bound to rivet every young girl's glance.
How shone his vest, how stiff each jacket pleat!
And how the gleam of his white leather pants
Strove to outdo the boots he'd fiercely polished,
Which with their hobnailed heels the street demolished!

How, swinging his gnarled stick, he kept in sight
The road that led out past the city gate,
While life was shining from the distant height,
Signalling that it would compensate
The lucky lad for toiling at such rate!
So off he went—when he came back at night
From giving life a thorough exploration,
O what a strange and puzzling transformation!

Of all those flowers there is not a scrap,
The hat itself has neither brim nor crown;
His coat and pants are half hole and half flap;
The boots that once had dazzled all the town
Creak, stripped of soles and with their heels worn down;
His feet are roofed, but there's a flooring-gap;
His walking stick alone remains quite stout—
It holds him up the while he limps about.

With his hat cocked, he walks his old town routes,
An object of compassion and of sneers;
At every corner he hears coarse salutes
From little boys who send him leers and jeers.
He calmly turns his nose up at their hoots,
And to him everything right good appears;
He doesn't note the crowd's disdainful mumbles,
For with too many *snaps*es how he stumbles.

In this apprentice, herewith brought to view,
My reader has for his examination
My hero's state in faithful illustration.
That heart of his was hollow through and through,
His faith and hope were utterly *perdu*
And he befogged from his inebriation.
Like that lad he was, if we relate
The lad's outward to Adam's inward state.

Attended by the reader's sympathy,
Ever nearer to his home he drew.
Already the church roof had come in view
Behind the low hills, brown and wintery.
Although the carriage drove on speedily,
He leapt off, every limb alive anew,
And on ahead along the slope he ran,
For down below his father's field began.

Far over land and fjord his eyes explore:
The Baron's gabled mansion and the mill
Beyond the distant wood are as before.
Lost in the sight a moment he stands still,
Then suddenly he turns from Vejle Fjord
And hurries to the path below the hill.
Into the cemetery this path leads,
And to a fenced-in gravesite he proceeds.

He was not wrong—it was his mother's grave!
"Margrethe Homo" on the cross it read;
Beneath, the years of birth and death God gave;
A painted hourglass stood upon its head,
From which, though, the hues were nearly bled.
He fetched a mighty sigh, this sight to brave;
It brought to mind how fast all comes to naught,
How soon a soul—the best, too—is forgot.

He reached the parson's gate, which gave a croak
As, opening it just a little bit,
On his father Adam's eyes first lit,
In greatcoat and a cap as gray as smoke.
A well-dressed lady stood there opposite
Him in the yard as he helped with her cloak,
And said out loud, in merriest demeanor:
"Come visit soon again, my little Trine!"

"Thank you, I will!" she answered, turning round
Toward Adam while those words of thanks were said:
The miller's rotund daughter Adam found,
Coming toward him, blushing very red.
He tipped his hat, as he ran with a bound
And on old Homo fell, who cocked his head
And looked him over from his head to toe
And then exclaimed: "It's you! What do you know!"

The pastor stretched his arm out like a hook
And, spreading wide his greatcoat from his breast,
He pressed his Adam gently to his vest.
His son and he in a brief hug partook;
Then they both went, the host trailed by the guest,
Into the warm and pleasant parlor nook.
Then there came a long interrogation,
All trustfulness and partial explanation.

There was grand shouting, in the Homo way,
When How the Great and Little Belts He'd Sailed
And countless other things must be retailed
To Homo till night closed their long parley.
Then they broke up, and by old Anna trailed
He found the guestroom where he was to stay.
She, with a candle and some bedding fraught,
He, with two letters that the boy'd just brought.

But these two letters had for months been pent
Inside the pastor's mailbag: there was one
The Vejle posthouse in September sent,
And one came on a January run.
He checks the address, by the same hand done,
Nor are the two seals any different.
He knows it's Alma's seal—he knows the hand,
But he has feelings he can't understand.

He paces in the guestroom in a fret,
Uneasy, like a sinner caught in cheating,
Old Anna meanwhile tucking in the sheeting
And turning the down blanket in a sweat.
"Tell me, Anna," he began, entreating,
"What's the good news here that I should get?
How are things? Do they go the way they went
When my late mother had the management?"

"No, little Adam!" stammering she addressed
Him as she looked up, working on the bed.
"No, this whole household just about stopped dead
The very day Madame was laid to rest,
And now we all have fogs inside the head.
Lord knows if we'll be any less distressed
With our new mistress, come the summertide,
When he will make the miller's girl his bride."

"What! His bride?" With that asseveration
Loud, our hero took a backward stride.
"One of Miller Knudsen's girls his bride?
Wherever did you get that information?"
"Oh, at the deacon's house," the maid replied,
"And, far as I know, it has good foundation.
But, my, the priest knows where to make a match,
That Trine's money makes her a good catch."

He stood there thunderstruck—inside his skull
The miller's girl set his mind in a reel,
Like water coursing round the miller's wheel,
Nor was there for reflection any lull.
"How does the deacon's daughter Hanne feel?"
The question helped to make his head less dull.
Old Anna answered: "How does Hanne do?
She does quite well, that I can tell you true.

"She has a post with the young Baroness,
She's her companion over at the hall,
Dressed up in silk and furs like a princess.
She has a skirt as wide as she is tall,
A plumed hat with a little velvet fall—
Yes, that's the way we people are, I guess.
But she's grown haughty, what with all those clothes,
And an unusually stuck-up nose."

Out of the room now agèd Anna went,
And Adam, staying back, absorbed in thought,
Eyed the letters which he had been sent.
He quickly sat down by the oven hot
And on the table placed the lamp he'd brought,
Then to the letter latest come he bent.
He broke the seal which Alma's words enclosed,
And read in silence what is here exposed.

"I write to you; although why I should write
When to my last I've gotten no reply—
Yes, I have asked myself the reason why,
And still upon no answer can I light.
I write, and meanwhile I am filled with fright
That what I last wrote you were injured by;
You found my last words very bothersome
And that's the reason that your lips are dumb.

"With this thought in my head to bed I go
Each evening when I, tired by long reflection,
No other reason for your silence know;
Only you know if it needs correction.
I can but tell you this, if that is so:
All I wrote I wrote in true affection,
Wanting you to take it lovingly;
If that wish failed—surely you'll pardon me.

"But how have you been? As to what you've done
Since our farewells I haven't heard a sound;
I sit inside my cot as if snow-bound,
A prey to cold and longing for someone,
And pine for you and for the god of sun.
Sometimes from my door I peer around
To see if there's a sign of one of you,
If soon this endless waiting will be through.

"You see, I trust the promise that you spoke;
Just a postman's cloak I have to see
And in the tender glow of hope I soak,
And what the letter holds smiles out to me.
My joy and horror lie in that red cloak;
It moves on closer to our property;
It goes by—at the next front gate bells sound,
And my high hopes are buried in the ground.

"Into the grave—yes, but the dead shall rise!
The old year's being rung into its grave;
Root and branch, its life now petrifies.
Above its trials and smiles the grass will wave,
For life to death is never made a slave.
The new year swiftly a new bud supplies
Which fresh as my love-longing will unfold,
Though both their flowers are hampered by the cold.

"Thus, every day I pray to the year's king:
Send me soon some warmth and some sunlight!
That life about me can be burgeoning
And hope within my breast can flower bright.
As gardener I have tended my hope right:
In every seed I send it scattering
That it might grow both tall and beautifully—
And should it not, then, send forth shoots in me?

"Yes! Like an infant snuggling to his nurse,
I hold my hope with that same tender grip:
I will not let one doubt its pinions clip
Or ever for my weakness *it* accurse.
Its promise every day my lips rehearse,
And at its glances oft my heart will skip
When they reveal, though tears be thickening,
That joy will come for certain with the spring.

"Yes, when the bright spring sun gilds all anew,
When golden rain weighs down the lilac tree,
When our yards bear a flowered canopy
And roses open for their bath of dew,
When birdsong fills our arbor's greenery
Where last year hand in hand we'd sit, we two:
Then, with that gladness, you come from afar—
So dreams, both day and night, your Alma Star."

Adam sat there, moved. He put the sheet aside
And opened up the letter from last year.
In it he learned that Alma's aunt had died:
In just one week a fever most severe
Had taken her and put her on her bier.
A postscript of a few words she supplied
About the house, and lastly she refuted
This or that which his last letter mooted.

He gets up from his chair; and to and fro
Along the guest-room floor again he paces
As, moved by that fair memory, his heart races.
Then, suddenly, ere he could even know,
In contradance his thinking about-faces
And past him Clara glided, Prince in tow.
He would have chased them off with this new mail,
But all at once the words in it grew pale.

What was wrong? *He* hardly knew aright;
He felt impeded each step he progressed,
So distrait, so addled, so depressed,
So heavy, yet so weak-willed and so light.
His sickness was (to this I must attest)
That he a stranger stood in his own sight:
A sickness to which often we're inclined
Once we have separated heart and mind.

For, clearly, we can be of fifteen minds,
Whereas of hearts we can't have more than one.
But life's coherence, which its basis finds
In the unity of both, soon comes undone
When mind, no longer held in check, unwinds
And, sundered from the heart, away will run;
When from its very self ego falls wide
And mind becomes confused without its guide.

253/

The mind then's like the captain of a ship
Who wanders round an unfamiliar port
And stops in every tavern for a snort
And into every dancehall has to nip:
From all life's chalices it takes a sip
And tastes of all the good things life can sport.
No sooner fixed, again it runs amok,
And, just as soon again, it's firmly stuck.

No more the inmost mind it once had been
That to the inmost heart in silence sank,
That high mind which once at the heart's well drank
The power for high undertakings in,
It lets each new impression play its prank
And, like a weathervane, is set a-spin;
So empty that it might as well desert,
It's twisted, turned, and changed just like a shirt.

For, in itself, mind's but propensity;
A lack of content causes its unrest,
And by that poverty it's always pressed
To find some other source of potency.
It would be charmed, uplifted, and possessed;
It wants to live—and hence its strategy.
If joy's used up, then woe will fill the void;
But in the end by boredom it's destroyed.

But, though the mind may often drain joy's bowl,
Its life is but penurious and afraid,
Since for the heart's own riches it was made.
Among its deeps, where dreams a feeling soul,
Where out from warmest wellsprings thoughts unroll,
There ego, often by the world betrayed,
Rediscovers its own faceless sources,
And mind acquires both power and resources.

When we called Adam stranger in his sight,
It was in this sense that phrase was selected,
That, with a worldly mind spoiling to fight,
He felt his limbs had all come disconnected.
"But," you will say, "but this must be corrected—
Upon a theologian it's a slight!
Such a mind might suit a hypocrite,
But here your judgment simply doesn't fit!"

But categories are not so granitic.
Contradictions are near commonplaces.
Don't we see some clowns with gloomy faces
And honorable men turned parasitic?
Don't we see a babe become a critic?
Aren't there male sopranos, female basses?
Don't we see skinny wives to fat men wed?
And jovial undertakers for the dead?

If that is so, then we might just come by
A theologian to the world inclined,
Who, every time his loved one came to mind,
Would quietly fetch up an honest sigh.
But then, no sooner did the small sound die
Than he pursued things of an alien kind
That made him give that sigh no more attention,
So that his love could not grow in dimension.

Still, it wasn't Clara who brought on
This situation, with its rifts and cracks,
For like a dream his passion had withdrawn.
Fled's the tension of its fierce attacks
As when, some morn, one walks the forest tracks
And tears a spider web. Where is it? Gone!
Once he no more could see her eyes aflame,
His love was left with nothing but the name.

But what now filled him daily with distress,
Distracted him and gave him no release,
What tortured him, was all that loveliness
The loss of which had robbed his heart of peace.
Each household scene made his despair increase:
What did this Jutland honesty possess
That could compare with Funen's *joie de vie*,
Which stayed in his mind's eye continuously.

What was the fir-plank sled against the sleighs
Departing to the ring of silver bells?
What were these geese and chickens with their smells
To swans whose white necks thrilled him in those days?
These silhouettes to family sentinels
In gilt-framed oils that lined the passageways?
This wretched yard, this grove, this plot of ground
To park lands such as Galtenborg surround?

255/

The parsonage—its walls that smelled of must,
How often they produced a sinking feeling!
This room where someone's hand could touch the ceiling!
How often he felt in a prison thrust.
The stove that wouldn't draw, but with a gust
Of east wind smoked to set you reeling:
Late and early, blowing from the shore,
It brought back the fresh air of Galtenborg!

And then the company that would enchant
The household! Knudsen, that old miller chap,
Who never from his head took off his cap,
And those dressed-up daughters, so *galantes*:
The normal-scholar, stiff enough to snap;
And the whistling tenant farmer Brandt,
Who rode on just a horse-cloth—what gentility!—
Compare to such a crew Funen's nobility!

But Sunday mornings, seated in his stall
Among ten farmers superannuated,
While father, in his black robes, depredated
Christian faith of flower, leaf, and all,
And neatly, with a smile to fit Old Sol,
Morality from dogma separated,
As with the Lord he'd chummily converse:
Yes, then it seemed that things were even worse!

Then very often to himself he said:
"Can this then be the goal toward which I toil?
To be a priest and open up my head
To such fine laymen of the Danish soil,
And, while the soul inside myself I spoil,
Turn everybody else's hours to lead
By reading them this great new bulletin
That Holy Writ forbids us all to sin?

"What's the reward? Let not my wits forsake me!
A tiny place to live and coarse rye bread,
A social circle that is sure to break me,
A deacon always making me see red.
But, it is true, a helpmate I can take me,
And live safe from the world till I am dead;
And if I live to reach my jubilee,
They'll take me into the Consistory."

Our wretched hero! So much to resent!
His call, his life, his lot were all decided;
Inexorable Necessity presided
Over his future of imprisonment.
A thousand wishes have his soul divided,
But no assistance was from Heaven sent.
His future path admitted of no change;
From the beaten track he could not range.

Every day these thoughts he ruminated
On his wonted walk along the lea,
Where the storks were nesting in each tree
And the lark with songs of springtime waited;
Where the earth its grassy carpet plaited
And the sun spread wide heaven's canopy;
Where life was budding forth in everything
And balsam came to him on winds of spring.

He let the fresh breeze do with him its will
And on that wakening life let his eyes dwell
Until at last he found salvation's well,
Which, strangely, from his own self he felt spill.
One day in the field he stood stock-still
And, breathing deep to make his weak lungs swell
With heady springtime air to cool the heart,
To himself did he these words impart:

"What a foolish life is this I've made,
For only outward powers I respected!
First to Destiny's blind god I prayed,
And then to Providence I was subjected;
Then to the games of Chance I was affected,
And now Necessity would be obeyed—
But what external power holds in fee
The power of freedom, throned inside of me?

"Does it not outweigh all? Let me but say
I *will*, and with a will maintain that stand:
Why shouldn't every barrier give way,
And I be rid of shackle, bar, and band?
That 'will' sets creativity in play—
Do I not hold my future in my hand?
Can I not form it, choose the way it's led,
According to the thoughts in my own head?

"If I wish to forgo theology
(As yet a choice I have by no means made),
Would not my will make this necessity
Of priestly calling go into the shade?
Were I to look outside the ministry
And forge a life that wasn't quite so staid,
A life a little way above the mass,
Would not the world stand back to let me pass?

"No doubt! My weakness only had one ground:
The low place I once gave my liberty,
Which I had thought lay in dependency
On life's external powers, which held it bound.
Praise God! I know now that idea's unsound;
I call my freedom now to work for me!
Each chain that held me I now break apart;
From here on in my liberty will start!"

He stopped, and joyfully looked out in space;
A smile, long missing from his mouth, now stole
Across his lips for anyone to trace.
His sick mind from that moment was made whole;
Contentment in his breast found resting-place,
And high of heart he soon was sound of soul.
He in his freedom owned a magic wand
To wave at all that once had caused despond.

He aimed first at the lightning bolts of Chance
That, flash on flash, had hid his prospects bright
Each time in Funen he'd but raised his glance.
And lo! changed to a flock of birds in flight,
Now round and round in air, red, yellow, white,
Before his eyes they flutter in their dance
Up, down, hither, thither, in the clouds,
And by the wind they're borne away in crowds.

He has no fear of them, these little fry,
For a penny you could purchase five;
They are the fairest little things alive,
For bad and good alike they'll prophesy.
Somersaults up there they can contrive
And turnabouts they have in great supply;
The wind, though, which their flights and twistings drives
From the power of freedom still derives.

258/

Indeed, whatever accidents befall
Turn out the product of the liberty
Of God and of the individual,
And tables turn when both of them agree.
It's hard to find a law of Chance at all;
For the product under scrutiny
Is a double freedom's consummation;
And Chance, then, has no part in its foundation.

With this hard question deftly put to rest,
He now took up that of Necessity,
From whose yoke he had just now burst free,
Though of its nature he was still in quest.
Night and day he spared no industry
As on with German logic he progressed,
Until Necessity he had so cinched
That into mere Reflection it was pinched.

Now he was untrammeled in his thought,
For no compulsion made him timorous
Now that Necessity itself was caught
And bound in chains, like old Prometheus.
His freedom set all outward powers at naught,
His strength and courage ne'er so copious;
His vision had the whole world in its scope
And always came back home to him with hope.

Filled by this hope, this sweet uncertainty,
Whose fullness almost made him overwrought,
And with a past that he had half forgot,
He planned to meet the future dauntlessly.
Its hidden stores would feed his destiny,
Nor would he know the nature of his lot:
Good fortune he would not anticipate,
For in suspension everything must wait.

His method brought him thus far on his way
When summer came with merry birds in song,
With purple clouds, with roses throng on throng,
And bade him take life's goods while yet he may.
Thus, one day he and father took the shay
And left the parsonage to drive along
Into the wood to hear the birds' sweet tones
And make a little stop at Hr. Baron's.

259/

An order on his tailor he'd bestowed
And with a neck-cloth truly elegant
And second-hand suit, very *à la mode*,
He looked to be a genuine gallant.
At the sight of this old Homo glowed,
As a father proudly cognizant
Of Adam when, slouched back as if to doze,
He used a silk handkerchief to blow his nose.

"Hear the cuckoo! Hear the cuckoo, Son!"
His father suddenly began to shout,
For now the pleasant woodland had begun,
Behind them now the dusty country route.
"That song told me my life had long to run
When last year I was racked with secret gout
And bade good God vouchsafe this life to me.
But you ask now—and hear the prophecy."

"Some prophet, who but answers bow with bow!"
Replied our hero, when the priest was through,
Whereon he sent his voice out loud and true
And through the forest rang his question: "How,
Hr. Cuckoo! How long shall I live from now?"
"Cuckoo!" the forest bird replied. "Cuckoo!
Cuckoo, cuckoo!" (Some long coo's and some shorts.)
"Cuckoo, cuckoo!" (Some thirty-odd reports.)

"Well, now," smiled the priest, "that's good to hear,
A granddad's age the cuckoo prophesies;
But say how many years," again he cries,
"Ere Adam at the altar shall appear!"
"Cuckoo!" the bird says. Laughing for disguise,
Our hero shouts: "What's that? You mean next year?"
But Homo, well content, throws himself back,
And bids the driver on along the track.

They reached the side road, down whose slope there rolled
A fancy carriage; and in velvet coat
A young boy drove, while, uncontrolled,
His hair flew wild beneath his red capote.
Beside him there sat stiffly, long of throat,
A well-dressed lady, tall and stout of mold.
The horses flew beneath the merry whip
And turned onto the track at furious clip.

"Who," Adam whispered, "is that in the trap?"
"Mille, she's the Baroness. Now hush."
Homo stops the driver, in a rush
To greet her with a low sweep of his cap.
The lady lets her eyes o'er Adam brush,
But the boy calls out: "So you're the chap,
Hr. Pastor Homo! Where you headed for?"
The pastor answers, "To the Baron's door."

"Delightful!" he replies. "I'll let them know."
Then, flourishing his whip high in the air,
The merry coachboy cries: "Geeup, now! Go!"
And drives as on a life-and-death affair.
But out the side the lady leans to throw
A roguish smile back to the standing pair,
At which on Adam's face red roses grew
That faded when the carriage passed from view.

"Well," he tells his father, "I admit
The Baroness's hat and plume stood tall."
"Indeed," the pastor says, "aren't your eyes fit!
That white plume's part of Hanne's folderal."
"What!" Adam cries, as Homo's sides near split.
"Who was the jaunty boy who'll say we'll call,
His red cap trimmed with finest braid, no less?"
"Ha!" Homo says. "That was the Baroness!"

Our hero sat astounded, and all ears
He was, as Homo had more news to broach.
"The Baroness not only drives a coach,
But in her horsemanship she has few peers.
A hunting rifle causes her no fears,
Though she gives wild birds much cause for reproach;
But, all in all, and letting such things pass,
She is a gifted and delightful lass.

"I know that there are people who will call
Her somewhat spoiled—but, by all that's divine,
The only daughter, last one of her line,
To whom the barony will one day fall—
She may have faults, but then so do we all,
And she's most healthy and her skin's quite fine.
Whom she selects for her hymeneal kiss
Could well be named the Pamphilus of bliss.

"A thousand-acre barony, the lot,
Besides the bog- and wood- and mill-tolls due;
Two hundred fifty farmers for a crew;
A herd of sheep with no pox, no foot-rot,
A dairy farm whose butter's widely sought:
How does that idyll, Son, appeal to you?
What do you think?" He gave his sleeve a twitch.
"Don't you think you'd like to strike it rich?

"You're blushing. You must think that I depict
A castle in the air, not for this earth,
That baronesses have ideals so strict
A priest's son would be of too low a birth.
But steady! I've great matters to predict.
Your looks are splendid and your mind has worth,
It wouldn't be a hopeless undertaking—
Trust me, we lie in beds of our own making."

Our hero cleared his throat. "And Hr. Baron?"
He asked, as half distracted his mind ran.
"The Baron," comes the answer, "is a man
Who both fears God and reverences the throne,
A good plain mind, upon the Jutland plan;
You hear the landed gentry in his tone.
There are two subjects on which he can jaw:
The new assessment and the old hunt law.

"For near ten years he's been a widower,
And he would go through hell and through high water
For his vivacious, roguish little daughter,
Who always makes Papa give in to her.
She'll plead and weep, she'll bait him and she'll purr,
Till she gets what she wants, the little plotter;
And if into her husband she would make you,
The Baron for his son-in-law must take you.

"So go right to it, Son! Go to, go to!
Such prospects are not granted every man:
A bride of nineteen, petticoats that span
All the glories I would want for you.
Go after fortune like a yeoman true,
And don't be worsted if its guardian,
The Baroness, should offer a hard fight:
A dog can bark and still not mean to bite."

He stopped before a gate along the road
From which they saw, atop a rising hill,
The red roof of the Baron's domicile
And broad fields stretching out round the abode.
They drove beside a woodland stream that flowed
Through leas where cattle browsed their fill
And up along the roadway till it swung
Around, through towering heaps of cattle dung.

Our hero can recall this barnyard vast,
And memories of that dairy dimly rise.
Now, as through the gates the carriage passed,
The attic and the gables he espies,
The staircase with broad balusters, iron-cast,
On which for twelve years he'd not set his eyes.
With Hanne, at the door like Old Affection,
He quickly re-established a connection.

As she preceded them to show the way
To what she called the Baron's hunting-booth,
And as she heard our gallant hero say
That she'd become a beauty since their youth,
Old Homo leaned in closer to convey
In whispers barely audible this truth:
"Yes, keep up good relations with the maid;
You'll gain her lady's favor with her aid."

They stopped when they had reached a parlor door
Which the maid threw open for the two
And, having done so, thereupon withdrew.
Through dark clouds of tobacco smoke they bore
And, passing a long boot-rack, came before
The Baron's frock coat of straw-yellow hue.
He sat upon a couch and fed a hound
That fiercely growled and bared its teeth around.

The Baron rose—a figure lean and tall,
With hair all gray and matted, shoulders bent,
His eyes good-natured and yet somnolent,
But with a hawk nose that looked down on all.
"Well, well! Good day!" he mumbled, well-content,
Letting his pipe upon the table fall.
"Damn good to see you in the neighborhood!
Sit down, Hr. Pastor! Sit down! Be so good!

"This must be your son—Dog, do be still!
Is that how you behave before your pastor?—
Just sit you down. You must try my canaster.
Before we dine we still have time to kill.
There's beer here and tobacco, if you will!
—Hush, Tyrras! Damn it! Heed your master!"
He then took hold of Tyrras by each ear
And out the door he kicked him in the rear.

All sat, and heavily the smoke soon hung
While priest and Baron sampled in duet
The finest fertilizer one could get
By mixing guano in with cattle dung.
Adam sat mute and, not a smoker yet,
Double curses on the Baron flung
For always blowing rank fumes in his phiz
And forcing him to blow it back in his.

Salvation came before he snapped his tether.
The lackey Ole gave the dinner call
And in they all went to the dining hall,
Which boasted chairs of old-time Russian leather.
There Hanne, in a silk dress got together,
From a sideboard came to serve them all,
Though she'd a longish walk to the round board
About whose cloth four sniffing hounds explored.

A door was opened—lively, plump, and red,
Bare of throat, and short and stout of build,
With brown eyes that were dancing in her head
And curls of jet that to her shoulders spilled,
In Milady, all in white, did tread.
Hr. Homo bade her sit, but he was stilled
When she cried: "No, I'll sit by your son here,
For on this day he'll be my cavalier."

With that she turned her snub nose instantly
Toward our hero, who was pleased with *that*;
He bowed low, as she curtsied rather free,
And soon beside the lady Adam sat.
The Baron sent the dogs off with a pat,
Then poured wine for the adult company
And dug into his food, while for his guests
His lively daughter laughed and made fine jests.

She put the pastor to full many a vault;
For when he thought some pepper would be nice,
For instance, she sent down to him allspice,
And when he asked for sugar, he got salt.
But mostly her poor father paid the price,
For with his every sentence she found fault;
Whatever might be uttered by hawk-nose,
Without delay the snub-one would oppose.

With Hanne she had much whispered exchange;
They'd signal to each other frequently
With smiles our hero found sheer roguery.
But now (as both the older people range
Through last year's charges laid upon each grange)
She turns to Adam with alacrity
And says: "I've known you long before this day.
We've been old friends since Hanne came to stay.

"A thousand things she's told me, even more:
How many times you felt the rattan sting,
And what was your examination score.
They say there's someone you'll be marrying,
A little gardener's girl whom you adore
Beyond all words. See? I know everything."
She laughed out loud; but Adam, face all hot,
Was thinking to himself: "You'd better not!"

"Oh," she went on, giving with her plump,
Her little, hand a hunting-dog a rap
To make it take its forepaws from her lap:
"Could be that Rumor is a lying frump;
At first sight I did not think you a chap
Who'd give up freedom for a flower clump.
Long live freedom!" Here her glass she drained,
And Adam cleared his throat, acutely pained.

Once the meal was done, coffee was on.
They all adjourned into the cool sun-room,
Where all the cups lay out for them and shone
And, filled by Hanne, gave off rich perfume.
The limping Baron to an armchair'd gone;
The pastor found the Baroness, with whom
He made chit-chat, while Adam went to study
Two engravings whose gilt frames gleamed ruddy.

265/

One was a full-length portrait of George Sand,
Of modern novelists by all odds queen,
In male dress, with a horsewhip in her hand,
Smoking a cigar with earnest mien.
The other showed the Germans' own Bettine
Before her mirror, at her writing stand,
Looking at herself as her hand spurred
A nimble pen whose squirts were all but heard.

Our hero stood before these famous dames
When Mille, in whom Homo'd caused ennui,
Rushed down to him to make this inquiry:
"Those are my heroines inside those frames.
What do you think?" "They're passable," says he.
"Passable!" she ardently exclaims.
"Why, these are women who have made men bow
When they would smoke and act upon their vow."

He managed to keep down his consternation
While asking what that vow of theirs might be.
"I speak of feminine emancipation,"
She bristled as she answered haughtily.
"The greatest idea of our century,
Which to weak brains has caused much tribulation;
A thousand women, though, stand resolute
To give their life and blood in its pursuit."

With that she looked him squarely in the eye;
But he, who'd never heard such forwardness,
And who had been discountenanced no less
By all the jokes at table she'd let fly,
Made a bow half meant to mortify
And answered sharply with a rare address:
"Oh, such a sacrifice would bear no fruit.
The whole idea isn't worth a hoot."

"A hoot!" And fierce the Baroness now grew.
Her eyes with some pretense of anger glared,
But little for their perils Adam cared,
Adding: "No, not worth a single *sou*!"
"What! Was the hoot not good enough for you?"
She cried again, as round the room she stared.
"Did you ever, Hanne? Did you hear?
At me and at my principles they sneer."

What to-do was there! Old Homo tried
To talk them into being reunited;
Hanne laughed, half anxious but excited;
"Mille, Mille," her weak father cried,
"This is too much! Please be more dignified.
My after-dinner rest must not be blighted."
But Mille answers with an ill-bred glare:
"Please, Papa! It's none of your affair!"

She turned upon her heel and with a rush
She yanked the garden door; and to the wood
She ran, into the matted underbrush,
With Hanne following, fast as she could.
Old Homo, furious, sent grim looks to crush
Our hero where, quite thunderstruck, he stood.
With a yawn the Baron said but this:
"I think some ombre would not be amiss!"

Again they went into his sitting room,
Where out the pipes and cards for ombre came.
And in the summer sun's pure golden flame,
Near hid from them by the tobacco fume,
Loss after loss plunged Adam in such gloom
He lost his senses as well as the game;
Four hours in that same chair he sat, outdone,
His back turned to the garden and the sun.

—Now over was this Tycho Brahe Day,
When on all sides our hero was disgraced,
And for whose memory he'd but little taste
As in the moonlight they rode on their way.
With taunts and sneers his father's talk was laced:
"You've made a fine job of it, I must say!
That savoir faire of yours can't be gainsaid!
You *do* know how to turn a young girl's head!

"But you perchance have other ties that bind,
To the Ideal, ties to Sublimity?
At table there was, it occurs to me,
Talk of a gardener's girl you left behind.
I do hope there is nothing of that kind,
A match like that would be sheer lunacy—
No, just be still! I do not want to hear!
A thought like that will never reach my ear."

Now here was one fine mess! A voice inside
Called to our hero: "Adam, be a man!
And speak the love you can no longer hide.
Let him question it as best he can!
He's hinting that you prove it bona fide!
Don't end this awful day as it began!
Free yourself. Your honor's still assured.
Go to it! You'll be either killed or cured!"

But unsuccessful was that voice at last;
For he sat silent, having grown too wise
To care much what such voices might advise
As often trip up an enthusiast;
To ponder on the fateful hints they cast,
Which form a very catalogue of lies
And superstition, for which he's no pleader.
Such were *his* thoughts—what are yours, my reader?

What do you think of voices deep within
Which in our times of gladness oft upstart?
Which often in life's trouble and chagrin
Greet us like music that restores the heart?
Which sometimes through our bones and marrow dart
Like thunderbolts that make a house near spin?
Which sweetly lure us with an "On! Go on!"?
Which harshly warn us with "Be gone, be gone!"?

And what would be the meaning you'd apply
To silent signs addressed to sense and thought?
That sometimes lead us right, sometimes awry,
But what they are and wherefore we know not?
Signs like hands that tug our coats, distraught,
Signs like stars that our fates prophesy,
Signs which come to us when we're alone,
And signs which in a crowd make themselves known?

Let all of this by common sense be tried,
Which judges fairly, does not pick and choose;
For faith cannot, nor lack of faith, decide,
And science is confounded in its views.
The stars, which can in daylight be denied,
Come forth the evening heavens to suffuse;
But he who 'neath perpetual sun might dwell,
Could he believe in starry skies as well?

Against the prose of day and earthbound sight
Many treasure ships have run aground
Which mind could claim if it could be made sound
By losing itself deep within life's night.
For in a thousand mouths does night abound
And with a thousand shining signs is bright,
But to interpret them and grasp their tongue
Requires a sense with no mists overhung.

What matters is that moths of time, and rusts,
Have weakened not your inward-listening ear,
And that amid the noise it still can hear
The spirit's voice and its ethereal gusts;
And that the voice, which to you only trusts,
Is carried to your heart still true and clear—
That voice which through the spirit-world has rung,
But speaks to each of us in his own tongue.

And if there quickly dart before your sight
An outward token you take for a sign,
It matters too, for you to judge it right,
How far your soul's seen in its pure design,
Whose truth does not come clear through reasoning fine
But can be grasped in one glimpse of its flight.
But if that life-sense should be in your keep,
Don't hope to sleep as the insensate sleep!

For where the world is lying dead and dumb
To common eyes and ears—there where it faces
Toward you, all alive, and from it come
A host of messages in thought's still spaces;
There where the masses find it wearisome,
Where after novelty the public chases
For some excitement and some recreation,
There is for you eternal stimulation.

—Adam, now home, found stimulation too,
Though from another source: a note had come,
And when he'd read the barest minimum
And found the signature had been scored through,
He thought the anonymity quite rum.
But what would put him in a proper stew
Was the content, which, as his heart skipped,
Proposed what follows, in a horrid script:

"Good sir! I do consider you a man
Who, though another's honor he offends,
Will also be the first to make amends
The only way that genteel persons can.
By the nut trees where the rill descends
Next Saturday at noon, that is the plan.
I'll bring the pistols. Be in mask disguised;
It would not do to have you recognized."

At this our hero felt no small surprise.
The letter's dating let him quickly know
It had been written one full week ago:
Tomorrow that same Saturday would rise.
The crossed-out signature he closely eyes,
Forward, backward, sideways, from below,
And, as he thought, he finds by this assault
The name that's written over must be *Galt*.

He calls out for the boy who took the mail
And sharply asks by whom the note was brought.
Why, it was in the Vejle postman's lot,
Who asked eight shillings for it by the scale
And was so paid, but as to more detail
The postman offered nothing, not a jot.
He bids the boy be off, and sets to pacing
Back and forth along the floor, mind racing.

He stops—again he makes his eyes descend
Upon the note, considering every word.
The words make sense, but he can't comprehend
Why the Kammerherre was so stirred
Just now that he should such a challenge send,
Now the affair was growing moss-befurred.
Can it only now have come to light,
And does his wife support him in this fight?

What must he do? —Must he prove cowardly?
Must he in utter wretchedness eat crow
And all the world's respect for him forgo?
No, no! Dishonored he will never be!
Then must they meet, although he does not know
A great deal about duelling weaponry?
It would be death without a hope of grace,
But how, how can he settle such a case?

Again he starts to pace about the floor,
Seeking a way out he could not find.
He seemed to hear demonic laughter roar
Each time a new idea came to his mind.
Not till past twelve was he himself once more;
And along the bed's edge he reclined,
Where dull and weary he dropped off to dream
While savage images before him stream.

He woke up as the morning sun shone bright,
And looked about him with a mind half dense;
But now he pulls himself back into sense,
Remembering the letter of last night.
The dawn that did that Saturday commence
Was of a bloody red, vermilion light.
He seized his hat and ran out to the yard,
Where dew had left the flowers all be-starred.

How beautiful the garden looked today,
An earthly paradise, unspoiled and clean!
The little patch of grass, so fresh and green,
The arbor over there, where peace held sway!
How merry to their nests the birds made way
And twittered out their morning prayers serene!
That life could be so fair he never knew—
And for him all this life might soon be through!

He dropped his eyes, and with a gentle tread
He walked down to the churchyard, deep in thought;
And there his mother's grave he visited,
And fixed the cross and wreath upon the plot.
A grassy slope beside that earth he sought
And lay down, weary, while kind looks he shed
Upon the silent mound with violets overrun,
Which sent him sweetness in the morning sun.

"Oh," he breathes, stirred by her memory.
"Mother, who on earth showed me such care,
Who with your love gave me such sympathy,
You went ahead—but I shall find you there!
The selfsame garland shall our two graves wear
If here beside you they will bury me;
Upon our bones the selfsame earth shall lie,
And both of us sleep 'neath the selfsame sky!

271/

"And you"—to Alma here he heaves a sigh—
"You who in my thoughts are very near,
Who more than anyone to me were dear,
Although at times my mind did set you by:
Oh, if into my deepest heart you'd spy,
I know you'd grant forgiveness to me here!
Yes, if we could for one more time but meet,
The bitterest of feelings would turn sweet!"

He dropped his head, as in his mind thus dawned
The memory of that summer evening
When he and Alma stared into the pond
And saw their future in it shimmering.
His face betrayed the depth of his despond
As long he sat, not thinking anything,
Although he sweetly smiled, unwittingly.
Then all at once he rose with gravity.

It was time! He hurried on his way;
But now the voice of conscience would be heard
To state the sentence murderers incurred,
And only ceased when loudly did he say:
"I'll gladly pay whenever I have erred,
But I could never bring myself to slay!"
He went ahead, with doubly brisk a pace,
But with no mask, for he thought masking base.

At the wood he gave his watch a look:
It was past twelve. He hurried on inside
Along the sunny smiling little brook
That through the forest fastness was his guide.
There, on the rising near the spring, he overtook
A figure whom a cloak and mask did hide;
Another mask appeared then to his gaze,
And both were wearing black velvet berets.

The world starts to go black—but now he braces.
He steps up to them, raising his hat high,
Announcing "Adam Homo!" to their faces.
The sitting figure to its feet does fly;
The second then counts off the fifteen paces
And says, "The pistols have been loaded, by the bye,"
And, adding to that: "You, sir, have first shot,"
Hands him the gun, and moves off from the spot.

Our hero viewed the scene, mute and compliant;
In deathly silence had a minute flown:
His challenger, still cloaked, stood on a stone
And seemed to him a terrifying giant;
Back there, one arm around a tree branch thrown,
The somber second stood with look defiant;
But he felt sure some words were warranted
Before he fired a shot, and so he said:

"Good sirs! As the offender by the laws
Of honor I'm forbid to offer the first shot,
And my own sentiments must give me pause
If I should vary from those rules in aught.
If then we cannot straighten out our cause,
I urge that you shoot first, for I cannot.
Second, do you hold with this decision?"
He's answered: "No. Ignore that one provision."

"Well, then," he says, while buttoning his cloak
And pressing back the cock upon his gun,
"Then I shall send this bullet to the sun!"
He aimed up toward the treetops; fire then broke
Loose from out the pistol, and the smoke
Was followed by a bang, as when someone
Uncorks a bottle that locked in champagne,
Though that's not how it strikes our hero's brain.

The shot has made him stiff and motionless;
But then the second calls: "Masks off for all!
This battle must in honesty progress."
Down from the stone, all of a sudden small,
Leapt, with her mask removed, the Baroness,
As from her shoulders she let her cloak fall.
Simultaneously, two more eyes beckoned:
The deacon's Hanne stood there as the second.

Our hero would not trust his eyes aright—
The thought of dying occupied him still
As down his backbone it was coursing chill,
And he kept peering down the line of sight.
It was too hard to swallow such a sleight;
He almost fainted—but then with a will
He pulls himself up proudly and thereafter
Finds his breath in a convulsive laughter.

273/

"Hush, hush, good sir!" the Baroness now cries.
"There's still a bullet waiting in my gun,
Which I won't waste. I am no simpleton."
"I'll stand my ground!" he doughtily replies.
"Unless," she goes on, "as I hope, for one,
For last night's words you will apologize.
Are George Sand and Bettine still just passable?"
"No," he smiles. "They're unsurpassable!"

"I'm afraid that answer too won't do,"
She goes on with the same jollification.
"If this bullet's not to enter you,
I want to hear a loud, clear declaration:
Do you judge feminine emancipation
As hardly worth a hoot, a single sou?"
With that she cocks her gun and draws a bead—
Comes his forced laugh: "I'm not brave. I concede!

"Emancipation I now take to be
A principle which nothing can withstand."
"Then," bursts out Hanne, "down upon one knee
And kiss the freeborn woman's lily hand!"
He stepped up, forehead bowed to her command,
Sank to his knee, and with humility
A kiss to both her hand and hem he brought,
While over him the lady fired her shot.

He quickly got up from the ground, but still
He felt some remnants of his dizzy spell,
On which account he made use of the well
And cooled his forehead with its water chill.
Some time he lingered there, head bowed, until
His thoughts back to their wonted order fell,
When Hanne pulled his coat sleeve from behind
And softly asked: "You think we were unkind?"

"The pistols just had blanks in them, I swear.
It was all a joke, to get you here."
"Of that," he mumbled, "I was quite aware
Soon as I read where I was to appear.
But I've grown hungry after this affair;
Without my breakfast I feel tired and queer."
"A problem of no major magnitude—
Here comes the Baroness with all the food!"

"See here, good sir!" the fair one's voice was heard.
"Your arms should bear these most delicious stores."
"My thanks," says he, "for the honor you've conferred,
Allowing me to be a mule of yours.
And might I know down which road I'll be spurred?"
"The one down to the Fjord of Vejle's shores!"
So all three tramped along the forest track
While both the ladies let their pistols crack.

It was a merry jaunt; the beaming sun
Lit up the forest leaves along their way,
And Adam's heart was once more light and gay,
Alive to life's rich music that had won
A triumph over mortal pain that day.
With hunting songs the ladies had much fun,
As over stiles and up and down each hill
They tramped off, in their velvets, with a will.

A boat lay waiting for them on the shore,
In which his balance was but touch-and-go
As Hanne set it rocking to and fro.
Thereupon both ladies took an oar
And chose our hero for the steersman's chore,
Who would, he says to them, much rather row.
"No!" Mille shouts. "The rudder stays with you,
While we brave chaps make up the rowing crew!"

And truly they went briskly to their chore,
Mille full of spirit, Hanne brave,
Each keeping perfect time upon her oar
So easily the boat slipped on the wave.
They can, thinks Adam, make a boat behave,
As he kept at the rudder evermore.
"You're self-assured young ladies," he avers.
"What ladies?" they reply. "We're mariners!"

In to the little island now they swung,
Where, as a screen against the sun's hot ray,
Leaves were piled which laden waves had flung
To form a chamber 'midst the bright sea spray.
They went ashore, and 'twixt two trees, where hung
A swing and where the aromatic hay
Invited unto rest each weary limb,
Sat Adam, with the ladies flanking him.

275/

"Behold here my beloved Sans-Souci,"
Mille says, while Hanne then unpacks
Onto the grass their hamper full of snacks
And pours the wine out for the company.
"Here I can breathe and let my heart relax,
Here I can dream of all life's poetry,
Here I leave the mainland far behind,
And here I'll toast you now you're of my mind."

He took the cup with thanks for her good will,
And both of them raised up their arms to hail
And clink their glasses, when a nightingale
Behind them in the brush began to trill.
"Hush," Hanna breathes, "a musicale. Be still!
Such omens I have never known to fail.
It's from above, and Heaven finds it good
To plight this friendship out here in the wood."

"Now that's my Hanne with her prophecy!"
Mille exclaims. "I think you ought to know
She started plotting quite some time ago
To join us in the closest amity.
This morning in the fjord as we swam free
As ducks, she said to me, malapropos,
She thought that we were made for man and wife!
She's crazy! Did you ever in your life?"

"When she was small she had a splendid head,"
Said Adam, as his cheek betrayed a smile.
"And I have not been sleeping all this while,"
The Baroness's handmaid commented.
"But I've a wish, which Mille's seconded,
That you would tell a tale in your best style.
Tell us one before we eat the cake—"
"Yes," Mille cried, "that's just the course to take!"

"A tale?" repeated Adam, while the two
Sat listening and on him fixed their glance.
"All right!" he said, with thoughtful countenance.
"Then hear a tale that might be known to you."
And so he told them the Undine romance,
The water sprite in whom strong fires blew,
About her love, by miracle created,
About the soul she got and abnegated.

The story won their deepest interest,
But it was also wonderfully narrated,
And Mille loudly and with great warmth stated:
"Undine, poor thing, you really should have pressed!
From water you were scarce emancipated
Before you were by it once more possessed."
But Hanne said, as to their cake they fell,
"With all that wet, a little dry goes well.

"Besides," she said, "to me at least it seems
That you'll soon have a suitor on the scene,
For you, Milady, swim like an Undine,
And here's a knight beside the ocean streams."
The fair one answered: "Off you go in dreams!
If you don't stop, I prophesy you'll glean
A padlock for your mouth, to keep it stopped—"
Then over to the swing she gaily hopped.

"Climb on, good sir," she urges from the ground,
And he, though much against his will, complies;
But hardly had he got the ropes wrapped round
When high up in the air our hero flies.
He hears the wind shriek at each upward bound,
And downward he sees black before his eyes;
But even higher the two ladies fling him—
Those two are heartless in the way they swing him.

"Now that's enough!" he shouted, tense and hot,
As earth and heaven mingled in his sight.
"No," answered Mille, holding the rope tight.
"By you we were in Undine's waters caught;
Now up in Ether-land will you be brought
So that in air you'll be as erudite.
Look around! Perhaps you will succeed
Up there in running into a *sylphide!*"

So with a heavenward ascension closed
That day which had predicted his demise.
Back to the forest shore their boat they nosed,
And there our hero said his swift good-byes.
He found his mind a little discomposed
As the lady rose before his eyes,
And cried aloud (as if to fix the thought),
"Living with her would be no hard lot!"

277/

With mind at ease homeward he went his way,
But from that time he knew but dislocations,
For almost daily, sometimes twice a day,
Came notes or messengers with invitations
To come up to the manor for a stay;
And from there they'd make their gay migrations:
On land, through forest, open field, and lea;
On water, over lake and briny sea.

He had to join the ladies on the chase,
And on their fishing trips he would be drawn;
He had to ride out in the phaeton
When over sticks and stones they made it race.
But in the days, weeks, months, that this went on,
All rushing past him at this giddy pace,
Their mere acquaintanceship could not last long:
They were companions (friends would be too strong).

It was odd, but he knew not one whit
Of how she felt or to just what degree;
And, though she drank from his glass willingly
And on the grass beside him she would sit,
Her look was never one of sympathy,
There never was a hint of love in it.
He'd lost the will to pay her court at all,
And that was how the game stood late in fall.

—There came one morning, and a harvest-fest
Up at the manor house was set for night,
To which (the reader will, of course, have guessed)
The parsonage was bid, as was polite.
In the parlor, at their daily rite,
Sat Adam at his breakfast while, distressed,
His father up and down the floor was ranging
With tense expressions that were often changing.

Suddenly he stopped and cleared his throat.
"My son! My son! My friend—" This was a strain.
He paused and wandered to the windowpane
As though the rest would strike too harsh a note.
"My good son!" (he had found the antidote)
"There's something which I feel I must explain:
I—ere time and age have turned me stony—
I—I—I'm giving thought to matrimony.

"Don't interrupt. I know what you will say.
You think I've put your mother out of mind—
How awful if things really were that way;
I'll never find another of her kind!
I know that I must seek a *pis aller*,
But nonetheless to that I am resigned;
And if you ask what grounds for it there be,
I'll answer you: it's sheer Necessity!

"You understand? What is Necessity
But small things by the thousands, all those grounds,
No one of which exerts a tyranny
But whose combined oppression knows no bounds?
This is how Necessity confounds:
Some weakness, gout, this wretched rectory,
Some old debt (but I'll soon pay off that score),
Disorderly parishioners, and more.

"But what a wife is worth one only knows
When he has tried to live a widower
And sees half spoiled his house and garden rows.
The miller's eldest daughter I prefer,
A comely girl who gardens, cooks, and sews,
And I confirmed her, as her minister.
With some funds she'll put me on my feet,
And when I'm old she'll make my last years sweet."

Here he stopped—upon his son he stares,
Who's troubled by the pause and observation;
But Homo, in still worse an agitation,
Asks straight out Adam's thoughts on such affairs.
"I do respect your choice," the son declares,
"If Necessity's not its causation;
My feeling is, dare I speak openly,
That in such matters action should be free."

"Free, yes, free!" the priest jumps hotly in.
"It is a most sublime, a golden word,
Almost too idealistic to be heard,
God help us, of a world so deep in sin.
Yes, if you're young, and if you're snug within
Four walls, belief in freedom's not absurd;
But when you're old with mankind's misery,
You take your hat off to Necessity.

"For it is not in any way the same
As that blind Fate which comes from heathen folk.
Were that the case, believe me, 'twould provoke
A Christian priest like me to blush for shame.
No, let Fate's cudgel batter my poor frame,
Long as Necessity spares me its yoke;
But since, for you, this concept seems quite new,
It might be best to use it upon you."

How glad the old man was to have got free
While slipping his son's head inside the noose!
"But," Adam parried, whom Philosophy
Would not permit to suffer this abuse,
"Logic governs your Necessity!
Its objectivity it can't traduce;
From there to freedom, by that concept's light,
The distance, which I've often run, is slight."

"A fig for logic!" Homo's voice now rose.
"We're talking here of that Necessity
That daily life evinces constantly:
That shows forth in a body with no clothes,
That screams from bellies caught in hunger's throes,
That beads the brow with sweating drudgery.
Respect for *that* Necessity, no other,
Grows as we know ourselves and one another.

"Yes, with the years we learn to know that curse!
But on you too, though young you yet may be,
Though you've read deep in human liberty,
Necessity lies heavy and adverse.
It's lying there in your impoverished purse
And in your appetite for luxury;
It lies in your desire to join life's feast
And your reluctance to become a priest.

"A choice is necessary—must be weighed!
Look! On the one side beckons happiness,
A barony to crown you with success;
And on the other side, here in the shade,
A parish church with annex (added stress)
And that's the tiny future you'll have made.
There, honor and high deeds of policy;
Here, duty and hard works of charity.

"The choice is yours! But you should understand
That if old leading-strings you still have on
And to the wrong side you are being drawn,
I'll rip them off from you with my own hand.
But you won't leave your father woebegone,
Or yourself open to a reprimand,
Adding guilt to loss of sure success?
Consider, and think of the Baroness!"

The pastor left him there to meditate.
Adam, in his dressing gown, sat bleak
And pondered as he rubbed his chin and cheek
And scribbled with his fork upon the plate.
His father's words had caused the lad much pique,
The pressure for decision was too great;
But in his heart they were deposited,
As was quite obvious as he now said:

"Yes, it is true, my priestly call is small,
And, though for Alma I'd be good enough,
What point is there in wanting to out-bluff
A whole world that won't have the thing at all?
On whose approval could I ever call,
If I my father's wishes should rebuff?
In weighing all these matters carefully,
I see what must be by Necessity.

"No, no!!' he exclaimed. "It's definite!
Necessity will not be at this wheel!
Necessity which I've contempt for—it
I cannot ever blame for how I deal.
Ev'n as I choose, my freedom I will feel,
Freely I'll decide, freely submit;
I'll think it through before my choice is made,
And every *pro* and *contra* I'll have weighed."

With that intent, until the daylight died,
Our hero touched on every pro and con,
And then a fancy-dress suit did he don
And in the coach sat at his father's side.
Off to the Baron's barnyard did they ride,
Where games and dances now were going on,
For even at the gate they heard the dins
Of clarinets and mistuned violins.

281/

They went inside the barn, where lamps were lit
And hung amid green wreaths along the wall,
And whose clay floor the clog-dance hurts no whit.
With all the locals they can't move at all,
For just as the old drover leapt to haul
Crazy Karen round the floor a bit,
About the ancient pair horse-laughter peals
To uproar as they flop head over heels.

Toward the guests there came two peasant belles,
Whose caps' red ribbons hung in coy display;
And one takes Pastor Homo's hand to say:
"How dost 'ee, fa'er! An't we two fine gels?"
"What! The Baroness!" the pastor yells.
"And my dear Hanne! Do I see right, hey?"
But, laughing, so fast both the ladies twirled
Upon their heels that round them their skirts swirled.

To Adam, Mille turns now, whispering:
"Observe the heavy vapor round my head,
I wouldn't let it go for anything;
It means tonight I'll dance unlimited.
Smell my hair. I wet it for this spread
With brandy and the extract for the sling!
Such attar lures the peasant lads to dances,
And while they dance it puts them into trances."

"Yes, that's all the imbibing one should need,"
Our hero laughs out loudly in reply;
But he's drowned out by music wild and high
That introduced a polka with all speed.
Mille's hand's lost to a passer-by,
And to the line the youthful pair proceed.
Surprised, he says: "Who was that man so eager?"
"Ah," answers Hanne, "Kammerjunker Kriger!

"Now, he's a very fascinating one,
Stationed here in Vejle recently,
One who, at least as far as I can see,
Would like this manor for his garrison.
Watch out! He understands how courting's done
With beard and spurs, and with dragoon's esprit.
And if he's mad, he'll split your head in two;
But now farewell: my steward's come in view."

Off with Steward Hansen she took flight.
Strong he was, and fiercely paid her court
As, in the dance, he whirled her in great sport;
Our hero, with a sulky face and tight,
Standing in a corner bathed in light,
Made a figure of but middling sort.
Hemmed in, he could not gain an inch of ground
As round him he could hear the footfalls pound.

The band, on casks raised high o'er everyone,
Cut into the hot air with its loud whining,
Into aromatic waves combining
Dust, sweat, brandywine, and farmer's son:
A steam of common sense and life homespun
Which Adam's nose refined was undermining.
He moved off toward the door; but he ran here
Into the Baron, who long bent his ear.

Then from far off, a roll on the drum pad;
There in the crowd he sees her ladyship,
Hands on the shoulders of a farmer lad,
Who grasped her very tightly on the hip
And did not gently swing his oread,
But heftily to both sides made her tip
Her legs and shoulders as he whirled about
His valiant lady, ever game and stout.

But suddenly the waltzers go their ways,
And swift upon them Adam's seen to steal,
And, with a humble bow to Mille, prays
She join him in a miller's dance and reel.
"Why, yes, indeed!" she says with smiling gaze.
"But first a drink to slake this thirst I feel!"
Here, puffing, Mille sat down on a bench
While Adam flew for punch, her thirst to quench.

When he returned, Lieutenant Kriger sat
Bent o'er the lady in all gallantry
And filling up her ear with flattery.
She took the punch and found it grand; with that,
She says to Adam, standing sullenly:
"Tonight I'm Grethe—yes, the thing is pat.
Hr. Homo, you the name of Hans must bear;
The Kammerjunker that of Mads. That's fair."

283/

With Hans's name he hardly was entranced.
He took a seat upon the bench in haste,
To talk of love, with country language laced,
With Kriger, who was Mads'd while he was Hans'd,
As Grethe fair enjoyed the punch's taste
And strong objections to them both advanced.
But now that rest renewed her dancing zeal,
She leapt up, crying out: "The reel! The reel!"

The music started up, and in the ring
With Hanne and the Baroness there trod
Our hero, who both ladies round did swing.
The gammers gave full many a gloating nod;
The young chaps screwed their eyes, but must applaud
Our hero's nimble form and easy spring,
And Hanne's rear that wiggles when she kicks,
And Mille's legs that whip like drummers' sticks.

Even wilder does the music sound,
And merrier grow the folk who watch their tricks;
Adam grows more free with every bound
And bolder too are Hanne's wriggling kicks,
While, ever more resembling drummers' sticks,
Mille's feet upon the clay floor pound.
And when they change one partner for another,
Like drunkards they keep weaving round each other.

Through loud huzza's in triumph now they pass
As, to her place, returning from the dance,
Grethe's led back by the lucky Hans.
Off he hurries to refill her glass,
But on returning, by the same mischance,
Once again beside her he finds Mads,
Who wins, by means of flattering address,
A miller's dance from Adam's Baroness.

Adam's cheeks now colored deepest red,
For this was something he could not ignore.
He wished that he could smash that Kriger's head
And stomp him just as flat as the clay floor.
To Mille with some bitterness he said:
"As for me, then, is there no hope more?"
"No," said the Lieutenant with disdain.
"No, poor Hans can spare himself the pain."

"Hr. Kammerjunker, who is this Hans chap?"
Our hero briskly asks, his forehead knit,
Pounding on the bench on which they sit.
"Oh," Mille cries, "now, what a fearful rap!"
But Kriger laughs: "Hr. Hans's eyes do spit,
He's giving both our faces one fine slap."
"Lieutenant!" Adam sputters, red and mad.
"Step out! An explanation will be had!"

He didn't get far. Mille made a dash
To stop him and to bring him back again
To Kriger, calmly stroking his mustache,
Who said politely: "Let's be gentlemen!
Forgive my joke! I fear I was too rash."
"My dear friend," Mille whispered to him then,
"When I call you my Hans and him my Mads,
You must know what's meant by that alias!"

She left with Kriger for the miller's dance
Just as a couple rushed into the lists
In time to all the others' slapping fists
And stamping heels, a choir of jubilance.
Our hero rubs his brow as he untwists
The meaning of her golden utterance:
"When I call you my Hans and him my Mads,
You must know what's meant by that alias!"

He felt relieved of all uncertainty,
And with his mind at rest now strolling round,
A thousand things of interest he found:
Back there a maid redid her finery,
And there a stocking garter was rewound;
There round a chest some gammers stood, to see
High upon its lid a hunchback sitting
With frills upon her bonnet most befitting.

She peered out on the dance without a blink,
Making the late crofter's wife *au fait*
As Adam passed them both along his way
To where the casks poured out their potent drink.
Some ten old farmers on a bench parley
Contentedly amid their tankards' clink,
While some, entranced by coachman Søren's lore,
Stand puffing on their pipes beside the door.

Eventually the throng made way for him,
And he fled through the barn's wide-open door.
But just outside his head began to swim:
A silence like a veil the landscape wore,
The sky above with radiant stars did brim,
Upon the ground the dew its pearls did pour,
With gentle winds the poplar trees did rouse,
And he could hear the trembling of their boughs.

He stood a while, by all this captivated,
As upward to the skies did his eyes climb,
Where, high above the earth, the moonlight plaited
Wreaths of eternity from things of time.
He woke, though, for the clarinets now grated,
And from his short dream in the night sublime
Once more into the barn our hero ran,
Where on the round dance everyone began.

Up to him then tripped little Grethe fair
And cried: "My hand is Hans's for this dance!"
He naturally would not forgo the chance,
And took it quickly, with a grateful air.
Into the circle more and more advance,
A ring in which both young and agèd share,
Where girl and boy, old goodwives and the lame,
Swineherd, pastor, and great Baron came.

To the music's din the entire skein
Was set in motion in that yawning space,
And on the floor was heard the heavy pace;
The girls first swung each other in the chain
As if to share apart the waltz's grace
Until each one was chosen by a swain.
But what most pleased them—when each waltz was done,
There came a clog-dance full of play and fun.

First Jens the Drover took the dunce's chair;
Then ancient Kirsten, blindfolded, fell down
At every step as they all tugged her gown;
Then Birthe smoked a pipe, with coughs to spare;
Deaf Mikkel on a fiddle went to town;
Lame Jeppe minuetted on a dare;
And then there came the game of fox and hen
And gay leapfrogs performed by the young men.

286/

The greatest pleasure kindled at the feast
Came from the laughs the Baroness provoked
When like a top she spun the flurried priest,
Who held her neck so tight she almost choked,
This while the Baron slipped and stumbled, yoked
To Hanne till the Holstein-waltzing ceased.
There was hilarity words can't convey;
Why, the goose-girl smiled, first time all day.

Our hero reached the peak of happiness;
For when once more the dancers circled round
And Mille's hand he dared gently to press,
A forceful pressure in return he found.
Upon his sunshine did no shade transgress
Till the coach and parting-time came round,
When he round Mille's shoulders draped her cloak
And then drove home from all the noise and smoke.

Once home, he threw himself upon the bed;
And, rocked to sleep, he fell into a dream
Where toward him visions of the future stream.
Long and deep he dreamed, then raised his head,
Demanding that all dreams be quieted,
Once more to consider his life's scheme,
And, calling upon hopes and memories,
To orient himself in view of these.

He was an honest chap—he'd not deny
That Alma's cause looked absolutely dim;
His double-dealing came to his mind's eye
And, as an honest man, it made him grim.
He had good sense, knew how to gratify
A world that was not really meant for him.
But he had feeling too—he deeply sighed
As he the cover of his desk threw wide.

He took out paper, pen, and ink to write
To Alma, giving her her liberty.
He wrote and wrote; the words came handily
And—broken was their bond, much to his fright.
But there was more, and he went on to cite
His reasons with the greatest cogency,
And with the chief (his father wished him to)
He bade the garden's lily fond adieu.

But while the wafer on it was still wet,
The address on the letter not yet dry,
He called the boy and him the errand set
To bring it to the Vejle post, and fly!
Up to the gate he kept him in his eye—
Somberly he turned and said: "I've met
The obligation which my honor claimed;
But oh! that letter makes me half ashamed."

The whole day through his nerves were in a knot;
He felt himself as anxious and as tense
As if he hunted for a lost tuppence,
But where he lost it he had quite forgot.
Next day he was much clearer in his thought,
And with that he regained his confidence;
For with his past behind him he could see
The beaming hope that lit his life to be.

Yes, now how bold and forceful would he be
When he could work from such a great foundation!
Not as a priest, for church and congregation,
But patron of all men in misery.
No more to feel his way so cautiously,
Amid the wealth that came with such high station
He wished to help, to ease, to gladden all,
Yes, God-like, call forth bliss on great and small.

It's true, he hadn't yet the barony
From which those great resources would progress;
But very wrong in all things must he be,
Were his nod not to bring him that largesse,
Were not the Baroness's hand and Yes,
With manor house, estate, and creamery,
His if only he would speak the phrase
To bind his fate to Mille's all their days.

And so our hero's life turned self-deceit,
And much as other people's who've transgressed
Against the role learned at their mother's breast
And heard in childhood at their father's feet.
But were he raised in freedom so complete
That his inner call could be suppressed,
Then actually it's about the same:
Whatever role he picks will bring him shame.

288/

Oh, on the stage of life let your eyes dwell,
And see, young reader, your reflection there!
See where the actors, pets of the parterre,
Go to the wall, and they deserve it well;
See ineptness without parallel,
Hear the lines which they failed to prepare,
See them please themselves in monologues,
But in ensembles go straight to the dogs!

And what's the reason for this wretched game?
The reason's lying in the wardrobe chest,
Because the role to which they could lay claim
Was found too small when given its first test.
With but a homely outfit that role came,
And they'd have liked to glitter when they dressed.
They sell themselves for tinsel and for plush
When into "roles beyond their powers" they rush.

For heroes they would be. With golden braid
Upon their cloaks they lean proud on their swords
And, beggar-kings among their wretched hordes,
They're wondered at and, what is more, obeyed.
Of the larger drama nothing's made:
Theirs is the only business on the boards;
And they're so heedless of collaboration,
They're sick to think of sharing an ovation.

Sad hour! when under hoots and stamping feet
They must evacuate the stage in shame
Where they were lit, in braid, by lantern flame
In parts and plays their talents did not meet.
Sad hour backstage! with sponges that delete
The greasepaint, yes, but hardly their ill-fame
When the play is over, and the joke,
And they are forced to doff the fancy cloak.

O dole! (for surely it must cause them dole)
In grief and penitence to call to mind
Their real and long-repudiated role
Which early to their lives had been assigned
And which to learn would now take heavy toll,
Since only scraps of it remain behind.
In any case, it is too late, that's certain,
To play it in a shroud at final curtain.

Not so, my reader? Frightful what comes later!
All right, then, look in your own breast!
For though you be content as a spectator
And far from noisy stages take your rest,
You'll soon be on the stage at life's behest.
Before your love of theater grows much greater,
Know your task! My own now is to see
To my own hero and his role-to-be.

His plan we know—although not expedited
Quite so easily as he had thought.
Yet, even when he had not been invited,
He'd show up at the manor like as not;
Yet, when beside the ladies he would trot,
He said such things his troth was all but plighted—
Not to mention that around the beauty
He flattered her beyond the call of duty.

For she kept on behaving just the same,
As though Miss Grethe's handclasp she'd forgot,
And with his touchiness he oft felt shame
From ugly laughs and jests passed without thought.
But what above all turned his high hopes lame
And made him, more than anything, distraught
Was Kriger's coming out upon his horse
Every other day to court, of course.

Oh, how that Kammerjunker earned his hate,
The way he would be preening his mustache!
As from his eyes the sparks of love would flash
When he would take her hand and kiss it straight!
Oh, well he knew that this young reprobate
Sued only for the Baroness's cash!
Oh, what a bother was that cozener
To him, whose love was, all of it, for her!

How deep he was in love he wasn't clear,
While in this fashion, sickened with dismay
And hemmed in constantly 'twixt hope and fear,
He saw whole months were slipping quite away.
—It now was winter, and the other day
The ice had formed beneath a frost severe.
Mille had a skating-party toward
And asked him to come join them on the fjord.

Once there, he strapped his skates on in a trice
And from the shore, with ice creaking below,
He dashed his way along the film of snow
That, fine and thin, lay on that bridge of ice.
He saw far out three skating to and fro
And knew the story without thinking twice:
Kriger's blue dragoon's coat that would be,
And upward roared the fires of jealousy.

In toward him on their skates the three came sailing,
Hr. Kriger, in his teeth a big cigar,
Miss Hanne, with her arms stretched out and flailing,
Barely keeping perpendicular,
And Mille, with a rhythm never failing,
Till, on one leg, no longer very far,
She slid to him, her other leg in air
In honor of his joining with them there.

"Welcome!" Mille called out, debonair,
Holding on to him by his lapel.
"I see this bitter frost finds you quite well,
You flew right toward us like a young March hare.
And how, I wonder, does your nose-tip fare
In these thirteen degrees of freezing-spell?
The rime has made your eyebrows twice as big.
But look! How do you like my powdered wig?"

She took her cap off from her dark-brown locks
In which, like flowers, the white rime was hung,
And at his cry: "The devil! You use chalks!"
Merrily on high her cap she swung.
But Kriger says: "The hyacinths in flocks
Despite the winter's cold have brightly sprung
By dint of the warm rose upon her cheek—"
"That's true!" she laughs. "It happens twice a week!"

"But as for now," she went on jauntily,
"Home to the island on whose coasts we'll land!"
With that she let Hr. Kriger take her hand,
And off they went along the frozen sea.
Adam then grabbed Hanne's, which was free,
And skated, though his heart stung like a brand;
But while those two like birds flew to their nest,
He with his lady like a snail progressed.

291/

Hanne's ankles nearly always bent;
Every moment, laughing, she must stop,
And wonders Adam often must invent
To pry a skate up from too deep a chop.
At last, after a long time, they both flop
Upon the coast, to Mille's merriment,
Who lit up her cigar from Kriger's own
And made sure that the smoke toward them was blown.

It was the second insult he endured,
But nonetheless he put on a good face.
When Hanne fell, he left her to her case,
While round in circles on the ice he toured.
Using only one leg for a brace,
He kicked high with the other, self-assured;
When all of this was over, he swung round
And slowly in a backward circle wound.

His lady has no more cause for disdain,
But up in smoke his triumph decomposes.
She was the Pharaoh, and he played her Moses
Whose miracles and wonders were in vain;
For Kriger, at his praise, great wrath discloses
And runs out imitating this campaign.
So from our hero Mille shifts applause
And makes it twice as loud in Kriger's cause.

Then Kriger said: "If you watch carefully,
You will behold an interesting sight:
Of your fair name I now am going to write
The starting letter, which, of course, is E.
Leaving them upon the surface white
With thin-packed snow, he skated free,
And then came back, and with the turns he made
He wrote two semi-circles with his blade.

And true enough! An $\mathcal{E}$ had been impressed,
So finely curved it was a joy to see.
Mille cried: "Oh, that's done cunningly,
How jauntily it bulges east to west!"
Our hero, who grew more and more distressed,
Regained his voice at this calamity,
And into this asseveration flew:
"Oh, nothing to it! I can do it too!"

He raced away; but when he'd come around,
Having made the letter $\mathcal{E}$'s first bow,
And was preparing for the second go
As on the ice his figure swung and wound,
The circle that he traced was far from sound.
Mille cried: "It must be fixed, you know!"
And gave him such a nudge that he was scooted
Straight ahead, while the Lieutenant hooted.

To Kriger she: "A point of exclamation!
It looks as though it's there your $\mathcal{E}$ to hail!"
But Adam, with his jostled back, turned pale
And found it hard to breathe in his vexation.
He skated on—he swooped, began to flail,
And went into a fearful oscillation;
His hat fell off—and Mille's laughter trills
As backward on the ice our hero spills.

And there he lay. At first our hero thought
He had a broken back from this collision,
But from the pain he reached a new decision
That he was injured in a lower spot.
Still, back upon his feet he quickly got
As Mille neared him, laughing in derision;
He snatched his hat, and with a bitter smile
He yelled good-bye, and rushed home from the isle.

With a stormwind's speed his skate-blades whirred
As on the lady he passed sentence grim,
Though on the ice she followed after him.
She called—but he feigned that he had not heard.
"Adam!" she cried—although the chance was slim
That so much as a look would be conferred.
He reached the shore, and once there he unbound
His nimble skates and took out on firm ground.

He hurried up the path, his forehead hot,
As from his seething feelings there arose
Demons casting fogs around his thought.
He felt like someone choked in poison's throes,
Like someone with a soul by Satan bought
Who finds that he has led him by the nose.
The mood he fell in was an endless pit,
His very anger was soon lost in it.

He got in, and at table father found.
When Adam came and drew his own chair near,
Homo filled a huge glass up with beer
And, having drained it, jokingly then frowned:
"You look as though you were half underground.
Our sick Mads's face looks just as drear.
Go at that pork! It makes the heart quite mellow.
I must be off now to prepare the fellow."

And off he went, with all his priestly wear,
To give last rites and get Mads's heart converted.
No sooner had he found the room deserted
Than at the window Adam took a chair,
Staring at the small yard, disconcerted,
And at the sunlit snow that glittered there.
Two whole hours he sat there at the pane,
Somber, stricken, no thoughts in his brain.

Already to its end slants the short day
And in the eastern sky the pale moon dwells,
When suddenly he hears the sound of bells
That through both soul and body makes its way.
He listens, as a cracking whip compels—
He sees it now—a horse with bright red sleigh,
Which, once past the dunghill, leftward swings,
The sleigh behind it, to which it lends wings.

And rearward on the sleigh, her cap all wound
With golden braid, with riding boots and dress
Of fur, there stood the little Baroness
Who looked about and made the whip resound.
With interest that he could scarce suppress,
His eyes pursued the sleigh as it drove round;
But hardly at the front door had it stopped
When quick into the parlor Mille hopped.

Congratulating him on his escape,
Despite his fall and that hard bump he took,
She added to this with a merry look:
"Away, young sir! Steal into your fur cape!
A sleigh ride will get you in tiptop shape!"
He rushed to get his cape from off its hook;
But, on returning, much against his will,
He found the lady's back-seat his to fill.

When he insists he take the reins in hand,
So as not to sit there like a sot,
The thought of it is more than she can stand,
But soon her opposition is forgot.
"Geeup!" she says; he drives at her command
While from the rear her whip cracks like a shot,
And round they swing, as out the gate they ride
With Spids and Morten barking alongside.

A bold turn at the lane's end brings them round
To where the church stood on the steep hillside,
And onto the main highway now they glide.
They fly like birds; the sleighbells loudly sound;
The sharp winds and the hoofbeats on the ground
Raise the snow around them as they ride.
It flies in Adam's mouth as powdery fluff,
And all that he can do is huff and puff.

From the open stretch of fields they bore
Down to the fjord, where everything went still,
And soon, o'erhung by hill on wooded hill,
They reached the ice-bedecked and snow-strewn shore.
The moon her shining silver rain let pour,
And, round her, thin and luminous cloud-veils mill;
But, suddenly unveiled, she hailed the sleigh
Which, in her cold smile, glided on its way.

Our hero sat in silence, drinking in
The brilliant glow spread out upon the night;
The evening hush, the wind that made no din,
Broken only when the whip cracked tight,
But flooded by the sleighbells silvery-thin,
Recalled that day of skating and their fight.
He looked about and found where he had tripped,
The very spot at which his blade had slipped.

Each track upon the white snow he can see,
His own wide semi-circle yet remains,
And tightly in his hand he takes the reins
And makes a bold dash over Kriger's $\mathcal{E}$.
"What!" laughingly the Baroness complains,
Observing this act of audacity.
"That was my middle that you just cut through!
Now, that repays the push I gave to you."

295/

"We're quits for both the damage and the shame,"
With a forgiving look he answers her,
While Mille snuggled deeper in her fur,
Just as a veil the moon's face overcame.
"Look!" she cried again. "Look, our coy Dame
Plays hide-and-seek behind her gossamer!"
And Adam stretched his neck far back to see
The Lady play her game of coquetry.

"That's just the posture of Endymion!"
Exclaimed the fair one with a knowing smile.
"Watch out! for Luna knows how to beguile
And Cupid's bowstring is already drawn.
Send her another look in that same style,
She'll swoop down from the cloud she lies upon—"
"Oh," laughed Adam, "when it's eight degrees
The darling's heart won't melt with any ease."

Once more he lifts his gaze up in content,
Still stretching out full-length upon his seat.
But Mille went on—while she forward bent
O'er Adam's brow, and kept his eyes in sight,
Which beamed at hers in warm acknowledgment—
"You really do disdain fair Luna's might?"
"Yes," he said. "Or she'd be here by this—"
But he'd scarce finished ere he felt a kiss.

At the touch the reins fell from his hand,
So that the horse at once stopped in its ambles.
Quickly Adam to his feet now scrambles
And waits for Mille with his arms out-fanned;
But what she wants she can't quite understand,
Though she's not caught for long among these brambles.
Lithe as a cat she slips into the sleigh
Which once again now glides along its way.

Since on the seat there was but room for one,
The fair one took her place upon his lap,
Which so sincerely overjoyed the chap
He flowed with gratitude for what she'd done.
Between the two of them a thread was spun
Of tender chat, which she was first to snap
By crying out: "Quick! Back to the estate.
We'll make arrangements there, and do it straight."

Like lightning they drove home. The horse's shoes
Struck sparks upon the road along the shore;
Then down the by-way through the woods they bore,
And in along the manor's avenues.
There down the stairs, emboldened, Hanne tore,
Receiving them with joyful, loud halloos;
But Mille cried: "Do wish me well this day,
For here, my lass, you see a fiancée!"

From Hanne's hug, to Adam she now turned
And with him in to see the Baron strode.
He, in his evening coat, sat unconcerned
At table with his mug. His pipe bowl glowed
From a drowsy candlestick that burned
Upon the table, and its thick smoke flowed.
"Papa! While you were slumbering away,
Your little daughter found a fiancé!"

"Fiancé?" in a drawl asked eagle-nose,
As he set the brimming mug aside
And from his place laboriously rose.
"Fiancé? And what, pray, might that betide?"
"What's this? Have your tastes grown so rarefied
You do not like the husband that I chose?
Here he is!" The Baron sighed aloud
As she drew Adam forth, who humbly bowed.

"Hr. Homo!" the man spluttered. "Won't you come
And tell me it's a joke? Dear girl, don't say
That you've been fools and gone so far astray!"
"Been fools!" says Mille, hurt and very glum,
At which she cries to Adam, who'd kept mum:
"You talk to him now that I've blazed the way."
But Adam's eloquence is no more grand
Than: "Hr. Baron, I beg your daughter's hand."

"Then it's in earnest? Satan's at his trade!"
The old man bitterly began to rave.
"It's true, we lie in beds that we have made.
I blame the freedom which to you I gave,
The way you gad about and misbehave!
From now on I will see that I'm obeyed.
You, Mille, from this parlor will not stir;
And you—you understand me well, good sir?"

As if he wished to underline his might,
He drank a mug of beer down one-two-three,
At which he gave his pipestem a hard bite
While Adam clenched his hat in misery,
And Mille took on, sighing tearfully.
Her whimpers set the Baron's wrath alight.
At last he said, in accent saturnine:
"To be a priest's wife would suit you just fine?"

"What? *I* a priest's wife? That I'd never stand!
You really think, Papa, I'm such a twit?
No, Father dear, just let me settle it!"
And now she takes firm hold of Adam's hand
And says: "If Father should your claim admit,
You'd drop this priestly whimsy you had planned?"
"Yes," Adam answers. "To that I'll attest.
It's certainly a reasonable request."

"Stop there!" the old man cries, and gives a rap
Upon the table, hard, decisively.
"And just what source of income will you tap?"
She laughs: "Why, Adam will be squire, wed to me.
And, after all, Pa! You're a well-heeled chap,
You'll help us settle on a property.
A son-in-law could lend your age a hand
And aid you in the manage of your land.

"Then, think," she gave the Baron an embrace
And hopped around him like a nimble bird,
"Then, think of his rare name, no more absurd
Than Juel or Brockdorff, which are no disgrace.
And yet the court's still missing Homo's race.
Think to what vexation you'd be stirred
If not upon a Homo I should fasten
But on a Nielsen, Møller, or a Madsen.

"Yes, you know how to sell your merchandise,"
Papa broke in on her, still just as cross.
But she went on: "Now, Father, please be wise!
Think if a starving, noble piece of dross
Had been your son-in-law! Now there's a prize!
He'd be your ruin, making up his loss
At cards, his debts, and there you'd be, quite stuck,
Once you had no more money he could pluck."

298/

That argument improved the situation.
And then, when Adam vowed, on Mille's plea,
To occupy his mind with crop rotation,
The Baron hugged his son-in-law to be.
Our hero was engaged, then, honorably;
From Copenhagen came swift confirmation,
As was expected, of his squire's estate,
His courtier-, junker-, hunt-certificate.

The Baron was a little out of face,
For he had sought a title to impart
To Adam, and he took it much to heart
That, from the halls of majesty and grace,
The grace was just a trickle at the start
And not the torrent proper to the case.
As for Adam, either would have done,
And Mille said: "It's really six of one!"

And, to be sure, just by the right to wear
Court uniform our hero's way was clear
Into life's elevated, grander sphere;
And, though he still stood on the lowest stair,
Each step up would ennoble his career.
He knew the great advantage he had there;
But, though his sights were always led on high,
His soul had greater things to clarify.

That freedom which was his preoccupation,
In whose idea his whole life was grounded,
Now stood, by no more barriers surrounded,
Realized in his imagination.
Now in pride he felt how his heart pounded,
Now with truth he knew his liberation,
Now with these means he had the potency
To turn his yearnings to activity.

For what is liberty, as an ideal
With all the feelings that belong to it,
Without the power that can make it fit
Into a world which, after all, is real?
It's no more than bar-assets which must sit
Unusable toward anybody's weal
Because the gold's not coined and lacks that splendor
Of design that makes it legal tender.

For Adam the ideal now had design,
For him it *was* coined by the potency
Which issued from the Baron's treasury
And to a thirsting soul was blessèd wine.
He thrilled to deeds in which he soon would shine.
His purpose was to live forever free:
This and *this* and *this* he wished to do,
And *this* and *this* and *this* he'd carry through.

This drunken freedom left almost unsung
The new bonds Eros twisted, strand by strand,
Which the Baroness's gentle hand
Round him and all his future days had slung.
Before his eyes like rosy wreaths they swung,
And if they stopped his soul from flights too grand,
Just as earth's vales were passing out of sight,
They bound him to life's pleasures twice as tight.

For on a common life, both brisk and sound,
The young pair now embark day after day:
To all the manor houses they ride round
To make their visits as new *fiancés*.
In a thousand tricks the two abound,
They're daily at new dalliance and play:
Good morning comes with wrangling, tiffing, spatting,
And for good night there's hugging, kissing, patting.

In this fashion, off with Time's ball flew
The whole of winter and a bit of spring,
In which old Homo had his wedding too,
With his new bride to ease life's evening,
The miller's daughter, who went feathering
The pastor's nest the whole day through.
The month of May came, and scarce passed before
Our Adam's wedding too stood at the door.

Early that great morning Adam raced
To don court uniform from toe to top
Which, sewn by Copenhagen tailor Popp
And then returned with word that there be placed
A bit more padding in the breast and waist,
Came late last night, sent back to him nonstop.
He put the breeches on, so blue, so dark,
To show the beauty of his strong calf's arc.

He looked down at his boots, and evident
Was his delight when he observed his spurs;
He donned his coat, whose braided fasteners
And brocade were to his heart's content;
His *tricorne* would delight the connoisseurs
(He gave one point of it its proper bent);
Around his slender waist he tied his sword,
Grabbed both his gloves—the image of a lord.

With his father, at just twelve o'clock
He mounts the shay and drives to the estate,
Where rows of servants on the staircase wait
And wedding guests through every doorway flock.
The priest is shown in to the Baron straight;
His son, who gives his dusty hat a knock
And seeks a place where he can clean his hands,
Is led upstairs to one of the washstands.

He washes up and waits now for the nod
Which to the manor's chapel sends him in;
He looks into the mirror, sighing: "God!
If only these good people would begin!"
He gets up from the chair in some chagrin
And, moving to the window, stares abroad;
From his coat he takes his porte-monnaie,
Jammed in his pocket by the jogging shay.

On opening it, a little note fell free
Which scarcely had he seen ere to his ear
Alma spoke out from the souvenir.
The now-old writing was an answer she
Had made to letters sent the previous year
And had long faded from his memory.
On folding out the note, his eyes first meet
These verses written on the topmost sheet:

Your Sunday letter I've just put away.
Halfway through, my Adam, had I read
When the old date on it ran through my head,
And what I thought then I'm about to say.

It has been told us that a gentle ray
Can shine down to us from a star long dead;
We have the light, though over night's dark bed
The fires of that black star no longer play.

301/

O, be not angry! When I read that note,
My joy in it by that thought was suppressed:
I wonder if he still feels as he wrote?

Aren't written words like light from that dead star?
The feeling they were born of in our breast
Is gone once they are read by one so far.

As large as life stood Alma by his side.
Her golden hair wreathed by a myrtle band,
She stood there in the white gown of a bride,
And toward him she reached out her little hand.
Down his cheek he felt a hot tear slide
And inward sighed in harsh self-reprimand:
"Why only now do you come in my head?
Of course it's you to whom I should be wed."

As when a dike which ocean waves torment,
Until its base is all but undermined,
Bursts open all at once and through each rent
The roaring billows pour in unconfined:
So in his heart, the memories long pent
Burst the artful chains which did them bind;
They leapt like prisoners out from their night,
Each one desiring freedom, life, and light.

A fearful battle tore him inwardly.
From every side it seemed as voices spoke:
"Undo the chains that bind your liberty!
Recall the costly promise which you broke!
Leap out the window! Quick! No lesser stroke
Than flight can save you in this misery.
Fly home! Take the express! Think of the smart
Which you have given such a loving heart."

Our hero stood there dazed—his forehead burned;
His eyes, which stared in space, grew twice as wide.
At once quick to the window he returned:
The gate was open on the park's far side.
He looked out at it with a gaze that yearned:
One daring run, and all was simplified!
But first he had to think the whole thing through . . .
Then—in his robes his father came in view.

302/

"Come," smiled the latter. "Sentence has been passed!
In chains you will be soldered to your bride.
They're all in chapel. Everyone's inside.
But look at you! Why do you look downcast?
What's happened? Tell me, son!" he said, aghast.
"Oh God," our hero with a sob replied.
"I can't deny it longer, I confess
I can't, I dare not, wed the Baroness!"

"What!" the old man shouted, truly frighted.
"Why? What's the matter? Tell me, but be brief!"
And Adam, goaded by this disbelief,
In a rush his broken vow recited
And ended with his lily crushed and blighted
Unless she could be spared from that great grief.
But Homo yelled: "The devil take your lily!
You can't back out of this thing. It's too silly!

"But you," (and here his angry voice turned gruff)
"You're saying things that quite astonish me!
Why, you're a philistine, that's plain enough,
If you still think of choice and liberty.
You'll be the cat who sniffs round fricassee
So long they finally remove the stuff.
Now show some decency and self-command,
And mind: Necessity holds the whip hand!"

"Necessity!" sobbed Adam in despair.
"Yes, that's right," the angry priest replied.
"That same Necessity which you've defied
Has tied you in a knot and left you there,
So be off to that altar down the stair!
You are not going? Can your ears abide
The scorn and sneers, contempt, and the disgrace?
The name of someone without faith and base?"

"Necessity!" once more came the lament,
And Adam looked out to the open gate
As he turned, preparing his descent.
"Stop!" cried the priest, for whom he did not wait.
"You must take *me* in tow for this event,
Me, whose sermon now won't captivate.
The one I wrote was full of fire and flash,
But one's excitement *you* know how to dash."

Into the chapel, where in pew on pew
Expectant guests awaited groom and bride,
Adam entered at his father's side,
Somber-eyed and pale as lily's hue.
There rose a murmur now that he was spied;
A whisper round the rows of ladies flew:
"Oh, isn't the old father so pedantic!
The son, though, oh how sweet and how romantic!"

Scarce his proper seat the bridegroom found
Before each head turned round just as before,
For on the Baron's arm, in satin gowned,
Which rustled as her long train swept the floor
And dazzled in the sunlight all around,
The bride herself stepped through the chapel door.
To all sides of the hall her glances darted
While from on high the organ's trilling started.

Behind the bride there came the bridesmaids two,
Each dressed in silk, and in the heart of each
A yearning that *her* wedding might come true
If only she'd a true-love within reach.
With lowered eyes, proud bosom, they went through
Their wedding-paces, which would surely teach
The way to walk when they too would be wed;
These two young maids were Vejle-born and -bred.

A hymn, ear-splittingly, had now been sung
And up before the altar stepped the pair
Where Pastor Homo stood, holding his tongue,
As he paternally surveyed them there.
All at once he forced air from each lung
And crying, "O!" brought all his wit to bear
Upon the bond—upon that bond which binds,
Which binds—and joins the male and female kinds.

He talked about the thorn, about the rose,
Of bliss's temple, opened and shut tight,
Of sorrow's sighs in life's strong undertows,
And of Hope's prospect from its gleaming height;
Of comfort shared, though bitterly Fate bite,
Of pleasure shared, what time love's blossom blows
Into a rose of sweet maturity—
And now his sermon went on swimmingly.

The service ended and, as is required,
Before the altar they exchanged a kiss
Ere Adam and his lovely Eve retired;
The guests assumed there was no more than this,
But, as will happen, they assumed amiss.
The door now opened and there came in, squired
By Steward Hansen in his Sunday best,
Hanne, on whose head a wreath was pressed.

Up to the altar now they fairly ran,
Where Homo, wakened from his little rest,
Upon his second sermon then began,
In which the first one's scraps were manifest.
But, though each morsel with an "O!" was dressed,
It was the work of a mere journeyman:
What once had soared now lumbered, thud on thud;
What once had been a rose shrank to a bud.

But Hanne's heart still with such pleasure swelled
At this snapped bud that never came to bloom
That in those eyes of hers the large tears welled
When she received the kisses of the groom.
Then both the couples rushed to the large room
(By a crowd like raging seas propelled)
Where they are treated to the salutations
Of everyone's "Congratula-tulations!"

Round Mille all her aunts and uncles swarm,
And friends with smiles and bows round Adam flock,
While on the dais trumpeters perform.
But 'mid these doings Adam got a shock
When, bowing for congratulations warm,
He chanced to see Lieutenant Kriger talk
To Mille in his old sarcastic way:
"So even you must bear chains from this day!"

Mille he heard answer: "Why, good sir!
Your senses must be in some sort of rage:
You think I'd let them put me in a cage?
To such alarms do let me minister.
My freedom, scant till now, I must aver,
Takes wings now that I've reached the married stage.
To Captain from Lieutenant I advance,
And captains always lead their mates a dance."

At this reply, which showed her cold heart plain,
Through Adam's veins he felt a rippling chill
But, keeping up appearances, kept still.
He led her to the feast, not showing strain,
And played the part that he was meant to fill,
Gallant to her, proud to the rival swain.
When, after eating, to the park all filed,
With Mille's arm in his he even smiled.

But she slipped out from it impatiently
And with her long train darted off to stay
With Kriger, to whom she had much to say
As arm in arm they walked the manory.
Our hero, wishing no more company,
Found a bench out in the woods a way,
Where to himself he whispered, much put out:
"But how could this have ever come about?

"My father's words I must admit are true:
I'm in the clutches of Necessity,
Necessity which I thought I outgrew,
Which was defeated by the will in me,
Which I had thought was just a bugaboo,
Which in my freedom was burst logically
And by that concept's strength was blown away—
Necessity's defeated me this day!"

With hanging head he long sat in debate,
Hoping in that dark some light to find,
Till up he started, half sad, half elate,
Exclaiming: "How we mortal men are blind!
What doesn't go together we must bind,
And what's united we must separate:
It's been said that logic makes us free,
But freedom comes from acting ethically.

"Let me once over ethics ride roughshod,
I lose the Paradise of being free
And suddenly confront Necessity,
Which indicates a Will apart from God.
Let there once be compulsion and the rod,
Our foot has left the path of decency;
But he who's wanted what his God has wanted
Is someone whom Necessity's not daunted.

"It's true, my principal mistake has been
To leave the narrow path that stretched ahead;
And so, though freedom's seed I might have spread,
The fruit of harsh Necessity I glean.
I must turn back, for I have been misled,
And though no miracles may intervene,
Henceforth the moral life will be obeyed:
I'll cleanse my will, my mind will be new-made.

"It will be difficult—I know, I know!
But in my struggle I'll be comforted
That, though from many wounds my heart's blood flow,
I nonetheless am moving on ahead:
Each loss will have brought insight in its stead,
To every pain the joy of thought I'll owe,
And every error I've—alas!—committed
At least will make me that much sharper-witted."

Strengthened, he arose and made his way
Up to the gardens, which were now deserted;
But down from the hall windows he heard play
Dancing-music bright and extroverted.
Scarce was he in before he was alerted
To his bride and Kriger, waltzing gay,
While, man and wife, the Hansens *hopsa*'s leapt
And men and women in wide circles swept.

A new set started, and when Adam went
To seize his bride's waist for the coming dance,
His rival thought to rob him of the chance
And whisked her off again, with her consent.
What else could Adam do in the event
But seek out Hanne to save countenance,
With whom he long whirled through the company
And forced himself to great hilarity.

At this on Hansen's brow deep furrows flared.
"Much thanks to you!" at last the steward cried,
And got his bride from Adam's arms unsnared,
Who to the table reeled as if pie-eyed.
While Mille danced and the musicians blared,
With two imbibing gentlemen he vied,
And not the least dance had been his and hers
At the departure of the revellers.

307/

The two brides left as fast as could be done,
Exchanging crafty glances all the while,
And Adam with Hr. Hansen too must run
Once Hr. Baron has warned them with a smile
To get some rest now in the proper style,
No need to get up with the rising sun.
"I'll keep watch," he continued, "in this room
So long as all those firecrackers boom."

Off in the same direction both men fly,
And, warm with love, hot with the wine before,
Our hero opens up his chamber door
And sighs out yearningly: "Mille, it's I!"
But there's no loving arm to draw him nigh;
He looks around—an empty room, no more;
He checks the wardrobe, shakes the bedclothes out,
But there was, and would be, no bride about.

He raised the table where the washbowl stood,
Beneath the bed he even sought his bride;
But something else was in that neighborhood,
And, balked, he flew back to the hall outside.
He found the steward there, who cursed him good
And bellowed like a stallion in its pride:
"What have you done with Hanne? May Old Nick . . ."
"What!" Adam yelled. "Is she too in this trick?"

A maid passed by them, letting drop a word
That to the park both wives had made a dash,
And thither both men took off in a flash,
Just as the booming fireworks were heard.
The moon smiled down, by lovers much preferred;
They scout the bushes where their game might thrash:
Two pale white forms they see walking alone—
They rush up and each husband grabs his own.

They lead them wriggling out into the field,
But see! on Adam's bosom Hanne lies,
And when Hr. Hansen's donna is revealed
It is the Baroness who meets his eyes.
Neither gentleman would touch his prize;
Each to the other does his lady yield,
And without ceremony are they led,
These lovely captives, to their bridal bed.

But in the quiet, softly moonlit night
Rose flash on flash the fireworks from the ground
Which poured their stars on all the scene around
And shot sparks of sheer wonder at the sight
Of two free women now in marriage bound.
Scarce had one died before one burst with light
Whose booms the great news told stentorianly
To mankind—viz., the local peasantry.

And so our hero was a married man;
He tasted joy, and not just from that name,
As dreamlike golden honeymooning ran
Along with summer in that homely frame.
Then came September, and the pair began
Their trip to Copenhagen, for the aim
Of Mille was to set up house in town
And get to know the city up and down.

In the open carriage with four bays
Noisily through Vesterport they pitched,
As up upon his elbow Adam hitched
Himself and swept the crowd with lordly gaze.
Behind them sat the servant, yellow-britched,
Who let his head on their maid's fair breast laze.
But Mille sat straight by her erstwhile groom,
In velvet hat and long white ostrich plume.

The rumbling makes her laugh, and she's elate
To hear the cracking of the coachman's whip;
And, when they draw up at the sentry-gate,
Around her on all sides her glances skip.
But, when the sergeant gruffly makes them state
Their names and business, Her Ladyship
Shouts for greater honor toward her house:
He'll know that they're the Homo's, squire and spouse!

The carriage moves on—but along the Vold
That very moment there came into sight
A woman, pale and blonde and dressed in white,
Whose green veil round her lily visage stole.
While they were busy with the gate-control,
Straight past the carriage she went tripping light;
She looked up—and at the sight stopped dead,
Aghast, her cheeks aflame with blushing red.

309/

With lightning speed the little parasol,
To hide her cheeks and eyes, she then unrolled
To be her shield against the eyes of all,
And shivered, listening to Mille scold.
She watched the noisy carriage pass the wall,
And long she stood there staring, stiff and cold;
She took a deep breath, and began to go
Out through the gate and homeward, very slow.

Just past the fence the garden gate is found.
She lifted up the latch, sighed heavily,
Let it drop back, then turned herself around
And took the Western Road out to the sea.
The sun was bidding farewell to the Sound
And over the waters breezes rambled free
As she walked up and down, her eyes downcast,
Head bowed beneath the heavy thoughts that passed.

The sun had long been down, and still her tread
Kept echoing on the deserted road
Till, startled, she looked up as from the dead
And, turning round again, toward home she strode.
The maid rushed out to meet her and hallo'd,
Crying: "O Miss Alma, quick! What dread
We felt on your account! You're overdue!
Your father's looked round several times for you."

She went into the parlor, with the vat
For tea, the candles, and her meal laid out,
Where, like a mandarin wrapped all about
In dressing gown, at chess the gardener sat.
"Where did you go, my girl?" glad came his shout
On seeing her. He brightened just like that.
"It's nearly eight, and in an hour or less
You know we must conclude this game of chess.

"Remember that you owe me for that mate
Your queen delivered to me late last night;
If I don't handily retaliate,
I will not sleep at all till morning light."
"Forgive me!" she replied, removing straight
Her hat and shawl. "Yes, you are right,
I stayed in town much longer than I ought to
And didn't notice where the time had got to."

310/

After she her father's tea had drawn
And answered every question with address,
She sat down, with her head bowed, and went on
To concentrate upon their game of chess.
The old man drank his tea as, motionless,
He eyed the board where she advanced a pawn;
The game proceeded as well as it could,
With Alma losing several men of wood.

Suddenly the old man cries: "That's breaking
Rules, for you to move with my black knight!
And what's this? Do I see your fingers shaking?
No, let me see!" He takes a candle's light
And to her face he brings it, shining bright.
"I'm right! It's fever, there is no mistaking,
I know that color for a certainty—
No, raise your eyes and just look straight at me!"

But Alma still refused to lift her eyes,
Lest he see thickly clustered teardrops there
Which copiously down her cheeks did bear
As soon as they had first begun to rise.
Without a word she got up from her chair,
The old man leaping up with this surmise:
"You heard some news of him back in the town!
That old affliction still has got you down."

When there came no reply, tense and distraught
He took to pacing up and down the floor,
Casting looks at Alma, while she fought
The tears her eyes continued to outpour.
Abruptly he burst out, much overwrought:
"What's happened to the home we had before,
This house to which peace once was bounteous?
That person has destroyed it all for us!

"Yes, once each morning there was such content
When down below I went out to my chores
And you flew to me with that look of yours
That spoke of wholesomeness and merriment;
When at your singing off my sorrows went,
When from your bowl you planted seeds outdoors,
When you would clear the walkways with your rake—
Ah, to our Paradise there came a snake!

"Oh, how we have been living these two years!
Unnerved, tormented, half alive, half dead,
As if on bliss had come a time of tears
And those were eaten with our daily bread.
For one whole year the traitor disappears,
Then comes a letter like an arrowhead:
A breach of promise to his chosen bride—
The man has been a cad unqualified!

"What has become of all the rosy graces"
(Here he straightened out her undone hair)
"Of which in their still beds I took such care,
Of which these cheeks once used to bear the traces?
By tears now watered in this indoor air
Grow only lilies, raised for burial places;
For this I must thank *him*, who has beguiled
And brought to ruin my beloved child.

"To him indeed I could wish all things bad!"
"Hush, Father!" Alma cried out suddenly.
"Wish Adam nothing bad; for, if you had,
When it struck him it would rebound on me.
But trust me, I shall heal, I shan't be sad;
Yes, trust me, when tomorrow comes, you'll see,
We'll greet the day with joy, like times gone by,
But just this evening give me leave to cry."

Here, with a sigh, she fell upon his breast;
She cried and cried, as in that tearful spring
She wished her very heart were perishing,
And soon to tears the gardener too was pressed.
Long in his arms, unmoving, she found rest
Till, sweetly bidding him good evening,
And as the long wick of her candle flares,
She climbs up to her room above the stairs.

On Adam's portrait long she stood and frowned
Before she took it down with saddened mien,
And then around its frame a cloth she wound
And set it on the table, wrapped, unseen.
She pulled a bureau drawer out where were found
Mementos meant to make her loss less keen,
And, when she saw that none had gone astray,
She boxed them up to put them all away.

312/

Into her wardrobe closet's inmost part
Box and portrait she slipped carefully,
And sighed: "He's gone as someone's work of art,
Now from the man himself I must be free;
He now belongs to someone else's heart.
It's shameful to be in such misery.
Each flower of memory of which I took such care
I must root out as I would any tare."

Toward the open window now she went,
Where darkness lay so thick she barely spied
The trees that grew along the garden's side.
But from the darkness up her gaze she sent
To autumn's stars high in the firmament,
And only there her thoughts were pacified.
"Oh," she whispered, "that light's made by Thee;
Thou hast no shadow of inconstancy.

"Up to Thy changeless order my eyes wend
Where Thou hast sent the planets in the night
To keep Thy plan which they can't comprehend.
They too know not the goal Thou hast in sight,
But at Thy signal all of them ascend
And take their fixèd pathways with delight.
Their courses they can faithfully fulfill
With no more than their knowledge of Thy will.

"Oh, teach to me that same fidelity
Lest from Thee my despairing soul should veer!
From Thy hands let me take the destiny
That, although dark, can yet to me be dear.
My broken journey Thou wilt mend for me
And, while there's nothing but confusion here,
While I am blind, Thou'lt lead me to my goal:
My will I shall devote to Thee heart-whole!"

She gives herself unto the Lord of Fate
Like a knight who, at a precipice,
When darkness thickens without interstice
And he the safe path out cannot locate,
To his steed the reins will relegate
In hope that it will lead him past the abyss.
She promises obedience complete
And therewith deals her own despair defeat.

313/

She sees it under her, all savagery,
But of its gulfs feels no more terrified,
Standing in the night's solemnity
And looking up to Heaven for her guide,
Down from whose heights flow peace and sympathy
Into her heart in an unbroken tide.
From sorrow's bitterness now liberated,
To suffering she now is dedicated.

She had gone through the first class of its school,
In which she had received expert tuition
In the nature of resigned submission.
She had understood its every rule,
But when, alone, she wept at her condition,
Caught in the meshes of those dark thoughts' spool,
Straight in the eyes of doubt did Alma look;
She sat there bent beneath her fear, and shook.

Like a bubble she had seen hope break
And, sudden as a dream, her joy undone;
She'd managed to lose everything in one
And her last treasure, with a sigh, forsake;
She'd felt the lures that her despair had spun,
By faith abandoned, left to weep and ache;
She'd learned that life can sometimes buckle under,
That it can splinter, shatter, burst asunder.

But here beneath the evening's starry mass
That built a bridge between the earth and sky,
She was promoted to the second class,
For her clear mind her soul did purify.
Gone was her suffering in the world's morass,
But to its synthesis she's lifted high,
In which what's burst asunder is re-bound,
In which all that's been lost will be new found;

Where there is shelter for the heart's deep shoots
Until once more they burst forth blossoming
And hope's crown is the same as memory's roots;
Where knowledge and surmise are but one thing,
Where dissonance which had been maddening
Into a lovely harmony transmutes;
Where life will be preserved in midst of death,
And suffering transfigured with one breath.

314/

But how could such things be, if there were not,
When suffering's school's conducted here below,
Another life, where thought can come to know
That joy and pain in one embrace are brought?
How could it be that we drink joy from woe,
Rejoice upon the stake which flames have caught,
And sing a martyr's song amidst the flame,
Unless from holiness all suffering came?

But all too rich is Heaven's holiness
To be exhausted through a single spring;
Therefore, divided, it pours its largesse
In torrents of delight and suffering.
Beneath all gladness slumbers our distress,
And gladness feigns death deep in sorrowing;
Alike in nature, they yearn to unite;
Unlike in form, they are in constant fight.

In their fight, on earth not ever done,
They waken feeling as our lives go by;
The soul, by turns attracted to each one,
Acknowledges their difference with its sigh.
Only for the twinkling of an eye
Do they in heart's content together run,
And he who's tasted them together, whole,
Has been extended Heaven's nectar bowl.

And from that bowl he's drunk down wisdom's sap,
Known holiness to hold both joy and pain,
That Heaven's blisses earth's distress contain,
That suffering has its home within joy's lap:
Upon all sighs this solace puts a cap.
Now these heavenly drops of nectar gain
On Alma's soul, as joy and grievous smart,
A single entity, suffuse her heart.

She still stood by the window as before,
With both hands tightly clenched against her chest,
As when doubt made its deep gulfs manifest;
Still, as the darkness o'er the earth did pour,
That endless comfort which the starlight bore
She drew and rooted deep within her breast;
It guided her into the realms of peace,
Where earthly hopes forever after cease.

315/

Our hero strides ahead—as heroes stride,
Though bullets may rain round their heads like hail,
Though friends and foes in battle may have died,
Though bolt on bolt of lightning may assail:
A word like "leap" may even be applied
To our hero's progress in this tale,
For since he settled down with his new wife,
He's leapt ahead a dozen years of life.

In this leap hard proof does Adam give
Of time's unspeakable velocity;
His nine-and-thirtieth year he'll soon outlive
And is half through his life, or practically.
That part of life, called the educative,
For then one learns how properly to see,
Now lies behind him, and we see returning
On him ripe fruits of all his life and learning.

Though he's surrendered many a youthful dream,
He strives toward the Ideal even now,
But well aware it's a delusive gleam
If to itself it cannot make life bow.
That earlier Freedom, which did not allow
Shape or substance to his mental scheme
And, when expressed, met only life's rejection,
He turned his back on: now he wants Perfection.

Already he'd acquired some rather small
Perfections he thought a necessity.
What was there in the world that could forestall
His gradual gaining on that victory?
At this point, as concerns him inwardly,
Our hero's twelve years older now, in all:
It may be asked, what changes time and tide
Have brought his life on the external side.

A downright transformation there occurred,
A transformation few would not desire;
For he not only had long been a squire
As others have been, as we've seen and heard,
But one who'd managed much cash to acquire,
A very rare and much-sought-after bird.
The Baron bowed to his mortality,
And to Mille went the barony.

The title was to pass to her first boy.
But she'd borne only daughters to this date;
And should she die, Adam would enjoy
Long as he lived the lordship of the estate;
But if he too made part of Death's convoy,
The holdings, skipping heirs he'd propagate,
Would pass entire to the collateral line,
As was the letter-patent's clear design.

Another, though less profitable, case
I'm bound to mention without any blame:
With the Baron his old father came
From the miller's girl's to Death's embrace,
Wherefore we must give up the commonplace
Of calling Adam by his Christian name.
As heir both to the name and dignity,
He will be Homo in this history.

My reader! Into Homo's residence,
Which rises in the capital, all brick,
The height of elegance and quite immense—
I'll take you up the side stairs double quick.
In his den, of quiet opulence,
With book-lined walls and with engravings thick,
Our hero's at his desk, bound to a book
On which he concentrates his mind and look.

How handsome he still is! The change is slight
In spite of all the time that's flown away:
Not one hair of his head has turned to gray,
His arching brow still shines a youthful white.
Perhaps a single wrinkle now may bite
Around his cheek and mouth, but they're still gay;
Still, in reparation time has brought
Its gift to his full manhood, a slight pot.

317/

But, please observe, it is not overdone;
Indeed, it is almost an ornament
To make his person look more eminent
When he was playing squire roles for someone.
His clothing—but I must be reticent!
If I start this, then on and on I'll run.
The proof of how he strives to be perfected
Lies in his clothing, perfectly selected.

What is he reading? Can I trust my eyes?
Demosthenes! And in the Ancient Greek!
And near him Marcus Tullius Cicero lies,
Quintilian too, who teaches us to speak.
First to the Grecian text Homo applies,
Then checks the Latin works for their technique
In order to observe how far and whether
Their theory and their practice hold together.

He studies with such zeal and industry,
Such intellectual pleasure does he find,
This must be something of a serious kind,
A matter that affects him personally.
Just look there how he makes a strict précis
Of what from this day's study he had mined!
His pen moves just as fast as his thoughts flock,
When suddenly he hears somebody knock.

No sooner does he say, "Now who will spend
My time on chattering? It must be Bentsen!"
Than through the study door comes little Jensen,
His childhood, boyhood, and his manhood friend,
Dashing without any diffidence in,
With just "Hello!" and there the honors end.
"How goes it?" Homo stammers, discomposed.
"Look!" Jensen cries. "The list has now been closed!"

And, saying this, a paper he unscrolled
Which he had carried rolled up in his hand
And on which was a list of names enrolled
So long it seemed perpetually to expand.
It's something Homo's most glad to behold,
He cannot wait to get the column scanned,
And both of them remove to the settee
To give this list their careful scrutiny.

While these two friends are thus in hot pursuit,
I will, dear reader, introduce you to
The background of all this, unknown to you,
But which, since it concerns you, I should moot.
You know that Homo's strivings have in view
Perfection such as might bear him much fruit,
And that he seeks its sum by adding sections
And always hunting after more perfections.

You know that by this date some rather small
Perfections Homo had accumulated—
As, for example, we might here recall
His skill at billiards, very highly rated,
His French, so good he might be estimated
To have been raised in France's capital,
His mastery of horse and spur and whip,
And his extraordinary marksmanship.

But this gave not the peace that he required;
A spiritual personality
Is the *Ideal* he looked to constantly
And of whose loveliness he never tired.
Two ways he tried to reach what he desired:
First, as the *cultured man*—the prodigy
With art and nature mixed in just relation;
And next, as someone trained in *declamation*.

To be a speaker he's for many years
Studiously read in rhetoric,
And in it to this day he perseveres;
Not even at the moderns does he kick,
While at the ancients avidly he peers.
For him Demosthenes is his yardstick;
That yardstick is the means to carry through
The plan of life he's always had in view.

Like every talented and noble mind
He wants to live on in posterity,
And therefore some great work he wants to find
Which, when the Ideal is from his mind set free,
Will then do miracles of every kind
When his own hand's led it to victory
(I say hand, though "mouth" I'd have preferred,
Since he would manage everything by word).

319/

General perfection is the thing
Which into every rank he would expand,
Into a circle ever widening,
For he excluded none from what he'd planned.
He'd force it by his powers of lecturing,
Would spread perfection through the state and land,
Would bring rebirth through total alteration,
And speak to rouse the spirit of the nation.

'Twas bold, but no chimera ill-advised.
What other role did Homo wish to play
Than what the greatest minds, each in its way,
Had in their lives and learning aggrandized?
But for the project to be realized,
With it he'd made an old dear friend *au fait*,
One who gave approval to his cause,
One worldly-wise—Hr. Jensen's who it was.

Our Jensen, who's a justice of the court,
Also a practical old bachelor,
Passionate and liberal to the core,
For twelve years gave the Homo's warm support.
He calmed them when their tempers grew too short,
He smoothed the husband's forehead evermore,
And smoothed the lady's path a thousand ways
(He is her cicisbeo, in her phrase).

With Jensen's help the plan would take effect;
For both the parties, after long debate,
Agreed at last that they would best erect
A speakers' club and at the soonest date,
Where hearts would lighten, talking on unchecked,
Where every rank would be free to orate,
And where, made more ideal than e'er before
By Homo's words, they'd all turn orator.

Once the crowd by his ideals and art
Of speaking had been suitably inspired
And with his matter method had acquired,
Then to the provinces they would depart
And everywhere branch speakers' clubs they'd start
In which the Danish population, fired
And eager, would, in total transformation,
Be moved to act upon each aspiration.

At once, as if by witches' sorcery
(For such a goal sets caution at defiance),
The struggle would break out, and force compliance
From the crafts, the trades, the farms, and industry,
From general opinion, church, and science,
With freedom, art, and Nordic poetry;
And from his talk Danes would not have protection
Until in everything they'd reached perfection.

This was the grand plan which the egoist
Might scorn, but the sincere friend of the nation,
The Christian and upright religionist,
Knows deserving of his approbation.
It was the speakers' club's first registration
That Homo studied from Hr. Jensen's list,
To whose zeal and whose exertions strong
Was owed the fact that this last was so long.

"What do you think?" cries Jensen. "Aren't there
Troops enough to see your whole plan through
And beat this country out a grand tattoo
Once people start declaiming everywhere?
But, just for fun, look at this retinue!
Look here! Of journalists a goodly share;
Of army men just three, not too well done;
Of pensioners, though, there are eighty-one!

"Say, forty poets and philosophers,
And people from the craft guilds and the free
Professionals a good one hundred three.
Twelve retailers—one from the wholesalers.
Ten doctors from the university.
Six from normal schools—not dodderers.
Five farmers. Eight householders from one *len*.
Attorneys—seven. Only two seamen.

"Shop boys, seventeen. Of students, three
And seventy. Of factory-owners, five.
Fifty folk whose rents keep them alive.
Of artist types in the locality
I've not a one, but some there's bound to be.
Two priests—I had hoped not one would arrive!
Ninety souls I can't call anything.
A round six hundred by my reckoning!"

321/

"That's wonderful!" says Homo, much content.
"My highest praise for helping with my plan;
But, tell me, though, by what strange accident
Is there no name here of a nobleman?
There's not a one in the whole instrument.
I think that I might place them under ban!"
His friend replied: "It's the democracy
That builds states now, not the nobility."

"Perhaps!" Homo replied. "But now we'll hold
A general convention for our cause,
So that we can determine on the laws
Whereby our young club's powers we can mold.
We'll keep the branch idea just as it was.
Each must be by the mother-club controlled;
For only it can reckon the accounts,
And impulse should flow solely from its founts."

"That's true," says Jensen. "Laws there have to be,
And punishment by ban must be projected,
And then the leadership must be elected,
Or else there'd be dissent and rivalry.
But first club spirit cannot be neglected,
And that concerns you, Homo, specially.
The convention, yes, you must require it,
Especially so that your words can fire it."

"I can assure you," Homo volunteers,
"I won't be going to it unprepared.
It's now—oh, let me see—some seven years
Since my first thoughts about this thing were aired.
Both day and night for this idea I've cared,
It is my very calling, it appears;
This work of mine I feel's a holy deed;
It rests with Heaven if it should succeed."

"It will!" Hr. Jensen joins in eagerly.
"It will succeed, praise to our folk and you!
Why, just what difficulty could there be?
I understand how people think, I do,
I know they would be flattered; hitherto
They've borne their yokes, provided they seemed free.
Just get club spirit going to full force,
Your great work will go forward in due course.

322/

"When, after ten, twelve years or more"
(On Homo's shoulder he now lays a hand),
"We see Perfection flower as ne'er before
And lay that garland over all the land:
Then—then, my friend, subscribers will command
A column for the great man they adore.
Here right before your house we'll have it sent
And it will top the Freedom Monument!"

"You're quite a prophet!" Homo smilingly
Arises in one motion from his chair.
"But come! You've stayed with me too long, *mon cher*,
My wife pines for your presence over tea.
Where are my gloves? I've little time to spare.
The *Réunion Française* can't wait for me.
Don't leave your hat! No, let the list just sit!
I might just want to look some more at it."

Across the room they briskly made their way,
While Homo said: "It's best that you not mention
This matter: it would only cause delay
If it were brought to my good wife's attention.
We'll keep what we've been saying in suspension
Until I visit you in court next day;
We'll hammer out those laws then, *tout de suite*,
And fix the time our gathering should meet."

Here he opened up the parlor door:
There on her sofa where the lamplight lay
The lady of the house prepared to pour.
Her hand Hr. Jensen kisses straightaway.
She is the same: her braided, fringed beret
Sits slantwise on her tresses as before,
And still between her ruddy cheeks there shows,
In all its jauntiness, her stubby nose.

But she'd long found, in just one element,
That time's incursions could not be withstood:
She had become extremely corpulent,
No doubt the consequence of motherhood.
But she'd not hang her head in discontent,
A figure gone was not life gone for good;
No, just as quick and just as debonair,
She still wants of earth's goods her rightful share.

323/

"My cicisbeo lacks all constancy!"
With customary gaiety she cried
When Jensen took a seat by Homo's side.
"My husband, who adores a mystery,
Has dropped you in his bag, securely tied,
And you've all but forgot the way to me;
And yet a thousand things were in my heart
Which to my friend I wanted to impart."

"Speak, dearest lady!" Jensen then replied.
"You'll find an eager listener in me."
"Oh, yes?" she said. "We'd better let that slide!
Three's a crowd and two is company.
Can my husband hear with decency
What to my cicisbeo I'd confide?
On two tongues confidential discourse runs—
But look—here come the darling little ones!"

No sooner had she spoken than the door
Banged open: first to spring upon the scene
Was the eleven-year-old bold Bettine,
Then Julle, ten years old, hops 'cross the floor—
Two pretty girls, as fine as any queen,
Cheeks red as if two rosebuds each face wore,
With stubby noses, hair which nets encase,
Cut rather short and combed back from the face.

Wearing middy blouses, in they leapt
On velvet shoes, and, since against disease
Current doctrine had weak children kept
Bare-legged, their skirts came only to their knees.
This style was just a fashion to accept—
They had no need for any therapies.
They ran around the table as if cursed,
And screamed for tea so they could quench their thirst.

"Hush, hush," the lady answered. "You'll get tea!"
But added in a tone a bit severe:
"Your manners are not all that they should be:
Come round and curtsey to Hr. Jensen here!"
Julle drops her head and wittily
Lisps: "Curtsey here for My Lord Chevalier!"
Then up she goes and snuggles to the guest
While Bettine runs to Homo's breast.

324/

While he was stroking down the darling's hair,
She called to Julle: "Look at Papa here!
Today he's acting like a cavalier
As if he had some compliments to bear."
"And see his shirt-frills!" Julle answered clear.
"Just the way he's drawn in our *Corsair!*"
Then over to the cupboard ran the two,
And from it the small *Home Corsair* they drew.

An explanation's owed. As mothers do
Who see in their own children their ideal,
The lady early undertook with zeal
To get her ducks to read until they grew
To quick and witty heads as sharp as steel;
And so she found a primer for the two,
The *Corsair*, in whose pictures her small fry
Found their first guiltless happiness to lie.

The journal's humor, though, did so awake
Bettine's and the little Julle's wit
That both of them had settled down to make
A *Corsair* that for them and theirs would fit.
What in the house they might find hard to take,
Each teacher who found more work requisite,
Each visit from the court and from the town,
Yes, Ma and Pa themselves, were written down.

Triumphantly they bring their journal back,
And in it, as we have just heard, we find
Homo, in such splendid frills outlined
His snug, crimped coat might well have sprung a crack.
With lips pursed, he has thoughts he must unpack;
Half bowed, it seems a kiss is on his mind.
And under him is this inscription shown:
"In the genteel world Pa sets the tone."

The lady laughed out loud, but Jensen snatched
Their *Home Corsair* as though it were his prey,
While Homo, who indeed had been dispatched,
Sat still, well-pleased, but sheepish anyway;
Well-pleased, because paternal pride attached
To children who intelligence display;
But sheepish, since to take the bitter pill
In Jensen's presence suited him but ill.

325/

He cleared his throat, a sign he was distressed,
But bore it otherwise in manful style.
Why, when they laughed, he almost gave a smile,
As though it was not he who bore the jest.
He drew his watch abruptly from his vest
And, mumbling as he stared down at the dial,
He rose up from the cushion of his chair:
"The *Réunion* awaits. No time to spare."

He said farewell and left. But now, when they
Had had all of the tea that they could take,
The children started fighting for some cake,
Competing as to who could loudest bray.
"Hush!" cried the lady. "You make my head ache!
Go to the dining room and whale away!
Go draw your pictures there, away from us,
There's something Jensen and I must discuss."

"Come on, Julle! Cover up your ear!"
Bettine yelled as to the door she flew.
"What happens in this room we dare not hear,
Or even see, if I've picked up the clue."
But Julle yelled, "Don't leave the *Corsair* too!
We'll draw Hr. Jensen knelt to mother dear!"
Then out into the dining room they've flown,
And with her friend the lady's now alone.

"Two clever children!" Jensen would begin.
"Oh, yes!" she answered. "Each a merry soul
And ready to rear up just like a foal
If anyone should dare to rein her in.
But to my news! You see me at the goal
Which all this time I've striven so to win:
The tale I have been working on is through—"
"And," put in Jensen, "worthy, sure, of you!"

"I'll let you judge!" she answered with some speed,
While fetching out two notebooks with a plea
That he would take them home with him to read,
For female style, she well knew, was not free
Of leaps of genius so high it might need
A critic's file to make it masterly.
"But," she went on, "keep this from any third,
And to my husband do not breathe a word!

326/

"He would be frightened if he came to see
That I've been playing the Promethean role
And that the fire for fictive poesy
From friends and from acquaintances I stole.
I've brought in all our circle, every soul:
My hero is Count Pruth, as you'll agree;
My husband is his rival; our old aunts
Play the silly flirts in my romance.

"What most amuses me as my ink flows
Is, above all, the opportunity
To tweak his many good friends by the nose
And hold them up for fools, though amiably.
If someone finds his portrait among those,
I'm sure he'll swear himself to secrecy.
And aren't I right to make life the foundation
For all the elements of my creation?

"All of us poor ladies, who must hide
What light we have beneath a bushel—we
Who, 'spite our talents, mind, and fantasy
Must look on church and state from the outside;
Who should, it's felt, be but a needle's guide,
But who in action only can feel free:
One choice we have—to sew slip after slip
Or rise in triumph through our authorship."

"Perfectly true!" came Jensen's compliment,
"But," she went on, "one fear is left still grinding
And often comes to cause me discontent.
When out into the world my book is winding,
Will fierce reviewers seize the innocent
And from the book leave me at best the binding?
Shall it be skinned and pinched and flogged and drawn
And I, its author, vilely spat upon?

"The better papers' judgment I don't fear,
Or Higher Criticism, which is found
To tend its business now on Danish ground;
But what alarms me are the stings severe
Of poisonous malice from which all steer clear;
Scandal sheets with tirades all around,
Gutter authors who attack with scum
And send us fleeing, spattered and struck dumb."

Abruptly she shut off this verbal blast,
And on her friend a questioning look directed.
He cleared his throat to get his thoughts collected;
He stroked his brow; and round his eyes he cast
As if they sought some counsel he'd expected.
And suddenly he found his voice at last:
"My dearest lady," came his whisper low,
"I know a way out. Do not worry so!

"Right now I cannot tell you of my tack,
But for your novel all your fears are through."
"Yes," she exclaimed. "I shall rely on you!
For with my cicisbeo back to back,
I'd take the world on, to the last man-jack."
Up from her chair her portly frame she drew
And said, on hearing carriage wheels outside,
"Now to the opera house we two shall ride!"

She seized his arm and forcefully she swept
Out of the room, where in the hearth soon died
The embers all. It seemed a house unkept,
Its scattered members self-preoccupied,
Its only sounds from household gods who wept
Within that silence from the ingleside,
Where oft they witnessed in their lonely keep
To music which into their hearts cut deep.

For there's a music to each family;
From feeling which unites a man and spouse
It issues and with sound all things endows
And gives life measure, beat, propriety.
Its stream forks for whoever there may house
And then regathers quickly as can be;
And from the common harmony upswelling
Comes the melody that fills their dwelling.

This life, though, in its musical condition,
Moving hidden through the household zones,
As well transfigures into forms its tones
And, seen from outside, builds an exhibition.
To architecture music makes transition,
Inward sounds to lines and cornerstones,
Whereby stand forth relations once concealed,
And all our *homes* as *houses* stand revealed.

328/

Woe to our town, woe to this age awry
If suddenly, by dint of witchery,
Those brick-walled houses which we all pass by
Were changed to those proposed now publicly:
Half ideal and half reality,
Expressions but of lives that in them lie.
What are those buildings with which we'd be faced?
Horrifying witnesses of taste!

Yes, what a drama would our fine streets show
If we saw family life out on display
In stiff symmetric columns in a row
Behind which, crooked, warped, the portal lay,
Or else façades stuck on any which way,
All crumbling, waiting only for the blow,
Or horrid shanties where the wind could spill
Through doors and window sashes fitted ill!

What wonder that *penates*, pushed aside
By absent warmth and by disharmony,
No longer hold such homes in custody,
No more than does the race which there reside?
But whither are these wretched gods to flee
When they're the sacramental bowl denied?
Will government assistance ease their way?
"The genius of the land will help," they say.

The genius of the land? Where has he got,
That strapping lad with fair and curly hair,
Bright eyes, as blue as the forget-me-not,
Who swings the sword and strikes the harp so fair;
Who'll steer a ship through any blustering air,
Though fields of golden sheaves are more his spot;
Who with a language smooth as wavelets playing
Can sweetly sing and keeps his speech from braying?

Where has he wandered with his cheeks so red,
His merry smile, his forehead rich with dreaming,
His simple temper, without show or seeming,
His soft love for the shores where he was bred;
His joy in foreign lands, adventure-teeming,
His mind to all the world wide-open spread;
Yes, where now is the genius of the land,
Whom north and south alike have raised by hand?

Alas, naught but an exile is he now!
He hardly helps himself in his distress.
Chased from the cities, scorn heaped on his brow,
A civil death is his, no more, no less.
In ragged clothes, with pains that make him bow,
Alone he walks the forest wilderness,
And with his nakedness to stare upon
He thinks about the insults undergone.

He minds that he's scarce left one laurel blade
From the wreath they wove in former days;
That they disputed every bit of praise,
Ev'n doubting that of stern stuff was he made.
He minds (his blood boils to be so repaid)
They've stained his honor in so many ways
That now he's pointed out on every street
As one past standing on his own two feet.

He minds (and here his heart bids fair to break)
That scorn had gone so far that people said
That even his own language was near dead,
His language, which did him immortal make!
Yes, counseled him that for his speech he take
A tongue which had for fountainhead
The Ginnungagap, the underworldly source
Where gibberish is spoken as Old Norse.

All he minds; and to forget his wrongs
He seeks a forest shelter from his rue
Where dense leaves hide both town and land from view
And where to comfort him rise wood birds' songs.
Here, alone, he feels that he belongs,
And here he weaves his laurel wreath anew;
Here he roves till falls night's canopy,
Then goes down to the cliff, beside the sea.

There he stands, with beech leaves garlanded,
Through which the evening wind soughs ruefully
And looks out where the waves roar on a sea
The moonlight colors with a glow pale red.
His mind is drunken with the sights ahead:
On sea and land he beholds victory;
He cries aloud: "My time will come again,
And put to shame the judgments of such men!"

Enough of him! My hero will not stay!
Who in his proper place now stands confessed;
For he, who's driven on Perfection's quest,
For the nation's genius leads the way.
It's nighttime, and with plans for the new day
He comes home from his promenade to rest,
Having thought his speech out, start to ending,
For the general convention now impending.

The structure and transitions are all there;
So clearly in his mind stands every section,
The whole speech, almost like a recollection
That need but be drawn up, lay in his care.
He only lacks the style for its projection,
And here he hopes there's no cause for despair.
Up the stairs he bounds, aglow with pride,
And in his room he throws his cloak aside.

Upon his escritoire the lamp's soon lit,
His pen and paper laid out in its glow,
And now in dressing gown we see him sit
To write away for a good hour or so.
A breeze! His fingers hardly hurt a bit,
And now he has the whole first part in tow;
Stretching in his chair to his full measure,
He leans back to peruse his work with pleasure.

A study for a painter! Shafts of thought
Are poised within his forehead's bow, the while
His cheeks record an intermittent smile,
Revealing his content with what he'd wrought.
He mutters, "Hum!" and answers on the spot
His "Hum" with: "This phrase might just need a file."
He stands up and he strides about the floor
And rubs his hands, elated with his chore.

"And so the time has come around at last,"
He says now to himself, "when over me
And my ambition sentence shall be passed;
When it shall show itself for all to see,
Now there's no bar to my activity,
How rich its fruits and substance are, and vast;
What in my lifetime in the mind I've sown
In time will come to lives beyond my own.

"How strange—" All of a sudden he stopped short.
"Indeed, how strange life can be, after all!
For I, who would not heed a priestly call,
Have now an entire nation to exhort.
But all of us are pastors of some sort
When on a public we let our eyes fall
From among whom we seek proselytes
To carry out an idea to its heights.

"My might's the might of spirit. In our age
People act by speaking for a thing.
But what in modern speeches makes me rage
Is that the speakers' styles are wearying—
That false gesticulation challenging
At every turn a taste well-trained and sage.
A master-teacher's needed by the nation;
But mastery comes but by long probation."

He struck the sail of his soliloquy
And on the console two lit candles laid
Before the huge glass very carefully,
Which, as the beams upon the mirror played,
Showed the figure that the speaker made
With every merit and deficiency.
He strode up—but had hardly had the floor
Before he went off flying to the door.

A fear came over him and to be sure
That no one would disturb him, come what might,
He locked the far door to his chamber tight
And tried the lock lest it not be secure:
He wanted protection from his children's sight,
Who often found that keyhole a grand lure
And even drew him in their *Corsair* talking
When, in his room, he sensed no danger stalking.

Now he's assured himself that vilified
Upon his spirit's flight he wouldn't be,
And once more to his mirror does he stride
And from his sheets declaims impassionedly.
Each gesture, though, which he thought fell far wide,
Each word which failed in point of euphony,
He tries again, and each new redeployment
Gives him, as orator, unique enjoyment.

He sometimes takes a sudden forward stride
And, stretching toward the glass his outspread hand,
Declaims with such a fervor and command
It seems as if his point were just denied.
Sometimes he speaks as someone mortified,
But sometimes he is flattering and bland,
Especially when indulging in appeals
To bring the crowd to trust in his ideals.

"My friends!" (As to the end he came,
With noble pathos, of the exordium)
"O, if we knew the happiness to come
Which the Ideal has kept for us to claim,
Its beauty would set all our hearts aflame!
What is it otherwise than, in its sum,
That true perfection, utterly neglected,
For which life and ourselves have been elected?

"O, that's a thought we never must forsake!
For even though our minds might thereby feel
The bond 'twixt earth and heaven sure would break,
The thought that wounds us all can also heal.
Toward the heights of life points the Ideal;
It shows us with a glance the path to take
And teaches us to go in that direction
Where peace and joy shall dwell in their perfection.

"Yes! He whom to perfection It has driven,
Though in the least thing which demands our strain,
Though in a work built but to fall again,
Who manfully pursues the task he's given,
Of him (when from this dust he is loose-riven)
We dare to say: 'He did not live in vain!
His soul beneath the ground knows no subjection;
Its home is the abode of all perfection!' "

He stopped and, moved, into the glass he stared,
Which did a figure in high transport limn,
Whose cheeks were flaming and whose eyeballs glared
As, from the inside out, they peered at him.
He drank his face in for that interim;
Then to the table he again repaired,
Resuming work upon his authorship
Before in his soul's flight he felt a dip.

333/

There in his solitude he shall remain,
This new Demosthenes, whose idiom
May veer off from the old one's traces some,
Though this their different matter should explain.
Away from him, then, as we've said, let's come,
And from the Ideal that he's sworn to maintain,
We'll rush to where Reality now calls,
One of the house's large reception halls.

There Mille sits, whom her divan enthrones,
In gown of velvet, violet-blue and fair,
While she, bent over toward Hr. Jensen's chair,
Reads out her novel in the loudest tones.
Like planets round a sun, around her stare
A ring of twenty literary drones,
Eyes fixed upon this lady of the pen,
Not looking, though, like perfect gentlemen.

Who were these men? What purpose to assign
To such a party in itself so rare?
They were the authors in the gutter-line
Whom Jensen asked to come to this affair
So that, with food and wine beyond compare,
To Mille's work they'd favorably incline.
Anonymously to this feast they came,
But here we'll freely give them, name for name.

On the right Hr. Smearer and Hr. Chatter,
As were Hrs. Nopanache and Emptybrain;
On the left, Hr. Slinker and Hr. Ratter,
With whom Hr. Twaddle and Hr. Talkinane.
Back in the shadows sat Hr. Muddysplatter,
Hr. Louse, Hr. Shameless, and Hr. Oralstain,
Hr. Yellowbile and still more carnivores
Who batten on the best names of these shores.

Half blinded from mirrors and the candles' glow,
Which robbed the guests of use of beaks and claws,
And won by liquors that deserved applause,
Whose vapors caused a pleasing vertigo,
They, while she read on, suppressed guffaws
And sometimes even mumbled a "Bravo!"
But to themselves they thought: "Is that good wife
Intending to go on with this for life?"

334/

She *did* stop going on. With voice afire
She read the final pages feelingly:
Her heroine writhes round in agony
And struggles between duty and desire
Until, burst out of her captivity,
A dirk in her freed breast lets her expire.
The closely written notebooks now removed,
A grateful murmur told her all approved.

They yelled a tempered "Bravo!" while they ground
Into their chairs and shrunk back as to hide,
Shot glances, smiled, and nodded all around
And wrung their hands, as if much gratified.
The lady licked her lips from side to side.
Then with her book she joined these friends new-found,
And with a twinkling eye, wherein awoke
Complacent hope, to all her guests she spoke:

"I stand before my judges. At your feet
I lay the fruits of my soul's authorship;
I even hand to you the critic's whip
If you should judge that punishment is meet."
A speech like this awakens further heat:
"To call the work delightful would be flip."
"If," someone says, "you wish a grade from us,
We'd have to give the work a firm A-plus."

Hr. Smearer adds: Within its category
He, as an author, had not reached such height.
Hr. Prater thinks it proper that this night
A golden laurel crown her work with glory.
Hr. Babbler volunteers: The Stagirite
Would gladly stand godfather to her story.
Hr. Twaddle makes a lengthy explanation
Of the work as Beauty's revelation.

Amid his twaddle, and the finest patter,
The dining room's great doors were opened up.
The lady gave her arm to Muddysplatter
And bid the whole contingent come and sup.
A table they beheld, to thankful chatter,
With pot alongside bowl, and bowl by cup:
Capons, oysters, cream, shrimp-stuffed filets,
Strasbourg roulettes, and truffles, and pâtés.

335/

Each one pushed forward, but the way is stopped
By crowding servants, all in livery,
Who worked the corks from bottles till they popped
And, at the sideboard, left a small path free.
With each pop of the bottles' corks hearts hopped
Inside the bodies of the company,
And, as if they'd already sipped the wine,
Their tongues went wagging, necks out, eyes a-shine.

On sitting down, hard was the lady's case:
To sit beside her everybody vied;
But she, with Muddysplatter by her side,
Bade Slinker come and take the other place,
At which Hr. Louse, though no doubt mortified,
Found himself in time a nearby space.
He scratched behind his ear unhappily,
Degraded now to a mere vis-à-vis.

The guests for some time only ate and drank;
All that could be heard was platters ringing,
On the table flasks and glasses ping-ing,
Forks hitting porcelain with a rousing clank;
The servants' heads swam, watching these men yank
The bowls away that they'd just finished bringing.
Hardly had one portion been ingested
Before another helping was requested.

Across the table Mille tipped a wink
To Jensen, who knew what her signal meant,
For in reply to it he gave a blink.
He stood (a call to silence his intent)
And 'gainst the bottle let his tumbler clink.
As from the plates their eyes on him they bent—
Sauce round their lips, at which their tongues still played—
This toast, his hand around his glass, he made:

"Gentlemen! We're living now in days
In which, compared with those of Jewry,
We've gone a step back, undeniably;
For while the Jews, exhausted by their frays,
Left judges off and turned to monarchy,
We, who've with royal justice parted ways,
Have gone and done the very opposite,
And reigning over our times judges sit.

336/

"Yet, what appears to be a backward stride
Will show itself a monstrous step ahead,
If we consider the effects it's bred.
Yes, as a fruit of crisis nationwide,
As freedom's triumph, I view it with pride
That judging has become unlimited;
That judges in our age"—he nodded round—
"Just like our journalists, are all self-crowned.

"Now Justice sports a badge of liberty,
The courts of journalists to separate
From those wherein our judges judicate
And Justice's scales are kept in custody
(Though never, let them fiddle endlessly,
Will they get the scales to balance straight).
You must know I speak from experience;
I'm an attorney—trust me to speak sense.

"Of such faint-hearted justice-fiddlery
The journalists—as all along you've known—
Who judge off-handedly are clearly free.
No witnesses are called up to depone;
Settlements, nay hearings, they disown,
And leave the arguments to sophistry.
Harshly to judge the age's vice and stink,
They need but take up paper, pen, and ink.

"The judgment passed, at once it's sent en route
On printed pages all across the land
For all the populace to execute.
But other papers' judgments come to hand
And, rubbed against them, it can then dilute
What blemishes and errors ought not stand;
Yes, judgments can be rubbed to such condition
They're all obliterated by attrition.

"In this war of everyone 'gainst all,
Of page 'gainst page, of this 'gainst the other one,
Arises what is called opinion
And what 'the nation's judgment' I would call.
Unlike the law, asleep it cannot fall;
Its conclusions can't be better done;
It is so sound that soundly it can rise
From judgments crooked, curious, or unwise.

337/

"And therefore, gentlemen, I wish to praise
With clinking cup the judge's call you heed:
Our love for you you cannot ever raze,
For you're the ones who that opinion breed.
A song might better help my toast succeed:
I may lack music, trumpets all ablaze,
But still our thanks in ravishment I bring—
In place of song you'll hear my heart's harp ring!"

He swung his glass, at which the lady clapped,
And toward the man did all the wine cups strain
When he invited them to get them tapped.
But in a thankful mood rose Emptybrain,
Who with a skoal Hr. Jensen's skoal becapped.
He spoke in a loud voice—but in what vein
A language with strict rules can't represent;
Of thought the speech was wholly innocent.

When he sat down arose Hr. Nopanache,
And, while they had this new scourge on them now,
Hr. Oralstain put forth with humble bow
A plan to underwrite his printed trash
And begged the lady sign, if she'd allow.
She took his sheet and pencil in a flash
And with a flourish turned him thrilled and green
By ordering fifteen copies sight unseen.

But now the talk and noise grew still more keen,
The lady using both her hands and patter:
Shamelessly she teased Hr. Muddysplatter
And drew his fork away from him unseen;
She rolled her bread into small balls of matter
And in Hr. Prater's mouth tossed this cuisine;
And of neglect of neighbor she was blameless,
For she threw sugared almonds at Hr. Shameless.

Alert she was, cute, in her hollow style;
More than once she nodded to the seat
Of Louse and to that of Hr. Yellowbile
Before she raised her tumbler to entreat
That they take wine with her, as most worthwhile
In helping them get down the salt-cured meat.
Her mouth all smiles, she fixed them with her eye,
And all three drank until their cups were dry.

338/

Now out came the champagne, and popping loud
Was heard from cork on cork, and glass on glass
Was joyously and raptly raised en masse
By all, who felt a drunk would do them proud.
Now songs began to rise up from the crowd,
Who all were reeling round; and at this pass
The lady—who'd enough of this uproar—
Stood up, and in this fashion took the floor:

"Before we all must part—and long with pain
I've heard the watchman's cry: 'Watch fire and light'—
Before these friends must leave me, as is right,
Whom I've been honored here to entertain,
I'd trust to you that infant of my brain
To which you've stood godfathers all this night:
I mean my story-daughter, dear sweet thing,
Who seemed to please you by her babbling.

"Heed the voice of her who bore the pet,
And heed the pact you with the child have sworn;
And, unlike some godfathers, don't forget
To tend the future of my latest-born,
When her black dress of printer's ink is worn
Out in the world so full of woe and threat,
Where she, who danced on roses heretofore,
Perhaps will walk in dirt from door to door.

"Care for the maid, if teases too deep bite;
Reach her your hands if she's in need of aid;
Lead her ahead if she's put in the shade;
Hold her up if she drops reft of might.
And now—before we part, new friendship made—
Fill up! Fill up! To close this happy night
I urge you drink the grape, drink hearty!
Skoal, sirs! Skoal! It's been a lovely party!"

Here she noisily pushed back her chair,
And at the table Jensen also stood;
The guests put on the best face that they could
And all arose, somewhat the worse for wear.
But now the lady really had a scare,
For, reeling half seas o'er, this brotherhood
Was stuffing every pocket full of cake
And rushing up to praise her, with their take.

The woman was manhandled in this fray
To grasp her hand and thank her for such food;
Why, Shameless really seemed a bit unscrewed,
Throwing his arm round her in that way,
While in a whisper of a voice he cooed
That her request he would of course obey
And willingly stand father to the child
And help her to get through a world so wild.

The hard-pressed lady's bosom fell and rose;
She hated to give up that evening's fruit,
But her resentment she could hardly mute.
Hr. Jensen came to save her from such beaus,
For everybody there did he recruit
To go to a café ere it should close
To put their skill at billiards to the crunch
And take a fine cigar and glass of punch.

This is an offer to which they all warm;
They let the lady go, find hats and capes,
And down the stairs without farewells they traipse,
Following Jensen like a roaring storm.
The lady fights for air as her mouth gapes,
Red-faced and furious at this breach of form,
And clangs for her four maids to come along,
To whom, when they arrive, she calls out strong:

"Throw open every window; that's your chore.
I want to see the house filled with fresh air.
And take some wet cloths and scrub down this floor,
And brush down the upholstery on each chair!
One of you heat a brazier up out there,
And take those table linens out the door;
For both these rooms, as if we'd all had flu,
Tonight will have to be smoked through and through."

So spoke the lady, giving thanks she owed
To God for bearing these festivities
Without a rupture with such guests as these.
She waited now to reap what she had sowed,
But only to behold this hope explode
When soon her book fell to her enemies.
The gutter-journals grossly slated it,
Not just attacked, but macerated it.

Who was the guilty one? That is the thing!
The critics wrote of course without a name,
And therefore no one did the hatcheting
And all heads were held high, all free from blame.
So it goes with authors now who aim
At refuge 'neath their small Maecenas' wing;
So it goes when poets pay the charge;
The old Maecenases had hearts more large!

But out with these Maecenases! I know
That you, my reader, hanker for the day
On which my hero, with no more delay,
Will take his most important plan in tow.
And you, for all the patience you display,
Will shortly say: "There's not much time to go
Ere Homo must make proof of his *virtù*
And show us what humanity can do."

You are impatient, yes, with this suspense.
One thing indeed I had forgot to mention:
Proceedings of the general convention,
With Homo's speech, were scheduled to commence
Within a few days—and, in consequence,
That Perfection, as yet mere intention,
Which his oration still has locked inside,
Within a few days opens its wings wide.

But just as Shrovetide always precedes Lent,
So, before Perfection makes its seat
In town and country, marketplace and street,
Fulfilling hopes and bringing heart's content,
A masquerade I want you to frequent:
For all of Copenhagen Homo's treat,
A party he's been giving once a year,
A notion which his wife put in his ear.

Again then to his home in town we wend,
From which, off in the brightly lit main wing,
There came out to the gate such hollering
You'd think the house had turned end over end.
Rumbling broughams and horse-hoof clatter blend
With lackeys yelling and dogs howling,
And as the coachmen "Mind your step now" shout,
The people from their carriages climb out.

341/

Up the staircase to where laughter reigns,
Dazzlingly becostumed and begowned,
The long chain of the guests curved round and round
Like a wreath from parti-colored skeins.
To move ahead, their feet not only ground
On one another's heels, but tails and trains;
And moans and groans had not died down before
The servants opened up the great hall door.

Banquettes were arranged against each wall,
As in amphitheaters, so that they
Who, unmasked, wished but to observe the ball
Could do so easily, out of harm's way,
And safely laugh at this masked free-for-all
Of people rambling round as though astray.
Already to these seats a crowd had gone
And still, through all the doors, the masks came on.

And what there was to see! There rises Night
In garments black with stars upon them glancing;
And round it Memory clad all in white;
There Hope, in rosy red, they could see dancing;
Gypsy-, gardener-, fisher-girls tripped bright;
There Harlequin in Pierrot's arms romancing;
There walked the Monk beside Turk and Tartar,
And here walked sailor, peasant, and hussar.

Such a throng one scarce believed it yet,
And therefore why not let our glances float
Up to the star-decked man on the banquette
Whom Homo talks with on a festive note,
Geheimeraad von Encken, who too let
His eyes rove round and sometimes cleared his throat,
And cast a look that could not see too far
Through his glass into this throng bizarre.

The man sat silent, almost impolite,
But when the noise had reached a fearful squawl,
The agèd sir rose up to his full height
(A most imposing figure, very tall)
And cried: "What an infernal caterwaul!
For older people this noise is not right,
Such humming and such drumming in my ear.
Young friend! Can we just get away from here?"

342/

"Your Excellency guesses my desire!"
Says Homo, bowing finely in reply,
Whereupon the two of them retire
To one of the small cabinets, nearby
But still as quiet as they may require.
But hardly had he stepped in when his eye
Beholds, stealing toward him 'gainst the wall,
A tight-masked fisher-maiden from the ball.

Von Encken she elected to ignore,
But grabbed for Homo's hand, which she caressed
So tenderly—and what is even more—
Covered with her kisses, ere, hard-pressed
By his astonishment, he could protest,
Then floated, like a spirit, through the door.
With piercing eyes he watched her move away,
But who that person was he could not say.

Above her lips the close-fit mask was set,
But on her shoulders braids of blonde hair wound,
And through the meshing of the fishing-net
He saw a figure at once slim and round.
He stood a second, guessing, in a fret,
Then came back in the cabinet with a bound
To do his homage to the reverend man
Stretching out at ease on a divan.

There, by themselves, we'll let the gentlemen
Remain, far from the crowd, a little space,
And take ourselves back to the hall again
Where, mouth to mouth, the sounds of gladness race,
Where masks rush round at such a merry pace
And burst with laughter when fools come in ken,
As over there—where someone takes the floor
And with this speech sets everyone aroar:

My name it is not requisite
To start with. I won't tell you it.
And my position, well, for that,
You may discern it by this hat,
By this collar made of paper,
By this scepter's zigzag taper,
By this towering coxcomb
In which fops would feel at home;

343/

And he who sees it also hears
It tinkling from these asses' ears,
Whose ringing bells will tell you true
That with a jester you've to do.
Oh, dear friends, hear of my woe!
How is it that we've sunk so low
Since those good days of long ago?
A jester's entertaining jokes
Are now misunderstood by folks;
His good ideas are shown the door
No sooner than they're on the floor;
Yes, even simple tommyrot
Is far beyond the courts we've got.
My life was gloomy—but in time
To keep from mouldering in the grime
Of dusty rooms with dusty nooks
Like ancient inventory-books,
And to keep safely from a fall
What some existence still may call,
I locked away inside a chest
A too-sophisticated jest,
And just to earn some gratitude
I worked my head off talking lewd,
And though it made me feel unclean
My language always was obscene.
I got back on my feet again,
For people understood me then,
And many folk of high connection
Offered me their full protection;
Yes, I've seen the eyes spit fire
On many a courtier and squire,
Forgetting title and high station
When that way went the conversation.
Now I was safe, or so I reckoned,
But luck can alter in a second;
And as the jug goes to the water
Till it gets just what it oughter,
Fate can turn things inside out.
At court they're suddenly devout,
What had been music to the ear
Now nobody desired to hear;
And when I came round with my sass,
All they would say was: Stupid ass!
And sometimes, too: You stupid dog,

344/

Lock your mouth, it's like a bog!
If you won't heed our words, my man,
You'll get a taste of the rattan,
And if that won't work in the least
We'll pack you off to see a priest.
Dear friends, what was there I could do?
The ways of fools are known to you:
If folly they're prohibited,
Then they might just as well be dead,
But neither would it serve my cause
To stay the very man I was.
Therefore I chose my strategy:
I drove away my irony,
My merry jests I firmly barred,
Though you may trust I took it hard,
And pinched my wit so flat and thin
That it was both a shame and sin.
I bought a costume that might pass,
And, when I looked into the glass,
Of all that makes a court-fool sort
There was but left: a fool at court.

With that in haste his jester's cap he doffed
And, in a modern suit, so chic, so proud,
Such as upon our streets we see so oft,
He hurriedly returned into the crowd.
But his departure scarcely cast a cloud,
For, instantly, his mask held high aloft,
Another figure bid for their attention
As he burst out with this high-flown invention:

Hail ye, my folk! You know me, I'll engage,
For I appear to you undominoed.
I am the artist, oft the city's rage,
At Kongens Nytorv, Thalia's abode.
Among the thousand toadstools of our stage
You found at least one noble nature strode,
And learned to treasure, with my mental vigor,
The posture of my admirable "figger."

My art's my self. On ancient theater-planks
The actor hid himself behind a mask;
We moderns, though, are equal to our task
And to the mask we say, "Thanks, but no thanks."

345/

What! This nose and this majestic look,
This brow, which in the cause of art I lay,
Surely more can be read in their book
Than in a vile piece of papier-mâché?

Upon the word the ancient stage was fed,
But what are words against delivery
That turns you deaf by its sonority
To what the poet thought and felt and said?
What is that preachment that makes ears despair
Against a passion's very incarnation
In looks, in postures, in gesticulation?
What myriad words, 'gainst one man standing there?

Of buskins and cothurni we dispute,
As though without their presence art must lose;
But my cothurnus, as you see, is a boot
And, as for buskins, I prefer my shoes.
Away, cothurni! Buskins, masks, away!
In our age it's the person takes the heart;
In that belief, my people, never sway,
And in the artist's figure love the art!

He smiled and left, but scarcely gone was he
Before, in costume most extraordinary,
There came a figure lissome as a fairy,
A small, slim lady of great gravity
Beneath whose mask a mouth peeked red as clary,
And round she pirouetted one-two-three.
With foot raised to depict in dance a flight,
She rather sang where others did recite:

Bow the fiddle, sound it spring-like,
So that wing-like
This gauze garment, tightly molded
And so brittle, round my middle
Comes unfolded!
That for hours this crown of flowers
In the dance can gently balance;
And then, chosen by the gallants
For the Holstein waltz beginning,
I'll undo my collar's pinning
And I'll close my spread fan's wings up,
And with eyes with flames long pent in,

As my breast with ardor swings up,
My cheeks blushing with winds rushing
And my foot in high style put in
Taut and bent in,
I'll float off, a gay smile shining,
On my partner's arm reclining,
O what sweeping, O what leaping
Down the great hall's gleaming floor!

While the chandeliers are beaming
Joy is streaming
On the dance floor all around me,
My heart's mended, cares have ended,
Dreams have found me,
On whose winging I am swinging
Like a saint to Heaven dashing.
Round me hosts of stars are flashing,
Soft winds cool me as I'm reeling,
Earth must have the selfsame feeling
On this spiral path I'm tracing
In my racing to the thronging
Of those yonder I see wander,
As I ride with, not collide with,
Planets pale and comet's tail,
That in longing,
Like me on the high air streaming,
Like me, though wide-waking, dreaming,
Fly a-glimmer and a-shimmer
To the music of the spheres.

I am done with woe, misgiving,
Dance is living!
Only what is fresh, eternal,
Glad emotion, hope, devotion,
Keeps hearts vernal.
Life's for youthful folk, that's truthful!
Out of fashion, with your white hair,
Take your footstool and sit tight there
While inside you sleeps the power
That is like a poor wallflower
Left alone on exhibition—
This world knows no worse condition.
God our Savior! Such behavior
Can't befall me! Let Death maul me

347/

After hours danced with flowers,
I'm submission.
I'll bloom yet, although He slays me,
And my gallant knights will raise me,
By whom, frighted, the pale blighted
Lily shall be borne away!

She tripped away, while fluttering her fan
As rapidly as wings on a tomtit;
But once she'd gone off, came her opposite,
A very old and gray-haired negro man,
Who pointed to his breast ere he began
And, sobbing, ground his dark hand into it.
Upon the crowd, which moved in close to see,
He stared hard, singing in a minor key:

An agèd negro you survey,
And what I've had to swallow
Enclosed within this mortal clay
I want you all to follow.

My mother sang this lullaby:
"Much evil will upset you,
Black William, if you blink an eye
And let the white folks get you."

I was a lad as black as coal
And wore a silver earring
When I was thrown down in a hole
On ship for Denmark steering.

I was a very modest boy,
In little I took pleasure;
In white things only was my joy,
Naught else did my eyes treasure.

With linens white I was impressed,
White vests brought me elation,
And white girls more than all the rest
Led me into temptation.

I stole white linen from our priest
(The rats I'd beaten to it),
But when his snow-white vest I fleeced
They locked me up to rue it.

The white girl's cruel voice distressed
Me as it kept repeating:
"Think you that this white lily breast
For your black heart is beating?"

Indignantly I went away,
My bosom pained with tightness;
And since that time my hair's turned gray
In thinking of that whiteness.

Soon of this life I shall be free,
But he would greatly grace me
Who, set to Bertrand's Melody,
Within a song would place me.

Then to the white girl's singing lips
While on her harp she's playing,
Before away his poor life slips
This black man would go straying.

Therewith he opened up his thick lips wide
And stole away, with all his teeth displayed;
But little heed to his lament they paid,
For now amid their circle they have spied,
In close march and brisk stride, a maids' brigade
Of maskers dressed for wandering outside,
Who, crowding one another as they mill,
Sing all together as though with one bill:

In cloaks and in hats in full feather
We come from the cobblestoned street,
But we're nimble despite the bad weather
And the heavy thick boots on our feet.

We are the women selected,
Who scorned the god Hymen's fair home,
And once were the Vestals protected
And reverenced highly at Rome.

There we bore the stamp of virginity
And wrapped ourselves up to the chin
And kept, in the temple's vicinity,
The fires of Vesta within.

But, her temple long time ago falling,
We spread over all of earth's parts,
And now, as we keep with our calling,
The goddess resides in our hearts.

Through our eyes she makes observation,
She won't let us rest from our routes;
And so round upon our visitation
We lollop in shoes and in boots.

In intimacy we are seated,
For chatter is good for our souls;
And while we get our hearts well-treated
We blow on the hearth's dying coals.

But if husbands the flame sets a-blushing,
And things for his wife get too hot,
Then out of the room we go rushing
And visit a different spot.

We wretched maids never know leisure,
The goddess devours our breast;
But won't someone melt? someone measure
Out comfort for hearts so oppressed?

With the wives we refuse to take chances;
We've seen them enough to know
That they watch us with sidelong glances
And would fain see our heel, not our toe.

The men, but especially those wedded,
With these words we'd like to implore:
Would a bond then be just so wrongheaded
With maidens who chastity swore?

It's friendship alone we're suggesting,
A marriage is not our desire;
Their wife's place we are not contesting,
We wish only a place by the fire.

And with them we'd pleasantly sit there,
To see the blest flame is well-drawn,
And keep the hearth properly lit there
While their wives from the cradle look on.

They heaved a sigh here like a *cri de coeur*,
But had to yield their place, uncomforted,
For now up did another masker tread,
A stiff and straight and agèd officer
Who suddenly unsheathed his rapier.
With dignity, as though a host he led,
With force, as though he'd just thrown off a weight,
He suddenly began to expatiate:

"I wish that it had never been,
This devil's age we're living in!"
In an author I once read that
(A major poet, to have said that).
Would he'd gotten what he aimed for,
And would we'd had a proper war!
For why these praises and these cheers
For valiant chiefs of many years
When nowadays, I need not hint,
Wars are only fought in print?
When daily at our doors they toss
A paper loaded with attacks,
At which some new newspaper hacks
Next day, with hatchet and poleax,
But without even one man's loss
(The girl who comes delivering it
Is never hurt the slightest bit).
Do you see this drawn sword shine,
Held within this hand of mine?
The day I was made officer
I swift unsheathed this rapier,
And while I with a lover's eyes
Its edge and point did scrutinize,
Full of youthful heart I swore:
"Someday this sword will feast on gore!
Before too many years elapse,
It will be full of nicks, perhaps,
Got from skulls in many battles
Where blood gushes and death rattles,
Where, while drummer boys are pounding,
Onward, to the trumpets sounding,
'Neath the scarlet Dannebrog
As thunderous cannon-lightning flies,
To fame and danger on we go!"
Then once again I raised my eyes

And with that same young heart I swore:
"Some day this sword will feast on gore!"
Alas, time came and passed, all wasted,
For gore this sword has never tasted;
As powerless as peace it hung
Along my side in its sheath flung
While I each morning on parade
Walked the streets in brass and braid,
And never did it get one gash,
Save autumns, when like lightning-flash
Out to North Field it was brought
To storm the foe's camp on that spot,
And hard for Vibenshuus we fought.
Alas, would it had never been,
This devil's age we're living in!
Now I am old and white of hair,
And out my life does quickly wear;
But how my mind with anger brims
That soon they'll bear my moldering limbs
In a cortège, and they will bid
Farewell to me beside my grave
As to a warrior fine and brave,
And there lay on the coffin lid
My sword which blood did never rust
To show the courage of my thrust;
Not one small nick there that could be
For all our valiant soldiery
A witness to my probity
And lend my coffin valor's sheen
To add unto its laurels green!

The agèd warrior gave his helm a tap
And, with his vizor down, away he stalked.
But someone came at once to fill the gap.
In, with an open book, a masker walked
At whom the group assembled was most shocked:
All cardboard was the head upon the chap.
Then quickly, as with such a man agreed,
From out his mouth there spurted forth this creed:

God and St. Ned!
An excellent head
I am and I'll stay,

As *people all say.*
I teach brilliantly
Whatever it be;
Each nut of a fact
I can hand you back cracked;
I solve with great ease
All your tough mysteries;
At every test
I have gone the duration;
My grades were the best
At each examination.
Yes, God and St. Ned!
I've an excellent head.
But one thing stumps me:
I can't judge worth a pea.
Why do I fall flat?
I've no answer for that!
The lovely, the good,
As well as the true
I've not understood;
To them all I've no clue,
And what judgments I pass
Aren't even third class.
As here, for example,
What rating is ample
For books like this one
In which I've been reading
Till my stomach spun?
I find blunders breeding
In here and that's all,
And it turns my blood cold;
But let me recall
The first section of it,
Which now is so old:
Aside did I shove it
And said, "A disgrace!"
But then, with red face,
I altered my view,
For folk by the slew,
Who had merited fame,
Gave the book their acclaim.
So now I am pensive
And most apprehensive

Lest my view of it
Should not really be fit.
Then do be the bailer
To rescue Per Tailor!
And teach me to judge
So that I won't fudge;
For once I have that
I soon shall come at
Each beauty and failing
For which I've gone sailing;
And soon will have news
If the book can amuse;
And soon from the deep
Bring up to the light
The true and the right
At its bottom asleep,
And show like a glass
What's weak there, what's crass:
Yes, not just keep awake
When some volume I take,
But to others make clear
Why it is à ravir,
Why it's to be toasted,
Unless I should hear
That the best judges say
That the book should be roasted;
For them I'll obey,
And I'll be and I'll stay,
By God and St. Ned,
An excellent head.

With this final word away he flew;
But as the crowd made way for this fine sir
There now appeared a masquerader new,
For whom they made room with much noise and stir.
Of walk and bearing like a conjurer
Whose ready tongue would always see him through,
The man stepped forth, and, hand upon his breast,
He bowed and to the crowd these words addressed:

Good people! You're aware that now things national
Are talked of everywhere by sages rational;
Allow me, then, a practical philosopher,

To *practically explain them to the amateur.*
In Greenland winter-fur, good people, you now spy me!
I feed on fat and whale oil, I get coarse and slimy;
But one-two-three, observe! I throw my fur coat off
And now I'm in a suit, a Scandinavian toff.
My brains are not so thick as they once were; my face,
No less than does my thought, conveys a certain grace,
And where the Greenland roughness went you scarce can guess—
My blood's phlegmatic, and my mind all friendliness.
This change, though, is not really after my own heart,
And, with permission, with this suit I therefore part
And stand now as a German, professorially gowned,
And watch the think-wheels in the brain-works go around.
But we grow bored with that, as no one will rebut:
Off with the German gown! In coat of rounded cut,
Busy, cold and clever, hands white, long and lean,
As an Englishman I pick my teeth all clean
And think of smoke, the noise of engines fed on coke
That make me steel and cotton goods with every stroke,
With which I inundate the world by sea and land.
Off with my coat! And now observe the way I stand,
For in a French suit I've a sanguine disposition
And have no small opinion of my French condition.
France, though, is not all. Off with the suit posthaste—
And in the Polish dress, pinched nicely at the waist,
I am a Pole in exile from his motherland.
The grieving eyes, though, are too much for you to stand,
And so off with the costume. I'll put a capuche on,
And in the long furs you'll soon recognize a Rooshian
Whose brightly polished skull uncrackably holds out.
My joy is brandy and my fear is whip and knout.
But as a hard-whipped back's deserved by the rapscallion,
I put my furs aside, and now as an Italian
I present myself at this distinguished fest
In what goes by the name of a Venetian vest.
I'm most accommodating, without any guile,
Frivolous; but if the wrong way someone smile,
I'm all afroth like wine and for my dagger start
And use my mouth to translate for my furious heart.
My drink's the blood of grapes, chestnuts my best meal,
But since they also have the same food in Castile,
I doff my vest, and in a low-cut camisole
And Spanish cape, I stand here now à l'espagnole.

355/

Now I am choleric in joy as well as pain,
But nobly, loudly, proudly beats this heart of Spain.
Utterly forthright am I, as you'll soon see,
For, turn your eyes away, the ladies hear from me.
Now I doff my cape, and now my little vest,
And only in my shirt you now behold me dressed.
I am no more a Spaniard; as you will agree
The shirt qua shirt is worn round universally,
Not just in northern places or in southern places.
The unit of the shirt belongs to all the races.
It is my deepest part, and with me constantly,
But, notwithstanding that, it isn't really Me.
No, underneath that shirt's universality
There dwells at ease my individuality,
My ego, my own person, which is mine alone,
And is too diffident to be to others shown.
But as to what concerns the so-called "national,"
About which people holler as if turned irrational,
You see there what it is: a costume we must don
When it won't do to walk round with just shirting on.
For though this world may be a suit, a man is not,
And true heart's ease and true lucidity of thought
We first perceive in some still corner of our house
When we, as individuals, wear but a shirt (or blouse);
For this assertion I make here with emphasis:
Clad in just his shirt a man can know much bliss!

Gathering up his clothes, away he went,
But up a flock of gypsy girls now draws,
Who, to music loud and vehement,
Swing themselves around and gain applause.
Before their clashing tambourines relent,
Let's seize the moment for a grateful pause
And make a visit to the cabinet
Where sit the two men at their tête-à-tête.

Together there the two of them converse.
A smile upon Von Encken's lips expands
As, peering at the bottom of his purse,
He crumbles his tobacco to thin strands.
Our hero seems to have come out the worse,
And seems to beg a pardon at his hands:
His cheek is hot, his forehead shows each vein,
He looks uneasy, features showing strain.

The agèd gentleman had thought to moot
The Speakers' Club (such was the new club's name),
Of which Dame Rumor, true to her repute,
Had put forth many a claim and counterclaim.
Our hero, innocent of any game,
Reported everything in terms minute;
But, livid, heard his project ridiculed
And, scorned from top to bottom, overruled.

"Your Excellency finds it all absurd?"
He shouted hotly. "What in every age
Is called Perfection and the ideal stage
Is but an empty, hollow, barren word?
You think the state's collapse is not incurred
If from the Ideal's track it disengage?
You think Perfection is but nugatory,
Along with loss of happiness and glory?"

"Yes," smiled the Geheimraad in reply.
"I'd print it as the substance of my creed;
And I'll go further: I would prophesy
That if these grandiose plans of yours succeed
And Perfection's temple's raised on high,
The end of all of us is guaranteed:
Throne and state would come right out of joint
And, if that happened—at whom would we point?

"You start—yes, you are consternated;
But your speech presumes—Use some reflection!—
That on the basis of our imperfection
The state's been founded and elaborated!
What need of rule, then, if those regulated
Looked only to the common weal's protection?
Were each soul like a heavenly denizen,
What, dear friend, would we need with clergymen?

"Why watchmen, law, police authority,
If people got no longer out of hand?
And, once from war and fear of war we're free,
What use the valiant soldiers of our land?
If all are healthy, doctors must disband,
And poets die where all is poetry;
A revolution which ne'er found its match
Would, if the plan succeed, our state dispatch."

357/

"I apprehend Your Excellency's jest,"
Said Homo, rather hurt. "But, if I might,
I'll put to the Geheimraad this request
To tell me on what means, then, I should light:
What cure will bring state power to its height
And save this country we see so distressed."
"Oh," said Von Encken. "I'm glad to explain!
The cure is hidden in the statesman's brain.

"But," he continued, "how our talk goes wild!
Politics talked at a masquerade
Is almost like a logic course purveyed
At parties honoring a newborn child:
One's own and others' time by both's ill-paid.
Oh, listen! Now the music has turned mild!
One moment, though, I must go to the hall;
My wife must miss her husband at the ball."

He stood up and, half turned to Homo's gaze,
He then appended: "One word to the wise!
See that Perfection's bird just flies and flies,
And ere you set your passion's heat ablaze
With those Ideals which only tell us lies,
Close down the Speakers' Club! And reappraise
This comedy in which you've been quite wrong,
And look into your mirror hard and long!

"It isn't right for you to agitate
The mob, who'll hardly make much sense of you.
Leave that to people out to dominate
A world in which their lives were turned askew.
I am a friend of yours of ten years' date,
Trust me! There are more things that you can do.
A noble and a fine young man you are,
But you're no demagogue—now, *au revoir!*"

There's Homo in a fine mess! But alone
He quickly got back on an even keel.
"No," he thought. "You won't turn me to stone,
You sly man with a slyness cold as steel;
Because you dare deny you're error-prone
And least of all are friends with the Ideal,
Should I too turn on it in treachery?
No, never, never! Faithful will I be!"

358/

He cast his gaze around the room with pride,
When, in a corner, lying on a chair,
He saw a handkerchief and grew wide-eyed.
"Ha!" he thought. "*She* must have left it there!
Except for her there was no one inside;
It is the fisher-maid's, on that I'd swear!"
He snapped it up and searched it anxiously—
Embroidered on one edge: "Helene P."

"What's this!" Homo exclaimed. "Helene P!
Helene, who is always dropping in
Since Mille's friendship put her in a spin,
And just two nights ago was here for tea—
To kiss my hand, like some crushed heroine!
But she might not have known that it was me. . . ."
Then in his ears he heard a tender sigh,
And—at the door again she caught his eye.

Although around her face the mask was wrapped,
An inner struggle showed forth vividly
Through outward signs. Just like a lily snapped
By rain, she stood adroop; just like a sea
In storm, she trembled, frightened and entrapped,
Her bosom swelling in like agony.
She took one step ahead, then one step back,
Sighing deep as if her heart would crack.

Suddenly she stood up straight and tall,
Suddenly he heard her sighs repeat,
And then, as though she'd let a burden fall,
Down she threw herself at Homo's feet.
From her shoulders slipped her fishnet shawl;
She stammered: "Adam—oh, my sweet, my sweet!"
She seized his hand. He wished she'd let him be.
Her mask fell off—it was Helene P!

"My God, Helene! What is all of this?"
Cried Homo, baffled at a thing so odd.
"Oh," sobbed out the young and lovely miss.
"Oh, ask that not of me, but of Love's god!"
"You love?" he stammered. "And whose is the bliss?
Tell me his name! I'll tell him of your nod. . . ."
"No, don't act as if you didn't know!
I know that you, like me, are in like woe!

"Against your destiny I've seen you fight,
Wound round with chains in which I know you sigh;
I've seen your lovely soul in its sad plight
When not one loving heart would heed your cry.
But this breast—What is there to deny?—
Has given you its sympathy outright:
The sight of you has lit a flame in me
That melts us into one, eternally!"

And with that her white arms, supple limbs,
Lovingly she twines about his knees;
But he stands stiffly and his poor mind dims.
He blurts: "You thought that you could hear my pleas?
You're wrong. . . . Dear, sweet Helene, these are whims!
Come to your senses! What if someone sees?"
He raised her up, and gracefully she swayed
Within his arm, which round her waist he'd laid.

Who at such a sight would not be won?
Leaning backward, eyes half shut the while,
She rested, wearing an ecstatic smile;
But Homo's virtue would not be undone.
His vow to the Ideal he'd not defile;
Reality's temptations he'd outrun.
Upon her lips he merely pressed a kiss
As thanks *galant* to her for all of this.

Footsteps coming! To the plush divan
The charming girl, all blushes, Homo brought,
And thereupon, his head and heart all hot,
Toward the door, full of alarm, he ran—
But there was no great thickening of the plot,
For it was Jensen who approached the man.
Unmasked, he held his domino in place
Before his masquerader's funny-face.

"Why," he cried to Homo, "are you here?
I have been looking for you low and high."
"Hush, hush!" our hero whispered in reply.
"A lady's had some pain. Rather severe.
A lady who to us is very near.
As host, I've other wants to satisfy.
You're darting round like fish caught in a net,
So would you please take charge of the poor pet?"

Off Homo fled. Hr. Jensen stared in fright
Upon the lady, finding there in view
A person he had tried to pay court to
And seen and met in company many a night.
But why, as though a prisoner chained tight,
Was he stuck to the wall now as by glue?
Why not leap to her aid? He had the will,
But his sound reason was his mentor still.

Suppose he dared approach to where she lay
And then someone came by to take a peep?
Immediately he'd be her fiancé;
And if the fair one, who was half asleep,
Awoke to find his sympathy so deep,
She must believe he wished more court to pay;
One word and then another would they speak,
And he'd be bound, for all of us are weak.

But he? Strapped by a thousand dalers' pay
(Good for surviving on, not thriving on),
To get a scanty household under way
By keeping track of where each øre's gone?
Such courage he could not rely upon!
Desire was scarcely all he ought obey,
For reason had commandments on its side.
He heaved a heavy sigh, and off he hied.

That horrid bachelor fraternity
That always has its heart up in its head!
There lay a sweet affectionate young she
Whose heart was full of longing to be wed,
But did not know to whom she might have fled
With all the feelings she bore constantly.
She lay there now and stared off into space
While reason snatched her suitor from the race.

Enough of the provocative Helena,
The latest shoot of ancient Grecian stock,
Who in the realms of Christendom now flock,
Who glitter with their talents in life's *scena*,
Who know their gospels to the last arcana,
But 'gainst the sixth commandment have a block.
Into the throng of masks, where she should be,
I'll take my gracious reader instantly.

The crowd, so recently diverted, made
A circle at the center of the hall
On sight of other folk in masquerade
With costumes that had caught the eyes of all.
Among them a churchgoing lady strayed
Who crushed a hymnbook close against her shawl,
Till, with a look which virtue evidenced,
She turned round to her public and commenced:

I've grown white hair,
And bed and chair
Are dear to me;
But Sunday morn
I'm not forlorn,
I'm worry-free;
For, early awake,
My hymn-book I take
And hurry there
Where bells do ring
And notice bring
Of public prayer.
Wrapped in my cape,
With veil of crepe
And feathered hat,
Folk by the score
At the church door
I first gaze at,
And then I teeter,
A sexton for leader,
To my pew,
For which a tip
To him I slip
When he is through.
Once I sit still,
I raise my veil's frill
And take my lorgnette
Through which I scan
Every lady and man
Not in their seats yet,
While organ-notes ringing
And joyous hymn-singing,
Full of delight,
From all this world's dole
Uplift every soul

On heavenly flight.
Then comes the priest,
My interest's ceased
In those next to me;
I see him standing,
Brow commanding,
And plainly see
Each noble feature
Of our fine preacher,
Testifying.
How hot he gets
Till his brow sweats
And needs a drying;
And how his eye
With thought rolls high,
Glows with coal's heat,
While each word slips
From over his lips
Like honey sweet.
When by his zeal,
So moved I feel,
I look to see
If other folk
With what he spoke
Were stirred like me;
If holy work
Had cleared the murk
Which worldly might
In life's rough churning
O'er souls in yearning
Had set tight.
Each tear I see
Brings joy to me;
In all those high
Court ladies' eyes
It gratifies
When, with a sigh,
A fat one leaks
Down lily-cheeks;
It makes me sure
That folk prestigious
Are religious
And heart-pure.
Yes, in the grand

I've often scanned
Devotion true
Which, all in all,
Among the small
Belongs to few.
In most of those,
I must disclose,
I see disgraces:
Candles out,
Hearts in drought,
And cold faces.
My eyes then do
A close review
Of all the flock,
Till the Amen
When once again
Outside we walk;
I go along
Borne by the throng
That goes to gaze
Upon the great
In winter state
Boarding their sleighs.
When with fierce din
Away they spin,
I rush to find
A lady friend
With whom to mend
My roiling mind.
Scarce in the door
Am I before
She speaks me fair:
"I heard it creak.
At church this week?
Were many there?
Come, let me brew
Coffee for you,
It's such cold air.
Do take a seat
And just repeat
What was said there."
And so time flies
In pleasant wise.
Back at my place

Visits begin:
The priest pops in
To show his face.
A too soon done day
Is dear Sunday,
Each one I've had;
But bursts the bubble
With Monday's trouble
And I am sad:
The long week hatches
Hours by batches,
An army of time;
The many tasks
That army asks,
It is a crime.
Dispirited,
Alone by the wall,
What the priest said
I can't recall.

She tottered off, brow furrowed, with a sigh
That gave expression to her mood downcast;
But now a man attracted every eye
Who, through their ranks, in dull-hued garment passed,
Whose one hand held a weighing-pan up high,
While the other held a yardstick fast.
With measured step, and nearly sunken chest,
He came and sang, without the slightest zest:

I've joined, a member in good stead,
A league for moderation,
Which, by our police allowed to spread,
Has all men's approbation.

By means of scale and stick our guild
Can save itself from tedium;
For the base on which we build
Is measure, mean, and medium.

In bad and good, in joy and woe,
Our rule is proof 'gainst treason;
Our good deeds always are so-so,
We cheat, too, within reason.

Day in, day out, we compromise
As we tell tales and prattle:
We strike the midpoint between lies
And truth in all our tattle.

In everything we take half-pains
To meet our obligations,
And save a good half of our brains
By halfway applications.

We count the jokes that we disperse
To crowds disposed to laughter;
We write some rather middling verse
And sing it middling after.

And, while we walk along our ways,
This one thought gives us pleasure,
That in the midst of our glad days
We're happy within measure.

The Globe is what we call the scene
On which our club's persisted,
And each whose life reflects the mean
Is for our Globe enlisted.

Here (in mid-speech, of course) he made a stop,
As though a plaster on his mouth were smacked,
And now another masker all eyes tracked,
Who leapt into the circle at the hop
And first-off seemed a minstrel by the fact
That he'd a lyre and clothing all a-flop.
That to a higher rank he did belong
Was evident when he gave forth in song:

Hark to a foreign troubadour
Who's changed his tongue, not his heart's core,
To visit Denmark's sons!
From France I came here by the sea
Once I had word that poetry
Earns cash here by the tons.

I needed help up in this game,
For near as naked was my frame
As joiner's planed-down planks.

But here I heard a poet loots
A royalty enough for boots
And trousers for my flanks.

In my mind with joy I hold
What, to my comfort, I was told
About a poet's fees.
They told me that they were so high
That with the money one could buy
A hat—plumed, if you please.

Besides that, hereabouts a man
Upon a laurel wreath could plan,
Though rather flat and scant:
That's fine! To show my wit can flash
I'll don mine like a knightly sash
Across my chest, aslant.

Then if, like Madame Potiphar,
The critics say I've gone too far
And can't stay where I am,
I'll prove myself as bold as they
And will like Joseph slip away
(The wreath I'll leave Madame).

The greatest joy, though, in my cup
Is that they're going to hang me up
In lithographs on high;
Then past them I shall walk along
To hear the voices of the throng:
"The troubadour's passed by!"

O flower-scented land so fair,
Where bard can live high on plain air
And carry his hat high!
True subjects of Dame Poesy,
For beauty's champions like me
Your best praise you've laid by.

For honor is the last reward
Which to the harp's sons you accord
For all the hearts they seize;
Yes, though their lives go all askew,
They know, at death, they'll get from you
Prodigious obsequies!

367/

With a La-la-la that mounted to a trill,
He jauntily leapt off. Then quickly back
The crowd moved to admit a chorus pack
And observe them in cothurni mill
With capes half off their shoulders hanging slack,
Be-wreathed, as though high games were on their bill;
And with a power they could hardly tame
Out with this choral song they loudly came:

We are all Bacchantes,
Enthusiastic aunties,
Creatures most ecstatic,
Figures from the Attic!

To our Queen Agave
We once said, "Peccavi,"
For her son's deboning
Amid our wild moaning.

With our flagons in hand
And our frenzy well-fanned,
With ivy-crowned hair,
In the drunken god's snare,

We now run, so zany,
After types that are brainy,
With great reputations
In all of the nations.

It's our very best luck
When we manage to pluck
A genius at times
Amongst those who make rhymes.

We bind up our victim
With roses we've picked 'im;
That his strength may decline
We provide him our wine.

Once he sips from our cup,
Drunk from buttering up,
And begins round to blunder,
Straight we tear him asunder.

And by splitting his heart
In his pain we take part;
By there raging around
We may get his soul found.

As we dance round and seethe,
From his laurels we wreathe
For ourselves a corsage
To charm our entourage.

No one gets the whole thing;
Little bits, though, we bring,
And with her little bit
Each of us makes a hit.

Once our spirits are drunk
From our victim's torn trunk,
We swoop off like a hawk
And a new victim stalk.

For we are Bacchantes,
Enthusiastic aunties,
Creatures most ecstatic,
Figures from the Attic!

Thereupon their flagons they swung high
And, looking round, as though they searched these parts
For other victims for their savage hearts,
Rushed off into the four winds of the sky.
Just when the last one's vanished from the eye
And once again the dancing-music starts,
Into the circle a new figure stalks
Who, looking at the crowd, politely talks:

What din and noise! What shouts and cries!
What sheen and splendor meets my eyes!
Observe in me an eremite
Approaching you with footfall light,
And let my cowl, let my waist-cord
A symbol of good thrift afford!
You laugh me off? You think that I
Don't know the joy life can supply?
To your relief I can report
I too engaged in social sport.
Where there were parties, I was sighted,

Where there were feasts, I was invited,
Art's charmed sun bathed me in its glare,
At joy's full table stood my chair,
And I partook of many a plate.
But what do you think was my fate?
Though every day I took inside
The finest food earth could provide,
Though constantly I drank of fine,
Of exquisite and rarest wine,
My health became, so strange to say,
More weak with every passing day;
Though writers and philosophers
Discussed over their porringers
The most sublime ideas with me,
While laughter at our trenchancy
Rolled round me, and thoughts by the bevy
Fell like snow when snow falls heavy,
While heaven, hell, and earth dissolved
Into the streams of words involved:
When I left the feast for home,
I felt my head an empty dome,
And, tired of all that witty gas,
My heart would sigh Alas! Alas!
But, most remarkable to me,
Though daily I donned finery,
And daily at galant resorts
Saw folk dressed fine enough for courts
With gold trim on them finger-thick,
The world made me more and more sick,
Till it turned such a loathsome sight
At last it drove me into flight.
Into the distant woods I fled,
To sleep alone within a shed;
There, mirror-clear, a river wound,
And there at last myself I found.
There by a clear voice I was greeted
That of me no reply entreated;
There I could find time infinite
For simple notions, lacking wit;
I found the peace beside that stream
To dwell within my heart's old dream.
My coarser fare, my sturdy bread,
Colored my cheeks once more red;
I thrived, not on the wine's bouquet,

But on fresh air of early day.
Dark forest paths I walked along
And listened, moved, to birds at song,
And should a sparrow hop to me
While I stood still beside a tree,
It would appear to me a play
Which made our stage seem workaday.
Blest simplicity around
Had poured on all her peace profound;
The verdant leaf, the yellow straw
I stared upon as cause for awe;
The wing-light golden clouds on high
Moved past like fables on the sky;
And when I lay in nighttime black
And listened to the storm attack
The shed's walls as if bent on crushing
And heard the forest echoes rushing,
Then in my head there rose the notion
Of a ship tossed on the ocean,
And to God on high I prayed
To send the sea's brave son His aid.
Full was my life, the earth was dear,
For Heaven all the time was near,
And while alone I sat out there
The world to me again turned fair.
Yes, in my breast did my heart race
To look upon a human face,
To cast a loving eye again
Upon my brothers, fellowmen.
I seized my staff and hither hied.
—But, turn my eyes to any side,
I see but masks, flat and degrading:
It is the same old masquerading!
The same old lies in polychrome;
And so good night, I will go home.

He turned and left—but Mille now ran on
In her fifth costume of the evening,
This time weaponed like an Amazon
With shield and lance which boldly she let swing;
But of her fancies we won't say a thing.
Let's listen to the trumpets' fanfaron,
Which at a sign from Homo starts to din,
To tell the crowd the dance would now begin.

Then dropped the ladies' masks which had concealed
Them from their dancing-partners' scrutiny,
And all night long the people danced and reeled,
Enlivened by the jaunty melody.
Only when the dawn rose vapory,
Dulled on cheer, away the guests all wheeled,
And to his alcove Homo too has flown,
Where, tired of noise, he took his rest alone.

While wings of sleep upon him cast their shade,
To you, my reader, this thought I submit;
To you, who just now saw a little bit
Of this age's grandiose masquerade:
Add to it! Call experience to aid
And say, hand on your heart, it's definite
That Homo has gone wrong in his projection
That we can have great longings for Perfection.

Has he turned downright stupid? Is he blind,
When for all life a goal he wants to claim?
Pray, what goal can any of us find
Save just that one on which he's set his aim?
Think of yourself! All people bring to mind
To whom this life is more than just a game,
And say if each of them with all his might
Does not toward that same goal join in the fight.

No doubt, most people's struggle scarcely dares
Break free from that small group in which they're penned;
Perhaps, though, they should stride out from their lairs
And push the whole world forward to their end?
But who can get the masses off their chairs,
If Homo's, if our hero's, not that friend?
Who else must work to make our bliss come true
Except one who most feels the pinching shoe?

Upon his shoulders he has borne the load,
And for that all of us are in his debt;
He for our nation's sake is sore beset,
And taunts upon him are not what he's owed.
He's just awake—the cock has long since crowed
Upon a day, so sad, so gray, so wet;
His grand plan's now awakened in his head—
Tonight's the night on which it's to be sped.

Brows knit, in *robe de chambre* habited,
Long he stood mute, letting his thoughts flow,
As past his lips escaped an anxious "O!"
(Though now and then "Alas!" came out instead).
But why should he have hung his head so low
Just as he stuck his leg out, leaving bed?
What had happened? What had drained his might?
Geheimraad Encken's words of yesternight!

The matter was: that what the man had said
Was, if not quite, then virtually the same
As something which had sometimes plagued his head
And would have left his striving spirit lame:
A doubt that he might well be brought to shame
About the plan that his excitement bred;
That he might lack the power of utterance
To give Perfection's triumph a real chance.

Such doubts he may have conquered yesterday.
Yes, with a puff from an excited breast
As light as chaff he blew them all away
When in Von Encken's words they were expressed;
But now when his starved stomach they invest,
Now when these morning jousts to him convey
The thought of what the evening is to bring,
The doubts he used to subjugate still cling.

He in his room kept pacing to and fro,
Till all at once he slackened in his stride
And stopped to take his speech out, just as though
By what it said he might be fortified.
With eyes intent but also weak with woe
He scrutinized his work, but often sighed,
And ended with the words: "How meaningless!
It keeps avoiding the main business!"

His heart seemed shattered with anxiety.
Having put his greatcoat on in haste,
Into the raw and foggy morn he raced
To battle with the inner enemy;
But with redoubled force, hardly outfaced,
Sharp stings it set upon him savagely.
Each person whom he met walking about
Shoved deeper in his heart the knife of doubt.

373/

At a corner Jensen came in view.
"Thanks for last night!" the little man declares.
"How lucky that I should run into you,
To tell you face-to-face of our affairs:
The burrow is all ready for our bears.
The hall at the hotel has been seen to.
The lighting I can manage on my own."
Away rushed Jensen—Homo stood alone.

His unease drove him down to the hotel,
Where the usual placards called attention
To a private general convention
To begin at seven by the bell.
He felt the ax fall at this written mention,
And down his spine an icy shiver fell.
His stomach ached, and forthwith home he sped
To sink down in his armchair, pale with dread.

With rigid eyes, with bosom iron-tight,
He eases his full heart in heavy sighs,
And as the sheerest folly he denies
The plan he'd made so bold to expedite.
Then suddenly the portraits meet his eyes
That lined the walls with men of fame and might
From the tile stove to the bookcase there,
And hurriedly he gets up from his chair.

"Ha!" he all but shouted, while he walks
Toward the great men, hanging there in dust.
"Ye paragons! How many of you must
Have suffered in your time these selfsame shocks;
How many must have borne, in self-distrust,
The weight of action, heavier than rocks;
How many must have fought with self-denial
Against the bitter doubt which was your trial!

"I feel more strong to see you roundabout!
I feel resolve grow by your memory!
Yes, like you all, I also shall win out
When power of faith, which was your triumph's key,
When faith's own shield against the stings of doubt,
I once again can find inside of me.
For you and me the way and goal are one.
What you once wished to do, I too wish done!"

374/

How bright the world became! As if on wings
His soul, released up in the air, now swept;
"All's well! All's well!" the voice of hope now leapt;
"All's well! All's well!" his high heart's echo rings.
Briskly to order his ideas he brings;
Back to his speech a second time he's stepped,
And with new faith reads over the beginning:
How true he finds each word now, and how winning!

For hours on he works, all industry,
To get his great oration memorized;
Only the end of it must be revised
So that the climax will strike properly.
He stays so long at his activity
He knows by heart each word he'd utilized
As well as every dot and stroke—and with Amen
His copybooks he locks away again.

He finds it's three o'clock. With mind set right,
Over to the looking glass he goes
And gets himself into civilian clothes,
With velvet vest and neckcloth, snowy white,
For as a speaker he could not impose
By bringing his court-uniform in sight.
That done, to the dining room he went
And joined his wife at table, much content.

To her he spoke with animated mien
While with manful power every trace
Of morning's agitation and doubt keen
He wiped clean from his words and from his face.
He laughed with Julle, bantered with Bettine,
Clasped hands across the table with Her Grace,
And added in a noncommittal tone:
"Tonight my angel will stay home alone."

When he was asked where he himself would be,
He answered: Jensen, one more friend, and he'd
Be playing cards—a little lie of need
Which he allowed himself, since he'd not see
Fru Mille made acquainted with his creed
Till he brought home the wreath of victory;
But, having given her that information,
He went back up to study his oration.

There, one more time he read his copybook,
Then on the bell rope gave a tugging bold,
Called the coach, and dressed to suit the cold.
Sharp at six o'clock his hat he took
And one last time, before away he rolled,
At his great men on high he cast a look;
But chiefly on Columbus's eidolon,
On Luther, Mirabeau, Lycurgus, Solon.

Homo made his way to the hotel,
Where Jensen lit the lamps in the great hall,
And saw the podium, at the farther wall,
Like a hilltop reigning o'er a sunken dell.
"What!" Jensen cried. "Are you beneath a spell?
Why are you here? You see that doorway small?
Go up and stay inside that cell's confine
Till all is ready and I give the sign."

Our hero went, but by that wretched room
With its one candle he was much repelled,
Though this idea helped mitigate his gloom:
That almost always in foul corners dwelled
The noble seed the world reaped in full bloom,
There took the force of life by which it swelled;
That almost always emanated darkling
The stars that set a nation's heavens sparkling.

By pacing up and down he kept at bay
The cold, and though the time was flying by,
He used it to rehearse what he would say,
But lost the thread of it, ply after ply.
He heard some noise below—the hue and cry
Of people storming through the entranceway,
First singly, and then all in one huge knot:
"They're coming! They are coming now!" he thought.

He hastened to the door, held it ajar,
And scouted with his eyes around the hall,
And he was right! That *is* just who they are.
The hall is packed at once from wall to wall,
But to him as he stares out from afar
Little Jensen tiptoes, with the call:
"It's time!" He whispers: "Come along with me!"
And Homo summons all his bravery.

As deacon priest, so Jensen led him out;
But as he walked along the dais then,
Past overcoated and frock-coated men,
Talking loud and moving all about,
With other words came these into his ken:
"Now comes the fun! Watch, we shall have a rout!"
His heart shrank 'neath his jacket then and there,
And, most upset, he took the speaker's chair.

There he stood with his Ideals, that race
Of children born within his quiet mind,
To loose them publicly from his embrace
With words that gave them over to mankind.
A shyness in near ideal form's defined
That moment in the features of his face.
Up from his stack of sheets, ideally slow,
His eyelids, like a helmet vizor, go.

Out over all that newly becalmed sea
Of men, a look inspired he sudden sends—
But with the sight of that humanity
His soul's so struck his self-possession ends.
A power ignorant of sympathy,
Toward the man a tight-packed phalanx bends;
He felt one 'gainst a thousand, sighed aloud,
And, to begin, more deep than usual bowed.

He raised his head back up and stuttered:
"Honored gentlemen! If—" But with that
The power to speak a word had left him flat.
It seemed his lips forbade that aught be uttered
And that his tongue became a wooden slat.
A blush of shame around his cheeks now fluttered
For his long silence, every speaker's sin—
Then from below they cried: "Begin! Begin!"

At that his voice seemed pushed up from his throat;
Suddenly his powers of speech were there
And on he talked as briskly as he wrote.
But now the reader I must make aware
Of a peculiarity which all souls bear
Lest what's to follow strike a jarring note:
Though with one entity the soul's endowed,
Its doubleness must also be allowed.

377/

From this it comes that someone when he talks
Is one thing, but another when he thinks;
That often he may follow all the links
In notions he may still find heterodox;
That in itself the heart a logic locks
Which from the head's contrary logic shrinks;
That often to his No a man says Yes,
And his own I as You will oft address.

In other words, there is within each soul
An inward soul which holds life's actual might.
To it, shell-like, the outward soul clamps tight
And oftentimes will play the inward's role,
Whose kernel, though, it never can get right
Although it acts as if it were the whole.
In the outward soul are skills and talents found,
In short, what's been called "the entrusted pound."

From this the reader's bound to recognize
(What would be else a lifelong mystery)
That Homo's soul was acting in this wise.
In his speech his outward soul rules free;
While *it* spins his thought to soliloquy,
Inside at its trade doubt's demon plies;
For when a demon is to play its role,
It's always held in by the inward soul.

There at his heart's root it scratched and bit
And shouted (while above this insurrection
Our hero stirred the crowd on to Perfection):
"Yes, watch out for yourself, you wretched twit!
For if no miracle reverses it,
You'll flop back in your chair in sheer abjection.
Just see that you come out well as you planned,
For, facing you, behold, your judge does stand."

When Homo, in much insecurity,
Announced the Ideal's ultimate conquest,
Back the demon shouted in his breast:
"There you go with all that idiocy!
Talk to the crowd, if that's what you like best;
Through all those layers of haberdashery,
Through all those brains in skulls too thick to feel,
You'll never penetrate with your Ideal!"

My reader grasps that, with this mutineer,
His words could not have had the least effect
When Homo's soul—reduced to mouth and ear—
In bearing, unity, and heat was wrecked.
His speech was cold as ice, as you'd suspect,
Too boring for an audience to hear;
And though, when read, the writing was unblotched,
That did not help with its delivery botched.

The gathering, which had till then kept still,
Felt they had had enough of rhetoric;
And to make clear that they had had their fill,
They pounded with umbrella and knob-stick.
But when he went on talking with a will,
The whole crowd greeted him with hisses thick,
And while he clutched the table, his head weak,
A man stepped forth, to be allowed to speak.

On seeing this, our hero turned dead white,
And found it very hard to keep aware
Of what the man was saying for all there:
That they thought *they* were speakers for the night;
That if he'd thought they came to hear and stare,
He hadn't read their wishes halfway right;
And that he seemed to cancel his own plan,
Aggrandizing the voice of every man.

Nonplussed, Homo stared out at the man;
Then down he sprang from his high situation
As up to take his place Hr. Jensen ran
And, while he gave the crowd an exhortation,
Interpreting the wording of the plan,
Begged them for God's sake to keep formation:
The speaker, who had had a slight attack,
Would soon have his old mental powers back.

He looked around—but saw the open door,
For Homo had already left the hall,
And little Jensen now could do no more
Than, on the sudden, to dismiss them all,
Vowing they should hear from him before
The day the next club-meeting was to fall.
When that was done, home to his friend he fled,
Whom he found lying, drained of strength, in bed.

"That was a damned poor showing!" Jensen cried,
While merrily he riffled his own hair.
"But, after all, you'd held the speaker's chair
For your first time. One's bound to get tongue-tied.
Ein Mal ist kein Mal. No cause for despair!
This first defeat we'll swiftly override.
Next week we shall again take up the chore—"
"No!" Homo interrupted. "Nevermore!"

"What!" shouted Jensen. "From that cause take flight
Which over many years you have worked toward,
Which you have thought upon both day and night,
Which you said was your mission, which you pored
Through books for, which once made your heart so light
And glad despite the blows from Fate's keen sword?
This you would unmanfully let fall?"
"Yes," Homo sighed. "Yes! Yes, for good and all!"

In vain his friend found good grounds to oppose,
In vain found proof for every hopeful word;
If Jensen had a hundred mouths to glose,
He wouldn't by our hero have been heard.
Like Icarus, a-swoon from wounds incurred,
Sent halfway through the heavens with such blows
As cast him headfirst, wingless, to the bay,
Buried deep in pillows Homo lay.

He entered now a period that's hard
To find the proper image to portray,
Unless my reader pays him no regard
And thinks himself at black-and-red to play
For something which he dare not throw away
And which he's staked upon a single card.
Red's the card the reader counted on—
Oh! Black's come up, and now the stakes are gone.

Deep melancholy had come over him,
Which, more than clamp his heart till it near bled,
Which, more than weigh upon his mind and limb
So that the strength from his fine figure fled,
Brought his nerves up to a pitch so grim
That he at this same time (what is here said
Has the ring of something rather crazy)
Was flabby and yet tense, restive yet lazy.

380/

For hours on end he could stand still and gaze
Down through his window at the thoroughfare,
As though half marvelling that folk out there
Could go along their customary ways
While there was not the least thing to declare
The dark he knew would overtake his days;
But if, behind him, someone tried the door,
He shrank as if some terror through him tore.

For nights on end he could lie wide awake,
Obsessed by others' scorn and mockery;
And there were people he would sometimes see,
Heads together, which began to shake;
At once he paled; it was a certainty
They did it for his failed Idea's sake.
And never would he dare to read a paper
For fear of finding jests at his mad caper.

At no price, though the pleas were more than kind,
Would he allow himself to go outside;
For why should he then summon strength of mind
To let himself by all the world be spied?
But when he took ill, being so confined,
When his physician showed up horrified,
The doctor's counsel he'd so far obey
As to take a coach ride every day.

He sat there with some sort of dignity
While in his carriage he went rumbling round:
Inside a barrier kept him safe and sound
From passers-by that he might chance to see;
Inside some peace from all of them he found
And, though imprisoned there, felt as if free;
For if familiar faces should approach,
He did have window curtains on his coach.

Fru Mille grew uneasy, and when she
Through Jensen learned the reason for it all,
She got the patient past the city wall
On an express coach for the barony.
But even there he could not feel quite free
Of that black gloom that kept him in its thrall,
And late in February back he came
Once more to drive round sadly, without aim.

Who knows how far his sickness might have spread
Were it not for a high authority
Which ordered that to court the man be led,
Where—he received a Kammerherr's gold key.
Geheimraad Encken stood him in good stead
And in high places spoke persuasively,
If on his own or at an overture
From Homo's friends—well, no one can be sure.

At least our hero got the golden key;
The cloud of gloom now disappeared from sight;
The closed horizon he could see spread free,
And, like his mind, his vision too grew bright.
But, it is asked, how could this key make right
The murder of his hope and dignity?
And even if one instant pleased him well,
What comfort was there in this bagatelle?

A lot! New hope springs from new avenues.
A man will sometimes take a street—not true?—
Whose end another street will run into
And lead him to completely different views.
He need but turn a corner for purlieus
In which he'd never had a rendezvous.
Thus Homo, when that golden key he got,
Now turned into another way of thought.

He'd keep the public from his enterprise,
Be with the nation and its welfare quit,
While in his thoughts he would direct his eyes
Toward a goal directly opposite
To that which he as speaker failed to hit.
Only *cultured* men he'd recognize,
Whose prospects still were of sufficient scope
For steady progress and continuous hope.

And with his new thoughts came the transformation
Of his perspective on life's goals and course;
But to know we need such alteration
Requires a shove first from an outside source.
That shove must make the heart thrill by its force
Before we wish for mental renovation;
For many to one way of thought are slave
And travel it from cradle straight to grave.

The path of many is docility,
Which one might well the church path choose to call:
Which, free from insult and from upset free,
Leads them toward the end which beckons all.
It isn't possible for them to see
New ways of thinking in with which to fall.
All turning round they think unwarranted
When all they have to do is look ahead.

Quite opposite, zigzagging out and in,
The paths of thought for all too many wind,
Who long for all the treasure they can win
To fill completely an unquiet mind.
They twist about in thoughts of every kind
Whene'er a former goal has worn too thin:
They want another prospect—answers new
To life's enigmas through new things to do.

But often in this fashion things so tend
That we turn right into a cul-de-sac,
An alley that is closed off at one end.
We stride ahead—we push on, but, alack!
Though 'gainst a wall we'd rush till our heads crack,
These can but say, "Stop! No! No thanks, my friend!"
And if we will not heed this prohibition,
Continued progress will bring inanition.

Then a man thanks God if aught befall
Which forces him to turn himself around;
Which brings that brow he strikes against a wall
Back to the air where nothing solid's found;
Then he will love those bumps because they hound
His thought out of the hole which held it thrall;
And that's just why Hr. Homo loves the key
Which gave his stifled thoughts their liberty.

But, as good fortune brings more in its train,
So it happened here. No time had flown
Since he had had, much to his tailor's gain,
The customary two gold buttons sewn
Upon his coat in back (but these pertain
To his civilian street-coat, that alone).
Scarce sat that rearward sign of honor right
When comes the cross in front, and he's a knight.

How was it done? All but *prestissimo*.
Three youthful Kammerherrer of this nation
Were to take part in a celebration,
And in full dress before the court did go.
Two of them had on a decoration,
And on the Chamberlain 'twould poorly show
To have the third there without any gloss;
And in that fashion Homo got the cross.

He goes straight homeward from the celebration,
That in the circle of his family
He might receive his wife's congratulation
And (with his features all complacency)
That Julle and Bettine might play free
With his new cross, sure to win approbation.
From them into his own room he withdrew,
Where he could get away from this to-do.

In solitude, his joy was unconcealed,
His soul felt freed at last from every band;
He thanked in his mind's quietude the hand
Which had both wounded and as well had healed,
Which graciously his heart had now annealed
And raised his spirit when he'd been unmanned.
Providence's finger he saw clear
And gave that Providence his thanks sincere.

"But," he thought, "mere words would hardly do.
True gratitude in action is expressed;
For someone who by Heaven's been so blest
Should give something to other people too.
To rid of woe the homes of the distressed,
To comfort hearts now overcome with rue,
A soul can do no better charity;
And therefore I'll do *good in secrecy*."

Some fifty dalers from his desk he's drawn
And, to assure that he would not be known,
Nothing but a duffel coat put on
Over which his winter cloak was thrown.
His eyes beneath his plain cap brightly shone
As through the gate he went to walk alone,
And up the street he hurried now along
Just as the dawn's light was becoming strong.

It was in March, and how the weather frowned
With rain and fog and winds of such a force
That he was all but knocked off from his course
And found it hard to keep his great-cloak bound.
At Kongens Nytorv, right around the Horse,
Two figures coming close to him he found,
Two skinny female figures, almost hags,
With slippers on their feet and dressed in rags.

The wind behind them blew their dresses in,
Detailing the full misery of each frame
As it went boring into bones and skin;
And now he noticed one of them was lame.
His heart warmed with a sympathetic flame
And, with his cloak drawn tight above his chin,
He let (although he did not break his stride)
A coin into the hand of each one glide.

"Oh, God bless you, sir," he heard behind.
But he walked quickly on, for now he had
Before his eyes his own self as a lad
In that dark time when he had been consigned
To roam the streets with his health undermined,
And, shuddering, he cried as almost glad:
"No, those women's misery was greater!
Thank God that my affairs got better later!"

With joy, then, in his present affluence
While others bore the brute force of distress
(A joy of which my reader would, I'd guess,
Have had at times some slight experience),
He strode along and did not spare his pence
At any outstretched hand of wretchedness;
And now his steps have led him finally
To where he could do good in secrecy.

Adress' avisen pointed him the way,
With pleas for loans to those in misery,
A midwife's heavy charges to defray
Or settle a late husband's funeral fee.
Three houses, where they suffered terribly,
He'd ticked off with a pencil that same day;
He climbs up, nearly to the rooftop's height,
The shabby stairs of one, flight after flight.

385/

In the hall he stops—his ears could catch
Much laughter, merry singing, shouts and noise,
And hardly does he lift up the door latch
When from the bench where they had shared their joys
Leap up two crones, one man, four girls and boys,
And one huge lad, his hair a thick red thatch.
A well-lit board with roast and flasks and punch
Astounds him quite as much as this gay bunch.

"I must be wrong," he says. "The paper said
That there had been a death at this address."
One of the crones replied, "That's true, yes, yes,"
Stinking of punch and glistening fat and red.
"Yes, it's true, the poor old scarecrow's dead,
And at his last he was in great distress;
He screamed and died there halfway through one shout—
But will the gentleman see him laid out?"

From a bench she snatched away a sheet;
There, skeletal, his features pinched up tight,
The dead man lay, his head of hair all white,
And, fussing with him, she talked in the heat:
"Born in Skagen, sewed till he was beat.
This sack was his last job, and it's not right—
One side's fine, but t'other isn't stout—
Now it's his shroud, it's his now to wear out."

Astonished, scarcely breathing, Homo stood
And on that hollow check let his eyes pore.
But she went on: "The poor thing! I'm heart-sore!
So many folk have come and been so good
And handed us a shilling at the door.
My husband, that's his son, did all he could,
And that he was well cared for I know best:
But won't the gentleman sit down and rest?"

Our hero, whose anger had begun to flame,
Motioned back the crone, who now fell still;
And, giving them a look that could well kill,
Rebuked them: why, they really had no shame
To ask for gifts from everyone who came
And use them to buy liquor and such swill;
Why, it was terrible to sit and souse
While there was still that dead man in the house.

They stood there looking shamefaced at this blame,
All except the youngster with red hair;
For he, who had been skimming passion's flame
From the bowl where they'd all had their share,
Answered Homo hotly: "That there shame,
Which this gentleman talked up so fair,
Means no more, if you understand his pitch,
Than that a roast's fit only for the rich.

"You think your shilling is so generous,
That with its help we'll come through our distress;
You think we'll scrimp and save, in thankfulness
That bread and water now is plenteous.
But when each day the cold is merciless
And each night we've just straw to cover us,
We need a day when everything is dandy,
And that is when *your* money comes in handy.

"You have it fine, you rich! Doves ready-cooked
Fly in your mouths, and life is cherry pie,
With lovely misses and fine wives you've hooked,
On velvet sofas in your castles high.
In your parlors pretty parrots cry,
But have you in such holes as this but looked?
If you'd like, just nose around our nests:
Rats and mice are all we have for guests!

"We dance upon the ruins, sir, our bunch,
In sorest need we open up joy's tap;
With our last shilling, yes, we make some punch
And even buy some raisin buns, mayhap;
While Death grins down, we drown both woes and lunch,
And trump his card before he springs his trap;
And if today we've chased away our sorrow,
We'll let the fiddle worry for tomorrow.

"Yes, look at me! And if you can't stay cool,
Go sling your cloak politely round your coat!
But we have newspapers in evening school
And our teacher knows just what's afloat.
A storm is blotting out the sun—I quote!—
And lightning soon will strike where rich men rule.
We little people know our catechism;
Be careful—and make way for pauperism!"

387/

"Hush, Jochum!" cried the woman. "Shut your face!
Oh, sir! Don't listen to his talking-back,
But mark the coffin that they're painting black."
Our hero, who just wished to flee the place,
Took out a daler from his money-sack
And put it in the dead man's hand—to race
Past Jochum's scornful smile at his retreat
Down the staircase and out to the street.

There he stood. Depressed, he went his route
And to a cellar came most cautiously
Where, if they could not pay the rental fee,
The family next Monday'd be thrown out.
But here he saw distress they talk about
As tickling to thin-skinned philanthropy:
Distress so without hope, so void of cheer,
That as a god a helper must appear.

He saw a pallid woman knitting hose
By candle in the dark and stuffy air,
While her husband, hunchbacked, cobbled there
And fixed bronze bottoms onto some sabots.
Four almost-naked children he saw doze
Upon the floor, which but for straw was bare.
He eased, with twenty dalers, their afflictions
And harvested a thousand benedictions.

Back on the street he stood, free, full of cheer,
Smiling at the thought of his good deed.
He rushed to find the mother in sore need
Who lived close by up in the fourth floor rear.
He climbed the staircase to an attic drear,
But, hand still on the doorknob, he must heed
A sound that struck him like a woman's sighing.
He entered—she sat by a cradle, crying.

Wrapped in his cloak up to his nose's tip,
Some words about the child he stammered first,
Then asked if at her own breast it was nursed
And if its health was good, poor little nip.
She did not speak, but round her face there burst
A blush of shame—and when he then let slip
Five-and-twenty bills near her child's face
She nearly clasped his neck in an embrace.

388/

She lifted up her voice and hand, elated.
"Oh!" she cried. "Down to this room so dark
A shining angel's flown from Heaven's arc,
Bringing help to one repudiated.
My angel's countenance, O! let me mark!
Let this breast betrayed and vitiated
Know its guardian angel, how he's named,
And keep that name till by Death I am claimed!"

It sounded like sweet music to his ear,
And one flap of his cloak he let fall free;
But—he would do his good in secrecy,
And nothing must with that plan interfere.
Rather than let his full face appear,
He wheeled about on one foot suddenly,
With one sweep round his shoulders threw his cape,
Rushed out, and down the stairs made his escape.

For the third time he was back outside,
Where now the wind and rain had been suppressed
And high above the moon, in snow-white dressed,
Down through the black clouds on the city spied.
Following the house fronts, he progressed
Toward Kongens Nytorv and its spaces wide
And, stirred, on Heaven's light he turned his look
While the heartstrings in him pealed and shook.

He'd brought relief to people in distress,
He'd done his duty as he had intended,
He felt the joy that no words can express
But to which every heart has been commended;
He walked as though half heavenward ascended
Till from his heart, as to his consciousness
The face of Alma rose, a sigh was drawn.
Where was she now? How was she getting on?

The Town Directory would surely say
Where she now lived! With this thought in his head
He walked on to a grocery down the way
To borrow one and find out what it said.
He found none there, and ran to the café,
Where one would have to be deposited,
And on his inquiry was made aware
The book was in the billiard room back there.

He stepped in, where in the cigar smoke's haze
A swarm of young men moved or paused to look
As with their hands and mouths and eyes they took
Joy speeding balls to holes across green baize
Upon the prompting of a cue stick's graze.
Our hero sat to one side with the book.
He opened it—though many names were listed,
Neither Star nor Alma there existed.

The old man, then, he thought, has likely died.
But what's become of Alma, the poor thing?
But here a noise broke off his pondering:
The crowd was in an uproar, goggle-eyed,
That in the game's heat one of them could bring
His ball to ricochet from side to side.
He pressed himself back deeper in his nook,
Picked up a paper, and laid down the book.

Cigar in mouth, he sat there, furrow-browed
(Around him people whistled, sang, and hissed)
And read the paper through his smoky cloud,
Where, in the news from Funen he had missed,
He looked as in a dream at the death-list.
Upon his vision fell a jet-black shroud:
His mind went blank at news of one demise
And scarce could he put trust in his own eyes.

He read: "The editor is sorely wrung
That yesterday's reports were not at fault.
At Galtenborg, the Lady Clara Galt
Met her death, though she was far too young,
When at a gate which she essayed to vault
Her horse tripped on a rock, and she was flung.
An officer who rode in company
Saw her tumble—she died instantly."

That was all; enough, though, to digest,
More than enough, for Homo. He'd a shock
As if a thunderbolt had hit his breast,
And for a minute sat there like a block.
In staying there he lost all interest,
And he strode past the merry-making flock
When from behind him as he beat retreat
A voice yelled: "Pahlen gets an aquavit!"

"Pahlen?" he repeated. He turned round
And there in the decrepit old *marqueur*
Whom he had hardly noticed earlier
The friend of his young manhood he now found.
But where's the gloss that kept him once spellbound?
The style, the figure, bloom, perfume that were?
The *rentier* had disappeared! How fallen!
Van Pahlen sunk into the *marqueur*, Pahlen!

With pale and oily face, his pate bedecked
With combed-together strands of dull-gray hair;
With vest of twill in filthy disrepair
Around a stomach flabby from neglect;
With pants that with his waist failed to connect
And showed part of his shirt—the man stood there.
Just one thing was the same for all his plight:
The bootstraps which still kept his trousers tight.

A dandy brought the *snaps* in on a plate
And everybody's eyes to Pahlen hied,
Who'd reached for it, impatient of the wait.
"—Get your hands away!" the dandy cried.
"Patience, *lieber* Pahlen! Theft denied
Until we get a joke that is first-rate."
The marker swiftly served them a salacity,
Took his pay, and thanked them with vivacity.

Our hero, with his mind half in a haze,
Dashed off from the laughing company
And went back to his own room presently,
Kindly welcomed by the moon's soft blaze
Which through the shining windows cast its rays.
He doffed his coat, and, bowed in memory,
He sat himself down in his rocking chair
As, 'cross the floor, the moonlight glided fair.

As from a fully sounded instrument
Which long preserves its chordal echoings,
Deep in his breast resounded the taut strings
To all that he that evening underwent.
His heart was like to burst with sorrowings,
And feelings he'd not felt to this extent
For many years engulfed him magically,
Whereby all life was shown forth tragically.

391/

Where had all those beings gotten to
Whom at one time his heart had so esteemed?
Where was the youthful happiness he knew,
The past that once so rich in hope had seemed?
Each hope was fled; each bond was cut clean through,
And every pledge of joy was unredeemed;
The name alone was left of ties destroyed,
And thwarted expectation, and a void.

His vanished life, in which no great works shone,
Struck him very nearly as if dreamed,
But dreams of high deeds now were very wan;
Through mists like ghosts upon the mind they gleamed,
And time, into whose depths he'd soon be gone,
A monstrous field of graves to him now seemed,
Which with a speed that filled his mind with fright
Would swallow all and cover all in night.

He sat there dark, while round him played the light,
Till to his rest he went with hurried tread,
Flinging off his clothing of that night
And setting down his slippers by the bed.
With Clara's face and Pahlen's still in sight
He pulled the covers up around his head,
As from the bottom of his heart so crooned he:
Sic transit gloria mundi!

Part Three

C A N T O   X

We make our choice—and what does that phrase mean?
Just what it says! We all of us abstain
From the Totality we can't attain
Save by ascent to the Idea's serene;
We make our compacts with the earth we've seen
And chase Life's Unity out of our brain;
We wander paths with other goals in mind
And learn more of ourselves and humankind.

We make our choice—we all of us were led
To think we would be what is called earth's salt;
We'd had it all but drummed into our head
That what we'd soon do would this world exalt;
With hope, the only wealth yet in our vault,
We paid the interest art and knowledge bred;
We'd be revered among the Idea's pastors:
We make our choice—and turn out burgomasters.

Hail, burgomasters! Masters all, at least.
But what of him who failed to choose? Where's he
Who steered now to the west, now to the east,
Toward art and science and to poetry,
Whose contemplation of his goal ne'er ceased
Although he overshot it constantly?
Like the fearful cat who shunned good cream,
With weak brains but strong faith, he botched his dream!

395/

We make our choice—we'd promised we would greet
A day whose sun would never have declined;
We had so firmly fixed it in our mind
That life's one goal was happiness complete;
We dared to hope all things for all mankind,
For we felt our desires with such great heat;
But soon hope's fires will into ashes flicker:
We make our choice—and give ourselves to liquor.

Our hearts were sensitive—we would ally
With all men, and we did, with vehemence;
Their oracle we had heard prophesy
And offered up both praise and frankincense;
We'd change our hearts for theirs and, flying high,
Give them our lifelong obedience;
But, when our faith is shattered, down we come:
We make our choice—and speak opprobrium.

We'd found, when through youth's spyglass we would peer,
Consciousness and good repute the same.
We'd thought that if in *right* we'd persevere,
Our *rights* to approbation we could claim,
For good effects out of good causes came.
How wrong we were is plain to eye and ear:
We hear ourselves impugned, dragged through the gutter:
We make our choice—we simply let them mutter.

But though the good may sometimes lead to bad
When we make choices from which we won't err,
And though we often in life's fray and stir
Can only by them keep from going mad,
We must reject convictions ironclad
In which our hopes and thoughts used to concur,
Since the Totality cannot be split
And one choice never covers all of it.

Our hero made his choice (for he rejected
The Idea which used to haunt his brain
And of whose fragments he was at much pain
To make a whole which then could be inspected)
And along new lines his life directed
Now that he'd grown much wiser, more humane:
Plunk in his middle age he changed his mount
And the Ideal did suddenly discount.

Why so suddenly? We're wont to see
That these things happen slowly, over years.
That's true of spirits from the lower spheres,
Whose coolings you can watch near hourly,
But in a spirit that has so few peers
Such a reversal happens one-two-three!
He'd hitherto just climbed—now he sank low,
Turned round forthwith, and let the Ideal go.

It had rewarded him with so much pain,
Such misery and torment did provoke—
Yes, while he languished 'neath its golden yoke,
Such poisons he digested grain by grain
That when he conjured up within his brain
The long years which had all gone up in smoke,
He found there were scarce ten days in a row
Which he could say were free of any woe.

But ere with the Ideal he'd ceased connection
By a decision ending every doubt,
His mind (whose service to his will is stout)
Provided him such excellent direction
He marvelled that till now he'd not found out
That there had been a catch in his selection.
If the Ideal were made Reality,
Then as Ideal it would cease to be.

Then it was never meant to be attained,
For ev'n in Art it stood off like a star
Whose pure light's only seen through prisms strained;
For life, however, off so far, so far,
It must be kept like something singular,
Much desired, but never to be gained.
Like a light in Heaven it should blink
And, graciously alluring, ever wink.

Vindicated then, no more distressed,
He let the light blink on, as free and gay
He made at home upon a bright June day
His choice, completely self-possessed.
Scarce was that done when, with his mind at rest,
He sees the roses shoot up on his way,
When all around him he can smell and see
The fruits of succulent Reality.

397/

From now on he wants but what can be had,
From this time forth content to meditate
Upon the lucky size of his estate
To make the autumn years of life full glad;
From this time forth he will not be made mad,
Entangled in the towlines laid by Fate;
From this time forth a man of cultured grace
And happiness is written in his face.

But, since a life with little to report
(Despite the splendor in which it passed by)
Of heart's *piano* or of passion's *fort'*,
Has little that can catch another's eye,
We now will cut its presentation short,
And very cursorily will we fly
Past seasons which but minutely had run
And which in years made up some twenty-one.

Our hero, as we've said, now had good days:
The summers he spent in the countryside,
But every winter in town he'd reside
To share in all the merry city ways.
He sometimes would drive round and sometimes ride,
And find himself at court or at soirées;
He would appear here, there, and everywhere
And be a part of every large affair.

He oft was seen in highborn company
Speaking in the tongues of several nations;
One saw him, with his bearing suave and free,
Taking part in many conversations,
Making or just hearing observations,
Till he'd developed that *présence d'esprit*
For lack of which he blamed his speech-disaster,
But of which now he'd made himself a master.

Yes, if that art was once for him a maze,
If just the practise of it too hard fell,
He now had got to know the art so well
He never had to cast round for a phrase
Or lose his thread upon some bagatelle;
He always knew a multitude of ways
To form an answer apt for anything,
Composed of both bee's honey and bee's sting.

/398/

But this advance did not end his aspiring,
For by means of a royal confirmation
He cleverly arranged for his creation
(Since now there was no chance of his acquiring
From Mille little barons of his siring)
As Baron, by which long-sought appellation
His calling cards thereafter made him known:
Homo, Kammerherre and Baron.

At this same time he had the joy to lead
Down the aisle in satin white as snow
Both charming daughters and see them proceed
Up to the altar proudly, all aglow.
Bettine with Count Magnus Gjede, a Swede,
And Julle with her rich Norwegian beau,
Whereby he'd done whatever done could be
To further Scandinavian unity.

But (I can hear the reader now exclaim)
What was he doing all those years gone by?
He worked (that does quite well for a reply),
He worked incessantly! He did not aim
Just to take his share of joys that came,
But by his zeal this world to fortify.
When something was promoted, shares were sold,
There he was, himself, his name, his gold.

But that whereby he crowns his grand ambitions
And ennobles his life's private sphere
Is what he does in his public career.
As member of a whole host of commissions
He talks with hosts of folk of all conditions
And sticks his nose up at what he must hear;
A host of letters he unseals, reads, writes,
Few of which survive two days and nights.

But through such business, full of fascination,
The days flew past like blinkings of an eye.
Time fell away, and entire years ran by,
Without there being any real cessation
Of his normal life, which kept up high
And grew in influence and reputation.
Through fifty-seven years he'd just progressed
When there's the Grand-Cross Star upon his chest.

How was it done? All but *prestissimo*:
Three elder Kammerherrer of this nation
Were called to take part in a celebration,
And in full dress before the court did go.
Two of them had stars for decoration
And on the Chamberlain 'twould poorly show
To have the third without that objet d'art;
And in that fashion Homo got the star.

He has a copy sewn on every suit,
That on his road of life he might have light;
But that was not the end of Homo's route,
For hardly four full years had taken flight
When, rumors of long standing bearing fruit,
A letter granting him Geheimraad's right
Was sent to "Baron Homo, Excellence,"
Which let him with his "Kammerherr" dispense.

And we will make a pause with this event;
His Excellence obtained, we will stand still,
To learn what's happened to the Lady Mill',
How things had gone with her and how they went,
If she had handled well or handled ill
The worldly mission on which she was bent,
If her emancipation-work proved void,
In short, how she had been and was employed.

She had remained the same—and what more praise
Can be delivered of a heroine?
She strove in all directions and all ways
Emancipation for her sex to win.
She'd written many novels through these days
And on a trip to Paris had she been,
Whence she'd brought back a Badge of Liberty,
A red cockade which was a joy to see.

Encouraged by the notice she could rouse,
She soon established a confederacy
Of women who found just their cup of tea
The manners she had brought back from *daraus*.
And this Freedom League spread mightily.
From membership in it she barred her spouse,
But little Jensen Mille did install
As ladies' secretary of protocol.

400/

On mornings her large drawing room was graced
With their attendance and their common chore
Of making Liberty Cockades, decor
Which, since its wear was up to each one's taste,
On hats, breasts, shoulders, or on backs was placed,
And monthly they would change the ones they wore
For others better from artistic angles
And decorate them, as with pearls, with spangles.

Then in the women's club the talk held sway,
In which the house's matron never lost;
Then at the mirrors many heads were tossed
And much approval for the fine array,
While chocolate was brought in on a tray;
Then came much laughter as Hr. Jensen crossed
The threshold with such nimble little hops,
Just like a cork that from its bottle pops.

Once he was seated, then the work could start:
The literary custom-tailoring
Which, as Fru Mille often would impart,
Was best done with the women visiting.
They sat at table and, wits quickening
To Jensen's pen and judgment in fine art,
Wrote scenes for novels, from which there would be
Whole books upon the stalls eventually.

There was a heroine in each creation
Rosy-red and yet as white as snow,
By whose doings readers got to know
The proud free women of emancipation.
They hoped to see a larger public grow
In support of their great inspiration,
Which, rich and fruitful, might yield annually
Two whole stories, some years even three.

In working for this cause they had embraced,
They felt alive and very well content,
As here, mouths open, over sharp pens bent,
They sat at table like the queens of taste;
And from the social circles which she graced
Each drew a person or an incident
Which all the noses of the ladies sniffed
Before they trimmed it to the novel's drift.

401/

So our lady lived, performed and dealt.
She managed to get many stories done
The same time that she briskly round would run
To get her genius in the wide world felt,
While the parlor, now used by no one,
No longer of the flowers of gladness smelt:
For who could tend domestic plants these days
When she and Homo went their separate ways?

They seldom met—in company, usually,
And when they came down for their evening meal;
For each lived his own life, and came to feel
That conversation was pure drudgery
When hers was fixed on A and his on Z.
But her good humor kept its even keel,
Although with time her voice was pitched still higher,
But—Nemesis, for that, had not passed by her.

She had become still fatter year by year
By virtue of the hearty appetite
She had for life, which made more fierce her bite
Into its joys before they disappear;
But now she groaned with fat—she could not clear
An inside doorway and she'd say outright:
Though day by day her mind grew more inspired,
Her body became heavier and more tired.

In spirit free—in body tightly chained;
Emancipated—yet beneath a yoke:
A contradiction! for which she bespoke
Physicians' counsel to have it explained.
The counsel was: a wheelchair's best for folk
Whose energies have by their girth been drained.
And from that time the lady was house-bound
With noise, with laughter, wheeling all around.

In wheelchair she would drink and she would eat,
In wheelchair she would entertain each guest,
In wheelchair she would her club members meet,
Who now of a wheeled genius were possessed.
In wheelchair she went to eternal rest,
For down to death she rolled in that same seat,
To pay the dust that she owed in arrears
On just completing six-and-fifty years.

In her chair at breakfast she was found
Among well-wishers and had bent her head
To find a *kringle*, fallen to the ground,
When all at once she gasped and turned beet-red:
All at once her eyes grew wide and round,
And from her chair she half leapt, so it sped
Backward, as, with lips that had turned gray,—
A râle—a roll—a râle—she passed away.

"Apoplexy!" each well-wisher cried,
But she remained as dead as dead could be;
For her the end came to life's comedy
And soon she joined the grave to be its bride.
Scarce widowered, off to the barony
Our hero pale and clad in black did ride
To tend to manor-business great and small,
Avoiding thus every condolence call.

—One year had passed since he received this blow,
And still he lived a widower, alone,
When someone wrote from town to let him know
That what he wanted most was now his own.
A stage director he was made, and so
From August twentieth he would be known.
This had been sent the twelfth; so coach and horse
He readied and from Jutland set his course.

A stage director! And his first time, too!
On this leap we shall have to dwell a bit,
For it's the greatest leap he has been through,
And in his coach he too must ponder it.
One wonders why it seemed so right to hit
On such a most unlikely thing to do.
A realist these twenty years now past,
Director for the Idea now at last?

Instead of seeking reasons recherché
For giving his behavior likelihood,
As, for example, that the theater could
A widower's deep sorrowing allay,
Or that this theater post was in no way
At odds with his proud strivings for the good;
Here is the reason we ourselves adduce:
His yearning to be of some personal use.

That yearning never ceased to haunt his head.
It had survived his every lost campaign,
And now he'd stand his country in good stead
And personally tend Art's holy fane.
That's why he wished the theater post to gain;
And to the eve of that great day I've sped
When to the boards his life he will engage.
And now once more I bring him on the stage.

In Homo's Copenhagen residence,
In the room with damask draperies,
The reader's longings after him we'll ease
By bringing him once more to prominence.
The door is opened—and His Excellence
(And servant with the French name, if you please)
In velvet robe comes from his cabinet
To finish up here with his day's toilette.

A noble figure! Who would ever guess
That sixty-two years weigh upon his back?
It's true, his once-flat stomach has grown slack
And of his blond hair there is somewhat less,
But in his look there is the same address
And 'neath his forehead's snow his brows are black;
His cheeks are red, his lips still moist and round,
His posture straight, his gait and bearing sound.

Up to the console with near youthful ease
He treads and looks into the mirror now.
"Jean-Jacques," he says, "my comb now, if you please!"
Jean-Jacques then hands it to him with a bow.
Though soft and sparse, his hair's combed anyhow
And then his neckcloth's straightened with a squeeze.
"Jean-Jacques! My ring and brooch! My watch and chain!"
These took no time to order, or obtain.

Jean-Jacques goes out, the coffee to prepare,
And by the table Homo takes a seat
Upon a huge and soft stuffed easy chair
To see what news the paper might repeat.
Outside the door he hears the tread of feet,
And then a rapping with an urgent air,
And hardly has he said "Come in" before
The nimble Dr. Flink stands in the door.

404/

"Good morning! May I cross the boundary?"
The little man exclaimed and bounded through.
"Last night Etatsraad Jensen said to me
That the Geheimraad's come back into view,
And here I am to greet Your Excellency.
Well, praise the Lord, you look quite well, you do!
You look rejuvenated! Yes, I vow
Your color's never been so good as now."

"Well, come sit down!" our hero swung around
And answered, somewhat condescendingly,
Briskly slinging one leg 'cross his knee.
"Come! Let's see if you find my pulse rate sound.
You know I'm going on to sixty-three,
A dangerous age—though my grandfather found
No harm in it (he lived to eighty)—I
Take after him, they say, unless they lie."

"If he reached eighty, you'll live ten years more,"
The doctor answered, grabbing *tout de suite*
Homo's arm to measure his pulse beat,
At which he cried: "Now that's a perfect score!
The blood was cooled by that last grief you bore;
Your pulse assures long years with joys replete.
Why, I'll prescribe to you, between us men,
That, if you want, you take a wife again."

"No, no, dear friend!" our widower then sighed
Involuntarily. "No, not for me."
"And, pray, why not?" Flink asked him earnestly.
"Do you think I'm in jest about a bride?
No, such a jest would be unsavory,
For marriage I consider sanctified;
And sad and lonesome in these walls, I hope,
You don't intend to sit about and mope?"

"No, not exactly lonesome as a fish,"
Our hero answered with a smile. "Dear, dear!
My good physician! You are lickerish!
I'm thinking I might have a woman here
To help me with whatever I might wish,
Someone whose body's sound and mind is clear.
I mean, a housekeeper I might engage;
Someone like that best suits a man my age.

"Somebody's recommended one to me,
Whom I this very morning plan to hire.
They say she's perfect, managed to acquire
Great skill in each branch of cookery.
Then friends and I will live to heart's desire
Once she's seen to my table's dignity
And kitchen, cellar have been redesigned;
For theater's all I wish to have in mind."

"Theater!" Flink repeated. "Oh, that's true!
The most important thing I don't recall;
Yes, my congratulations, sir, to you,
Though sharper to congratulate us *all*.
A golden age of theater you'll install;
A wind will blow in from direction new.
No more spectacles, we'll have great plays!
The public waits for miracles these days."

"The age of miracles, dear Flink, is gone.
But here's Jean-Jacques with coffee fresh and fine!
Do have a cup! Jean-Jacques will see it's drawn."
"Thanks," stammered Flink, "but it is almost nine;
'I vant to zee a bit uff Cobenhawn,'
As the man said when your police and mine
Approached him on the street. How time does fly—
Your humble servant—I must say good-bye."

He left—but only to have Homo spin
Round to Jean-Jacques and say: "Where was your mind
That, unannounced, you let the doctor in?
Do that again and you won't see me kind.
You're to announce first even kith and kin
And, when toward an audience I'm inclined,
No one from the anteroom you'll bring
Until you hear me give this bell a ring."

Jean-Jacques, who was a jokester, bowed his head
And, not even attempting a reply,
Announced, abashed, Miss *Frisk* had visited
And in the anteroom was standing by.
"Ha," Homo smiled. "Doctor Flink and I
Just spoke of her. Well, now, that was well said.
Have her enter!" Seconds later he
Subjected her to careful scrutiny.

406/

With her hat and shawl and checked silk dress,
With dark-brown hair and with so fresh a face,
So fresh it seems to promise something base,
She gives a curtsey as she makes ingress,
While from two eyes, like fair suns out in space,
She sends him looks of such bright forwardness
That he soon sees how tight her dress betrims
The rounded breasts, the strong and strapping limbs.

"Sit down, my dear!" whispered His Excellence,
Indicating courteously a chair.
"Of why you've come I'm perfectly aware.
You wish employment in my residence,
And, with Etatsraad Jensen's reference,
I don't see any hitch in the affair;
But first I should make very clear to you
The kind of thing that you will have to do."

The register of duties he then traces
For housekeeper and maid, respectively:
The latter in the kitchen Homo places;
The former will do service at high tea.
He last asks if her expertise embraces
Dinner parties and French cookery,
To which questions Miss Frisk's answers go
No farther than: "Well, now, I should think so!"

"Bien!" Homo smiles, and far back in his chair
He throws his shoulders, most baronially.
"Then we can leave the household business there
And take up a new subject, namely me.
Here, my good woman, there's a snag, you see—
As master I am apt to overbear—
Take my fine linens. I will have you know—"
"My wash," she breaks in, "shines as white as snow."

"Bien!" he repeated. "But there's more to weigh,
Like conduct, tact, good sense, and dedication;
For though I'm not quite old, despite this gray,
I'm still not of the younger generation.
And many evenings I seek recreation
In playing several rubbers of piquet;
But where to find a partner who'd agree
To play with me in perfect privacy?

"Is that a thing to which you could adjust?
Could you, Miss Frisk, take on a partner's role?"
"Yes," she replied, with laughter arch and droll,
"I thank His Excellency for his trust,
Though I'd be talking nonsense, on my soul,
To say that cards were aught with which I fussed.
I scarce know how to hold them in my hand,
But I can learn what I don't understand."

"Now, that was well said! That's the way to talk!"
Exclaimed our hero, while his purse he scanned
Till he drew forth a gold coin from his stock
And placed it gently in the Jomfru's hand:
"Let this coin as earnest-money stand,"
He said. "Do save your thanks until I knock
Your wages higher should we come to find
That we're contented being so combined."

He stood up, and Miss Frisk, intoxicated
By his condescension, got up too,
Whereat his jests continued unabated:
"Go down and give the house your overview.
Size up the pots, pans, glassware, kitchen crew,
And learn where everything is situated;
But don't forget, when you go home, dear soul,
You've bound yourself to serve my needs heart-whole."

"No," she answered, blushing deeply: "No,
Your Excellency, I'll not vacillate,
I'd not deceive a man of such high state.
But with your leave I ought to go below
And give your maid directions apropos
Of current modes in kitchens of the great."
She stepped out backward, curtseying to the ground,
And only at the doorway turned around.

Homo stared upon the closing door
And then broke out in this soliloquy,
Slowly pacing up and down the floor:
"For painters hers could Juno's figure be!
Eyes, bust, size, shape, nothing to deplore,
And though she's simple there's no crudity.
A few choice words to her and I can claim
A truly splendid partner for my game."

He sweetly smiled—but lets his face go slack
When suddenly in rushes his valet
Announcing the return of Homo's flack,
Who had been sent out earlier that day
And from the theater this report brought back:
The actors, authors, actresses all say
Tomorrow when it's twelve noon on the dot
He'll find them in the lobby, the whole lot.

The message lifts a stone from Homo's heart.
From Jean-Jacques he receives, in great elation,
Three letters (three of them!) of invitation,
Two of them to luncheons, very smart.
He set these in his mirror frame, apart,
While muttering: "Now here's a situation!
They're fighting over me! Today I'll caper!
But what's the meaning of this filthy paper?"

Jean-Jacques, to whom he spoke, puts in his hand
An envelope, grotesquely thick, and swears:
"The crone who brought it's standing on the stairs.
She says that what she wrote at heart's command
Would not be scorned by one so proud and grand."
The seal our hero from the letter tears,
Blows off the yellow sand to clear the text,
Goes to the window, where he reads, perplexed:

"Great sir, hear my petition! In the grip
Of greater reverence and humility
Than any with which I've acquaintanceship,
I come secure before Your Excellency.
Twice before I brought my quandary
Before your porter; but such ugly lip
He used to me that I intend to do
Without the porter and go straight to you.

"Your Excellence! Is every memory
Of me expunged now from your heart? If so,
By God above, then, it is up to me
To make that recollection grow,
And put aside for now all modesty;
For I can find no other place to go.
But, sure, your breast will swell, so deeply stirred,
When once my tragic story you have heard.

"My name is Lotte Sørensen, the same
You were acquainted with in your life's spring,
When Your Excellency was studying
And with the tailor lodged, Hr. Frank by name.
His wife taught me to sew within a frame,
Stitch neckcloths she'd turned with new bordering,
Spin, knit, mend boots, along with which there went
Waiting on the three who paid her rent.

"Then Sundays were like any other day,
For Madame Frank was strict in everything;
But I was innocence upon a fling,
And in my veins the blood was coursing gay.
At that time you enjoyed my merry way
And, with that, my life took a different swing:
My lily snapped—but love's rose paradise
Was that same instant opened to my eyes.

"Alas, we all are human, sad to say!
And women's hearts are tender, as we know,
And to another cannot bar the way
When men's affections are not simply show.
But never had I dreamt there'd come a day
When you'd become such a magnifico;
No, I'd no eye out for great recompense
When to a friend I gave my innocence.

"Yes, you had this heart—may I lose here
This tongue of mine, if that should not be true!
But love's brief paradise was quickly through
And at the rose life's thorns began to spear.
A hostile destiny did me pursue
Until I wound up in a fourth-floor rear,
And life soon took a still more fearful spin
When I was entered at the Lying-In.

"My child, the angel, died—and I was saved
A little while by public dole, till I was flung
Once again, abandoned and so young,
Out in a world which its young victim craved.
'Twixt virtue and necessity I hung
Till that position grew too hard. I caved:
I fell when I thought virtue closest me
And hurtled down to sensuality.

"My guardian angel turned away in pain,
And in his garment of a lily-white
He waved farewell, while I my lamp profane
Swung round, just like a drunkard, with delight.
My heart sank ever deeper, stain by stain,
While my soul grew to ever greater height:
For it's the truth: Not just my heart's abscesses,
But all I am, I owe to those distresses.

"Each morning I sat at my vanity
Or lay stretched out upon my bed
And books got from the lending library
With joy almost delirious I read.
Smollett, Wildt, de Kock, but specially
Spiesz in my life's night a new light shed,
So that before a year and day had flown
The knowledge of mankind I'd made my own.

"Down in passion's crater I now stared
And saw far into the heart's mysteries;
For ever in my mind I now compared
Life as it was with these authorities.
The students, soldiers, clerks, not one of these
Could blind me now with words of love declared;
Into mankind's dishonor I could read
And at the root of every soul found greed."

His Excellency stopped here and exclaimed:
"She's raving mad, the devil's on her back!
I won't read more words from a maniac
And, with such scrawling, how could I be blamed?"
He skipped two pages so dense they were black,
And at the final page his eye he aimed
To learn at last how all of this would end,
And read the following, which *there* was penned:

"It was cold comfort, yes, I am aware;
Each time I grabbed the flask, I understood;
But, Lord above, it was the last that would,
The very last that would some comfort spare.
Each day I took that comfort where I could,
Each year the tempter grew less hard to bear.
But what a well-bred sort must undergo
In such a tempter's company, you well know.

411/

"Along with shame I suffered injury;
For though I never steal or ever cheat,
Near every moving-day out on the street
My landlord would throw my few things and me.
Then, homeless, round the town with naught to eat
I may have acted up nights noisily
With cries for help to save me from disgrace
That threatened from the watchman's gleaming mace.

"Enough! Johannes Wildt long time ago
Taught me about us women's earthly lot;
And here, a pauper with a poorhouse cot,
On me the smiles of life don't sweetly flow.
On us it's only order they bestow,
But as for pleasure they allow it not,
And my position pinches horridly
Among the horrid crowds of paupery.

"One being only have I chanced to find
Who gave my soul a sympathetic ear:
Pretty Line she was called, poor dear,
Although her days of beauty lay behind.
I must conclude by putting you in mind
Of what she told me when her death was near:
That she too had the privilege immense
Of being known once to Your Excellence.

"My wreath upon her fresh-dug grave is laid
With roses and with lilies richly chained,
And from her heaven she beholds displayed
A witness to a friendship past, unfeigned.
The day I wove them I first ascertained
What honor to Your Excellence was paid,
Just as if, moved by my condition, Fate
Intended for my loss to compensate.

"Yes, it is Fate that leads me now to you.
Oh, to my life's wreck pay some kind attention.
Smile graciously as humbly here I sue
For just a little, miserable pension.
Save this lost one with your intervention!
And while you give rest to the weary, do
Bring her the joys that once were known to her:
Some coffee, some tobacco, some liqueur.

"O Excellency! Here I clasp your knee,
A female pauper, for that's how I'm classed.
If a pension you should grant to me,
You bind this heart to you forever fast.
All the precious memories of our past
I call upon to aid me in my plea,
And sign myself (if only it brought ruth)
Your Excellency's Lotte of your youth."

Here the letter stopped, which with this yell
To bits His Excellency therewith rent:
"Would that a thousand miseries befell
The shameless crone for this thing that she sent!"
His wrath, though, he moved quickly to dispel:
"Give her a few marks for her document,"
He tells his servant. "—Stop! You must wait, though!
I first must fetch out my portfolio."

Brisk but grave, he goes to his desk-drawer
And passes five rigsdalers to Jean-Jacques
With these words: "Tell the woman that this stack
Is hers if she will not come to my door
Again and never writes me one line more.
Say you have orders, should she try this tack
Of haunting my home, mixing in my affairs,
To seize her and convey her down the stairs."

His servant left, and Homo, overwrought,
Stayed with the letter, all in shreds, behind.
His recent happiness he could not find
And hardly could he fetch the breath he sought.
That youthful sin which he had quite forgot
Renewed the pangs of conscience in his mind,
And with a furrowed brow and downcast eye
He contemplated all the reasons why.

He needed rapid aid, thus panic-struck,
For five times had he sighed out in his woe.
But aid was near, for in did Jean-Jacques show
His spiritual adviser: Doctor Buck.
The tall man entered—with his head bowed low
Whereon a smooth black skullcap had been stuck,
While a simple suit fit modestly
Around the thin waist of God's deputy.

413/

He stepped up warmly, as though peace were nigh,
And Homo, sad of heart, in agony,
Darkly clasped hands with the deputy
Who, looking at him, broke forth with this cry:
"I come upon a man whose mind's not free,
A man who would the world or God defy.
Yes, though the grounds I don't ask be explained,
I see it clear, Your Excellency is pained."

Our hero shrugged and gave him this reply:
"Sit down, Hr. Pastor—Doctor, I should say!
You come as though you'd heard me call today.
I'd just been thinking of the luck whereby
The Catholics living where the Pope holds sway
On shield and buckler of the Church rely.
If they have sins—the Church's lye will scourge them;
If they have griefs—confession booths will purge them.

"We Protestants," Hr. Doctor Buck replies,
"Have not forbidden shrift from our belief.
To us can come all those adrift in grief,
And we have comfort too for sinners' sighs.
If those of all your reasons are the chief,
Then from the luck of Catholics turn your eyes,
And—though this is no shriver's interview—
Your spiritual adviser's here for you."

"All right," whispered Homo. "Let it be!
You'll know the rankling, secret and severe,
Which darkens every lovely day for me."
And now, with hems and haws which to the dear
And worldly reader are no mystery,
He tells the priest that tale of yesteryear,
Of Lotte's fall and its sad consequence,
Nor does he hide the letter's evidence.

At this confession Buck sat up all ears,
But now he lifted up his eyes to state:
"Yes, certainly the sin is very great,
Seducing people of such tender years.
And, in hearing you, it deeply cheers
Me, knowing that you also feel its weight:
Though the world may think that sin but slight,
It's murder—murder of a soul outright.

414/

"What must be the church's servant's course
Before he dare to let such sinners go
Is to look for genuine remorse—
I think that's something which you ought to know—
Although, when my ears hear you sighing so,
You surely feel it with excessive force.
Besides remorse, the church as well expects
You do your best to ease the sin's effects.

"Understand me right! You have my praise
For having sent her letter no reply.
Those five rigsdalers you'd no need to raise:
Such gifts a noble heart might typify;
But she will drink them up in the cafés,
And all their value will be lost thereby.
It's natural to help, ev'n tempting, say,
But Nature's not always the Christian way.

" 'Twere sin were help on such a one bestowed:
She's unredeemable, beyond recall.
But if she's lost, that is not true of all
Who took a slide upon a slippery road.
There are some people who—though low they fall—
Can be helped to shed their sinful load;
In fact, to plead for such beneficence
Was why I came to see Your Excellence.

"A Home for Magdalens, to be precise,
Is something I should like to superintend,
And who would help me break their chains of vice
I should call virtue's genuine good friend.
His sin with one won't find me overnice
If toward her like his help he would extend;
And with his kind support we'd save the lost
Who on the thorns of life are wildly tossed."

Forth from his breast an envelope he drew
From which he takes out a subscription plan,
And with these words: "If it's all right with you?"
Trustfully he gave it him to scan.
"I gladly will contribute what I can,"
Sighed Homo, penitent, as, mind askew,
He snatched his quill pen up to volunteer
A hundred dalers to the Home each year.

"No haggling! That's your magnanimity!"
Cried Buck in contemplation of the sum.
"Self-sacrifice, though, acts more potently
To help the true sense of remorse to come.
If I requested it, would you agree
To give yourself a patron's martyrdom?
And, what would please most, would you consent
To take a place within the management?"

"What? In the Magdalen Home management?"
Cried Homo, horrified. "No, no, my friend!
To such a Home I'm not the one to send!
Why should the Magdalens need this old gent?
What for?" "To raise the tone, that's evident!"
Buck answered gravely. "Help them to amend.
Raise those who plunged down giddily transgressing,
You'll reap their thanks as well as Heaven's blessing."

At "Heaven's blessing" Homo must give in.
He promised all, to get out from his slough,
And, much moved, Doctor Buck received his vow
And moved him with this comfort for his sin:
"You've done, dear friend, all that you could do now.
You're pardoned for what sins there might have been.
Not only can you hope that you'll be graced,
You must believe now that your guilt's erased.

"No matter what doubt whispers in your head,
Your belief in this must never cease;
And in this way your mind will be at peace."
Slowly he rose; across his brow he spread
His hand, wiping it of every crease—
A wholly different man stood in his stead.
Of theologian there was not a trace;
A sleek sophisticate was in his place.

Retracting power and authority,
Back and forth His Excellence he drew
Adroitly, chatting of X, Y, and Z,
Retailing all the gossip that he knew
And finding out, and with real pleasure too,
What he'd not heard: His Excellency and he
Were dining at the same place that same day,
And he was sure that it would prove quite gay.

416/

He said good-bye—and Homo was alone,
His brow unclouded and his heart now light
Which had just been weighed down as by a stone.
For should he be in sin in his own sight
If theologians did not think it right?
And could he think that any stain was known
Still to remain upon the tally sheet
Which Pastor Buck himself chose to delete?

Having thus got out of his late fix,
He went to dinner in a merry mood,
Restored his senses, stuffed his craw with food,
And took, at ombre later, all the tricks.
Everything is cleared up in two flicks
When through the sharpened eyes of age it's viewed,
For age unties, like bows, with effort slight
The knot which for our youth is much too tight.

But true it is—if, as the saying goes,
Youth and wisdom hand in hand don't go—
With age and wisdom too we can't suppose
One always is the other's *quid pro quo.*
But what's the meaning, then, of that long row
Of years and days until a life must close,
If at the end we still are destitute
Of—tiny though it may be—wisdom's fruit?

When comes the feast-time and the harvesting?
The rule, I think, is in our fourth decade.
What we do not have then, life could not bring
Though through another hundred years we strayed.
We take the stock which in those years we've made
As we move onward in our wandering,
And what at that time's not begun to sprout
Will never in our lifetime open out.

Though that rule be by miracle undone,
It's *Nature*'s course on which we've commented,
Since mankind too is sown and harvested
And time and measure are for everyone.
That play, which can divert us and can stun,
Of shifting seasons is in us inbred;
For what else are life's ages if they're not
The life of Nature, into us re-wrought?

417/

The heart thus has its spring, its summertime,
Its harvest time, its fall of wistfulness,
Its winter coating it with chilly rime
As death's metamorphosis does progress.
All Nature's life in hearts does coalesce
And only through them to the soul can climb,
For which this Nature were a mystery
Had not our hearts provided it the key.

For the soul dwells in a tropic sphere
Where spring and summer are as one with fall,
Where growing plants bear foliage all the year,
Where land and coast are spared the winter's pall:
It learns of changes from the heart—the gall
Of loss and grief, the bosom's hope and fear—
Which knows the sting of death and passion's violence,
Whereas the soul is throned in endless silence.

But—as has just been said—if this heart beat
For thirty years and could not find the way
(Through all the trials of living day by day)
To spiritual life, it's met defeat;
And with the soul still ignorant in its seat
That same long time, then I would have to say
That something (say, a will without corrective)
Made any unity quite ineffective.

Neither, then, will wisdom's fruit mature,
Whose rarity's complained of constantly:
From it alone we unity procure,
Which *is* the soul's central commodity;
Unripe, the heart seeks this or that amour
Until sensation gains ascendancy,
While in its silence keeps the soul its throne,
Lost in vain abstractions and alone.

But let's go onward from such lucubrations
Which put no smiles upon our hero's face,
And down in everyday life's habitations
Find him furthering the Idea's case
Through wardrobe-ladies and illuminations!
For Homo the great day has come apace
When his theatrical career commences,
His greatest day, too, from its consequences.

418/

He has just gotten up, his soul elated,
And dressed in his blue coat and star, and vest
With knightly snow-white ribbon decorated,
In tight black pants, 'neath which few could have guessed
Were spurs; in yellow gloves, as for the rest,
And hat in hand. Outside a carriage waited,
And, once inside and comfortably placed,
Away he rolled, nay, like a comet raced.

He came at twelve precisely, as was planned,
And at the portal of the theater
Was warmly welcomed by the manager
And by his bowing second-in-command.
He left the carriage—for a while he scanned
The house's wall—the hue he called a slur
Upon art's noble body, an outrage,
And let himself be shown up to the stage.

With loud song he was greeted by the choir,
Gathered in the orchestra's deep pit,
From which the melody rose ever higher,
Roaring up to him with welcome fit.
Leaning 'gainst a wing, he harked to it
And said with thanks that won their hearts entire
That, dear to him as was their music's art,
Its artists were no less dear to his heart.

"God Save the King" the orchestra now played
While up to him the manager now took
A motley-hued theatrical brigade:
Mechanics, ticket-takers, porter, cook,
Light-man, barber, with that picture book
Of power, the choir and extras of the trade.
Our hero pledged them to their tasks in art
And with a gracious nod did then depart.

From them he went round with the manager
To visit every corner of the hall;
First down the prompter's hole he had to crawl
And courteously but firmly did aver
That loges and parquets had ears like all,
To which he added that he'd much prefer
That those who stumbled and were ill at ease
In roles would give them all their energies.

419/

From the hole he quickly went along
To the cashier's desk and window, where
He put a ban, in few words but quite strong,
On holding back on tickets which were there,
Which treatment of the public he found wrong.
If all the tickets were sold fair and square,
It could encourage people then to buy them,
And so his orders were not to deny them.

These orders he had scarcely inculcated
Before into the wardrobe room he went,
Where the theater's tailor had long waited
With his lists of stage-habiliment.
At Homo's bidding, costumes were uncrated,
But when on them our hero his eyes bent,
He touched some riding-breeches there arrayed
And told the tailor, very much dismayed:

"A whole leg clad in tights I won't abide!
It is unseemly and it must not be.
The gentlemen can stick their legs inside
Loose trousers which will reach down to the knee
And which are fit for good society;
But such underfittings as don't hide
The naked form may not be worn in here.
I forbid them—dear sir, is that clear?"

He left—and came now to the little rooms
In which the theater ladies change their clothes
And where the pretty mistress of costumes
And her assistants gave him their hello's.
He talks to her about the way she grooms,
In every room and mirror sticks his nose
And on a maid's cheek tries a make-up stick—
But, oh good heavens! it is much too thick.

The mistress, when he leaves, gets this advice:
"My good woman, please do get this down:
When you are looking after someone's gown
Don't stop at seeing that the fit's precise;
Recall that modesty's a woman's crown.
For form's sake one cannot be overnice!
On top the actresses should not be 'raw,'
Nor dancers on the bottom—that is law!"

She only shrugs her shoulders, while her eyes
Disclose some doubt about the law's effect.
"Well, if it's seen as something to despise,
If stiff-necked folk won't give it their respect,
Say I'm the one who was its architect.
The ladies will accept it if they're wise."
A friendly nod he gave, to disengage,
And then he walked back over to the stage.

Here he found the theater's painter waiting
And, skipping over the amenities,
Discusses all the arts of decorating,
Perspectives, houses, city-streets and trees.
To make sure of a thorough inculcating
In that art of well-kept mysteries,
He orders several backdrops lowered fully
By a mechanic stationed at the pulley.

Like a connoisseur he eyes the smears,
Though lingering but a short time at the best,
For it's his duty, above all, to test
What could be done with all these ropes and gears.
He bids—and a ferocious lion appears
On all fours, almost human, on request;
He bids—with thunderclaps the house is racked,
It rains, a storm is raging, lightning's cracked.

He waves—and down the cloud is seen to fall,
Rocks rise, as if half puzzled, into space;
He waves again—the princely golden hall
Is changed into a hermit's dwelling place
Over which sway palm trees cool and tall,
The hermit stretched out flat upon his face.
He has the man stand up. He's liked the test
And all,—the lion less, though, than the rest.

The manager came by to let him know
That there's long been a crowd in the foyer,
So doubtless it was time for him to go
And speak of just where his intentions lay.
Homo did not like *lèse-majesté,*
And answered sharply: "They'll wait longer, though!"
At which again he had the thunder roll,
As if to show them who *was* in control.

While this thunder frights the manager,
Our Zeus betakes himself to the foyer,
Where wide the door's flung by a servitor,
Through which, in perfect ease, he makes his way.
His standing here now sets his mind astir,
For in Art's shrine he's still an *émigré*;
But, though the sight some others might dumbfound,
Dumbfounded he was not as he looked round.

The bright lights of the art had filled the hall;
To his left the actresses all shine,
Velvet-clad, with looks and smiles benign
Which the high Ideal of theater recall;
The solo dancers stand the last in line,
Each with her Flora-skirt and Zephyr-shawl.
The whole row bowed, as if upon command,
As with a bow he turned to face their band.

To his right, with that, he pivoted
To take the greetings actors offered him,
And singers, whose trills, this time, were not shed,
And dancers who gave greetings with each limb.
His third salute he gave, but straight ahead:
Where at the far wall, on their pillars slim
Which lift, yea, bear Parnassus on their bases,
Our poets humbly nod back from their places.

He spoke—but still his speech's poetry
One must not think that he'd had time to mold;
It was the present moment's fruit of gold
Which he produced with poise and fluency.
But that his mind was up to deeds so bold
Was due alone to his *présence d'esprit*,
Which stood the test and was exhibited
Brilliantly to all, as when he said:

"Good people! I've had you called to this hall
To see you here beside me on this day,
This day when to my lot it was to fall
To make, as your director, my entrée.
With greatest pleasure I salute you all;
With true content I see in our foyer
The stars and comets of the stage at hand
To light the finest poets of our land.

"But here, where greatness seeks its counterpart,
What do I want, what am I seeking, pray?
Quid Saul inter prophetas? you will say—
And, truly, I do not take it to heart
If you think that into the realms of art
There isn't any public right of way.
Before, though, to that question I reply,
There is another thing I'd clarify.

"Another thing! And that the theater's own!
The theater's purpose! And unto our shame,
As certainly high Heaven must bemoan,
We all too often have forgot that aim.
What's the intention these boards should proclaim?
What's to this day the theater's cornerstone?
To tend the Idea, make Its imagery
So clear the gallery can't fail to see!

"The Idea—entity of highest birth
Which not just philosophic foreheads bear,
But which from Heaven has come down to earth
Transformed into the good, the true, the fair;
Which through all times and countries everywhere
Has moved, worked, fought, and judged our worth,
Which in us has made Its own being real,
Yes, given us Itself, in the Ideal.

"The Idea, my good women! my good sirs!
It goes about the world dispirited;
Its presence in life's dramas is gainsaid;
It is disowned by social arbiters;
In the tableaux of Church and State It stirs
(I've seen It) like a cripple, underfed,
A sight which brought conviction absolute
That with this life the Ideal does not suit.

"And does It suit then with our personal 'I'?
Alas, good sirs! Not one of us is fit
To find the way up to the Ideal's sky;
For though our words forever fight for It,
In actions we do just the opposite,
Nor do we have the power to reach that high.
And with a sigh we are forced to agree
It is too high for weak mortality.

423/

"But where is It of use then? Only there
Where life's a play in which mock struggles rage:
In art's high sphere, upon the theater's stage,
Where we can end our struggle howsoe'er;
Where, deeply sober, we can still engage
With passion's flames and hearts full of despair;
Where all temptations are imaginary
And all tears spilt are only honorary.

"Yes, there—and by my *there* I do mean *here*—
Yes, here the Ideal has fit dwelling place,
Here where It's shown upon the curtain's face
In Edens of all trees of knowledge clear;
Here where It is expressed in speech of grace;
Here where performers make the Ideal appear,
Where, with his pathos, each of them confers
Its outline in those mighty characters!

"But, ladies, gentlemen! I say to you
That if I am not wrong in what I've said,
If each of you for artist's garlands sue
As friends of the Ideal, thoroughbred;
If this ship of theater sails ahead
On time's stream to the Ideal and its course true,
To well-tuned lyres of poets singing clear—
Why am I here on board? Your course I'll steer!

"Perhaps somebody here will now object:
'What is the purpose? Everything goes well.'
But does it go well? May we not suspect
That many times the ship can't breast the swell?
If on appearances we'd not be wrecked,
Is all we need momentum to propel
When now and then distress-shots we should hear?
—Well, that's the reason why I want to steer!

"By what right?—True, a poet I am not,
Indeed, no sort of artist. That's quite true!
But many years' experience will do.
I've looked for the Idea in every spot
And, though truth orders me to say to you
That I've not found that wholeness which I sought,
All the clearer stand before my eye
The thousand places where it does not lie.

424/

"Thus on our voyage I shall be the shield;
For standing at the rudder I shall roar
Each time the ship approaches such a shore,
Each time an artist goes too far afield:
'Watch out! The Idea was not here before!'
And when we skirt each rock by me revealed
And, in addition, do not sail quite blind,
The proper course we may at long last find.

"Good sirs! Hope is the anchor for our trip.
Good ladies! Climb up, do not be dismayed,
Upon the light planks of our theater-ship:
And should they sway, you need not be afraid!
Farewell to artists caught in envy's grip,
Farewell chicane and spite which so degrade,
Farewell our public stranded at low tide:
Upon our course to the Idea we ride!

"And to continue with these similes
Which, I must say, have riveted my mind,
I wish to have the poets all assigned
The sending of a favorable breeze.
Let's sail out on the lyre's brave harmonies,
So that the sea of ardor runs unconfined
And its white foam across the main deck laves
As our ship plunges down deep in art's waves.

"I stand at the helm, the wind blows free,
And every which way there upon the hop
Are all the actors of the company
On sails and rigging, on the shrouds and top;
And while the singers' verses go nonstop
To stir the crowd toward Ideality,
On high the corps de ballet nimbly race
With flag and banner telling of our pace.

"So by illusion's lamps we go undaunted
Along the clear wave-tracks of fantasy
To seek the golden fleece which once had haunted
The minds of Jason's hero-company.
And when we have then found the thing we wanted,
When the Ideal's on board successfully:
That Ideal which finds no welcome ground
Though for a home It searches all around—

"Then, when on art's breast It finds Its bed,
Then, gentlemen, about It one can say
What often of the youthful maid is said
Who at her parents' death in sore need lay,
Who wandered, by her fellows pushed away,
Who almost had to beg to get her bread:
Lo! Destiny is overhauled for her!
She's cared for—she's gone into the theater!"

Here Homo stopped—and his left hand, complete
With hat, he had stretched out while, on his breast,
Upon the star he made his right hand rest.
His look, his arm, the placement of his feet,
All went to give his speech's fire more heat,
And scarcely had his last thought been expressed
When all around there came approving mumbling
In which was drowned a single poet's grumbling.

Our hero stepped away now and displayed
His trim form to the ladies' retinue
As, gallant courtier, he began to woo.
Each got a word, round which a sweet smile strayed,
But 'twas before a chosen very few
That he his thoughts on art and nature laid.
Those few would play the major roles, he vowed,
And, as he left the ladies, finely bowed.

He wheeled round to the actor-retinue,
Moved on past the heroes and the kings
To lovers, herds, seducers of young things,
Pronouncing on the mimic arts his views.
He ordered them to mind their p's and q's
And pay no heed to critics' crotchetings
Which oft ran counter to the needs of art,
Then from them to the poets did depart.

The hands of two or three of these he pressed
To thank them for their various submissions,
Then told them of a plan of interest
On which he had pinned all his stage ambitions.
His plan was this: put on only the best,
Convert the better class with these renditions,
And by its taste the worse will be so led
That from good work it dare not turn its head.

426/

"And therefore, gentlemen," (he's nearly through)
"Go straight to work! It is your obligation.
Dramatic work's far worthier to do
Than seeing a good book through publication.
Think of the great reward awaiting you—
I don't speak of financial compensation
But of rewards in public eulogy,
Rewards which to you are no mystery."

As he was speaking, both the doors swung wide
And lo! with tables, trays, and napery
In a throng of dapper servants stride
In Homo's livery, as all plainly see.
They place their stores amid the company:
With a pop the champagne corks are pried,
Buckets full of oysters meet their gaze
And wine, sweets, ices, chocolate, and pâtés.

Homo ambled over to the board,
And, with the art's practitioners around,
He gallantly beheld them like their lord
And in this fashion started to expound:
"When we've put our day's duties in the ground,
It's wonderful to have refreshments poured;
When one is tired by a director's post,
He feels himself relieved by playing host.

"As your host I stand before you here.
Think me just a gentleman, please do!
Just as this moment I don't think of you
As artists but as guests whom I would cheer.
'Not Just For Smiles' may o'er our stage appear,
But in the lobby that need not be true:
Here *just* for smiles we'll drink and talk our fill,
And so—I bid you: Go to with a will!"

Gasps and whispers greet these strange advices:
"A splendid man! Why, never has our corps
Known a director like this one before!"
The men the oyster-table most entices;
The ladies, though, assembled round the ices,
And spirits lifted all around the floor.
There was much merriment, much conversation,
Which, with the champagne, rose to jubilation.

427/

Our hero made a toast to all the fair,
At which the last cloud in the exalted sky
Of the director's gravity must fly
Before the thanks the ladies' smiles declare.
His dignity achieved a lighter air;
The great refinement rumor knew him by
In bearing, word, and gesture's now expressed
In such high charm as captures every guest.

All friends of theater were deeply proud
To see united here in harmony
Administration, art, and poetry,
Whereby a golden future was avowed.
Much jest and witticism was allowed;
But when a comic actor got too free,
Familiar to the point of disrespect,
His watch, with some discomfort, Homo checked.

Lest he should bear a grudge against a guest
Who showed himself too tactless in his wit,
He thought it safest that he should be quit
Of these gay games while they still had their zest.
He bade farewell abruptly: it was best,
He claimed, to ride his horse and keep it fit.
He hurried down into the cool street air,
Followed out by everybody there.

Here, with his groom, the horses stood at rest,
But leapt like Pegasuses fiery
When up upon the saddle of the best
Homo swung with youth's alacrity.
It reared, as though high Heaven were its quest;
But Homo tamed its spirits masterfully,
And, waving at them as they stood and wondered,
At a trot along the square he thundered.

He brought the beast back to a walking-pace
While making sure the reins did not go slack,
And stroked it as he let the horsewhip smack.
"It's just the same," he sighed, "as in this case,
The way to handle all the artist race:
Stroke them while your whip cracks on their back."
Reins tighter, with more speed he rode along,
Trailed by the groom and gaped at by the throng.

People craned their necks, wishing to see
His Order's ribbon on his velvet vest.
And you, my reader! Give yourself a rest
And watch him on his horse, high as can be.
Him whom you've known from his nursery,
Whom, as a boy perhaps, you liked the best;
For though he'd then done things that were quite bad,
Still, such grand emotions he had had.

You thought he would go far, and never more
Than when, engaged, he'd gotten to dry land;
You came to doubt, but with that doubt did stand
Hope, until his years had reached two score.
Observe him now! He'll never be more grand.
But has he any meanness to deplore?
Just look as people bend their backs to him
While he himself but touches his hat's brim!

Has he deceived you? No, I dare reply
On your behalf, if white your hair now grows;
For you have learned, in all the time gone by,
How with us, most of us at least, life goes.
And if you're still a youth, let some time fly,
Till on your chin a bit more whisker shows,
And see what's fallen to your good friends' part
To whom you have ascribed a head and heart.

Indeed, to press advantage at this pass,
And force you now to your sail's lowering,
Behold yourself in your own looking glass!
Bring more to bear than someone else could bring
On each detail and weigh—this is the thing—
Past with present, silver spoons with brass,
And tell me then if it is right for you
To take of brother Adam a dim view.

No, quash your sentence and walk down the street
Where, all decorum, he rides, figure taut,
And with him to the Esplanade retreat
Where he stirs his blood up with a trot!
Yes, see, past Østerport he now has got
And views the Shore Road's glories from his seat
As o'er him gentle summer breezes pass
And he breathes in the scent of new-mown grass!

The dustless highway, newly watered down,
Drives from his mind his kinship with the dust;
He feels he's free, new man from foot to crown,
And where he looks the world is fair and just.
They plant, they pave, on sand they build a town;
They milk cows where the clover grows robust;
There with their passengers the buses rush,
And here a bird sings finely in the brush.

Where all things hint a future golden age
Twice as lovely is existence found,
And Doctor Flink he hears again presage
That for long years to come he would stay sound.
Beforehand he enjoys life's lengthened round;
He runs through his career upon the stage,
Guiding the Idea along Its way,
Onstage, behind the wings, in the foyer.

His vision spreads—the horse gives out a groan
That instant as a blow falls on its shanks.
He sees support from all the nation's ranks
Who'd been awakened from the sleep they'd known;
He sees the King applauding him with thanks,
A ribbon blue and watery in tone;
He looks about him and from side to side—
Oh, this fine prospect, how it satisfied!

You can see Landskrona from here quite clear;
The Swedish coast is at its loveliest!
How charming does that country house appear
With its veranda running east and west!
It would be a joy to settle here;
It would be nice to buy that little nest
And in the summer, when the season ends,
To use it Sundays to receive good friends.

He sees—he has a strong imagination—
Himself with those good friends on one fine day
Sitting outside, dinners put away,
Their coffee cups in hand, in conversation.
At their cigars he sees their matches play,
Sees them look round with exhilaration
While rows of people on the highway course
Toward the woods, on wheels, on foot, on horse.

He sees his good friends go back into town,
And only Jomfru Frisk remains behind
To bring him candles, slippers, dressing gown,
And play cards with him till the sun's declined.
In his gown he deals the cards face down,
And on the game she concentrates her mind,
Yes, struggles long, her thoughts in turbulence,
Till the game ends in deep confidence.

Upon this earth he sees all this and more,
But all these sights must be the reason why
He had forgot to look up at the sky
Where thunderclouds had now begun to roar.
The air was dark that had been bright before,
An army of black clouds now marched on high;
Some heavy drops came down—and in his ears
Strong blasts of wind now and again he hears.

What was he to do? This riding tour
Which lured him from the city to excite
In him his dinner-hour appetite
Threatens him with a cold-water cure.
Would Bellevue's stables serve him in his plight
As shelter long as this storm should endure?
But then he'd have to miss his dinner-fête
And therefore, home! before it gets too late!

Coat buttoned up, he swung his horse around,
But scarce had done so when the storm broke out;
The rain rushed down as from an immense spout,
And with its broom so fiercely swept the ground
That treetops all along the road were downed,
While on his neck cold raindrops ran about.
Down he clamped his hat, near forfeited,
And spurred his horse on, giving it full head.

Charlottenlund he reached, soaked through and through;
But what good now the shelter he might find?
As thunder rolled and lightning made him blind,
Without a stop he hastened on anew.
At Vibenshuus his linen was soaked too;
At Østerport his hood was undermined,
His hat was just a mat atop his face,
When to him the town watchman raised his mace.

431/

Alas, how changed from when he first set out
Was he as now he rode back into town!
His clothes, as from the clouds, were dripping down;
His posture made him look like a wash-clout.
A sailor's wife, 'neath her umbrella's crown,
Shouted at him: "You poor roustabout!"
And to his home he came so sore beset
As only you know who have been that wet.

If only he'd put on new linen, though!
But there stood someone from the barony
With letters he must answer, instantly,
Since his agent wished to let him know
His oat fields had been mown some time ago,
The rye and barley of such quantity,
Especially the whole strip by the moor,
They'd lack the room to keep the grain secure.

He cast off just his outer clothes, therefore,
And as wet as he was, nay, drenched all through,
He went, pleased with how much the harvest bore,
To his desk and wrote this word or two:
"Now that the grain supply is in plain view
And there's enough to last a few years more,
To make sure it won't spoil then, I advise—
Immediately increase the side-barn's size."

This note once done, he sent the man away;
And only now he changed his wet clothes straight,
Whereafter, dressed up for the feast that day,
He dashed out to it, lest they have to wait.
He turned from hot to cold, though, as he ate;
The best food in his stomach heavy lay,
The best wine could not make him feel more hearty,
And early he returned home from the party.

He went to bed, but with half-addled brains
He wakened from his sleep round twelve o'clock;
His blood made such a pounding in his veins
As though it had to fight foes by the flock.
In his left side he felt some shooting pains,
His brain felt swelled as though he'd drunk much hock,
And anxiously he waited out the night
To send for Doctor Flink at dawn's first light.

432/

Fleet Doctor Flink came bounding through the door
And lifted up his hat, exclaiming thus:
"What's this! Stretched out in bed like Lazarus,
Our rich man, leader of the theater corps!
Who gave His Excellency all this fuss?"
He felt his pulse and mumbled out, before
Our hero ever got his symptoms told:
"A simple rheumatism! You've caught cold!"

"What?" Homo smiled. "You mean to say that's all?
I can assure you I took quite a fright."
And now he spoke of how he'd felt all night
And riding through the country in a squall
That soaked him through, so hard did the rain fall.
The doctor then denounced that ride outright,
But added cheerfully: "Be on your guard,
Drink elderberry tea, and just sweat hard!"

He left, and Homo sweated all the day,
Even felt, though tired, much at ease
For having soaked the sheet through all the way;
But night came—and still worse grew his disease,
The pain redoubled by anxieties.
He tossed and turned, but never right he lay,
And as a savior Flink he credited
When in the morning he stood by his bed.

Muttered Flink: "Now what are we to think?"
Putting thumb and fingers to his wrist.
"Of course! A fever, but it won't persist;
We'll pack it out the door in just a wink."
To comfort him—no more the optimist—
He made out a receipt, and with a blink
He asked him with a snake's insinuation:
"How is it going with elimination?"

"Just fair!" His Excellency makes reply.
"That's what I thought!" the little doctor yells.
"*Da liegt der Hund begraben!* That's what tells
What side the foe can be assaulted by,
And I won't spare him, knowing where he dwells."
He sent for oil; on that he would rely:
Down his patient's throat he swilled the lotion.
Hope's nectar Homo swallowed with the potion.

433/

Much eased again he takes the doctor's hand
And says: "My good man, let me please entreat
That you in all haste get me on my feet.
I can't be sick and let my work just stand.
The season is upon us. All I've planned
Mills round my head—I need my brain complete!
But your sure looks such confidence instill!
A doctor's smile does wonders for the ill."

"My word of honor will I pledge to you,"
Flink answered, "that before this week is done
As easily upon the boards you'll run
As I do out the door now." Off he flew;
And Homo set to using, all day through,
A laxative, with which much ease he won;
But night brings the old fever, fortified
With violent pains which sting him in his side.

Next morning Flink again stood by his bed
And said: "Well, is our business now ended?
Has the Geheimraad scoured well, as intended,
And made the foe turn tail, discomfited?"
"Alas, dear Flink!" his patient sighed, and said:
"My sickness to my side has now descended,
It's all gone wrong!" A full account he gave,
And suddenly the doctor's face turned grave.

He took his hand and felt round Homo's side,
While asking: "Is this where you feel the pain?"
"No, not there." "Then might it here reside?"
"Yes, here precisely." "Yes, that would explain!
But down to work! This we will have to rein
Before it takes the lung on in its tide,
And though His Excellence might hate the cure,
I'll have you bled at once, of that be sure."

"Have me bled? No, do not think you will!"
He cried out, drawing up his coverlet.
"Part me from my blood! Much thanks you'll get!
In my condition that would do me ill."
"But," answered Flink, "the doctor knows his skill,
Inflamed lungs aren't cured by a tête-à-tête."
"Inflammation!" Homo shrieked. "Good Lord!
But you're responsible when I get gored."

"With pleasure!" Flink said, as with lancet keen
He cut down in his patient, whose heart dropped
When high in air twelve inches or thirteen
The blood so lightly, frolicsomely hopped.
Six cups were filled with this headsman's cuisine,
When Flink said in a whisper: "Time we stopped!
But when I get through testing out this sample,
We'll need another portion just as ample."

He left as soon as Homo's wounds were dressed
And he'd talked to him with authority,
And Homo lay a half-day most distressed.
He felt that he had worsened drastically.
He dozed, he shook, his mouth went leathery,
And bitter doubt arose within his breast.
His doubt prevailed—he sent out, overwrought,
For agèd Stink, and to him he was brought.

The agèd doctor came, who earnestly
Took the patient's hand and his confession.
His grade was: Most Unsatisfactory.
The cure he took destroyed Stink's self-possession:
He found blood-letting a great indiscretion.
Why, when he glanced toward the table, he
Exclaimed, astonished: "Is the man quite mad?
Six cups of blood! Just two would have been bad."

This cry, like lightning, made our hero shrink,
Especially when he went on: "At your age
Such a procedure I call an outrage,
It is as good as tipping death the wink."
Just at these words in bounded Doctor Flink,
And Homo, furious, threw down his gage
With this challenge: "You disgraceful man!
What have you done? Defend it, if you can!"

Astonished, Flink approached His Excellence
And asked, in friendly fashion: "You're still ill?"
"Get out of here!" he cried. "You're going to kill
Me with your tappings, sweats, and effluence!"
"Well," Flink thought, "now I must take offense,
And I know whom I owe this new ill will."
He went to Stink and asked him pointedly:
"You set my patient quarreling with me?"

"And if I did," came coldly Stink's reply,
"I'm glad to tell you why right to your face;
Inflammatory's how you qualify
This fever—but a hemorrhoidal case
Is what it is, it leapt out to my eye."
"That judgment," Flink smiled, "lacks the slightest base!
I'd think myself a fool were I to hold
That this man suffers from the 'vein of gold.' "

"And if my judgment's baseless," Stink replied,
"That baseless judgment you'll still have to hear;
It's possible you may be edified.
Your bleeding was an error most severe
For which the world had made you pay full dear
If from it the Geheimraad should have died."
"Hush!" whispered Flink. "Your judgment's without base,
But don't say that before the patient's face."

This message was delivered all too late,
For Homo listened anxiously and grim,
Though what he heard rather persuaded him
That such help left him in a sorry state.
"No," he thought. "With you two, hopes are dim!
I'm not your guinea pig to perforate.
Go find more victims for your arts of night,
Into a hospital I'll take my flight!"

He rang, and when the servant came inside
He whispered a long message in his ear
So softly that the others could not hear,
And like a wind away the servant hied.
Meanwhile the doctors' breach was rectified
And covered with collegial veneer;
And both of them like brothers once again
Stepped up to Homo on his bed of pain.

"We have conferred upon it," started Stink.
"These symptoms I now rightly understand
And calmly trust them to a doctor's hand
Who watches out for Nature's slightest wink."
"Yes," he was joined now by the little Flink,
"Our cart will have a second dray-horse spanned.
We'll try a second arrow in our bow:
Tonight into a tepid bath you'll go!"

436/

"Fine, gentlemen! I'm much obliged to you!"
With a sidelong look he made reply.
Then both doctors bid the man good-bye
Until the morning came, and so withdrew.
Before the sun had vanished from the sky,
Homo's servant's news came, welcome, too,
That the sedan chair, green as hope, would ride
Him to the hospital, and stood outside.

Into the hospital our hero's brought,
Into death's courtyard—he who recently
Climbed on stage toward Ideality
And laughed to see his golden future caught.
Sunk so low since his proud ride was he
That, shoeless, with a load of blankets fraught,
In just his nightshirt he's borne down the street;
Extremes, as known to everybody, meet.

And here, my reader! pause before the fence,
The hospital's black grillwork fence, wherethrough
Homo's taken from his residence
And down the pathway soon is lost from view.
Those gates you must observe with diligence
On which another motto stands, it's true,
Than the "Abandon hope!" the whole world knows,
For here we read: "We patch folk like old clothes."

You stand before the fane of flesh and bone,
Which, sad and low, has no *éclat*, no spark,
And different thus in any outward mark
From that of which prayer is the cornerstone
And over which the spirit's way is shown
To Heaven by a high spire rising stark;
For here they take no note of inspirations,
But only threnodies and lamentations.

Here peace is what of all things most you lack,
Here courage feels itself put out of face;
But, if that virtue here is out of place,
Forbearance all the more takes up the slack.
With our demands we learn here to hold back:
A bit of barley soup, some milk, for grace.
Such is our wish, our prayer, our cry in scope;
And yet we are here filled, and rich in hope.

437/

For in an image hope lives constantly
And what image is as near a soul
As that wherein its being we may see?
That body lying there out of control,
That form, emaciated, no more whole,
Still gives expression to its entity;
That living symbol which to us makes plain
The soul, as what it is and what it *will remain.*

But here, where on that form we stiffly stare,
We should instead discover its true state.
For, if that truth of it we could translate
Into faith and make it our hearts' care,
That tale the world would no more have to bear
That bodies do but die and suppurate;
Then at this life we'd not so fiercely clutch
And, though we're racked, not mourn its loss too much.

Then in our faith we'd know how to translate
That language which from symbols' bonds is freed
And even in disease know how to read:
That this hand, though so powerless its state,
Which in its weakness cannot do one deed,
Is pledge unto a spirit ever great;
Is pledge that what we grasped on earth below
Throughout Eternity shall with us go.

Then we'd know what that foot has signified
Which cannot take a step for being so frail,
Would see ourselves to that goal ever stride
On Nature's ground which cannot ever fail.
And then those lips which with our death travail,
Through which earth's water never more will glide,
We'd take as promising the nectar cup
From which a spirit ever blessed will sup.

Then we, rejoicing in such faith as this,
Would bind these two worlds which are separated
And build a bridge across death's wide abyss;
And there find not only that form instated
Whose shell we daily see more desiccated,
But warmth in that breast which has come to bliss,
An eye that to new light wakes and rejoices,
An ear now open to familiar voices.

438/

Then we would imprint upon our mind
That in the soul is form's eternal ground,
Not to flesh and blood alone confined
Like one last anchor without which we're drowned,
Like those last rotted planks to which we're bound
One little hour ere they must be resigned
While we sigh: "What I have is what I've known;
But what I'll get, I never have been shown."

We've had instruction, yes, so plain and pure
That we can't doubt when we do not want to:
There's been pronouncement, one so loud and sure
That all that's needed is to hear it through;
We've gotten such assurance, wise and true,
That to see that it remains secure
We need but lift—as all symbols require—
The covering which is the thought's attire.

Our hero, who now takes the stage once more,
Did not lift up the cover where he lay,
Though for a week his fever blazed away
No less intense than it had been before.
His will to live remained in his heart's core,
The best hope that his doctor could essay,
And daily bulletins were handed down
Which gladdened all his friends and all the town.

He found a new routine. Each morn, before
His doctor came and his nurse went away,
He looked through all the cards from yesterday
From people who'd asked for him at the door.
Each noon the theater manager would stay
A while with news of Art's home and its corps;
Each eve Etatsraad Jensen would come down
And please His Excellency with news of town.

In his routine full fourteen days had flown.
The sick man's attitude continued stout;
The inflammation had found its way out—
But suddenly his strength was overthrown.
So fast a pulse, indeed, he'd never shown;
He gave his doctor much to think about.
And I request the reader walk tiptoe
As to his sickbed now we two shall go.

How dark in this high chamber, how austere!
While outside vibrant morning now displays
Her crimson in the bright sun's golden rays,
The shining sunbeams all die out in here;
For tight green blinds shut out the morning's blaze
And window shades drawn down make it more drear.
His bed is in the corner. There he lies,
And in that chair his wardress shuts her eyes.

He's sleeping deeply as from battle shocks.
On his table medicine's arrayed,
His gold watch, telling time with its tick-tocks,
His signet ring, its Latin phrase displayed:
Esse, non videri—and, inlaid
With silver, his Order's black jewel box
In which his stars, with diamonds inset,
Are kept with other treasures rarer yet.

Upon the chair, the bed, yes, on the floor,
A mass of closely written notebooks lies.
What reason can these papers be here for?
What are they? Not prescriptions, we surmise.
Oh, my dear reader! Turn away your eyes
From what concerns the theater, nothing more.
You see ten plays which were sent in of late,
Which the director now must ruminate.

The dramatists wait now for him to tell,
So earnestly do they desire to know,
If in or out their dramas are to go;
And their uneasiness he knows full well.
He'll spare no efforts, though he's very low—
O model for official personnel!
Each moment Nature leaves him free of need
He uses to evaluate and read.

But, still, the dramatists must wait, and long!
Ploughing through them's more than he can do;
Rest, rest is what he is entitled to—
How can a sick man find ways to be strong
For deeds that make a sound man's health go wrong?
If he won't keep his need for rest in view,
That need is quite clear in his doctor's mind,
Whom coming through the doorway we now find.

Once he came in, the wardress did not stay.
The doctor then approached the ailing man,
Who sent his eyes around, as if distrait,
To search out papers he had yet to scan.
The doctor, from the bed, swept them away
Before our reader could pursue his plan,
Whereupon he said: "Have done with it!
His Excellency's health will not permit."

He took his pulse, examined either lung,
Requesting that his patient raise his voice,
And lastly looked with sharp eye at his tongue
And at its coating he did not rejoice.
His word to Homo's far from his first choice:
"We all of us must climb back rung by rung."
But to himself he thought: "The fever's worse.
Damn, this toff's prognosis is adverse!"

He'd make a new draught. Homo hoarsely bade:
"Hum, roll the shade up, would you, just halfway.
Open one pane! So fine the fresh air played
Upon my soul and body yesterday.
I'm tired, as if I'd just been soundly flayed."
"A small request I'm happy to obey,"
Replied the doctor. "It's as good as done.
This room shall be filled with golden sun.

"Has the Geheimraad aught else to request?"
"Just one thing more," the ailing man replied,
"One thing that up to now I have let ride:
This wardress puts my patience to the test.
The other two were hardly of the best,
But this one's been a real thorn in my side."
"What?" cried the doctor, staggered at this word.
"You understand, this wardress is your third!"

"But not the right one," Homo then returned.
"Each time I wake, I see her nod her head.
If on an errand for me she is sped,
Her hallway gossip never is adjourned,
And I lie waiting one good hour in bed.
Yesterday she gave me oatmeal, burned,
And almost never follows your routine
For giving draughts. What's more, she isn't clean."

"Oh, now, damn it all!" the doctor cried.
"But," he went on, "if you are so averse
To all my women, I'm forced to decide
To save you from the clutches of this curse
And give you in her stead my private nurse."
"Who is she?" Homo would be satisfied.
"Ah," he was told, "she's splendid every way,
But of her there is little I can say.

"I met her through my wife; she's on in years
And poor, although I'd not say indigent;
In tending to the ill she has few peers
And, since our patient is so eminent
And is in trouble up to his sick ears,
I know she'll help him to her full extent.
As I am sure that she will take this case,
I'll send a message to her dwelling place."

He left, and the Geheimraad stayed in bed,
Who with his tired eyes, his face gone pale,
Looked round in all the light the morning shed
And with real pleasure now seemed to inhale.
Through his dry lips he drew the gentle gale
That from the open window round him spread.
And on the doctor's statement his ears hung:
"We all of us climb back up rung by rung!"

He hardly knew how long the still hours wore,
Lying thus alone, till suddenly
Someone lightly tapped upon his door.
"Come in!" he whispered. Gently as could be
A woman came, and in a moment more
The doctor, late from some emergency.
"Here, Excellency!" he spoke from where he stood,
"Here's the nurse I told you was so good."

The little nurse (for she was rather small
Than tall) came halfway toward the bed,
But, deferential, said no words at all
Lest she interrupt what then was said.
For Homo'd asked the doctor to recall
To him the parts to which disease had spread.
And while, upon this subject, they converse,
We shall, my reader, pay heed to the nurse.

442/

In a black wool dress she's standing there,
The creases round her waist a little tight,
Upon her head a small cap, snowy white;
A simple scarf alone is her neckwear.
She stands there, on life's staircase at some height,
With worthy bearing, as we've heard declare,
Features fine, skin lily-white in hue,
With melancholy eyes, lively and blue.

Her fair hair has turned gray, and on each side
It's covered by the cap which frames her face;
Her candid forehead time has sorely tried
And on it pensiveness has left some trace;
Her neck's held high, her small hand keeps its grace;
Her color, though, can more than words betide
That here below we must do what's required—
There she stands: collected, calm, retired.

The gentlemen have stopped their conversation,
And now the doctor turns around to her:
"On you Geheimraad Homo I confer
And leave our patient to your ministration.
With his consent I sent my messenger;
His Excellency knows your dedication. . . .
But what is wrong, nurse? Are you feeling weak?
The blood is rushing up into your cheek."

The pale cheeks of the nurse, it was quite clear,
Were clad in crimson mantle suddenly;
She laid hold of a chair which she found near
And dropped into it with alacrity.
The doctor brought her water cold and she,
With one gulp, seemed no longer to feel queer.
With lowered eyes and barely heard "Alas!"
She gave him back, with many thanks, the glass.

Nothing had our hero seen or heard.
To him the chief thing was his own condition,
And tired of all that had that day occurred,
He lay consumed in febrile inanition.
The doctor left his nurse upon her mission
To follow through the day his every word;
And in the chair behind a screen they'd spread
She sat alone, at one end of the bed.

443/

She sat there still, in the profundity
Of silence where the sick man dwelled,
And wiped away her teardrops as they welled
And choked her sobs before they could break free.
The wakened pain she would have wanted quelled
Rose unimpeded from her memory:
That it was he who needed ministering
She had expected least of anything.

So Alma sat—for why go on to hide
A fact that you've already entertained?
But Alma to such humble work constrained?
How can such a fall be justified?
The information you'd have me provide
Is quickly given and is soon explained.
While she herself sheds silent tears of grief,
I'll tell you of her destiny, in brief.

Some ten more years, since we had seen her last,
With her old father she had left to spend
Till suddenly their life came to an end
And he into eternal springtime passed.
Their house was closed—but when debts they'd amassed
Were paid, she'd little on which to depend:
A house, two-windowed, in which to reside
Beyond the fields was all the will supplied.

She moved in, still in close proximity
To memories of her youth which now was done;
For she still saw the garden filled with sun
Where as a child she had played merrily.
From her window, stirred, her thoughts would run
Along the byways of her reverie
Through every path, through every arbor dark,
Though she no more could set foot in that park.

She had to find a way to earn her bread
And live so that the house would stay her own;
For in this wide world she now stood alone
With no kin who could have contributed.
She soon got straightened out upon that head:
For pay she took in things that must be sewn,
She copied scores, she colored land maps in,
And did it with great skill and discipline.

But though her needle, pencil, pen she plied,
For her this handiwork was no vocation;
The thread of thought was to her needle tied
And with her paints bloomed her imagination;
She heard sounds while she worked at her notation
As of a vibrant tune, half lost inside,
As of a lonesome sigh whereby a heart
Once more suppressed a newly wakened smart.

In this way days had flown by in a throng
And far she had advanced in time and years
When weakness overtook those eyes once strong,
And with her needlework it interferes.
With fine wash in its place she perseveres,
Which to her home fine families send along,
And to the doctor's wife was recommended
By whom, as it turned out, she was befriended.

The wife caught typhus, and to tend her bed
She asked for Alma, who all night and day
Stayed by the ailing woman on death's way
So faithfully, the doctor often said,
That nursing plainly was her true métier.
Soon afterward he was accredited
To the hospital, and, needing aid,
His wife's old nurse was the first choice he made.

She accepted and she bade good-bye
To the little house she still held dear,
Moving closer in to Toldbodsvej,
Since to the hospital it was quite near.
There she heeded many a painful sigh
And saw death in full frightening career;
There she learned the helplessness of men,
And another world came into ken.

My reader with this little information
Must make do till the canto coming on.
But let me add, in further explanation,
That Alma never once had come upon
Her former lover, till this confrontation
After all those many lonely years had gone.
She knew a bit about how life had served him;
She'd heard of him, but never had observed him.

445/

Desire to do so takes the upper hand,
And softly she walks to the bed beyond.
There before him sleeping does she stand
To see how well his features correspond
To those of which in youth she'd been so fond.
Scarce o'er her sobs can she exert command:
His profile, haughty, cold, inspires near dread—
Where had the soft, warm, gentle features fled?

With fear of recognition, overflowing
Grief and trouble, was her soul distressed.
That fear in this case might be laid to rest:
The day dragged on in sadness thoroughgoing;
The patient dozed, exhausted and unknowing,
And only looked up once or twice at best.
He called her "nurse" when he would say a word,
For just her dress stood out; all else was blurred.

Where could she turn, with her warm heart so stirred?
Where seek relief? His life's wreck, that alone,
She marked out in his look, as cold as stone;
And in his words but memory's pain she heard.
Three days and nights she watched him, undeterred;
When on the fourth morn day's bright candle shone,
Three doctors made a long examination
And such a number gave some consolation.

So consoled, he lay that eve revived.
At his headboard stood the oil lamp lit
And he'd received what drops were requisite
From Alma's hand, when someone else arrived
—Herr Jensen. Alma silently contrived
To reach her nook, while Jensen went to sit
Beside the patient, who reached out his hand
To him, struggling hard to keep his self-command.

With warmth his friend clasped Homo's hand extended,
While fixing on our hero such a stare
As made him start at what might be portended.
But when Jensen let his hand stay there
In Homo's, when he grew more solemn in his air,
That tense expression on his own descended.
"What's happened?" Homo asked. "Is it about
Something in town?—Well, speak! Just spit it out!"

446/

"I must give you a piece of information,"
His friend replied, somewhat uneasily.
"But maybe it is best I let it be;
You may be too weak for a conversation.
It would upset you for a certainty."
"What?" he asked. "I want an explanation!
The last drops gave me strength enough to cope.
The theater hasn't burned down then, I hope?"

"No," he whispered. "All's well on that score!
But—" Here again he took hold of and squeezed
The hand withdrawn by Homo just before.
"Compose yourself! 'Twas long before I guessed
That this was true. . . . This place is yours no more;
In no great time you will be dispossessed."
"The manor has burned down!" the patient blurts.
"You're right, such a disaster really hurts."

"Oh, you mistake me," Jensen heaved a sigh.
"You know the ancient adage, 'Flesh is grass.'
Both Excellencies and the beggar-class
Are covered by that law—alike they die!"
"And will you tell me why you speechify?"
Homo asked. "On your own sea, alas!
You soon must set your sail," replied his friend.
"Your life's called in—you're very near the end."

"You jest, and very rudely too!" replied
Our hero forcefully. "The last strong gust
Has, praise God, left me all the more robust,
And now my head is greatly clarified."
"But surely your own doctor has not lied,"
Continued Jensen. "That old Doctor Rust
Who came this morning? As his dinner guest
I heard him say that it was manifest.

"Don't think I'd hoax you. Too grave an affair
Is this, and painful too for me;
But all your business you must now prepare,
Since at the end we may act foolishly.
The news that you must die was mine to bear,
A service due long camaraderie—"
"Your sense of friendship's most mysterious!"
Homo cut him off, bitter and serious.

447/

Scarce was this said when toward the wall he flung
His body, leaving a white slash betwixt
Him and his friend, where the undersheeting clung.
It was as though a poison Jensen mixed.
Suddenly his thoughts became unstrung,
His heart sank, and his eyes were staring, fixed.
His pulse raced, and within his ear the din
Resounded like a storm: "Your life's called in!"

He heaved a sigh—but soon turned round to where
His friend sat, half sunk in a pit,
Observing the extended strands of spit
He sent unconsciously into the air.
"My friend!" he whispered. "We've had much to share.
Why then be angry, why be badly bit
Because you've stayed the same right to the end?
No, let not friendship break though death descend!"

"Ah," answered Jensen. "Just leave all to me!
As *executor testamenti* I
Shall serve you after death most faithfully.
And to that end might I ask, by the bye,
Whom will you leave your townhouse when you die?
It's not connected with the barony.
We also have to settle what you owe.
I'll question you, you answer yes or no."

A pencil and some paper he withdrew
And at a sort of rough draft he now went,
Mumbling: "My last will and testament."
Then he began to question Homo, who
Fetches forth a deep sigh subsequent
To each condition to be followed through
By an executor who'd be around
When he himself had been put underground.

When Jensen finished with his cash supply,
His debts and loans and suchlike obligations,
He asked: "Would there be charity donations?"
Our ailing hero let some time go by,
Then whispered to him: "I endured privations
In my student days . . . donations . . . aye,
To yield a thousand dalers annually
Split 'mongst ten men at university.

"Take care of the form of the donation,
I'll make it out to the Consistory.
Oh, that's right! Lest it get away from me,
Remember that I want an allocation
Of a hundred dalers annually
To one of whom Jean-Jacques has information.
Her name is Lotte, she's a pauperess,
I know the poorhouse was her last address."

"Fine!" mumbled Jensen. Homo sank anew
Upon his pillow, tired by such long talks;
But Jensen took his Order's jewel box
And with another question turned the screw:
"But who's to have these diamonds under locks
And for the other jewels give thanks to you?"
"See that my daughters get them," so sighed he,
"And in my name you write them lovingly."

"And this gold watch?" the other man went on.
"That," he answered, "you hold to your breast,
In memory of the friendship we possessed.
My horses, too, my chaise and phaeton
I also give to you when I am gone,
But see you give my saddle-mare the best."
"Oh," Jensen cried. "It's more than I have earned.
Your kindness on that mare will be returned."

He turned a page, again the questioner:
"Your marble bust, where shall it be directed?"
"That," he husked, "I give the theater.
I'd hate to have a thing like that neglected."
"Fine!" said his friend. "That wish will be protected,
And I shall write your daughters, my good sir,
And all your staff shall have gratuities.
Now you can go into your grave at ease."

He stood up, but just then he saw the ring,
Which on the table earlier we saw,
On Homo's index finger sparkling,
And he remarked: "You do know that the law
Forbids interment wearing anything
Like jewelry. I know we might say pshaw,
But it would still be best if this would show
To whom you wish that signet-ring to go."

Till then our hero heard him patiently,
But now he felt he'd had enough of it.
He turned around with some hostility
And snapped: "You really ought to wait a bit,
They haven't yet sent round the hearse for me."
He looked down at his ring, his eyebrows knit,
And deeply sighed: "This one last souvenir
Shall go with me when I am on my bier.

"Who do you think it was possessed this stone?"
He turned and asked his friend out of the blue,
Who had no time to answer on his own:
"My former sweetheart, whom of course you knew!
This A and H was her idea alone;
The wreath's from a design that lady drew.
I had the stone set into this gold ring
And put the motto on as the last thing.

"I've worn it on my hand both day and night,
Though her I kept in near oblivion.
But oh! how strange, when now my life is gone,
More clear than anyone she's in my sight.
I can recall those cheeks with roses bright,
Her eyes in which the violet had shone.
Bring her the message, if she can be found,
That with me went her memory 'neath the ground."

"I'll gladly honor that particular!
Serving you is all that counts for me.
I do remember little Alma Star,
Though, it is true, she'd now be elderly.
But she'll be found, though she be very far.
Farewell, my friend! Tomorrow noon I'll be
Back with the papers, you can be quite sure.
I shall come round to get your signature."

He went to go, but Homo made him bide.
"One more thing!" he whispered, much upset.
"Your words before I didn't rightly get.
Was the doctor's word unqualified?
Was there no hope to wreathe the goblet yet
That holds the bitter drink of death inside?"
"None!" answered Jensen with the deepest rue.
"Fool Flink left neither blood nor life to you."

450/

"So," said Homo, "my farewell I'd . . ." "No!
No!" Jensen broke in. "Farewell I won't say.
Tomorrow I'll appear around midday.
We can talk then, if you will have it so,
About your funeral, how you'd have it go,
And take, like brothers, each his separate way.
Then, too, you can advise me when I'm here
If you'd like spiritual comfort near."

He left. From Homo, in a dreamy mist,
Some minutes later all began to fade;
Till now he woke because he was afraid,
But now his eyes closed, powerless to resist.
His sleep was deep, when Alma, who had stayed
Behind her screen and heard all, rushed to assist,
For from the bed there reached her suddenly
A muffled cry, as though of agony.

She took the empty chair and sat there waking
Beside the patient, who moaned heavily
As terrors on his dreaming soul were breaking
And showed in outward signs of agony.
His hands were tightly clenched, his lips were quaking,
His chest was heaving wildly, like a sea,
And beads of sweat on cheek and brow were quivering
When wide he opened up his eyes, still shivering.

Alma's hand, which toward him she'd extended,
He seized with all his strength and groaned: "Oh, no,
Oh, hold me, save me, let not my life be ended!
Its horrid maw it stretched out for me! Oh!"
He got his thoughts' disorder somewhat mended
And looked around with wide eyes high and low;
He calmed himself—he sensed just where he was—
And then on Alma his eyes came to pause.

"What?" utterly dumbfounded he exclaimed.
"Does another dream now take command?
Does that star rise which once upon me flamed?
Is this a holy spirit dropped to land?
Aren't those the eyes that oft at me were aimed?
And this hand—is it not Alma's hand?
If it is you, let your voice make it known!
If you are Alma, speak in Alma's tone!"

451/

But Alma was unable to confess
The feeling for which no words could be found:
The pain in which her memory was bound,
The joy in which there was but hopelessness.
She pressed his hand her answer to express.
She shed a tear and down her cheek it wound,
And on him tenderly she turned her eyes,
And only thus could bear out his surmise.

"Then you have come to me amidst my woe?"
With trembling voice he spoke to her anew.
"You know our meeting must be brief, do you?
Now that you've come I find that I must go.
Here, right before your eyes, sits death, you know;
Some hours I still have left, so few, so few!
If there are charges 'gainst me you would read,
Then speak up now! It must be done with speed."

"Don't talk that way!" she sobbed. "Do not refuse
The comfort which I take from seeing you.
What reason do you give me to accuse?
You were my happiness these long years through.
What's past there's no good reason to pursue!
Think of the magnitude of what ensues!
For me each hurt by this hope is made sweet:
That soon beyond the grave's edge we shall meet."

"Beyond the grave," said Homo, to whose mind
The terrifying dream came suddenly.
"Beyond the grave's edge, Alma! Won't we find
But fear and dread, horror and penalty?
If to its depths you'd found yourself consigned,
And in the dark abyss had tried to see,
And felt the failure of your hope, your power,
You too would tremble for the final hour!"

"Yes, if we saw with our imagination,"
Alma answered, "where would we find rest?
We would be helpless in our desolation
As terror of the unknown gripped our breast.
Forget these visions of intimidation!
Behold those distant shores which faith knows blest!
There mighty powers of life are gathered all,
And, when you sink, they'll come to break your fall."

"Which powers are those?" asked Homo, and he sighed
While his eyes searched round as they had before
(For now his mind was greatly occupied
With that dream-image, rising evermore).
"Where is that power whose rule all must adore,
Which o'er all things and all men must preside?
When back upon my life I've lain here musing,
Everything about it is confusing.

"There standing watch upon my way is Fate,
Which grimly drives me to the abyss's lip;
There Chance insidiously lies in wait
Until into his net I helpless slip;
There cold Necessity with its strong grip
Keeps me in those chains it loves to plait.
Which is the greatest? On which must I call?
My life is theirs—they've had me one and all!"

"Do you see no powers, then, but those?"
Asked Alma, much moved, while his hand she passed
Between her own two hands and held it fast.
"No candid Providence among these shows?"
"Alas," he answered with a look downcast.
"I see it when its hand upon me froze.
I see it there far back, away back when,
But it is now so long, so long since then."

Our hero sank back, mulling these things through.
But she, to lift his heart from misery,
With her caressing voice began anew:
"Seek sustenance then from your liberty!
That last friend has always been with you
And, safe with it, you tremble needlessly.
Through it this world's united with the next—"
"My liberty?" he broke in. "I'm perplexed!"

"Your liberty—the will in your own breast,"
She answers him, and on her pallid cheeks
A rosy flush arises as she speaks.
"Have you not felt great joy at will's behest?
Even in the dark, where no star peeks,
Still in it light's own comfort is confessed.
Deep in your will assistance you must find,
For there your future's sure to be designed.

453/

"Is there not something which you wish for most?
A yearning wherein every hope's contained,
A goal that all through life has yet remained?
When by that will of yours you are engrossed,
Like bird of passage o'er the waves unchained
It bears you to Eternity's far coast.
If you are borne by all your power of will,
Arrive you must, and wonders happen still."

"Ah," Homo stammered, "is what you say true?
I do wish, but it isn't clear to me,
I've willed so much . . . and nothing it's come to.
My wishes have become a mystery.
Ah, Alma! From this earth I cannot flee!
My dearest wish is to remain with you;
You haven't failed me in my weakest hour,
But do you think the will has so much power?"

"Yes," she answered, stirred. "I would propose
With our creative powers it's coalesced;
For what else is the will within each breast
Than the root from which our being grows?
Can the meanest plant or flower that blows
Be not of any trace of will possessed?
All life is willing—will is the first trait
Of every soul, how little or how great."

"Yes," Homo sighed. "If I but knew before—
When on my road a backward look I take,
I see the plans I made like bubbles break,
And what I wished for once I wish no more."
"Collect your thoughts, then, ere your life is o'er,"
Alma interrupted. "Naught forsake!
For your salvation let us both now pray,
And what we pray for will be on its way."

"Yes, you are right," he whispered. "It is true,
Yes, let us pray before it is too late.
But my heart's well is empty at this date,
My powers at this last just will not do.
Let me lie still a while to meditate
And turn my thoughts unto their proper view.
If I fall asleep and my strength slip,
Then promise me you won't relax your grip."

454/

No sooner was this said than he had lain
Back on his pillow in a sleep profound.
His soul and body were in slumber bound
Until the morning sun shone through the pane.
He raised his eyes, intent to ascertain
That Alma's hand around his own was wound,
Offering protection as before,
Which having seen, he fell to sleep once more.

Alma would not ever leave his bed
Although a dozen doctors came that day
In Danish and in Latin to parley
And judge him ripe for kingdoms of the dead.
They felt his pulse, and they were heard to say:
"More drugs or doctors are unwarranted,"
"His staff is broken," "Failed are his life-powers,"
"All is done—he's going within hours!"

At noon when Jensen had come in the door,
He from his slumber wakened once again,
And, though his friend's words he can grasp no more,
He takes a firm hold on the proffered pen
And scrawls his name (a messy specimen)
Upon the document which Jensen bore.
With "God be with you! Hold on to the end,
Then it is done!" off steals his saddened friend.

The dying man with Alma was alone.
She sat, with a cool drink that she kept ready,
By the bed, and with her eyes held steady
Observed how hollow his dim eyes had grown,
Preparing for the end she had foreknown
When the convulsions through his frame would eddy.
The prayer for which he now had no more power
She said for his soul in this silent hour.

Till now he'd borne death's burden silently;
Only the visions woven by his thought
His hand would brush away as though he fought.
But now he rose up, eyes all shadowy,
And, as though Alma's witness he besought,
He said, his voice without vitality:
"Where did the long time go which I had won?
I lived for scarce a minute—it is done!"

455/

He wished to take her hand back thereupon,
But gasped instead for breath, which had near passed.
His hand seemed to his pillowcase bound fast.
Down on the bed he sank, with all breath gone,
His lips went blue, his eyes had seen their last,
And his final heavy sigh was drawn.
The silent memories of the drama ended,
Of eyes now dimmed, on Alma's heart descended.

A while she stood, observing, mournful, mute,
As the interns wandered to and fro
Attending to the corpse with eyes acute,
And shuddered, listening to their *bons mots*.
Once the professor had arrived there, though,
And had the table brought for his pursuit,
She knew exactly what he'd use it for
And, sighing, went out in the corridor.

Poor Homo now was treated ill indeed.
He was hauled forcibly out of his bed,
Stripped, and on the board deposited
Where, with sharp weapons, he was autopsied.
All in him was exposed for all to read
And sliced through, twisted, drilled and fully bled.
The hospital's report on him was formal:
A man in all respects completely normal.

This information much pleased Homo's friends,
For as a comfort to their grief it came;
For Jensen, specially, who apprehends
His own opinion in the doctor's claim.
He runs all over town, as he commends
His friend with that approval lame
And shouts: "How's that for an unlucky death?
He was normal, even with no breath!"

But that's the least of how Hr. Jensen stirred.
To Homo's daughters a report he sent,
Had the papers print up the event,
Made arrangements to have him interred,
The costs of a proclama he incurred,
Had read and certified his testament,
Got hold of Lotte, got the duties paid
And also the donation Homo made.

456/

But in this last grant he came out the worse;
For in its terms he made an oversight,
Forgetting every medieval curse
On those who break testator's word and right.
The trustees did not bring this lapse to light
And after some time found they could reverse
The grant, which was hereafter instrumental
In helping teachers' widows with house rental.

But Jensen had a great deal more to do
Than bring down curses on each last trustee.
The funeral, with pomp and panoply,
Is taking place, and we will get a view
Of Homo's manor, his last rendezvous,
Where now the dead march sounds out mournfully.
But there we find policemen wielding sticks—
So to the street where all the locals mix!

There's the procession—reader, over here,
And though you're much grieved by the sight, be stout!
From Homo's house they're carrying the bier;
Muted trumpets sound a dirge devout;
With veils about the mane and nose and ear
Six horses black now draw the carriage out;
Upon the velvet cloth with golden braid
Rises Homo's coffin, laurel-laid.

Look there at the mouths with grief indented
On black-clad men, their eyes upon the ground!
There's Homo's bust, with black crepe ornamented,
Which the theater's chorus stand around;
And on a red silk pillow, ribbon-bound,
Rest the insignia he'd been presented;
These the actors follow, whose tears burn
To see their second father's burial urn.

But what a crowd! Just see it twist and bend
Along the street and up into the square!
All the town's worthies, all its reverend,
Mix in the cortege with mournful air;
On priestly capes the uniforms attend,
On hats and helms, the shakos' scarlet glare,
On knightly cross, the star—Peter on Paul,
And countless carriages behind them all!

Where are we to end it? Where begin?
Therefore, dear reader, it's high time we lit,
At this point where the crowd is getting thin,
Down through this side street here, lickety-split!
And through the church door let us hurry in!
Up to the loft! There we can breathe a bit.
But what a crowd of well-decked-out grandees!
The ladies throng the church's galleries.

The organ is preluding—all eyes screw
Upon the door in curiosity,
And each nods to his neighbor hurriedly
As comes at last the coffin overdue.
Ah, what a shame the corpse is not on view!
They'll have to make do with the eulogy
By a priest, for eloquence renowned,
Who paints his subject's worth and soul in sound.

He signals—and the choir begins to sing
A last farewell unto the man now dead;
But for my reader too faint does it ring,
And over to the churchyard let us head!
If you would come, across the field we'll spring
Out through the gate, and on the wind be sped.
We'd not arrive to find the burial past:
We must put everything in at this last.

We picked the proper moment to depart:
The undertaker's driving on ahead.
Let's take this path! For by it we'll be led
To where the burial is about to start.
Cross on cross we see, which moves the heart,
And stop now where the open grave is spread:
How deep and dark! Once Homo's laid down there,
He'll have a long search for some sunlit air.

Why are the workmen standing so intent
Around that huge stone lying on its side?
Aha! That's Homo's marble monument
Which Jensen had ahead of time supplied.
His friendship saw the chisel early plied:
To no unmarked grave would his friend be sent.
Look at that stone! A man could surely rest
With such a roof securing such a nest.

But hush! Behind that hedge of barberries
The long procession's coming near at hand.
The nimble sexton fussily oversees
The coffin set down on the yellow sand.
Down it's lowered underneath the land,
The priest steps up for final obsequies;
He takes off his calotte, as black as night;
All deep into their hats direct their sight.

From the sexton he now takes the spade
And says, while throwing down some clumps of ground,
Words to point the coffin's hollow sound:
"From earth taken, to the earth you're laid,
And from the earth you'll rise again new-made!"
The funeral party to the grave go round,
And at the coffin with this thought they stare:
"Thanks be to God that I'm not lying there!"

Into the hole their quickest looks they sent,
And back to town they hastened well away
As from a long excruciating play;
Just Jensen with his good faith and lament
Stayed with the workers at the stone that day,
And we will keep by one so excellent.
On his friend's grave, he helps with his own hand
To get the marble monument to stand.

O friendship's final, touching obligation!
O holy bond the grave cannot divide.
There lies the stone, and Homo fortified
'Gainst worldly care and human defamation.
How fine, when we approach it from this side,
That gold inscription shines for contemplation:
HERE LIES ADAM HOMO PEACEFUL 'NEATH THIS LAND,
BARON, GEHEIMERAAD, AND KNIGHT OF THE WHITE BAND.

CANTO XI

Let's bid our hero, reader, our farewells!
For he has left this worldly isle behind,
Where his estate of faults and bagatelles
Is to his race in surety assigned.
His plans the wind blows round like husks and shells,
His virtues are in blackest night confined.
Till Canto Twelve he shall sleep in his tomb,
And so for Alma Star we now make room.

How were things for *her* since all this sped?
What does she in her quiet dwelling place
Since she looked on the dying Homo's face
And closed his eyes for the long sleep ahead?
Does she alone and grieved, uncomforted,
Sit in her home and stare off into space
And let the tears flow down incessantly
To savor, bittersweet, each memory?

Ah, no! Though she might well appreciate
Some time for grief, it really would not do;
There was too much work to be gotten through
For her to fold her hands and vegetate.
From early morning until evening late
Back to her labors at once Alma flew,
To all the wash that people had been sending
And, long untouched, required her attending.

While at the hospital she'd kept her station,
Back home the linens simply came and came,
And getting them done now must be her aim,
For she'd not disappoint folks' expectation.
Alma has long had this occupation;
Her principles and duties she'd not shame,
And with *them* one must not let work stand
Until death comes and rips it from one's hand.

As soon as the first daylight reached her bed
To her sewing-table Alma sets,
Preoccupied with scissors, needle, thread,
On well-bred ladies' ribbons and manchettes,
Capes, and dresses, corsets, collarets,
And like goods which had been deposited.
All must be looked through and repairs be made
Before into the washtub they're conveyed.

She stands bent over it for half a day,
Untired by work and assiduity,
Treating every piece most carefully
Lest any by her hand should start to fray.
And from her eye should one teardrop break free,
She scarce finds time to wipe it clean away;
For on time passing she must steal a march
If she's to iron, ruffle, flute, and starch.

Thus anxiously the busy day she'd spend,
Nor did night bring the ease it brought before;
Once, when her day of labors reached its end,
With them all of her trouble too was o'er;
Then such pleasant thoughts her rest would send
That she felt free beneath the yoke she bore,
And scarcely was the lamp out by her bed
When over her closed eyelids sleep would spread.

Quite different now. Once it is night,
Her body worn from laboring all the day,
Her soul demands with doubled force its right
To memory, which is hard to drive away;
Then what she'd known returns in that dim light,
And half the night she stands, beneath its sway,
Before the open window—toward the burning
Evening heaven of September turning.

As, all around her, earth the dark night dims
And slumber's bandages around life wind,
As cold sends shivers over Alma's limbs,
She stands there with a moved and dreaming mind
And listens, as to distant spirits' hymns
Among the murmurs of the breeze entwined.
Within the Infinite in which she's thrust
She feels released from kingdoms of the dust.

461/

Into the gulf beyond the starry hosts
She focuses her eyes as if to scout
The paths she might conceivably make out
That lead departed souls to Heaven's coasts.
In those orbs that shimmer all about
She sees the homes appointed to those ghosts
And asks, with all the stars up in the skies,
Might he live there—the one for whom she cries?

She stands there night by night, while day by day
She puts her powers to an activity
To be pursued with greatest urgency.
But cold nights make her flesh their icy prey;
Her day-work never ceases: sooth to say,
That day by day she loses energy.
It seemed to her herself she could forecast
That this work she had now would be her last.

She does it all the more assiduously;
When she feels the work is over, though,
The fabrics dazzling with the shine of snow
And in each least detail as they should be,
Her strength is finished with her drudgery.
But still she dares not let her burden go;
She has to bear her wash all over town,
Though these last steps are bound to wear her down.

Scarce home in evening darkness had she wended
When, tired as though through many miles she'd pressed,
Straight to bed she went to find some rest,
Feeling that her life was almost ended.
In fevered dreams she watched as night progressed;
No sleep at all upon her eyes descended,
And with a deathly languor overspread
She lay there as in chains, bound to her bed.

But she did not search long for liberty;
It was a mere four days that sick she lay.
When her neighbor, Grethe, the fifth day,
Came early to inquire how she might be,
And with the drink that she'd made previously
And with her usual morning-greeting, "Hey,
How are you, Alma?" turned to face the bed,
There Alma lay with her hands folded, dead.

From earth in silence she'd been borne away;
From mortal struggle which had been but short
She'd gone to where eternal peace held court
One week from Homo's burial to the day.
Her neighbor found this most hard to support.
It seemed to her more harsh than words could say
That she should see the kind miss never more
To whom so long she had dwelt just next door.

She had assisted Alma to the last
And did so now; she went out and bespoke
A coffin for her friend, of sturdy cast,
A good one, most secure, and made of oak.
She knew the many goods she had amassed;
And furniture was worth so much to folk
Its sale assured a funeral that would
Be talked about all through the neighborhood.

The coffin brought in, straight to work she went,
Once the room was scoured and laid bare,
To dress the body in the proper wear.
But here she stood in a predicament:
Though shelves and closet she looked through, intent,
And in each room no effort did she spare,
No more than two black dresses were in view,
And dressing her in black just would not do.

She tried the dresser, tense with expectation,
But there was nothing there to give her aid;
The top drawer, where some papers were arrayed,
She pushed shut with a sigh of desperation.
A try upon the bottom drawer she made
And gave out with a shout of jubilation.
There—she scarcely can believe her eyes—
A wreath of artificial violets lies.

There lay a ball gown that one still might use!
A muslin gown, which, yellowed just a bit,
Still had no tears in any part of it;
A stomacher; a pair of white silk shoes;
A string of pearls. There leather gloves still sit!
In short, the garb in which Alma debuts
At the fancy ball in Canto Five,
Where Adam first learns Alma is alive.

463/

She'd saved the dress to have the memory,
And often looked at it with much delight
Until upon his passing, finally,
She put it in the drawer and locked it tight.
But Grethe's forehead visibly grew bright;
To find such clothes was a felicity.
She gathered up the garments one and all
And dressed up her dear miss as for a ball.

When she is through and nothing more remains
In any nook or cranny she must do,
She goes ahead to shine the windowpanes;
But, since the old newspapers were too few,
The papers in the drawer must see her through.
Bunch after bunch of them Grethe obtains
And uses up too much of these by far,
For Grethe has no notion what they are.

In her innocence and busy haste
She does not dream that Alma's memory,
Yes, all her mental life had been encased
In that drawer she had emptied, practically;
That here were feelings left in surety
By that heart which death had just embraced.
No, what the drawer held Grethe can't surmise,
For she'd have left it all there, otherwise.

Now her hands are rummaging inside,
And memories of a past rich with lament—
Letters started which were never sent,
Sighs that on the lyre's strings spread wide,
Observations, fruits of days that died,
The thoughts, the fancies, the emotions blent—
Grethe offers up to gods of cleanliness;
But then the panes turn out a great success.

But to what end? Night has begun to fall;
In haste upon the rod she sticks the nip
To light the sconces all along the wall,
For soon she can expect companionship
From neighbor women she has asked to call
And see how she had gotten things in grip.
In the hallway all of them now loom,
And Grethe bids them step inside the room.

They stand dumbstruck—what glorious bright light
To those poor eyes in darkness long kept back!
There on the floor, upon two footstools black,
By which two pots of flowers watch that night,
The coffin rests, round which they tightly pack.
Candle-lit, dressed in her gown of white,
Her wreath of violets smiling broken-hearted,
With roses in her hand, sleeps the departed.

How lovely to behold! Completely gone
Is every wrinkle time had brought to her;
Death's laving every mark of woe did blur,
And round her mouth her youth's bright smile was drawn.
Alma is returned to her young dawn;
Yes, as she lies, eyes closed, and does not stir,
With just the slightest tilting to her head,
She's almost like a child asleep in bed.

The women were much moved at this perfection,
And toward this sight their glances they all bend,
Which, as they look on, sends back a reflection
Of a peace eternal, without end.
They'd thought of her as one who was their friend,
For she had long been dwelling in that section,
And though she'd lived a very quiet life,
She'd always a kind word for each goodwife.

So round this coffin stood this sisterhood—
But you, my reader! you who wish to seize
What in the dresser drawer might still have stood
Of Alma's many private memories,
For you know there remained a few of these:
Come with me and receive this precious good!
I've gathered up the pieces I could find,
But Grethe hadn't left too much behind.

In two collections I will give you here
All the surviving lyrics Alma wrote,
The first part being of that time remote
When her beloved's faithfulessness was clear;
The second, used to keep her life afloat,
Penned at and in an age that lies more near,
The whole, or fragment (as it's come to be),
I give in order of chronology.

A L M A ' S R E M A I N S

I / LYRICAL POEMS

You do not write—you do not know of yearning:
That state in which the soul is in the sway
Of something which has wandered far astray
And to which day and night one's thoughts keep turning.

With fevered thirsting after news he's burning,
To hear it his own life he's given away;
It's as he fiercely pleaded, "Say, O say!"
And hope, the more it pled, received but spurning.

The certainty which his last hope forecloses
Leads either to that feeble-mindedness
Displayed in endless waiting nonetheless;

Or else the soul's uttermost depths exposes,
Down which from realms of day and sunshine bright
We must descend like miners into night.

—————•—————

It's come—I hold the letter in my hand.
The worst of any news has come to me;
I've been relieved of all uncertainty.
It's over, over—here the words do stand!

The storm cloud has now loosed a lightning-brand
To strike my proud house down in savagery
And burn my glory in a flaming sea:
All I have known and dreamed and planned.

Where are those pangs of poverty I feared
Here in this shelter comfortable and thick
To which I fled when my world disappeared?

Here in this flame-proof cellar do I dwell,
Built of my recollection's sturdy brick,
And o'er and o'er my priceless treasures tell.

———•———

What good is fighting! There's no strength in me.
If on another's life one builds his own,
If one is bound unto one man alone,
Then he's no longer able to be free.

All in vain I strive—my fantasy
Keeps giving shape to what's already flown;
But he who to me my own life had shown
Is the sarcophagus where I must be.

I live in him but cannot breathe aright.
I call but no one harks to my appeal.
I search—my eyes see nothing but the night.

With life's sensations I am still astir,
But only that cold heart can I now feel
Which serves me, still alive, as sepulchre.

———•———

Once more, false hope, you surprise
'Mid its despair my heart with your rocking;
After the pains of its knocking,
Up like a glittering star you arise.

No comfort I take from that gleaming,
It will not bring back all the joys I had sounded;
Dark, by whose depths I'm surrounded,
Is lying in wait for me, spying and scheming.

Plunged in the waves of deep ocean,
None die at once, though in vain they are striving:
Raised twice on the sea-current's driving,
Down to the bottom they sink with its motion.

———•———

On high, O God, You exist,
Sitting in glory while, staggered by hurt,
Crushed and bent low in the dirt,
Here in Your sight like the serpent I twist.

Might it then meet with Your pleasure,
The pain of Your creature exhibited here?
Have you a musical ear
To find moans of agony something to treasure?

Is it their beauty, perchance,
Which brings delight to You, hearing my groans?
Might it suit Heaven's own tones,
Suit Heaven's harmonies, this dissonance?

———•———

As when the steed shying sudden away,
Feeling the whip, to its calm pace returns,
It's through that blow that it learns
That peace is what pleases most its *chevalier:*

Such is the ease, Lord, I find,
That, though my prayer may not now meet success,
It has been heard nonetheless,
It will be eternally borne in Your Mind.

Hard though the woes You command me,
Still You are near! I've Your pledge in Your blow;
Still You are with me in woe
And utterly, in my distress, understand me!

———•———

Sighs every thought sets a-wing,
Where is the power that holds you enchained?
Sorrows that can't be contained,
Where is the force that has dammed back your spring?

The torrent that rushes and beads
Through the canals wanders calmly its way;
Limpid as pearls is the play
Of moss-covered waters enclosed among reeds.

Art as my helper appears!
Nature, the errant one, it shall set right,
Shall, to my ease, put to flight
Longing's complainings and solitude's tears.

———•———

The songbird has hovered on high;
Blossoming, powerful, I was the tree.
Where now that brave buoyancy
Which once could uplift me as far as the sky?

Gone is the joy, I despond
At this waiting and peer out in search of its end;
Downward forever I bend
Like a willow bent over a pond.

Life which had once been detailed
To my eyes very clearly, and brought me delight,
Heaven, now lost to my sight,
I seek through these images veiled.

———•———

I'll never forget all he said!
Never the happiness he would proclaim!
Sweetly he called me by name,
Waking the echo of my voice long dead.

Here I am lonely, forsaken,
A mountainside, soundless and silent, am I;
I would as before make reply—
The voice is not here which my echo could waken.

To a memory that voice is consigned,
Deep in the mountain's breast now it sits bound,
Ne'er to be freed; and the sound
Here to my heart I eternally bind.

———•———

In days of our youth we reached shore
Upon the far island which Love's king enthrones
And back to the continent's zones
Which we sailed away from we shall go no more.

What though our hope be declined us?
What though we find that the woodlands are banned?
Fight we shall and win that land,
For the road home we have closed off behind us.

Away from it are our hearts turned;
We were like the hero whom honor commanded,
Who, beholding his warriors landed,
On the seacoast behind him his sailing-ships burned.

———•———

Songs, oh! how lively you are!
Songs, on the musical wings I have wrought you!
Know you how dearly I've bought you,
What it has cost me to bring you so far?

The bird tells at what price you're sung
To which Nature's law this strange urge did impart:
That out of the blood of its heart
The pelican must make the food of its young.

Out of the wounded heart drain
Thoughts upon thoughts, as I'm all the while bleeding:
These are what go to your feeding,
Musical children of my muffled pain!

———•———

As at the sunset to fits
And to chills of a fever Dame Nature must yield,
Meadow and deep-furrowed field
Steaming while fog on the dark beaches sits:

So we quake, feeling depart
The gladness which leaves in its wake only pain;
Fear in our souls then has reign,
Trembling and unrest then seize on our hearts.

But when with gladness the jars
Of our souls fade away, we are greeted by ease;
But when the sun has slipped under the seas,
There rise, as the fog sinks, the unfailing stars.

———•———

Roses so bright, of such cheer,
Lovely you blossom from odorous patches,
Wishes that our own heart hatches,
Sweet are the vows you've breathed into our ear!

Still, you possess little matter!
You'd have to be reaped in a hundred-pound crop
Just to make one single drop,
Out of all of you there, of rose attar.

How many, how many desires,
Alas, must this heart of ours learn to deny
Just to bring forth the one sigh
Which the power of almighty Heaven requires?

———•———

Just as the stiff-frozen snakes,
Long brought to stillness as autumn leaves fall,
When gentle October days call
Are lured back once more from their crannies and brakes:

So come, if one blissful smile show,
Whims which had fled before menacing fate,
Error sore need did abate,
Wicked ideas we'd repulsed long ago.

Are we blinded by each ray of morn?
Is, then, our punishment ne'er to be finished?
Must we bow, be brought low, be diminished,
Ere even the smallest delight can be borne?

———•———

When on others we have been depending,
Potted plants we turn, watched lest we fail;
If we lack for attention, we ail,
Always in need of much comfort and tending.

Out from my shelter I'm tossed
Just when the flower began to grow ill:
Back with the plants of the hill
I'm set out in the storm and the frost.

Now I share in the lot of their train,
I must take all the weathers, whatever befall;
Clouds high above my head sprawl,
From Heaven I expect naught but sunshine and rain.

———•———

To honor men early we start:
First it's our parents who win our acclaim;
Then our admiring flame
Feeds on kings and heroes of war and of art.

The world then our homage demands,
Incense we bring which will greatness betoken,
Till the gods we ourselves have bespoken
We plunder, their charms taken off at time's hands.

What we take back from men such as these,
Honor and trust and that love we would swear,
We to the pyre now bear,
Seeking therewith but our one God to please.

———•———

Farthest back in the dark galleries,
Plagued by the heat of the theater, I sighed;
The door of a sudden swung wide
And in to restore me there came a cool breeze.

471/

You presented yourself to my eyes,
Friend who will free us when we're without breath:
Comforting idea of death,
You came and your image within me now lies!

When despondent I sit, languishing,
Here in the heat and the burden of day,
Come like a cherub my way,
Hover about on a soughing, chill wing!

———•———

When the soldiers return from the war
And their dust-covered feet wear the cobblestones down,
The fife and drum lead them to town
With music to bring in the staggering corps.

The playing gives heart to them all,
And each one forgets the road back and its length;
To powerless limbs it gives strength
And joy to each soul overcast by a pall.

They are mankind as they go,
Led by eternally governing thought!
Whereby to the human heart's brought
Courage and cheer for our wanderings below.

———•———

You little bird, who hop about so light,
Whose merry twittering now meets my ear,
You go about your business with good cheer
Though instinct's net is tied around you tight!

Bound to your day-work, nothing daunts your flight
Home with corn and straw you commandeer;
We people, who enjoy our freedom here,
Do not conceive such faithfulness aright.

Free as a bird! For us that goal does stand.
You live, and our obedience is shamed!
For you, desire veers not from command.

Free as a bird! Had we your diligence,
At God's least signal we would be inflamed
And for us instinct be obedience.

———•———

472/

O busy life, with only work to ply,
From early morning till the sun descend;
With pen and brush I labor, and then mend
With needle and thread. All must be done well by.

O busy life, you'd make me drop my eye;
You'd stop my thoughts before they apprehend
The heavenly Jerusalem at their end,
The life and the delight to be, on high.

My solace is the soldier, bold and tried,
Who in the trench his orders has obeyed,
Working forward and not terrified.

Once he has made sure that the path is free,
He sets the ladder 'gainst the palisade,
Bursts in and swings the flag of victory.

———•———

How far hope reaches to our younger eyes!
As far as to our vision's far frontier;
With it all life abundant does appear,
The vast base on which all that plenty lies.

But we behold that basis shrink in size
As we go forth upon our life's career
And, as it is diminished year by year,
The life spread on it shrivels up likewise.

At last no more remains than one small dot
And, wonderingly, when all our strength is spent,
We look at the result of all we've wrought:

No longer hope spreads round as once it did;
In its place stands as life's monument
Resignation's stolid pyramid.

———•———

The soul is brought to life but by hope's might,
Which, given over, our lives must run out;
Resignation from its rock redoubt
Compels bound hope unto eternal night.

Life ceases—death upon us presses tight,
Our soul goes pining in the land of drought;
No Moses makes the rock with water spout
And moves the stone to make the streams run bright.

One blow no longer frees us from despairing,
But God a miracle of aid has sent
In that last power of soul, that of forbearing.

It works inexorably, but very still;
And slowly through hard flint forces a rent
From which, in drops, life's fountain starts to spill.

———•———

O Hope that disappoints when we look back,
That is believed in when we gaze ahead,
Whose promises once made are oft gainsaid,
Shall I call you a spirit white or black?

Your comforts lies, which also mock us, lack.
Though your assertions be discredited,
You must be true yourself; for you have sped
A pledge of endless joy amidst our wrack.

Yes, you who disappoint me hour by hour,
I will believe the vows that you propound!
Your Heaven *is*, although no eye can con it.

Thus points the needle by magnetic power
In the direction where the magnet's found,
And, were it lengthened, it would rest upon it.

———•———

When in his sleep the invalid turns round,
Feeling how his ancient wounds still bite,
His dreams send him wild visions of the fight,
And once again he knows the bullet's sound.

Again his struck leg burns, and he is bound
In his own blood to lie again that night,
To drink the bitter cup of pain he's plight
As through the bone the surgeon's saw is ground.

So do I feel when all is at its best:
One word, one sign, is all my heart requires,
And in it all old sorrows come to nest.

Such is the fruit of battling as he did!
The old wound still retains its painful fires,
But who is so brave as that invalid?

———•———

474/

How short a summer has our North so chill!
Yet summer's name is always being said:
We must make plans, for summer's just ahead!
We'll take a ship this summer, yes, we will!

Until next summer! we say when we thrill
To find hope's music not completely dead,
Ev'n when the sun's by winter fogs o'erspread
And snow turns white and frozen field and hill.

Only in fall we sigh as summer parts;
But scarce beneath our foot crackles the leaf
When dreams of summer once more lull our hearts.

Why do we lament long winter's stay
When hope clings to what's gone to Time the thief
And in our minds it's summer every day?

———•———

When with true laughter our hearts do resound,
A little sigh's heard later from the breast
As if that laughter should have been suppressed
In which the soul one moment's freedom found.

As if we should have been at school, not clowned,
When we by such a gladness were possessed,
And smoothed the knit brows of a world distressed
Where bearing crosses is what makes souls sound.

But why was laughter granted then to man?
What can it do for us who must be stirred
To tears amidst this earthly tragedy?

Its time's not come till past is our life-span,
Till, turned a hymn of liberty, it's heard
Rejoicing at the Heavenly comedy.

———•———

What splendor in the night on Saturday!
All the neighborhood with work was flushed:
Around I saw the preparations rushed
For all the joys that Sunday would display.

Back from the pump their water they convey;
The windows are all washed, the basins brushed;
And each at his own business now keeps hushed
Resentments at his neighbors down the way.

O Sabbath evening when alike we shine!
Your doings tell all men how to behave
Who for eternal Sunday gladness pine.

And are your doings scorned, then let tongues wag!
Though at your work you like a mule must slave,
You lift your head up proudly like a stag.

———•———

How many vanished years behind me lie!
How far my youth and its vivacious spring!
Today a brand new year is opening,
And forward once again I turn my eye.

I think about the camel who gets by
On just one long drink in its wandering:
Through the sands it goes, not famishing,
Not falling to the desert floor to die.

I too have drunk deep at the fountain's side
Which long the inner thirsting can dispel
When once that thirst is fully satisfied.

Onward through life's desert still I tread
While far behind me now I leave love's well
To reach the palmy gardens of the dead.

A L M A ' S   R E M A I N S

II / RELIGIOUS OBSERVATIONS

Our crops, just as our God, we *magnify*
By plowing Nature down, that the Divine,
The shoot of Grace, can rise up strong and fine;
But with what do we *serve* the God Most High?

Why should He need the sinew we apply?
He made the world with no more than a sign.
Yet we can catch souls for His realm benign,
And that's the service God has in His eye.

His use of us that of the hunter matches
With his tame elephants and duck decoys
When traps or bows would be but useless ploys.

And to that service our reward attaches,
Reward for which the heart thirsts in the breast:
Worship—best of things and holiest!

———•———

Christ died and has redeemed us by that deed.
That sacrifice brings us Eternity;
God's love it keeps for us eternally,
Though none in that locked mystery can read.

But out in Time the message did proceed
Of that salvation this world longs to see,
And as Master, Helper, Healer, Teacher, He
The Christ stands in the midst of mankind's need.

Redeemer who the world's sins can negate,
Who bears our punishment upon His head,
Him it's past our power to imitate;

But from the *Savior*'s burden we can't hide:
He'd have us take the cross up in His stead
Like Simon of Cyrene at His side.

———•———

Strange! At sight of vice we pale and quake,
At words of falseness we cast down our eyes;
And see we faith that seeks not any prize,
We feel contentment for another's sake.

Can we in others' guilt or worth partake?
Can it be that back the grave's edge lies
A conscience universal, great and wise,
That through the dust-strewn realms does work and wake?

Its voice sprouts hidden in each human breast,
But seldom here, where each has much to clear
From his own conscience, does it reach our ear.

But *when* it's heard, to much does it attest:
That with each other we must stand or fall,
That the palm will go to none or all!

———•———

Can beings made by God that same God flout,
And what's the outcome of that pantomime?
The Evil One has freedom, he has time,
And God's time of triumph he draws out.

But God, Who o'er the power of time is strong,
Keeps to the far depths of Eternity,
And in the thus-created vacancy
He makes time for the sinner very long.

What use his scorn? What does his wrath conclude?
With God's own weapons, he his God does flout;
And if he kept on drawing the time out,
Still his revolt can't burst infinitude.

———•———

Why do these demons upon mankind press?
Might they, because far-distant from their God
And cast into the darkness by His rod,
Wish to restore their long-lost holiness?
That lift of soul, that joyousness and power
Which they had had once in a splendid hour,
That surge of life which one time they could mark
And thought would aid them in the realms of dark;
That wealth, though, they thought waiting to be used
At their first touch into a lump was fused;
The plenty which unending they had dreamed
From life's wellsprings to them no longer streamed:
Their might had ceased—dry in their very core,
The flood of blessedness would flow no more,
And there was naught but memory to follow.
Thereupon they felt empty and hollow,
And with their terror they were taken first
By savage hunger and by burning thirst:
They must retrieve the fresh life that they lack,
The lost abundance—but how get it back?
Then, spying downward like the birds of prey,
They saw mankind in his primeval day,
Who, new-made, unbowed, frank, and free and bright,
Moved bravely in his hopeful, youthful might,
And furiously upon him they descended
So that their thirst and hunger might be ended;
For—as the Scripture says about their legions—
They wander through the parched and desert regions.
They would avoid the ways of ruination,

478/

They'd fill their empty selves to satiation.
Then, with the crowd of souls they'd hold in tow,
They'd fly to Heaven, faces all aglow,
Back to plenty's home, to holiness.
In their longing onward still they press,
Abandoned to the wilderness, unblest;
When Christ expelled them from the man possessed
And cleansed man's nature with His own, divine,
They sought a refuge in a herd of swine;
And from its shores into the sea they raced,
Still terrified of every arid waste.

To be saved there is but grace's way;
The devils who down other ways would press,
Who burst in and put souls beneath their sway
Thus to regain their squandered holiness,
Are thieves and robbers, neither more nor less.
But though they're given room to sow their strife
And though they have their playground here in life,
They know well that their power has its date.
They tremble and believe, as Writ doth state.
And though their battle seems near permanent,
Their overthrow is yet a certainty,
For their hosts gave these words of prophecy:
"Have you come ere your time, us to torment?"

———•———

By Jesus' victory the Devil's downed,
Yet still he can entice the human breast.
He works away—and goodness is suppressed.
How can it be? What new strength has he found?

For the Church that victory lay the ground.
It's built by souls, like Satan's throne unblest,
And for each soul won, one stone God does wrest
From that throne to which it had been bound.

The Church arises. Down the proud throne crashes:
The stone hearts Satan gloats so to acquire
Take life and shoot forth penitential flashes.

At last, when life has entered every stone,
When on his Church Lord Christ erects his spire,
The throne is gone—the Devil is alone.

———•———

At Satan's fall the world in woe still tossed.
When with his home of light the Devil lost
The highest thing a creature can possess,
That life which fosters blessed happiness,
Then by furious doubt he was attacked
With his "All ruined, wracked! All ruined, wracked!"

Then—not to be destroyed in his distress
And eaten up by his eternal loss—
His pain into the world's arms did he toss.
The ghost of sanctity he would see laid
And called disorder to come to his aid.
To drown it deep within oblivion's lake,
Unsanctity himself he'd have to make,
Drag the world down in his own collapse,
Seduce, betray, destroy it in his traps,
And, ever from his own self taking flight,
In others' natures his own nature losing,
His own Hell for all other creatures choosing,
Storm unsteady down the paths of night.
In the Devil's busyness and burning,
No moist melancholy comes, no yearning;
Hope laves him not in his apostasy;
His sorrow is a wizened leaf torn free,
Whirled round in winds that never cease to shriek;
And his despair is like that wind so dry
On which his mind must onward, onward hie,
Drying the tears forever from his cheek.

When once the fallen hear the call of grace,
When there are no more left him to abase,
When there is no more world to make his own
Where he can rage and from himself be free
While others bear his thrust-off agony,
When in that Hell he sees himself alone
Which he for all mankind would have prepared,
When in that waste he sees himself ensnared
Where not the slightest signs of life remain
(Where, as in Africa's Sahara bare,
Not one thing can grow for lack of rain
And, reversed, no rain can come down there
Where nothing grows), when in that drought
Satan now sits, his power all played out,
Forced to turn his vision in to find

What he had wished to fly from, his own mind,
When after an unceasing augmentation
He finally inside himself is pent:
Then only comes his time of punishment,
When life for him is one with desolation.

———•———

Blessèd is to feel yourself newborn
And feel hope's Paradise surrounding you;
But holy is to be of your self shorn
And in the spirit bring forth something new.

Up to that double heaven do we soar
When for existence we give thanks to God,
When from our hearts our hymns of praise we pour,
In music send our joy in life abroad.

But if our voice is all that we can hear,
It goes with us as it with Satan went.
The beauty of his music took his ear
And God did not receive the honor meant.

He sings no more—and muted utterly
Those joyous strings wherein the sound had lain;
And the heart's text, lost in melody,
He tries to recollect, but all in vain.

But when in Heaven should the fugue be sung,
The great fugue whereby life itself rejoices
With all the lines around each other slung
Although we can distinguish all the voices;

When God, Who fills up all, shall hear His praise
Bursting forth from each heart's poetry:
Might not the Devil join it phrase for phrase
And so complete the mighty harmony?

———•———

In medieval castles, as we know,
Upstairs the dancing and the feasts went on
While in the wretched dungeons down below
The captives lay still, manacled and wan.

Such was the Heaven of which many dreamed.
The holy sat on high in pomp supernal
While down below the damned men howled and screamed
And suffered in deep darkness pains eternal.

Who could have borne the dance's merriment
If dungeon groans had reached the castle hall?
Who in a Heaven could find his content
Believing still eternal doom must fall?

———•———

Of the damned I read in Scripture's pages
That deepest darkness serves them for their cage
In which the snake dies not and fire e'er rages.

Is *this* our woe, that fires must ever rage,
That the snake not die? No! Life's clear sign
Is that torment which looks back yearningly,
Relights the stifled flame of memory
And forms 'gainst termless death a battle line.
In that night of pain without relief
Another soul can come, threatening more grief:
The restless spirit, doomed always to be,
Whom agony keeps waking while he spies
Down on perdition's pitch-black sea,
Still shuddering if a judge should meet his eyes.
He sees the face of Heaven's God reversed,
Within the depths of his lost life immersed;
He sees, transported by his own fierce dread,
A dreadful spirit at which he must start;
He sees a God, Who shows the fearful part
Of Him alone, which will avenge the dead.

Lives there no hope then where the damned are held?
Who owns the power by which they're compelled,
Who wakes the anguish which is permanent?
Does the Archfiend send them punishment?
No! That one but to tempt them can aspire:
He puts the sinner at the abyss's rim,
But God's the one who punishes, not him!
Inside the bowels of the damned like fire,
Like the snake that stings without cessation,
Almighty God has made His habitation,
For He would be perceived in His full ire.
That flame of life whereby all things are bred,
That heat whereby suffused are all their hearts,
That burning fire which holiness imparts,
Is felt here like a pyre to which they're fed.
But even there one hope remains entire:

However fiercely burns that inward fire,
How deep the terror where the damned must dwell,
God—Heaven's God—is what they know as Hell.

———•———

We liken death unto a corn of grain
Laid in the earth only to rearise;
A pupa which through its cocoon soon pries
Wherein, enfolded, its life once had lain;
For death a birth to come always implies.
Life by Nature's force is new empowered
Just as its old form Nature has devoured;
Its bonds will be undone by putrefaction:
Death's demands the worms do not ignore,
Each worm takes its due, as creditor,
And toward renewed life does its little fraction.
The soul, though, does not heed this savage action:
Deep in its own being concentrated,
With its own works and doings captivated
(For forming a new body is its deed),
It sits quiet—like that Archimede
Who, while all around him war was blazing,
Kept busy on his system through invasion
And, thus absorbed, could work out his equation
In the midst of Syracuse's razing.

This first death is a death we comprehend;
But the second death which comes our way,
Says Holy Writ, upon the Judgment Day,
What is that second death that has no end?
To it what other name should we extend
Than petrifaction? when, just like a stone,
Dead to the world and dead to itself grown,
Unmoving and unchanging and alone,
Robbed with its action of all hope and yearning,
The God-forsaken soul, in dark cell turning
To one life-sign left, its consciousness,
Waiting for its freedom, powerless,
Is ever kept in darkness and damnation.

From second death is there, then, no salvation?
There life still is hanging by Time's thread,
That Time that's but the batting of an eye
For life which in the grave long time must lie,

483/

But which it never would wish forfeited,
Considering eternal tribulation.
From that death is there then no more salvation?
When stones are broken, sometimes folk have found
A living toad, they say, within them bound
Which, perhaps whole centuries locked away,
Sat there and waited, hidden from the day.

So too it is my hope that some day God
Will shatter into bits each stony case,
Blow death up with the lightning of His Grace
And from its prison send the soul abroad:
The lost soul which, in weakened, helpless state,
Just like the toad could only sit and wait.

———•———

Our nature has two urges side by side:
We want to feel we're free, we're undirected,
And yet by Providence we'd be protected,
For on our road we do wish for a guide.

How reconcile two contraries like these?
That God could do it Who did make our mind:
He gave the soul its freedom—or, if you please,
He holds it in elastic bonds confined.

At every slightest movement they give way,
They stretch as far as any road it takes,
And if the soul should plummet as it may
Down to the depths—never the bond breaks!

———•———

How shall we take election save by Grace,
Which doctrine has left many of us shaken?
Will only *some* souls by Our Lord be taken?
Will He think what is called the world too base?

The answer in the heavens I could trace
When night's resplendent stars did all awaken
Against the Milky Way of mists forsaken,
A chosen few among the throngs of space.

No light we see within the Milky Way,
And, as space here, so time conceals from sight
The ones who will by Grace be resurrected.

But time and space fade in Eternity,
For God the Milky Way is stars alight
And every soul by God has been elected.

———•———

To be elect—that is not to go proud
With Heaven's or earth's honors in your air,
Is not as badge of worth our cross to bear,
But to wish that we beneath the cross be bowed.

It is to be in God's vineyards allowed
And at the break of dawn be called to share
In the day-labors till we're worn with care
While in the market stands the idle crowd.

The time to do this work the few are granted,
But many are yet called while day runs on
And all ere the eleventh hour is done.

God's kingdom with the help of all is planted,
All paid alike; for first and last are gone
Where all's eternal—payment ever won.

———•———

Who has not sometimes felt the prideful forces
Whence comes the notion that we scarce touch earth,
That the world belongs to us from birth?
To life's high springtime they trace back their sources,
To the abundance which, new-made, we'd known,
To that well-being, which we owe alone
To ancient noble blood that through us courses,
When in our minds this thought takes solid root:
"I'm made by God, the Master Absolute!"
This pride, though, ere we're swollen, must be caught
Lest in His work the Master be forgot;
Its growth, before it towers, must be lopped;
For, as conceit, it will grow wild, uncropped.
The Holy Ghost must treat it properly,
From raw stuff into finished must transmute,
Must gentle it into humility:
Humility is of true pride the fruit;
Deep inside it feels the shoot's fertility
Which then reveals itself as sensibility.

———•———

485/

Where is our hidden man? We're satisfied
That he is there and is our property;
But if he's found in us or if he be
With God, there's no sure answer to provide.
Sometimes we see him standing by our side
Like fragrance from a flower we pass by;
Sometimes as a no longer pent-up sigh;
Sometimes as a sound he comes—or breeze
Heard only when he nears and when he flees.
Although the sight of him we cannot win,
He can be sensed and felt and be breathed in.
Yes, oft so plainly is his closeness known,
Our very heart becomes for us too tight
And we can feel his being as our own;
But then again far from us he takes flight,
As if his bond with us he wished to sever,
As if not merely hid, but gone forever.

———•———

What is our hidden self, which, quick to flee
And just as quick to come back nonetheless,
We've known since first we came to consciousness?
What words describe its nature properly?

It can be named as the identity
Which came with us as part of God's largesse,
The spiritual name we each possess
Since rising from that night of vacancy.

Our Nature lets us do what suits our taste,
Our race's legacy we can forsake,
Our gifts, our talents, and our powers waste;

But that eternal name, in us inwrought,
Our liberty can never put at stake;
If it were lost, we would be turned to naught.

———•———

Will that identity again be found
From which we by our birth were separated?
That self we lost, if not annihilated,
When we came to the world in old sin bound?

From the cradle we went searching round;
Our loss by human praise was not abated,
In nature's bounty 'twas not dissipated:
Without its hidden self, the soul's unsound.

486/

When comes that treasure we want most of all,
Which as the soul's security we'd claim,
The trust fund God set up when we were small?

When truly we're of age! When we've half learned
What God has given as our inwrought name
Through the intensity with which we've yearned.

———•———

Just how that self which here has been revealed
Will at our true self's birthing cease to be—
How we win back our hid humanity:
The answer to that question Heaven must shield.

The Holy Ghost its exploits keeps concealed
And, ere a person can think lucidly,
All born, baptized, and named by name is he,
And knows but the effects that Grace can yield.

Of those effects our doubts are put to shame
By that hidden man who plain appears
And not just as Creator God reveres:

With truth he calls Him by a father's name:
As Heaven's child he has God's Son for brother;
As soul reborn, the Holy Ghost for mother.

———•———

What comforts us—us who've not reached the goal,
Who drag along our stock's oppressive dower,
Who never can come into our own power
But everywhere see Nature in control?
We who still wait to be born anew
Take comfort from what God said of that birth:
"Ever that new Heaven and new Earth
I keep within my sight," "I knew of you
Ere in the womb I made you what you are."
Each soul, eternal and particular,
Exists not just in possibility,
But *ready-formed* before God's sight. I'm here,
My own unique humanity was here
Ere it was born below, distortedly,
And God beholds it as it will appear.
O, bounteous comfort for us in life's sphere
Where oft it seems that all has come to naught!
But comfort too to Him by Whom we're wrought:

His eye upon our unique selfhood cast,
Which He sees ere in us it has its birth,
God in His Holiness is not aghast
At human sin that cries up from the earth.

—•—

Like a sun the words shine in my mind:
God in His own image shaped our race
And on us stamped the image of His face
When He created man and womankind.

God's Being then with woman's is entwined,
Who shares with man the burden and the grace;
But where in God's profundity to trace
Our ancestry, our female source to find?

Its wellspring in the Holy Ghost I find,
Which from Eternity conceived the Son
And in time gives the soul a new existence;

Which comforts, leads, admonishes to mind,
Which, sighing, praying, comes to everyone
And is disheartened when it meets resistance.

—•—

Where'er we look in books of history,
Where'er in Nature's book we turn our eyes,
God's works must ever fill us with surprise.
We startle as we see them, joyfully.

But only life's bare surface do we see,
The meaning of these sights we can't surmise,
And without that our interest soon dies—
Like babes who leaf through picture books are we.

By the Holy Ghost we're fortified,
Whose sight can pierce life in its full extent
And all its contents gathers and maintains.

Motherlike it sits down by our side
And in the book Our Father did present
The pictures in it points out and explains.

—•—

When the Holy Ghost moved mightily
Within the Church while this world it re-laid,
When flowed its gifts in an unstemmed cascade,
We worshipped not Mary's divinity.

488/

But when the Spirit left the clerisy,
Pious thoughts and feelings 'gan to fade,
Just then when for the race of earth Rome made
Mary Queen of Heaven's monarchy.

But we who to Her halo's beams are blind,
Who, seeking for the womanly eternal,
Can't think it made by the Creator's hands,

We must ascend to Heaven, there to find
The inspiring, the gracious, and supernal
Madonna who deep in the Spirit stands.

———•———

Would we the Holy Ghost as being know
And see that life in it in which we share
And of its independence be aware,
To it our thoughts in prayer will have to go.

If God the Father, to whom our prayers flow,
Were the one who Heav'nward did us bear,
Who answered our hearts' prayers which He put there,
He would deceive Himself with such a show.

But prayer's devotions the soul owes alone
The Holy Spirit, which down to us bends
And, praying with us, does our prayers bless;

Which fills us with a holiness its own
And up to God the Father our souls sends,
Is one with Him, yet different nonetheless.

———•———

We love the Son and Father, but that third,
The Holy Ghost which our discomfort quells,
Unknown to us in our hearts ever dwells
Though all our prayers to it are never heard.

For every time we seek it we're deterred
And turned away, while out of its own wells
Of love it fills us and our hearts impels
To seek the Son's and Father's kindly word.

For itself it wants not thanks or laud;
From itself it waves the voice of love,
For it is but the agency of God.

489/

Alone to Him it pours out the deep sigh,
Takes its ease and the world's from God above,
When in His being's depths it comes to lie.

———•———

As God let His Son wear a crown of thorn,
Let Him feel homesick in the human race,
So also He sends forth from His embrace
The Holy Ghost when souls cry out forlorn.

Though it may seem that it of honor's shorn,
As messenger it does the acts of grace
And, though at baptism its name's last in place,
The Bible shows what love to it is borne.

God can forgive him who does blasphemy,
Ev'n the worst, 'gainst Him and Christ our Lord;
But 'gainst the Holy Ghost, then damned is he.

For though as Holy Spirit it's conceived,
Which neither seeks for honor nor reward,
God's heart won't bear that it should be aggrieved.

———•———

What redemption is can words convey?
It might be called: the Son's path out from God,
From His paternal home, that led abroad
Into the world, to tread that godly way
Which later would be taken up by all
Who in a shepherd's voice had heard Him call
As from the world He homeward went to God.

Redemption is the Son's walking abroad
And turning home—His blazings point the track
To which the Word will call each of us back.
But is redemption only earth's affair?
The many mansions which we recognize,
The great paternal house that blinds our eyes,
Is there no trace of Jesus' wanderings there?
He's at the Lord's right hand, that we would swear:
He must still be a-doing here below,
Still His love by high deeds He must show!
Though gone to Heaven, to the earth He's near
And, working up above, he still works here;

The separate worlds His power can combine,
As once upon the Mount they saw Him shine
And stand forth as the visible Messias
Who'd spoken with great Moses and Elias.

———•———

Redemption by the Son's peregrination
From God to world and back to God again,
To draw back all creation in His train,
Makes Time in its divine signification.

In Christ Time is His long excruciation,
His loss of Heaven's magnificence—his pain,
The world's yoke on His shoulders to have ta'en;
For Him Time's trudging, trouble, tribulation.

In the world are discord, doubt, and sinning,
Minds at odds, by wants in disarray,
Minds bemused, which lusts unnumbered feed,

Which wish to stop eternal life's beginning,
Which block the Son upon His homeward way
And the swiftness of his steps impede.

———•———

While we can't stop the clock's hands going by,
While we can't hold external time in fee,
In the internal world that time, we see,
With heart's need and desire does comply.

Our weakness the Redeemer has in eye;
When our souls beg time go less recklessly,
He slows it like a clock with sympathy
And to our powers its passage He does tie.

Our prayer brings Him beneath the yoke of Time:
When we as our Redeemer Him invoke,
He pauses from his longed-for homeward climb.

A power from His patience we're bestowed;
For His love we tug upon His cloak
That He might take us with Him on His road.

———•———

491/

If the planets from their rounds forbore,
Time in the outward world would have outrun;
And Time within the spirit's world were done,
Were Will but one—its purposes no more.

Without these changes Time's rule would be o'er,
It's bounden to the war of dark with sun,
To fear and hope, to peace, both lost and won,
To mind which holds so many wills in store.

This alternation of the dark and light
Must cease, though, when that one light shall abound
And shine down in the sun's place from above,

As must the soul's unsteady, faltering plight
When what is requisite at last is found,
When we find rest at last within God's love.

———•———

As Time's mark, which its ending prophesies,
The fullness which its vacuum will replace,
Throughout the universe (which is Time's face)
Christ, the hand upon the world-clock, plies.

His word's the warning this world to advise
That it return to Eternity's embrace;
The circle along which He has to pace
Leads home: the hour when sleep will close His eyes.

So long as forward that clock hand does wend
We wait upon our Savior, our Lord's Son,
Who still is pointing toward the mighty end.

But comes that end whereby Christ's journey's crowned,
Then peace becomes eternal, Time is done,
And deep bells of Eternity resound.

———•———

Since God is Love, His nature then involves
That from Eternity He should be more than one;
But Love all differences of will dissolves,
And thus God from Eternity is One;
The difference between those Persons three
Is Love's proportion—is its harmony.

492/

If that first Doubleness is apprehended
Of which the Son is thought no attribute,
The Love is taken while it is extended
And the Son is seen to be Love's fruit.
With Him, in Whom the Two to One are bound,
The Trinity's internal world is found.

But is that heavenly nature which is born,
In which the Father can His image see,
Through which He's to the Spirit ever sworn,
And in which Love finds its epitome:
But is this child, the sole born to His Sire,
Not He Who's ever outward to aspire?

Who's looking, with His eyes in yearning drawn
Out from the Trinity, fain to explore
The world which He had yet to come upon
But which, in longing, He had seen before;
Who begs His Father that world to create
Through which His vast Love can expatiate?

——•——

Out over the Creation God's eye wakes—
He sees His work, He sees its aim and end;
But with a cold love, so we apprehend,
And in His eye judicial our heart quakes.

A kindness in the Father's eye first breaks
When He knows that world redeemed which did offend;
For when upon His Son's deeds His eyes bend
Who for His Father's heart's approval aches,

Then for His Son's work love He does accord
Forever to His world which had lost beauty,
But which once more magnificent does stand;

Then for His love He garners the reward,
When that world which His Son asked as His duty
Is given back to Him at His Son's hand.

——•——

"I thirst!" down from His cross Our Savior cried,
Seeing at His feet Creation spread;
His thirst for love, though, was not satisfied,

Although the world with His own blood was fed.
As He spreads out His arms to take in all,
For thanks He's given vinegar and gall.

But to His thirst the Holy Spirit bends;
When Christ reborn the world shall know divine,
As comfort's soul its soul's fruit it extends,
Extends to Him the world as "the new wine,"
Whose strength within His breast shall be dispersed,
Whose warmth forever shall refresh His thirst.

———•———

The world of the Creation's fully wrought
But through the hands of each of the Highmost:
From Father on to Son and from Him brought
Back again to God by the Holy Ghost;
And then, as life achieves its consummation,
The Cross reveals its true signification.

Then does the Son spread from the Trinity
Once more His arms, as they were spread abroad
Toward the world, pierced by Love's mystery,
In all His striving, pining, after God;
And in the Spirit's total revelation
Its form receives as well its explanation:

The Cross, which, as our hearts spread endlessly,
Is seen then in the regions of the blest,
Is truly Christ's own form, whose agony
Shines out here as the sign of love confessed,
When those arms stretched out wide and cruciform
Open for the world, forever warm.

———•———

When all's locked in the bosom of salvation,
When in that consummation we shall rest,
Can no new error put us to the test?
How is it that there comes no more temptation?

Of God's face none have had the revelation:
Not angels who in arrogance transgressed,
Not men whose number can't be even guessed
Who broke free and go darkling through Creation.

494/

But God will stand revealed to piety,
And once our sense beholds Him in His might,
The soul can never more from Him break free.

Its vision must confirm its holiness;
When of its Father's splendor it has sight,
All freedom in His love must coalesce.

———•———

In Heaven where at last our home we make,
Where time and where all struggle's at an end,
Where with our hands to no more work we bend,
With sweet eternal rest we'll ease our ache.

But in it, feeling we do not forsake:
Deep joy, which longing cannot comprehend,
Which as the heart beats ever will ascend
Each time that we, in love, a breath do take.

Beside the soul which our heart there regains,
In light which is the Trinity's creation,
At life's well, in the lap of sanctity:

With our Redeemer's blood within our veins,
Lost but in God and in His contemplation,
Filled with the Holy Spirit, calm are we.

C A N T O   X I I

From church into the theater! The transition,
When abrupt, must cause perplexity:
From hearts flying Heavenward in psalmody
To fancy's parti-colored apparition!
From sober Scripture which no soul can flee
To airy figments born of inanition!
We must prepare ourselves for such a leap
And, ere we take the step, we must breathe deep.

Breathe in, my reader! ere you onward stride
To the drama you're about to find;
And, in the meanwhile, let me call to mind
That truth, though only one, has many a side.
While church may only one plain truth provide,
Upon the stage you'll see the motley kind;
But, choose what form you will, poems didactic
Are duty-bound to make the truth their practic.

We left our hero once the man was dead,
Once he within his grave's embrace was put,
That person who, while still his life he led,
We followed on his wanderings, foot by foot.
Now I ask my reader: would you dread
To tear aside death's curtain, black as soot,
And, while in earth upon his corpse worms sup,
Go to another place and look him up?

'Twould do you good! A little stir, I fear,
Might also be produced within your mind;
There might be things that you will get to hear
That in your heart their proper target find.
But down the same road you yourself must steer
When your own life you have at last resigned,
And, as in plays the actors first rehearse,
You could practice that road you'll traverse.

You could put yourself in Homo's place,
And with those words in which, most justly, he
Beyond the grave's dark edge describes his case
And with those things which *he*'s allowed to see
You could think: This I must closely trace;
It has to do with him, but also me:
Should my heart's clock come to a sudden halt,
Then I myself will be laid in a vault.

What's more, dear reader! Well aware you are
That there are clever people who'd delight,
So curious they are and erudite,
In being set upon a nearby star
And looking down through telescopes so far
On earth and all its vapors in the night;
They would maintain, and very rightly too,
That there would be great pleasure in the view.

But if the earth, observed in just that way,
Can please good people, which is not denied,
Surely it would make them yet more gay
When, coming round upon Death's other side,
They let their eyes so gently backward glide
On life and on its figures made of clay,
Who leap and run and hop and stand stock-still,
And the extraordinary roles they fill.

Then only we'd be able to make out
The mass confusion here in which we go;
For there, apart from the sublunary rout,
We'll stand upon the mountaintop aglow
As all the fogs part for us, as they show
The farthest prospects spreading all about,
Revealing what was too close for our seeing,
So that we can distinguish its true being.

But what might be most tempting there for you
In wandering, never stopping, never tired,
Along with Homo after he's expired
Is the circumstance, added thereto,
That such a journey is indeed required
For this long epic's story to be through.
So quickly let us draw aside death's curtain!
Of how our hero fares we must be certain.

He in that other life just opes his eyes,
In new-made form just takes a look around
Among the wondrous things there to be found,
Which he's both pleased and most astonished by.
The sense of life, which death's bath had raised high,
Set the blood within him all a-bound,
And toward his heart there was a gladness brimming
In which his being blissfully seemed swimming.

"You'll never die!" there sounded in his breast.
"In this new form a pledge you plainly see
Of life, which has arisen brave and free.
Raised from the earth, you are no more distressed;
Here in the dawn of immortality
Death's last chain has been lifted from your chest.
Forever youthful, onward will you go
To Paradise whose fruits forever glow."

He'd reached out for the fruit, but then a roar
Broke forth from deep within him like a spring
And in its volume grew but more and more
Until it burst his soul with bellowing.
A backward look, unthinking, did he fling
And instantly upon his ear there bore
A thunderous voice which he would not have greeted:
"Now, Adam Homo, judgment shall be meted!"

When on his ears he heard his full name fall,
With great authority to talk that way,
He hardly could interpret such a call
As something he did not have to obey.
He paid the voice heed and walked on—but all
Who keep him company heed what I say:
While this inset-tale is pertinent,
The Judgment Day is not the judgment meant.

The judgment we have here's the special one
Which, like a first crop, waits for one and all
When from the grave's night 'neath the dawning sun
Of conscious life we look round as we crawl;
When memory, which was wrapped within death's pall
And only slowly got its weeds undone,
Like sudden lightning into thought is hurled
And calls back life which vanished with the world.

Homo took the place assigned to him.
Looking up to Heaven, he was dazed
By Heaven's sea of light, which he twice praised
When, letting his eyes linger at the rim
Of Hell's abysses, down in fear he gazed
At endless depths of blackness, threatening, grim;
But 'fore and back of him, on even ground,
Two never-ending avenues he found.

He stood himself before a monstrous scale
Whose index pointed straight up in the air,
So evenly were both pans weighted there
Between the streaming light from Heaven's vale
And, beneath his feet, Hell's dark despair,
And first in earnest did his courage fail;
For clearly, as if stamped on steel, he read
His name, upon one pan exhibited.

He nearly swooned, and bothering not his head
He sat right down in front of his own name
On what he felt the bench where sinners came,
And now a while he sweat the sweat of dread.
But, after being so dispirited,
He looked up slowly, though his fear the same,
And suddenly beheld upon the scale's far side
The advocates by whom he would be tried.

There at the bar before him they stood still:
The advocate for Man stood on the right,
Who would the role of chief defender fill,
Looking as if victory were in sight.
To give his client courage in his plight
He smiled with confidence and great good will.
His face showed infinite solicitation
Together with a tradesman's calculation.

To his left his colleague in debate,
At sight of whom each nerve in Homo flared,
And rightly so; for he in truth now stared
Upon the prosecutor, Devil's advocate,
By whose expressive features he was scared,
For like a hard and heartless profligate
With diabolic eyes he cut him through
And plainly loved the fright he put him to.

The victim sought relief from the defense;
His hopes to his compassion he addressed,
Whereon he summoned all his confidence
And steeled himself to meet the bitter test.
All was at stake—and with great violence,
Therefore, his heart was pounding in his breast
When the Devil's advocate began
With a voice that smooth as honey ran:

"Pursuant to the office which I hold,
And with full powers from my Principal
(By no exceptions thereunto controlled)
And bowing to the law majestical
For which before this bar I make so bold,
I put forth in this hall judicial
This finding: On the person by the name
Of Adam Homo, Hell has rightful claim.

"Supporting my contention I adduce
Defendant's vita from his natal day
Till when in death within his grave he lay;
For my contention shall not prove obtuse
When, even if the law be taken loose
In its strict rules, his life we weigh.
To prove that this assertion's justified,
I herewith set the lawbook to one side."

Here he paused; but hardly had gone mute
Before the advocate of Man set to:
"My mind is confident in this dispute
Now that we've heard my learnèd colleague's view;
His proof is truly puzzling to construe,
His finding is of all fact destitute.
He Homo's life under the law arraigns,
But what law? Does he mean the law of Danes?

"If that is so, his case cannot be won.
Were Homo's life to Danish law assigned,
My client would shine brightly as the sun,
Untouchable, unpunished, and unfined.
His legal fortunes can the better run
As that court long ago was left behind
Which could have tried him, unlike any others;
For fines are gone for making unwed mothers.

"But if Mosaic law my colleague mean,
If he'd drag all the prophets into view,
It's plain he's looking only to undo,
And with objection I must intervene:
My client cannot be judged as a Jew,
And by another court he must be seen.
Thus to the moral law I here repair,
For it alone I recognize as fair.

"But first this observation I'd put in,
To parry that law's first blow ere it land,
That Homo was born with Original Sin,
Long before he could move foot or hand;
But to him we would scarce wish to make stand
The charge of that sin, from whose origin
Flowed most of his mistakes and divagations,
Which were but that First Sin's manifestations.

500/

"Furthermore—I say it with regret,
For I would hate to hurt someone revered—
Furthermore, when one is poorly reared
At home and school, but is especially set
Some bad examples here and there, all met
When one's susceptible of being steered
To good or bad, youth's callowness can claim,
I do believe, a good share of the blame.

"And finally my major argument,
Which now by no means ought to be neglected,
Since surely it by none can be rejected,
That if a person in a different,
But fair way, strictest judgment underwent,
His times as well would have to be inspected;
For people in their doings and their pain
Are products of their era, in the main.

"But how did Homo's age turn out to be?
Was it ideal, heroic, and prophetic,
Was it romantic, courtly, and poetic,
Was it an idyll of sweet Arcady?
Worse luck! It was all strife and obloquy;
It was an age that might be called 'cometic,'
For its tail was in the lead role cast
In its low drama, which, praise God, is past.

"It was a time when mediocrity
In broad thick strokes was everywhere expressed;
A time the young evicted from the nest
The old whom they'd first bitten, shamefully;
A time when souls found peace sheer ennui,
But found war too of no great interest;
A time whose weakness was especially glaring
Whenever it attempted something daring.

"A time when people joined into a crowd
To bring forth something great and worth acclaim,
And parted full of glee and huzzahs loud
When from their actions nothing at all came;
A time when lips were bitten in deep shame
While honor was besmirched and disavowed;
A time when wild conceit and obloquy
Stopped up the mouth of plain morality.

"And now just put yourself in Homo's place!
That is to say, now that you see him plain
In time's perspective, one link in a chain
Which did a multitude of links embrace,
Then you will know the great worth of his case!
No doubt he was caught up in his times' skein,
No doubt, like them, in weakness did he sprawl,
But, oh how noble he stands, all in all.

"How he rose above his generation
In morals! Where in him did spite reside?
Where malice, character-assassination,
Conceit which over all the world would ride?
Where demolition recklessly applied?
How great his industry and application!
How honest and how earnest and how strong,
Even when sometimes he acted wrong!

"Yes, how to judge him! He who ne'er desired
To judge the world or offer condemnation;
He who never failed an obligation
Although he didn't do all it required;
He in whose smile and eyes friendship respired,
Who clearly showed a kindly inclination;
He who had plans to benefit the rest
And whose intentions always were the best!

"No! For a nature of so sweet a kind
To Hell it is impossible to fall.
Few of this time's children come to mind
Whom, on the whole, I would dare better call.
If he's condemned, condemn them one and all;
And I am easy that this court will find
That Homo here, joy of his friends and race,
In Heaven's majesty will take his place."

And so concluded Mankind's advocate
And over to his client gave a nod,
Who in a fearful and a dreamy state
Hung on what he said, and with an odd
Confusion waked when he'd ceased to orate.
Our hero was relieved to hear this laud
From his defense, but sore his heart was stung
By the sharp charge his adversary flung.

He on the pointer cast an anguished eye,
Upon whose movement would depend his fate;
But, on scrutiny, it still stood straight
And both the pans remained equally high.
His name smiled brightly at him from its plate
And up again, encouraged, his eyes fly
To watch the Devil's advocate prepare,
Whom then before the court he heard declare:

"If Heaven were for apologies awarded,
If we could dream ourselves to Paradise,
Then to this sinner I too had accorded
The palm he's owed in his defense's eyes;
Just one thing I give him for his prize,
The birch he's been by moral law afforded
(For from my speech it was quite evident
That moral law was just the law I meant).

"About the law, then, as I now begin,
My colleague and I agree on that detail;
But in his plea our sinful origin
He thought was to our man of some avail,
Since he considered it the well of sin
From which we later draw up pail on pail:
Since at the well's first digging he'd not been,
Homo thus escapes a share of sin.

"A pretty proof! My colleague in this case
Must think that he can call for equity,
Which like the cloak of love most certainly
Is needed by the wretched human race.
But here what equity, pray, can there be
Where of inequity there's not a trace?
No, where the righteousness is absolute,
Equity's not needed in the suit.

"That primal sin my colleague understood
By a familiar error in his thought
As able to do Homo here some good
Is only added to the sinner's lot.
That sin, if we use logic as we should,
Does not mean that in no guilt are we caught,
But only that men do not hang alone
But all together—but that's *long* been known.

503/

"So much for primal sin! As for the age,
To which example and one's education,
Stepchildren of what it thinks fine and sage,
Must by sound logic be put in relation:
Since time's been dragged into this disputation,
Impartially to treat it I'll engage,
And use no mask as did my counterpart
To wash a dirty sinner clean of heart.

"When Homo's vessel at full speed was sailing
It was an age like any you might find,
Had its advantages, and many a failing,
Had its weakness and its strength of mind,
And in it Hell and Heaven were combined;
It was a mirror (all times are) detailing
In an image clear and organized
A social spirit dimly realized.

"And if we keep that image in our eye,
When did we see a better? We've long lists
Of failings of the races lost in mists,
And if into the sinners' rolls we pry,
Prophets, wisemen, poets, aphorists
Give us for every age a full reply:
Every writer who's still worthwhile reading
Has found his own age not worth special pleading.

"But let's call Homo's age bad through and through:
What, I must ask, does that say for his case?
The charges that our sinner has to face
Have nothing with his age, day, taste to do.
It's his life as a free man we pursue,
The moral power of the human race;
We're not concerned here that his gifts were grand:
His moral, his true self's the point at hand.

"From that his horoscope Homo can cast
While I, who've finished with my refutation,
Perform some little acts of emendation.
We heard his charms from his encomiast,
And those we give him with joy unsurpassed,
For if they moved the ladies of the nation,
It is a certainty (I do lament)
They didn't make the angels much content.

"So many charming people make their way,
As well I know, down to the fiery pit,
And all his charms won't help him the least bit.
His pure resolves or, as they often say,
His good intentions also will not stay
His plunge down to the depths of it:
For with what has the road to Hell been paved
We all know, even those who have been saved.

"His virtues—here's the list on which they're shown:
He did not judge—because his soul was light
And egoists care only for their own.
He was honest—till he felt need bite!
He was impassioned—for the cheap and slight!
He strove on—yes, to keep the truth unknown!
He worked hard—yes, to be more glorified!
He did good—to his tailor, once he'd died!

"No, now there's something else that he must hear!
Just like the ringing of the headsman's ax
Morality shall whistle in his ear!
And while the pyre's flame for the sinner cracks,
While all his limbs are paralyzed with fear,
The law that measures him will not be lax.
This is the moment! Now he needs some aid!
Win or lose, now shall his life be weighed!

"Here I hold the law by which proceeds
Conscience's judgment on a life entire;
Which does not only weigh a person's deeds,
But voids an act we'd otherwise admire
Because it comes from an unjust desire
(For godliness, not good works, he most needs);
Which asks heart's purity and which extends
So far that every thought it comprehends.

"Here I hold the law which bids us give
An unconditional obedience:
Obedience in which we breathe and live,
Which we fulfill though its cost be immense,
Which raises no doubts howe'er fugitive—
Perfect obedience in every sense,
Not after choice, reflection, calculation,
But as an unconditioned obligation.

505/

"Here I hold the law which binds delight
Eternal to commandments ever kept,
While, unmoved by remorse which too long slept,
It disperses those to endless night,
To judgment, punishment and pains unwept,
Who from the smallest duty took their flight.
By that law Homo's life will be assessed;
We now shall see if it can stand the test."

He ceased, and went to work with devilish haste,
Opening life's volumes suddenly,
And with more force the law's objectives traced.
Our wretched hero, sunk in misery,
Shook on the sinners' bench, for he could see
The scale-pan to the dark being displaced.
But his defender still was standing by,
And quickly raised the pan with this reply—

To Satan's advocate he shouted: "Stop!
We have not yet concluded with our test!
Your measuring and weighing you must drop!
My client is a Christian man confessed
And raised above the law jurists have blest
As being justice's unquestioned top.
From Law, whose measures are as hard as steel,
Homo to the Evangel will appeal."

"That's something else!" the other then replied,
As hurriedly he put the law away,
And then—just when our hero grew bright-eyed—
He took the floor again, with this to say:
"If I'd known that, I would have put aside
That speech of mine, for it has gone astray.
If under the Evangel Homo stand,
He isn't subject to the Law's command.

"And thus—" He stopped abruptly to impart
A look to Homo which, so kindly done,
Made him think a stone rolled from his heart
And made his face as radiant as a sun,
With hope that now his process might be won.
"And thus," he went on with that friendly start,
But with a smile that showed a hellish plan—
"We'll see if Homo is a Christian man.

"He may be startled, but that won't stop me
From catechizing him, 'spite his distress;
For him full, perfect justice there shall be,
But for my principal not one whit less.
From the Evangel I would only press
For faith and hope and charity—those three
Essential parts of Christian creed;
And, as for faith, our combat must proceed. . . ."

"And as for faith," spoke he for the defense,
Cutting off the learnèd prosecution,
"Since the assertion's made with much good sense,
Although your morals think it a pollution,
That with the age's faith we must commence
To judge faith's part in Homo's constitution:
Though virtuous we can be on our own,
It's most unlikely to believe alone.

"No! When faith is weak on every side,
And superstition is no more a vice,
Miracles from Heaven are the price
Mankind exacts if faith is to abide.
But look at Homo's age, just for a trice!
Consider all that trash who faith denied!
Most believed in nothing, and the gist
Of what the rest believed was lost in mist.

"Those their faith had not completely shamed
With their Christianity compounded,
And of its dogmas those alone they claimed
Which to their reason did not seem unfounded.
God's very wonders by their doubt were bounded
And, with the angels reason had defamed,
They put aside as well the Devil's cause,
Even when they felt his scratching claws.

"In such a faithless age, who could expect
That Homo, much too quick to gather moss,
Who read all of his faithless age's dross,
Could find some solid thinking to reflect?
But yet his faith was not a total loss,
Its light in him he'd now and then detect;
For more than once he saw at his right hand
A Providence did very plainly stand."

"Delightful!" cried the Devil's advocate.
"My colleague's left me little more to do.
What I have learned I'll take as revenue,
And, if his charity is as first-rate
As is his faith, then Homo's case is through.
Then his defender I'll interrogate
Who in his client's interest shows such labor,
How dearly he loved God, how deep his neighbor."

"And how can someone look for charity
To any great degree?" came the reply.
"An age which keeps emotion under key
By so doing leaves it cold and dry.
Once charity's cold universally,
The individual's the worse thereby;
For, when in a cold room you have to stay,
Your inner heat must vanish quite away.

"And yet his charity was far from nil;
It always smoldered, though one can't compare
It with his hope, which naught could ever kill
But from his shining eyes would beam out fair.
Each blow of fate that hope of his could bear;
The stars of hope did all his heavens fill;
By hope he lived, still there though sorely tried,
And hope he carried with him when he died."

"Yes, there's a sight!" the prosecutor cried,
Pointing to our hero scornfully,
Who now was in extreme anxiety
And in whose face and features all life died.
"No," he went on, "his hope is nullified!
His faith, his charity, were fantasy.
With all of the defense's hollow eggs,
I soon suspected he stood on weak legs.

"He is no Christian, that's a certain thing!
He is a son of Adam, and is tied
To Adam's laws, by which we will abide,
And he must be content with what they bring."
"Halt!" the advocate of man then cried:
"My client need do no surrendering:
He yearned to reach the land of true Perfection,
And he appeals now to the Ideal's protection!"

"Well, I like that!" his counterpart replied.
"Now that's taking the issue far afield.
The Ideal, in which his form is revealed
But in eternal shape and clarified,
This is the judge whom he would have decide.
But when he sees it, keep your eyes well-peeled,
Lest he, to seize the palm that he requires,
Goes from the frying pan into the fires!"

He looked up, where beams of light now played,
And Homo too, who followed with his eye,
In Heaven's depths, with sharpened sense surveyed
His ideal form, clear, though far off so high,
Which showed him as a being fully made,
And round it bright eternity did lie.
Though blindingly its perfect beauty shone,
The image he could see there was his own.

At first his heart was wonderfully stirred
But, looking at its luminous perfection,
Which showed the meanness into which he'd erred,
He shut his eyes in shame and great dejection.
What his defender said he no more heard,
It passed like sounds with which he'd no connection,
Nor any longer would he contradict
The prosecutor's discourse loud and strict:

"This time of trial we feel has now expired,
Bright truth has cleared all smoke screens quite away;
Admission of his guilt, though not required,
We've seen the frightened sinner's eyes display.
Defense looks rather drawn, nay, overtired;
Now that in court his client's had his day
And each appeal's but proven his fault base,
Before the court I now shall rest my case."

All stopped; a hush fell round their neighborhood.
Both the advocates turned round to stare
At the judicial scale, as if they would
Discover Homo's fate and sentence, where
The pointer's tip was quivering in air.
In Homo's heart the doom already stood;
Scarce moved the tip, a-shuddering he fell,
The pan that bore his name sank down toward Hell.

509/

With that the clammy hands of desolation
All but kneaded him to nullity
Till every life-sign felt the strangulation;
A nausea drained away his potency
And in the faint of his heart's suffocation
And in the swoon which his soul could not flee,
He poured out all his anguish in a sigh:
"Then Grace's light forever's passed me by!"

He would have very gladly died once more,
But was awaked to life—'twas singular;
For like a light deep in a mountain's core
He saw before him, still unearthly far,
The glimmer in that instant of a star
That even greater light and splendor bore
When at its height its long beams were withdrawn
And it but as a splendrous image shone.

Its forms were flowing round still incomplete,
But soon its perfect body was made clear,
Rushing with a bird's haste him to meet,
With newborn hope his sunken heart to cheer.
It was young Alma's visage, ah how sweet,
And, too, old Jomfru Star did there appear;
It was a vision, bright in Heaven's field,
In which both memories' beauty stood revealed.

'Twas Alma, who of her clay mantle free,
In form which her own beauty had bestowed
With splendors of that Heaven where she abode,
Hailed him on the road to Eternity.
Touched by eternal love which in her glowed,
As past the bar she glided easily,
And, covered by the shield of innocence,
She sat by him to speak in his defense.

O now what hope inspirited his breast!
O, with what solace did his soul rejoice
To see those features wherein was expressed
That perfect trust, when with a heavenly voice
These words she spoke, to the court addressed:
"In life and death this soul was my sole choice!
Him I have chosen as my own, my all;
His lot is mine—let his fate on me fall!"

"With greatest pleasure! I do acquiesce,"
The Devil's advocate did then declare;
"But," he continued, "if there's nothing less
Than his salvation urging this affair,
Then Scripture's view of Heaven I must stress:
But one does have the key to enter there,
But one, the Savior, from the deep abyss:
No soul created saves a soul for bliss."

"But from perdition it can make him free!"
Alma used her sweet voice to expound,
Which had the warmth of deep love in its sound:
"Where two accept the same grief willingly,
And in a common suffering are bound,
Where two are one, then no Hell can there be.
The great law of compassion consummates
The law of justice, and the two equates.

"It is for every age and ever race,
Yes, will abide throughout eternity:
And as one suffers for another's case,
As sin and grief, despair and injury
Can like a plague be spread to every place,
So too with peace and joy and sympathy,
With hope and faith, salvation's road is clear;
And in accord with that law, *I* am here.

"What I've received of grace, I herewith bring
That soul I swore on earth my faith entire:
Grant of reprieve, which is my breveting
Into the seraphim's most holy choir,
With rights to victory's wreath and gladness' wing.
Here's the reprieve!" And thus afire
The notice on the scale-pan Alma threw,
Which, sunk with Homo's name, now upward flew.

Scarce was that done before the pointer drifted:
In a circle backward did it fly,
And just in that same twinkling of an eye
When down with the reprieve the scale-pan shifted
And Homo's name up from the depths was lifted,
Both pans came to rest equally high;
Homo's fate could lead him just as well
To Heaven's kingdom or the depths of Hell.

He sat uncertain, looked round without aim;
But at a sign from Alma's hand he stirred,
And from the court by her, without a word,
He was led out, but not the way he came.
As to the bar he turned his back, he heard
The Devil's advocate cry: "What a shame!
The sinners' bench is vacant! Off he strolls!
Damn, but they stick together, those two souls!"

But Homo hurried off—he strode away
Like a criminal slipped through the gate
Who in his terror can't for some time say
If he had actually escaped his fate.
But he was saved; in his recovered state
He looked with all the awe that in him lay
Upon the gentle seraph he saw stride
Earnest, calm, and silent at his side.

How that sweet sight brought solace to his breast!
How it called back so fresh to memory
Those days when life on earth was happiest,
When briefly they had lived so gloriously!
What joy their walk together did suggest
Of nameless solace in eternity!
The worst that could befall he'd risen above
And now was reunited with his love.

The sum of happiness seemed infinite,
And when a far red glow shone in his face
To Alma he then turned and asked of it:
"Is Heaven's entrance through that shining space?"
"No," Alma gave him answer definite:
"The glow comes out of Purgatory's place.
Its portal right before us you see lie;
We have no other way to Heaven's sky."

"What's that!" he stammered loud and much afraid.
"Then has the hour of grace not come around?
Saved from darkest Hell but to be bound
In fires of Purgatory for me laid!"
"Fear not!" she answered. "Be calm. You're conveyed
To flames in which your soul's again made sound.
Comfort in your suffering won't forsake you;
Through the flames my own hand now will take you."

512/

"You?" asked Homo. "By you be protected?
Back to Heaven then you will not wend?
You, who in a glory without end
Participate among the souls elected—"
"Oh," she said, his strong but gentle friend,
"How little of Love's nature you've suspected!
How little of election! Of me, too!
Yes, I'm elect—to be of aid to you."

With sure steps she pursued their destination
And he, who let himself be led by her
Whose trust to his unease did minister,
Soon reached the home of pain and of purgation,
Whose gate swung wide for them without demur,
While past them flitted round a shadowy nation
That as a choir of Purgatory's throng
Greeted them with this, their welcome song:

Here we're enwrapped in high crimson fires
Which with stuff of the earth we must feed;
Here what hurts souls itself soon expires:
All that thinking which wordliness sires
And to Heaven, the pure, can't proceed
Here is torn from these bosoms of ours;
To the fierce flaming flood are returned
What had once been in nature our powers,
And it seems as though we ourselves burned.

All about we see seas of flames race
That like gold wish to cleanse all our souls,
That our markings do threat to efface
And in ashes our honor abase
And burn down all our splendors to coals.
The heart's melted armor recedes,
At our finery fires mockingly stroke:
Our laurels, our virtues, our deeds
Go up like a nothing in smoke.

High up in the air the flames swing
As we are pulled down on the pyre
By the weight and the worth that we bring
Till our souls, each a poor and small thing,
Rise up from the pain of the fire.
Set free from that burden of shames,

513/

On wings of their longing they roam,
Become still more light than the flames,
And ascend to their heavenly home.

N O T E S

p. 3 *aesthetic:* Paludan-Müller uses the Danish cognate *(æsthetisk)* in its literal sense, "concerned with material things" (Gk., *aisthetikos,* "of or pertaining to the senses"). In the 1840's there was still some objection to the word's now current meaning of "relating to the appreciation of the beautiful."

p. 7 *Vejle:* The town of Vejle is located on the east coast of Jutland, at the head of Vejle Fjord.

p. 13 *Dean Matthias Holm:* As Dean (Dan., *Provst*), Holm would have, in addition to his pastoral functions, administrative responsibilities for the priests in his sector of the bishopric.

p. 14 *Dr. Strauss:* David Friedrich Strauss (1808-74) argued in his controversial *Leben Jesu* ("The Life of Jesus") (1835) that the figure of Christ was almost wholly the invention of early Christians, who translated their passionate desire for a Messiah into the fact of his actually having come.

p. 17 *Bowls used for honor. . . :* See II Tim. 2:20-21.

p. 21 *a mark, four shillings:* There were 16 shillings in a Danish mark. Some idea of their respective buying power in the mid-19th century may be had from Hans Christian Andersen's notation in his diary for 1835 that he had spent one mark for a three-day supply of coffee and two marks for one pound of butter. French bread for the same period cost him two shillings, and he paid 12 shillings for the services of a washerwoman. See Hans Brix, *H. C. Andersen og hans Eventyr* ("H. C. A. and his Fairy Tales") (Copenhagen, 1907; rtp. Copenhagen: Gyldendal, 1970), p. 89.

p. 33 *to the deacon once a week:* The task of giving children elementary instruction was not uncommonly in the hands of the local deacon. *Dannebrog Man:* The Dannebrog is the Danish flag. In 1808 King Frederik VI reconstituted the 200-year-old Order of the Dannebrog and, following the model of the new French *Légion d'Honneur,* added to it a new bottom rank, that of *Dannebrogsmand.* The rank was awarded to anyone judged to have contributed to the welfare of his countrymen or community.

mutual teaching: The "monitor system" put into practice in England by Joseph Lancaster (1778-1838) and Andrew Bell (1753-1832), whereby older or better pupils were entrusted to teach younger or slower ones. Its success in England in the early 19th century led to experiments with it in Denmark and elsewhere on the Continent.

p. 34 *Horsens, Aarhus:* The main road north from Vejle to Aarhus, 45 miles up to the Jutland coast, passed through the coastal town of Horsens.

Deacons just get damp. . . : The original Danish proverb, *Når det regner på præsten, drypper det på degnen,* actually is used to mean that even lesser folk get some share of the world's bounty. Hanne, in her proud defense of her father, twists the proverb to mean that he is actually better off in his lower station.

p. 37 *Homo flens. . . :* Lat., "Homo [or, A man] weeping! O monster of a man! Unworthy mind!"

p. 39 *Cornelius Nepos:* The Roman historian (first century B.C.), author of *De viribus illustribus* ("On Illustrious Men").

"*Rego,*" "*Nego*": Lat., "I rule," "I deny."

Adjunkt Stæhr: An adjunct teacher is one not permanently attached to the school faculty.

The Danish phrase, *grå stær,* means "cataract," and the compound *stærblind* means "blind as a bat." Paludan-Müller seems to have chosen the name to suggest the adjunct's grotesque incompetence.

p. 40 *Thule:* The Roman name for the more northerly reaches of Europe.

patronne: Fr., "the wife of a proprietor."

p. 46 *Fourth Class:* The lowest Honors category.

ars amandi: Lat., "the art of love."

p. 47 *His passport:* Passports for travel within the kingdom were required of all Danish subjects until 1862.

Sjælland: The island on which Copenhagen is situated.

p. 49 *in sano corpore . . . :* Lat., "in one healthy body, one healthy mind."

Etatsraad: An honorific title, placing its bearer in the third of six ranks of social precedence.

Kammerherre: Another honorific title, placing its bearer in the second rank of social precedence. Along with the title went a special uniform which had a gold key suspended from its right coat-tail.

Paul with Peter: See Gal. 2:11 ff.

Conferensraad: An honorific title, placing its bearer in the second rank of social precedence.

p. 53 *Vejle mail:* The mail boat serving Vejle and the cities situated on the Danish islands.

forty dalers: A daler was a rather large silver coin worth two-thirds of a rigsdaler. See note, p. 61.

p. 58 *Sodality:* A student club.

p. 59 *the Vold:* The Vold had been the landward ramparts of Copenhagen and was torn down almost entirely by 1860. Even before that date, however, the open land around the ramparts had been made into esplanades and pleasure-grounds.

p. 61 *Justitsraad:* An honorific title, placing its bearer in the fourth or fifth rank of social precedence.

Kammerraad: Another honorific title, placing its bearer on the sixth and lowest rank of social precedence.

rigsdalers: Coins worth one and one-half times the daler. In 1832 Hans Christian Andersen's mother required one rigsdaler to buy herself a pinafore (Brix, p. 230). In 1848 one hundred rigsdalers would buy roughly one acre of choice farm land (See Vilhelm La Cour, *Danmarks Historie* ("The History of Denmark") (Copenhagen: Berlingske Forlag, 1947), II, 345.

p. 62 *rentier:* A man living on the interest of his capital.

p. 64 *jeune premier and ingénue:* The young romantic leading man and leading lady.

posteier: Open-faced sandwiches spread with liver paté.

p. 67 *Aabenraa:* A Copenhagen street not far from the University. The Danish pronunciation would be approximately "Aw'nraw."

p. 68 *Holm, Steen, Øst, Mehl, Grist:* The first four names mean respectively "island," "stone," "east," and "meal." The translator has substituted for the unrhymable original fifth name, Møller ("Miller"), the name Grist as, for one thing, it sounds vaguely Nordic and, for another, it keeps the bucolic allusion in the list of names.

p. 72 *the Rampart:* See note, p. 59.

p. 74 *Bellevue:* A beachfront hotel and restaurant at Klampenborg, 10 miles north of Copenhagen.

p. 78 *konditori:* A pastry shop where light refreshments are served.

p. 80 *du:* I.e., they had permanently dropped the formal term of address, *De,* a sign that they now considered themselves to be intimates.

p. 83 *Pylades:* The companion of Agamemnon's son Orestes on his return to Mycenae after his father's murder.

écarté: A card game for two players.

p. 84 *Nørreport:* North Gate, one of the old gates through the city ramparts.

p. 85 *Teutonic Knight:* A member of the fierce medieval military order which controlled and harried much of the Baltic region.

p. 87 *laude:* Lat., "with praise." Adam had passed his examination with honors.

p. 91 *de Fix:* The adjective *fiks* in Danish means "chic."

p. 93 *Jacotot:* Joseph Jacotot (1770-1840), professor of French at the University of Louvain, proposed in his *Enseignement universel, Langue maternelle* ("Universal Instruction: The Mother Tongue") (1832) a teaching method whereby knowledge of a language could be gained through a thorough study of only a few sentences in it. In later books he demonstrated how his method could be used in a wide variety of fields. His first book was translated into Danish in 1837.

Lancaster: See note, p. 33.

p. 94 *Cimbri:* In 102 and 101 B.C., at the battles of Aquae Sextiae and Vercellae, the consul Gaius Marius defeated and slaughtered the Teutones and Cimbri, the first of the Germanic tribes to invade Gaul and Italy.

p. 96 *Abelard:* Peter Abelard, the 12th century French theologian, who fell in love with his young student Heloise despite the threats of her uncle, Heloise's guardian. After a clandestine marriage, Abelard spirited her away from her uncle's house. He was arrested on the uncle's orders and castrated. He went into a monastery and she became a nun.

p. 97 *Venus's brat:* Cupid.

p. 100 *Lex Canuleia:* A Roman law of 445 B.C. which recognized the legitimacy of marriages contracted between patricians and plebeians.

p. 119 *nervus rerum:* Lat., the driving force.

p. 120 *dry Hesperides:* The safe North African garden where grew a tree that bore the golden apples given by Ge to Hera on her wedding to Zeus.

p. 121 *Danaidae:* The daughters of King Danaus of Argos who were condemned to Hades for having killed their bridegrooms, all sons of Danaus' brother and enemy. Their punishment was to go on forever pouring water into jugs which, because of holes in their bases, could never be filled.

p. 131 *Langebro:* Literally, "Long Bridge." The bridge connects Copenhagen proper with the island of Amager.

p. 142 *ombre:* A card game, usually for three players.

p. 143 *peppermint pastille:* Peppermints were popularly thought to afford some protection against cholera.

p. 144 *Vesterbro:* Literally, "Westbridge." A district of Copenhagen outside the city walls.

p. 157 *Østergade, Amalienborg:* Østergade (East Street) was (and is) a fashionable residential street. Amalienborg was the royal residence.

p. 162 *Candidate:* The title for a student who has passed his final University examinations and is now ready to practice in his chosen field. Adam is a "candidatus theologiae."

p. 171 *Deer Park:* A wooded pleasure-ground just north of the city.

p. 173 *The Slip:* A lane in the city, no longer in existence.

p. 183 *Amor and Psyche:* A five-act dramatic poem (1834) by Paludan-Müller, based on the tale found in Apuleius' *Golden Ass.*

p. 189 *Korsør:* A port on the west coast of Sjælland, from which ferries leave for the island of Funen.

p. 190 *the Belt:* The Great Belt, the strait between Sjælland and Funen.

p. 194 *Galt:* The Danish common noun *galt* means "a castrated boar" or "hog." As an adverb *galt* means "wrong." Both the Kammerherre's moral and physical condition seem to be aimed at in his surname.

p. 196 *Nyborg, Fyn:* The ferry from Korsør docks at Nyborg on the east coast of Funen (Dan., *Fyn*).

p. 201 *of Randers mold:* Randers, a town 25 miles north of Aarhus, was noted for the manufacture of fine gloves.

p. 202 *"Ils sont passés, ces jours!":* Fr., "They are gone, those days!"

p. 203 *Cimmeria:* A region along the northern coast of the Black Sea.

p. 204 *"Varus, give me back my fallen legions!":* The emperor Augustus' exclamation on hearing that his general, Varus, was defeated by the Germans after a bloody battle in the Teutoburg Forest (9 A.D.).

p. 207 *reading club:* A private circulating library.
     spills: Twists of paper used for lighting lamps, etc.

p. 209 *sugar-pear:* A sugar confection in the shape of a pear and sometimes enclosing festive messages on slips of paper.

p. 210 *Ninon de Lenclos:* The celebrated French beauty (1615-1705), mistress to a succession of eminent men, and leader of Parisian society in the latter half of the 17th century.

p. 222 *Epicurean scepter, Pyrrho:* Pyrrho, the contemporary of the philosopher Epicurus (3rd century B.C.), developed his skeptical philosophy upon the basis of Epicurus' hedonism.
in nuce: Lat., "in a nutshell."

p. 223 *Oremus:* Lat., "Let us pray," the first words of the opening prayer in the Latin mass.

p. 226 *ius proponendi:* Lat., the right to propose candidates for church posts.

p. 228 *Lolland:* A Danish island to the south of Sjælland.

p. 229 *Moses' socks:* The white portion on the lower leg of a horse is called a sock.

p. 231 *the Thotts:* The Thott family, still flourishing in southern Sweden, died out in Denmark in the 17th century.

p. 241 *bischen:* Ger., "a little bit."

p. 246 *Middelfart:* A port on the extreme western tip of Funen, just across the Little Belt from the Jutland town of Fredericia.

p. 250 *Little Belt:* See note, p. 246.

p. 252 *red cloak:* Postmen wore scarlet uniforms.

p. 256 *Consistory:* A priest with the honorific title of *Konsistorialraad* ("Member of the Consistory") was placed in the sixth rank in the order of social precedence.

p. 259 Reflection: Hegel uses this term to mean an intellectual construct as opposed to an actually existent thing.

p. 261 *Pamphilus of bliss:* The original gives the name as "Pamphilius," but standard reference works yield no one by that name. Most likely, Paludan-Müller was thinking of the character Pamphilus in Terence's *Andria*, a young man whose father attempts to force him into marrying his wealthy friend Chremes' daughter, Philumena. Pamphilus, already in love with the prostitute Glycerium, is saved from having to abandon her when it is discovered that she is actually the long-lost sister of Philumena. At the end of the play he is doubly blessed with a wife whom he loves and who is wealthy to boot.

p. 266 *George Sand:* The French novelist and feminist (1804-76).
Bettine: Bettine von Arnim (1785-1859), the self-styled intimate of Goethe. Her edition of *Goethes Briefwechsel mit einem Kinde* ("Goethe's Correspondence with a Young Child") (1835) was doctored and embellished out of her own imagination. She was an ardent political liberal, passionately supportive of the cause of the exploited and oppressed.

p. 267 *Tycho Brahe Day:* An unlucky day. The phrase comes from the 16th-century astronomer Tycho Brahe's determination (by astrological chartings) of the unlucky days of the year.

p. 279 *a pis aller:* Fr., "a makeshift expedient."

p. 282 *Kammerjunker:* An honorific title which places its bearer in the fourth rank of the order of social precedence.
The name Kriger means "warrior" in Danish.

p. 283 *Grethe, Mads, Hans:* Characters in Johan Hermann Wessel's burlesque tragedy, *Kærlighed uden Strømper* ("Love without Hose"), first produced in 1772 and still performed regularly in Denmark. Mille, representing herself as the marriage-hungry Grethe, gives Adam the name of her preferred financé, Johan (Hans), whose untimely absence has driven her to make arrangements to marry at once the much less splendid Mads Madsen.

p. 286 *the game of fox and hen:* A children's game representing in song and dance the efforts of a hen to keep her chicks safe from a marauding fox.

p. 289 *"roles beyond their powers":* See II Cor. 8:3.

p. 292 *an Ɛ:* Mille's Christian name is Emilia.

p. 298 *Juel, Brockdorff:* Two distinguished Danish families. The Brockdorffs were Holstein nobility who provided the kings of Denmark with officers and diplomats. In the early 19th century one of the line married into the Juel family, among whose eminent figures were the statesman Jens Juel (1631-1700) and the admiral Niels Juel (1629-1697).
Nielsen, Møller, Madsen: All commonplace names and therefore, Mille implies, belonging to commonplace people.

p. 307 *hopsa's:* The *hopsa* is a waltz-like dance in ¾ time which requires a hop from one foot to the other.

p. 309 *Vesterport:* The West Gate through the city rampart, at which customs officers and police were stationed.

p. 321 *len:* A county or barony.

p. 323 *Freedom Monument:* Erected to commemorate the emancipation of Denmark's serfs in 1789.
Réunion française: Fr., "The French Club." In the original, the club's name is the *Réunion francophile.*

p. 324 *cicisbeo:* A gallant who attends upon a married woman.

p. 325 *Corsair:* Meir Goldschmidt's satirical political weekly (1840-46). Lord Byron's verse narrative of the same title was published in 1814.

p. 327 *Higher Criticism:* The textual and historical analysis of literary texts.

p. 328 *ingleside:* Fireside.

p. 329 *those proposed now publicly:* Bad economic conditions during and after the Napoleonic War had led to a standstill in housing construction and to the consequent overcrowding and deterioration of housing stock in the capital. In the 1840's proposals for the renovation of the city were broached with increasing urgency until, in 1852, a royal ordinance permitted destruction of the Rampart and the expansion of the city beyond its former limits.
the genius of the land: Here begins Paludan-Müller's heated contribution to the nation-wide outcry against the ideas of the literary historian Niels Morten Petersen (1791-1862), who, by the 1840's, was convinced that Denmark was "a historical nullity" and could only survive by merging its cultural identity with those of the other Scandinavian lands. In an important essay of 1845, *"Den nordiske Oldtids Betydning for Nutiden"* ("The Relevance of the Nordic Past to Modern Times"), Petersen strongly suggested that the various Scandinavian languages be subsumed into a single literary language.

p. 330 *Ginnungagap:* In Scandinavian mythology, the empty vastness out of which the human world arose. By 1840 N. M. Petersen was strongly arguing that Old Norse should replace Latin as the basis for all instruction in language and literature.

p. 335 *the Stagirite:* Aristotle, who was born in Stagira, a city in Macedonia.

Strasbourg roulettes: Goose-liver dumplings cooked in claret.

p. 342 *Harlequin in Pierrot's arms:* Harlequin, then, would be a woman dressed in male attire for the masquerade.

Geheimeraad: Literally, "Privy Councillor." In the course of the 18th century the title had become entirely honorific, placing its bearer in the highest rank in the order of social precedence. At the time Adam Homo receives the title, it was no longer in use, having been eliminated by a royal ordinance of 12 August 1808.

p. 345 *Kongens Nytorv:* Literally, "The King's New Square," the location of the Royal Theater.

p. 346 *buskins and cothurni:* The half-boots worn by ancient Greek and Roman tragic actors.

p. 349 *Bertrand's Melody:* A popular song about General Henri Bertrand (1773-1844), who accompanied Napoleon into exile on St. Helena and who, in 1840, was permitted by Louis-Philippe to bring the Emperor's remains back to France. After a trip to the Americas (1837-39), Bertrand published a pamphlet on behalf of the abolition of slavery, *La Détresse des colonies françaises* ("The Distress of the French Colonies"). In 1842 he was again in the New World, concerning himself particularly with the cause of the blacks.

p. 352 *Vibenshuus:* A northern suburban district of Copenhagen, containing the open land known as North Field.

p. 361 *øre:* A medieval Danish coin remembered in the language as something of small value. The øre was reintroduced in the currency reform of 1875 as a coin worth one-hundredth of a krone.

p. 368 *Agave:* Daughter of Cadmus of Thebes and leader of the Bacchae, the female worshippers of the god Dionysus. At one of their religious orgies, they tore Agave's son Pentheus to bits. She carried the remains in triumph into Thebes, not knowing that they were his until after her frenzy had passed.

"Peccavi!": Lat., "I have sinned!"

p. 378 *"the entrusted pound":* See Luke 19:11-27.

p. 380 *Ein Mal ist kein Mal:* German proverb, "Once is never."

p. 385 *the Horse:* The common name *(Hesten)* for the equestrian statue of King Christian V (d. 1699).

Adress'avisen: A newspaper which, after uncertain beginnings, was published uninterruptedly from 1749 until its demise in 1908. From the early 19th century on, its sole function was to provide advertising space for those seeking and offering employment and other kinds of help.

p. 386 *Skagen:* The northernmost town in Denmark, at the northern tip of Jutland.

p. 391 *marqueur:* A scorekeeper and general factotum in a billiard hall.

snaps: Aquavit.

p. 399 *the Grand-Cross Star:* The Grand-Cross was the second-highest rank in the Order of the Dannebrog. All four ranks were awarded a star as an insignia.

p. 400 *Badge of Liberty:* The red cloth insignia worn in remembrance of the days of the barricades (February, 1848), which ushered in the Second Republic in France.
daraus: Ger., "abroad."

p. 403 *kringle:* A pastry braided into the shape of a pretzel.

p. 406 *Miss Frisk:* The Danish word *frisk* means "lively" or "fresh."

p. 411 *Smollett, Wildt, de Kock, Spiesz:* Lotte's taste in reading runs to the slapstick and cruelty of the novels of Tobias Smollett (1721-71), to the sensational Gothic novels of the Dane Johannes Wildt (1782-1836) and the German Christian Heinrich Spiesz (1755-99), and to the somewhat risqué social novels of the Frenchman Charles Paul de Kock (1793-1871).

p. 413 *Dr. Buck:* The Danish common nouns which are homonyms of this name mean "he-goat" and "(formal) bow." The name may have been chosen to suggest a prurience beneath Buck's civilized veneer.

p. 423 *Quid Saul inter prophetas?:* Lat., "Is Saul also among the prophets?" I Sam. 10:10.

p. 427 *'Not Just for Smiles':* The inscription, *Ej blot til Lyst* ("Not Just for Amusement"), appears over the stage at the Royal Theater in Copenhagen.

p. 429 *Esplanade:* The open land outside the Citadel in Copenhagen.
Østerport: The East Gate through the city ramparts.

p. 430 *Landskrona:* A Swedish town situated on the Sound separating Sweden and Denmark.

p. 431 *Charlottenlund:* A forested tract just north of Copenhagen.

p. 432 *Dr. Flink:* The word *flink* in Danish means "clever" or "nice."

p. 433 *Da liegt der Hund begraben:* German saying, "There's where the dog lies buried." In other words, "So that's where the trouble lies!"

p. 436 *"the vein of gold":* A literal translation of the Danish locution, *den gyldne åre,* for hemorrhoids. Cf. Lat., *vena aurea.* The reason for the expression is that it was once believed that bleeding from this vein was a healthful occurrence.

p. 440 *Esse, non videri:* Lat., "To be, not to seem."

p. 445 *Tolbodsvej:* Tollbooth Road. This street ran close by Frederiks Hospital, the most respected hospital in the city at the time.

p. 448 *executor testamenti:* Lat., "executor of the will."

p. 449 *Consistory:* A committee of University professors who, under the chairmanship of the Rector, serve as liaison between the University faculty and the Ministry of Education.

p. 456 *proclama:* A notice in the newspapers for any creditors and/or likely heirs to make themselves known.

p. 459 *Knight of the White Band:* The ribbon of the Order of the Dannebrog is white with red edging.

p. 477 *Simon of Cyrene:* See Matt. 27:32.

p. 478 *They wander through. . . :* See Matt. 12:43-45.

p. 479 *They tremble and believe. . . :* See Jas. 2:19.
"Have you come ere your time. . . ?": See Matt. 8:29.

p. 480 *"All ruined. . . !":* See Jer. 9:19.

p. 482 *deepest darkness:* See Isa. 66:24.

p. 483 *Archimede:* When the Romans finally succeeded in taking the Greek city of Syracuse in Sicily (212 B.C.), they found Archimedes working at his desk and killed him on the spot. It was he who had designed the defensive weapons which had allowed the Syracusans to repel all prior Roman attempts on the city.

the second death: See Apoc. 2:11.

p. 487 *"Ever that new Heaven. . . ."*: See Isa. 65:17.

"I knew of you. . . .": See Jer. 1:5.

p. 494 *"the new wine"*: See Luke 5:37ff.

p. 500 *the fines are gone*: These fines were removed in 1812.

STEPHEN KLASS, a native Bostonian, is a professor of English literature at Adelphi University. While both his graduate degrees from Yale are in the literature of eighteenth-century England, he has studied Scandinavian languages and literatures to the point of specialization. He "discovered" this classic, until now inaccessible and virtually unknown to the English-speaking world, while on sabbatical leave in Denmark in 1972.

DR. ELIAS BREDSDORFF, the distinguished literary historian, has recently retired as the Head of the Department of Scandinavian Studies at Cambridge University. In addition to his translations and studies of D. H. Lawrence, he is the author of many books and articles on 19th-century Danish literature, his latest being *Hans Christian Andersen. The Story of His Life and Work* (1975).

Designer: Cynthia Krupat
Copy Editor: Madeline Kripke
Cover Illustrator: Povl Christensen
Proofreaders: Albert McGrath and Sidney Green
Typist: Jeanne K. Widmayer